Shattermoon

DOMINIC DULLEY

Jo Fletcher
BOOKS

First published in ebook in Great Britain in 2018 by Jo Fletcher Books
This edition published in 2019 by

Jo Fletcher Books
an imprint of Quercus Editions Ltd
Carmelite House
50 Victoria Embankment
London EC4Y 0DZ

An Hachette UK company

A CIP catalogue record for this book is available
from the British Library

PB ISBN 978-1-78648-605-9
EB ISBN 978-1-78648-604-2

10 9 8 7 6 5 4 3 2 1

Typeset by CC Book Production

Printed and bound in Great Britain by Clays Ltd, Elcograf S.p.A.

Praise for *Shattermoon*

'A riptide of excitement . . . totally swept me away'
Daniel Godfrey, author of *New Pompeii*

'Big screen space opera at its most entertaining.
With a welcome hint of an updated *Stainless Steel Rat*,
Orry Kent makes for an engaging and savvy protagonist.
A very impressive debut novel!'
Gavin Smith, author of *The Bastard Legion*

'Imaginative world-building . . . a lively sci-fi romp'
SFX

'For those in need of a gallivant through space with
a bunch of mismatched chancers, *Shattermoon* should
be at the top of your list'
SciFiNow

'This book builds and builds with so much action
that it kept me entertained to the very end'
Dyslexic Reader

'[A] fast-paced read from start to finish, a total page turner,
which I read almost in one go'
Bookish Outsider

'A fun and fast-paced heist novel'
I Should Read That

'An action-packed space adventure, Dominic's debut is a blast!'
Laura Patricia Rose

'An exciting read with a capable and cool-headed protagonist'
Blue Book Balloon

For my family

CONTENTS

1

THE BOOK GAME

The press of sweating bodies crammed into the ballroom made for an oppressive atmosphere. Musky perfumes and pungent local spices caught in Orry Kent's throat as she gazed longingly at the open doors to the balcony. Beyond them, Tyr's bloated yellow sun hung low on the horizon, reflected perfectly in the still waters of an artificial lake set in landscaped grounds. After more than a week planetside Orry had adjusted to the lower-than-standard gravity, but she still couldn't get used to the heat.

She fanned herself as a pair of uniformed footmen threw open the grand double doors to admit the Count of Delf. Milan Larist Soltz was a tall, painfully thin man in a dark, form-fitting tunic, unbowed despite his advancing years. His skeletal frame, short grey hair and smooth-shaven face put him at odds with the corpulent gentlemen who immediately flocked towards him, fingering extravagantly curled moustaches and beards, drawing attention to hair teased into gravity-defying styles. There were women in the press of bodies too, proudly displaying the ersatz youth provided by the latest gene treatments.

Orry curled her lip at the scrum of pampered prigs competing for one of the count's thin smiles. It was clear to her that here on the capital world more than anywhere, the Ascendancy had lost its way; Delf's austere personality was a rarity among the decadent Ruuz aristos, where restraint was pretty much a lost virtue.

He's here, she subvocalised, watching minor nobles, magnates and high-ranking members of the Administrate alike being expertly deflected by Madam Costanza, the count's major-domo; the severe-looking middle-aged woman stood out amongst these birds of paradise in her sombre charcoal-grey trouser suit relieved only by the crisp white stock around her neck.

Yeah, I know. I'm into the security substrate. Orry's integuary rendered Ethan's words with such clarity that her brother might have been standing beside her rather than huddled in a ditch beyond the estate's distant boundary wall. *Ready, Sis?*

Where's Konstantin? She glanced around the packed ballroom, searching for the count's grandson.

Still with his sick little chums. He hasn't realised you've arrived early.

She stared thoughtfully at Delf. *Okay, do it.*

Executing now . . .

She saw Costanza hesitate. The major-domo's eyes glazed for a moment as she focused on her integuary, then she glanced towards one of the ballroom's several exits. Leaning close to Delf, she murmured something. The count nodded and Costanza strode away.

Orry started making her way around the edge of the dance floor. The dark wood parquet looked ancient; she supposed it had been transported from Earth along with the rest of the estate.

The ballroom running the length of the Delf mansion had

2

tall windows overlooking the extensive manicured grounds. Lights burned in crystal chandeliers suspended from the high ceiling, illuminating the laden tables lining the walls; they left the centre of the long gallery clear for the immaculately tailored aristos to dance to the music of a string quintet. After watching the dancers for an hour it was Orry's considered opinion that somebody should remove the broom handles from their backsides.

She was nearing the count when a young man in an under-lieutenant's uniform stepped into her path. The waxed tips of his moustache were drooping in the heat and his face looked a little florid above his high collar, which bore the silver insignia of the Grand Fleet. He snapped to attention, clicking his boot heels together as he jerked his head into a stiff bow.

'Your servant, miz. Lieutenant Varin Ivchenko at your service.' She tried to move around him but he blocked her. 'I wonder if I might have the pleasure of this dance?'

Orry gritted her teeth; she needed to keep an eye on Delf. What was this idiot doing approaching her, anyway? Any one of these simpering Ruuz society girls would be wetting their gussets at all the gold braid on that dress uniform, let alone the sabre dangling from his belt. Why couldn't he bother one of them?

'I'm flattered, Lieutenant,' she said in her best highborn accent, 'but I fear I must decline.'

She stepped to one side, but he moved with her, his smile vanishing.

'I must tell you, miz, that I am accustomed to getting what I want.'

3

She patted him lightly on the cheek. 'Not this time, sweet-heart.' She pushed past the startled officer.

Problem? Orry frowned at the tension in her father's voice.

Just a Ruuz who thinks he's God's gift, she told him.

Don't they all? Okay, you know what you have to do. Just give Ethan the time he needs.

I know, she replied testily. Her father had been drumming the plan into them for the past week, which was troubling – she couldn't remember the last time Eoin had been this uptight about a job.

Delf hadn't moved far, but the false security alert Ethan had planted in the mansion's substrate wouldn't delay Costanza for long. With his major-domo otherwise occupied, a number of strutting peacocks were pressing for Delf's attention, so Orry snagged a silver platter of shellfish as she passed a table and used it to forge a path to the count.

'Buttered redspine, Your Grace?'

He frowned down his long nose at her. 'No, thank you.'

She turned and handed the tray to an obese gentleman with a walrus moustache and a pair of soot-black goggles covering his eyes. The man took it automatically, smiling at her – then spluttered with outrage as she returned her attention to the count.

Get nearer, Ethan told her.

'Do you not care for redspine, Your Grace?' she asked, pressing closer. Delf smelled of expensive cologne and the local brandy he was drinking.

Better, Ethan sent. *His pattern's copying now. Stay right where you are.*

Orry hid her exasperation and smiled up at the count.

'Who are you?' Delf asked. Another man might have been amused by her intimate proximity, or have seen it as an advance. The count just sounded irritated.

She dropped into a curtsey. 'Lady Jade Flint, My Lord.'

He narrowed his eyes. 'You look familiar,' he said. 'Do I know you?'

'Oh no, sir,' she replied with a girlish laugh. 'I am entirely unimportant.'

Delf frowned at her a little longer, as if trying to place her, then blinked. 'Well, if you'll excuse me, Lady Flint . . .' He tried to edge past.

Keep him talking! Ethan sent.

'This is a wonderful ball,' she said quickly, standing her ground.

Delf sighed and took a sip of brandy. 'Your first, I take it?'

'Does it show?'

'Perhaps a little. Now—'

'You should hold them more often,' she blurted, and immediately cringed as the murmur of conversation around her faltered. Since the death of his son ten years ago, grief had turned Milan Soltz into a recluse. Orry didn't feel much sympathy for the count; her mother had died ten years ago and *she'd* managed to get over it.

Delf squinted down at her. 'Who did you say you were again?' he asked. His voice was dangerously quiet.

She smiled sweetly again, trying to think of a way out of this, but rescue came from an unexpected quarter.

'There you are,' a familiar voice said from behind her, and she turned to see Konstantin, his full lips drawn back into a strained smile. The young viscount was dressed in a frock coat

5

and cunningly tailored waistcoat which went a long way to disguise his ample belly. He bowed to his grandfather.

'Did *you* invite this young lady?' Delf asked.

'Yes, Grandfather.' He shot her a hard look. 'I'm sorry if she was bothering you.'

The count waved a dismissive hand and turned away.

I need one more minute, Ethan sent.

Konstantin leaned forward and kissed Orry's white glove. Glancing up into her face, he murmured, 'What the fuck are you doing?' The singsong tone belied the anger in his eyes.

'I was being polite, of course,' she said, trying to sound hurt, ignoring Konstantin's fingers pinching the bare flesh of her upper arm as he marched her towards a side door.

I've lost Delf, Ethan sent.

Did you get it all? her father asked urgently.

No.

Dammit, Orry. You have to get back to him.

She turned her face from Konstantin to hide the integuary-dullness in her eyes. *Are you kidding me? Let's just finish the book game and regroup. There'll be other opportunities.*

Like when? It's taken me years to— He stopped himself, then spat, *Shit on it!* Orry had never heard her father so angry. He remained silent for a few seconds, then announced, *Okay, you're right. Let's just get this fiasco over with. Try not to screw anything else up.*

She flushed, determined not to retort.

6

2

HIGH-ROLLER

'Do you have it?' Konstantin demanded quietly. His breath reeked of wine and sweetsmoke.

Orry forced a smile. 'Of course,' she said as he opened a door and ushered her through. She coughed, her eyes watering in the sudden fog of scented vapour. The room was small, with hunting trophies hanging from every wood-panelled wall. She recognised a couple of rare species among the heads and horns, although she thought she'd struggle to name their native worlds.

Three Ruuz lordlings were sprawled in chairs around a circular table in the centre of the room, watching a writhing tangle of glistening limbs. The two women on the table wore nothing but the odd scrap of sheer silk, which if anything made them look more naked. The sweat-slick bodies rubbed together amid moans of pleasure, but Orry could see the emptiness in the girls' eyes. She'd seen it on a dozen worlds or more: women and men driven to desperate acts by hollow bellies – but to witness it here, in the heart of the obscenely wealthy Fountainhead worlds, filled her with fury. She looked away in disgust.

'Kostya!' one drunken young man exclaimed. 'Back already?'

'Get out,' Konstantin snarled.

The man hesitated, then a knowing smile spread over his face. As he leered at Orry she imagined his eyes penetrating her gown to the flesh beneath. Resisting the urge to shrink away – or to plaster the lordling's nose across his face – she kept her eyes on the tiled floor. She suddenly, desperately, needed to take a shower. The three men made unsteadily for a door on the far side of the room, taking the girls with them.

Orry took a seat and watched Konstantin drop into the chair opposite, his eyes blazing. The viscount was a striking young man who might even be handsome if he cleaned up his act. Good bone structure, she reflected, spoiled by puffy, translucent skin and deep shadows under his eyes.

'Show me,' he snapped.

She reached beneath her layered skirts, extracted the bundle tucked into her garter and placed it on the table.

Konstantin ignored the flash of leg and snatched at the package like a starving man, long fingers fumbling to remove the protective fabric bag. He yanked the book free and stared at its dog-eared cover, drinking in the faded colours.

Orry thought of the white cotton gloves the curator at the Tannhauser Foundation on Manes had used religiously whenever he handled the book. The week she'd spent as the old man's assistant had been the longest of her life, constantly dodging his wandering hands as she waited for an opportunity to lift the valuable volume. Konstantin licked his bare forefinger and flicked through the yellowing pages, and her mouth twitched as she imagined the look of horror on the curator's face at such cavalier treatment.

Folio fever was an expensive obsession among the sons of the noble houses, although few outside of the super-rich Fountainhead systems could afford to play. The hobby was incomprehensible to her; yet another example of the privileged classes having more time and money than anyone had a right to. The excesses of the Fountainhead made her want to puke. What she was doing might be criminal, but to her the real crime was *not* relieving these inbred pigs of as much of their inherited fortunes as she could.

'My fee?' she prompted.

Konstantin dragged his eyes from the book and blinked as if surprised to see her still there. He pulled a soft leather pouch from his frock coat and pushed it across the table, immediately returning his attention to the book, poring over the ancient pages. A pendant dangling from his neck brushed the tabletop and Orry found herself automatically appraising the dull green gem encased in a simple golden setting – antique, she thought, at least a century old, but it was the stone that had caught her interest and, as she looked more closely, her heart quickened. It looked exotic, pre-Withdrawal at least.

You okay, Sis? Your heartbeat is elevated.

She cut the biometrics feed her integuary was sending to Ethan.

And now you're dead, he observed dryly.

I'm fine, she told him. *Just do your own job and stop distracting me.*

Loosening the drawstring, she let the pouch fall open on the table. An exotic fragrance rose from the pinch of fine brown powder flecked through with luminescent green. She began salivating as the rich scent of spice paragon clung to the inside of her mouth.

9

Bellonna was notorious in botanical circles for resisting all attempts at cultivation anywhere but its natural habitat deep within the reflecting caves of the moon Hestor; it flowered only once every seven years, when the moon was in the correct alignment, which made spice paragon, derived from the stamens, one of the rarest and most valuable substances in Ascendancy space.

Figures scrolled in Orry's peripheral vision as her integuary projected the results of its analysis of the spice onto her visual cortex. She smiled coldly, almost pleased that Konstantin had come up short.

'This is less than we agreed,' she said.

He glanced up, irritated. 'I find myself temporarily embarrassed this month. My grandfather' – a scowl – 'is less than generous with my allowance.'

'Not my problem.' She performed a quick mental calculation and tried to keep the anger from her face: Konstantin's 'less than generous' monthly allowance was more than most citizens would earn in a year.

'You can wait a week, can't you?' He waved his hand around the richly furnished room and sneered, 'I'm good for it.'

Stick to the plan, Orry, her father told her. *Don't get clever. Just take the damn spice and get out.*

She reached for the book.

'Wait!' Konstantin slammed his hand down on the volume.

Orry looked at him expectantly and he licked his lips, glancing round the room. 'Take something . . . *anything*. My grandfather will never notice.'

Orry . . . Eoin warned.

'Let me see your pendant,' she said.

'No.' Konstantin closed his other hand around the green stone. 'Not this.'

'Fine.' She snatched up the slim volume and began replacing it in its bag.

'If you like jewellery, Mother had hundreds of pieces far nicer than this one – you can take your pick.' Konstantin watched the book disappear into its bag, his brow lowered. 'This is ridiculous – I *demand* you give me that book.'

Orry closed the spice pouch and slid it back across the table.

Aurelia Kent! Eoin snapped, making her feel about five years old.

Konstantin ignored the pouch and leaned closer. 'You know who I am,' he said quietly. 'You would do well not to make an enemy of me.'

She gazed levelly at him. 'Threats, Your Lordship? Do you really want to go there?' She smiled. 'I wonder what your grandfather would say if he found out where we first met, or how much you spend on your various vices.'

The viscount's eyes flashed and she waited for him to master his fury.

'You noisome little quim.' He reached up, removed the pendant and set it on top of the pouch.

Costanza's on the move, Ethan told her. *She's heading your way.*

Orry grabbed her prizes and tossed the book to Konstantin. 'Nice doing business with you. I'll show myself out.'

'You do that. Fuck off back to your hovel.'

'Charming as ever.' She curtseyed, and slipped from the room.

Her integuary bracketed Costanza immediately, providing

biographical data as the woman strode across the dance floor. She looked furious.

Orry ducked into the crowd and threaded her way around the edge of the ballroom. As she passed through the double doors leading to the entrance hall she glanced back to see Costanza enter the smoking room.

Outside, the early evening air was heavy and languorous, scented with orange blossom. The sky was a darker red than usual in the late twilight and Perun, the larger of Tyr's two moons, was already visible as a vast crescent above the trees. The lights of habitats and processing stations glinted at the moon's edge; drive-flares marked the passage of ships coming and going. The sky above the capital world was a busy place.

She tapped her foot as she waited beneath the carriage porch, watching the latecomers arriving to distract herself. An elderly couple clambered stiffly from a driverless limousine and it hummed away to make room for the next arrival: the bug-like autocar Ethan had subverted that afternoon. She smiled with relief as she climbed into the back seat and arranged her skirts carefully around her.

Home, James, she told her brother.

Yes, modom.

Cut it out, you two, Eoin sent.

The autocar drew away, gravel crunching beneath its honeycomb tyres. The burning torches lighting the long driveway cast flickering shadows as it passed.

Okay, Costanza and Konstantin are on the move again, Ethan reported. *They're heading for the gate, just like we thought. Damn, we're good.*

She saw the lights of the crenellated gatehouse up ahead. A

personal flyer sat on the grass beside the stone structure and three figures stood in the road, blocking her way. The autocar's headlights illuminated Costanza and Konstantin as it slowed to a halt. A muscle-bound footman holding an extendable baton accompanied them.

Orry took a deep breath and let it out slowly as the three approached the autocar. She lowered the window.

'I believe you have something that belongs to us,' Costanza said.

'I'm sorry, who are you?' Orry enquired.

'My name is Madam Costanza. I represent His Grace, the Count of Delf.'

'Just give it back—' Konstantin began, stepping forward.

Costanza held up two fingers and the young man fell silent, face flushing.

'Return the pendant and the spice,' she told Orry, 'and you may leave.'

'Not keen to share this with the count?' Orry asked, playing for time. *Where the hell is Dad?*

'His Grace does not need to know every detail of his household's business.'

'And if I don't give it back?'

There was a snap as the footman flicked his wrist, extending the baton to its full length. Konstantin grinned, but Costanza's face betrayed no emotion.

'I see,' Orry said. 'In that case—'

She stopped as headlights played across the scene, dazzling her. Costanza and the others shaded their eyes as a black high-roller turned through the open gates, barely missing the top of the stone archway. The interlocking plates of the vehicle's single giant wheel reminded her of a lobster's armoured back. It stopped and the plates slid over each other with an oily rasp, deforming the wheel to lower its small central cabin to the ground. A gullwing door hissed open and her father stepped out. He wore a crisp grey suit and was clean-shaven for once, his tangle of sandy hair slicked neatly back.

'This is private property,' Costanza told him. 'You'll have to leave.'

Eoin reached into his jacket – making the footman raise his baton – and produced a gold arbiter's badge. The footman paled and lowered the weapon.

Costanza stepped back as Eoin approached Orry. He peered at her, looking genuinely pissed off, then straightened. 'This woman is under arrest,' he said.

Konstantin glanced at Costanza.

'On what charge?' she asked.

'Dealing in stolen antiquaries. We've been following this one for weeks.' He held out a black-gloved hand to Konstantin. The viscount stared dumbly at it and Eoin sighed. 'Give me the book and I'm sure we can keep your name – and His Grace's – out of the newsfeeds.'

Konstantin stiffened. 'I don't know what you're talking about.'

'Just give it to him,' Costanza snapped.

'But—' He flinched as she stepped closer and reached into his coat. She withdrew the book in its protective bag and handed it to Eoin.

'I can see you're sensitive to matters of state,' she murmured. 'This person is in possession of an article of jewellery – a family heirloom – together with a substantial quantity of

14

spice paragon. You may keep the spice as evidence, but I must ask for the return of the pendant.'

Orry held her breath as Eoin glanced at her. She wouldn't put it past her father to hand the damn thing back just to teach her a lesson. His lips twitched and he turned to Costanza.

'Are you trying to bribe a member of the Arbiter Corps?'

'What? No!' For the first time, Costanza looked flustered.

'Any items the detainee has on her will be processed and marked as evidence. After her trial you are free to submit a written request for them *all* to be returned.'

Costanza closed her mouth. 'Very well,' she said heavily.

He opened the autocar's door and Orry climbed out. She kept her eyes on the ground, looking subdued, as he led her to the high-roller's cab and placed her in the back seat.

'Thank you for your cooperation,' he told Costanza. 'I'll be in touch.'

The vehicle swayed as he got in. Orry kept silent as the wheel reformed, hoisting the cab a metre into the air. The engine hummed, and the high-roller pivoted and moved slowly away. The last thing she saw as they turned out of the gate was Costanza berating Konstantin while the footman, clearly uncomfortable, tried to pretend he wasn't there.

She slumped into her seat, feeling the tension drain out of her.

'Even short, that spice is worth at least twenty grand,' she said with satisfaction. 'Not bad for a few weeks' work.'

Eoin switched the controls to automatic and twisted in his seat to glare at her. 'This was *never* about the damned spice. I wanted Delf's integuary pattern.'

'*Why?*' Orry asked angrily. 'You still haven't told us *why* – but anyway, it was impossible—'

'Never mind.' He clenched his jaw and turned away.

'Look, I did my best, all right? This whole thing was way too complicated from the start. Whatever happened to "keeping it simple"? That's what you always taught us – so what's changed?'

'Forget it,' he said. 'We'll just have to find another way to get the old bastard's pattern.'

She stared at the thinning hair on the back of his head. The growing bald spot made him look vulnerable somehow, no longer the infallible, indestructible figure of her childhood.

'Is everything okay, Dad? You've been acting weird since we landed here.'

'I'm fine.' He turned to face her again. 'And another thing: what the hell was that with the pendant? What have I told you about going off-script?'

'Come on, he was short,' she said defensively. 'If I'd just taken the spice he would've smelled a rat.'

'Don't give me that! You just wanted the pendant. I'll bet it's exotic. What is it? Departed?'

They sped along the boundary wall, the ancient bricks illuminated by the soft glow of the high-roller's lights.

She pouted. 'I don't see what the problem is, Daddy. We got the spice and we've got the book back. The pendant's an added bonus. Maybe we can use it to arrange another meeting with Delf.'

'Don't *Daddy* me. You're not eight years old any more, Orry.'

She slumped back in her seat.

'Although,' he continued with the ghost of a smile, 'your idea might not be the worst one I've heard today.'

She grinned.

Any chance of getting me out of this ditch sometime soon? Ethan enquired over the family channel.

Anyone following us? Eoin asked.

Nope. They've gone back to the house. Ethan chuckled. *I wouldn't want to be in Konstantin's shoes.*

You couldn't afford *Konstantin's shoes,* Orry pointed out.

Not even with my cut?

Maybe one.

Her brother sighed. *At the moment, I'll settle for not being in a ditch.*

Five minutes, Eoin told him.

Orry pulled out the pendant and stared at the stone. She stripped off one long glove and brushed the ball of her thumb over its surface. It felt silky, frictionless. Definitely exotic – *could* the Departed have made it? The thought was tantalising.

She reached up and fastened the pendant around her neck.

3

KONSTANTIN'S END

Konstantin Larist Soltz, 3rd Viscount Huish, stumbled onto the lawn at the rear of his family seat and whirled to stare up at the light streaming from the ballroom windows. The music sounded muted out here, battling with the constant chirp of the stemhoppers.

He raised his bottle in silent salute to the distant figures taking the air on the balcony. His frock coat and waistcoat lay somewhere back towards the house; purple wine stained his shirt as he lifted the bottle to his lips and swallowed.

Stumbling, Konstantin turned his back on the house and staggered towards the lake. Perun was still visible over the far horizon, illuminating the night with its ghostly blue light, while Veles, its smaller companion moon, climbed from behind the mansion's elaborate chimneys, lending a surreal rusty glow to the landscape.

'Bitch,' he muttered, slurring the words, then laughed. He hadn't meant to say it aloud. 'Fucking twister,' he added for good measure. 'Fucking . . . fucking *whoredog*.'

As much as he wanted to believe he'd known something was

wrong about her from the start, the truth was, he'd not had a clue. He *lived* for those ancient books – they might have become the gentry's latest obsession, but even his so-called peers didn't understand the *smell* of them, the feel of the paper against his skin, the covers and illustrations – and the *words*. Of course, many of the books were available electronically, some were even still in physical print, but that was hardly the point: *these* volumes had been made on Earth, the rarest of them predating even the First Expansion. His heart quickened at the thought, even through the numbing effects of the wine.

He hoped the arbiters took her to the fucking cleaners. The thought brought a twisted smile to his lips. Costanza had given him the usual tongue-lashing and made it plain he was to keep the whole affair quiet to avoid any embarrassment to the old man. That was a shame. If only there were some way to give evidence, to twist the knife and guarantee a hefty sentence. It was a pity they no longer executed antiquities runners.

For some reason Costanza had been particularly angry about the loss of the pendant – fuck knows why. Sure, it was a family heirloom, but the mansion was full of the damn things – and anyway, *he* was the heir. He did like that trinket, though. Something about the dull green stone made him feel – what? Powerful, he supposed, when it was around his neck. Hopefully the arbiters would hand it over once that bitch had been incarcerated for the rest of her thieving life.

A warm breeze rustled the trees as he reached the lake's edge. Bulrushes lined the shore and Konstantin could make out the dark shape of the boathouse some distance away. He raised the bottle again to drain it, coughing as he took too much of the velvety wine. He spat out the dregs and flung the bottle out over the water. It spun in a lazy arc before raising a white splash in the darkness.

Damn, but his head hurt. He frowned as the throbbing in his skull grew suddenly worse: overindulgence had never made him feel like this before. He gripped his forehead as a sudden pain stabbed behind his eyes and turned, trying to walk back towards the house – but his legs gave way, pitching him to the soggy ground. He groaned as the pressure in his head built quickly until he thought his skull would burst. Mud oozed wetly between his grasping fingers, sticking his shirt to his belly. He tried to scream, but his muscles wouldn't respond. His vision blurred, greying at the edges.

A red glow in the trees caught his attention as it moved lazily, trailing a streamer of light, and he gasped as a tall figure wrapped in a cloak stepped from the shadows to regard him with eyes like burning coals. A short man appeared beside the dark figure, keeping a stubby, pistol-like device pointed at Konstantin.

The viscount opened his mouth, only to have it fill with muddy water. He managed a gurgling whimper before darkness overcame him.

The pressure was still there when Konstantin awoke, but at least now the headache was bearable. He opened his eyes and blinked rapidly. Everything looked wrong, and it took a few seconds for his befuddled brain to make sense of what he was seeing. Suddenly his fuzziness and the sharp pain in his ankles made sense: he was hanging upside down – in the boathouse, by the looks of it – dangling a foot above the floorboards.

He squirmed wildly, and discovered his hands were bound behind his back. 'Hey!' he yelled. 'What the devil is this? Let me down!'

He fell silent at the scrape of boots on the wooden floor behind him and twisted in an attempt to see who was there, but succeeded only in sending spikes of agony through his legs. His anger died, replaced by a sour fear deep in his belly.

'Who are you?' he demanded, hiding behind bluster. 'What do you want? Do you have any idea who I am?' He flinched at a light touch on his lower back.

A man appeared in front of him, trailing his hand over Konstantin's body. 'Hush, My Lord.' The man smiled to reveal a set of perfectly formed teeth one size too big for his face. One of them was gold, glinting dully in the dim light. He was a runt of a fellow, wearing a padded jacket that made him look like a child in his father's coat. A ratty goatee clung to a pointed chin; hollow cheeks were pockmarked with acne scars. His close-cropped hair was bleached white, apart from a black streak running down the centre.

Konstantin opened his mouth to tell Rat-boy just what he thought of him, but something about the man's sunken eyes made his throat close up. They were dull, like a river shark's. Inhuman.

'That's better,' said the man. 'Now . . .' He stopped and slapped the heel of his palm against his high forehead. 'But where are my manners, Your Lordship? I haven't even introduced myself.' He performed an execrable, mocking bow. 'Morven Dyas, at your service. I believe you saw my companion, Jericho, by the lakeside. I've left him outside.' He leaned closer and lowered his voice to a conspiratorial whisper. 'Between you and me, he's not fucking right' – he tapped his temple – 'up here. You know what I'm saying?'

The man nudged Konstantin and winked, and he glanced around, close to panic. *Where's Costanza? Hasn't anyone missed me? I'm the count's grandson, for fuck's sake!*

Morven Dyas was looking expectantly at him.

'D-Delighted to meet you,' Konstantin managed.

The man stared at him for a moment, then burst into laughter. 'By Belladonna's crusted teats, this is going to be easier than I thought.' He reached out and gripped the front of Konstantin's filthy dress shirt. Buttons clattered to the floor as he ripped the shirt open, exposing the viscount's mud-streaked chest.

'What are you doing?' Konstantin asked, his voice quavering.

Dyas reached behind him and produced a long, curved blade. He crouched in front of Konstantin, tapping the knife's point with his forefinger. 'There's something I want from you, My Lord.'

'Anything,' Konstantin breathed, unable to take his eyes off the knife's edge.

'A pendant – I'm sure you know the one I mean: a green stone in a gold setting. I admit I was a little nonplussed to find you weren't wearing it, as I was assured you would be. Where is Madam Costanza, by the way? I expected to find her here.'

Sweat was trickling into Konstantin's eyes, making them sting. *Costanza? That treacherous bitch!* No wonder she'd been so keen to get the pendant back. He blinked rapidly. 'I don't have it any longer.'

Dyas stopped tapping the blade and his piggy eyes rose to stare at Konstantin. 'Don't lie to me, Your Lordship. I know all about that particular gewgaw. Even you would never sell it.'

'I didn't sell it – she stole it!'

'Who?'

'A girl . . . woman. She approached me a few weeks back, said she had a folio. She came here tonight and took my pendant.'

The man studied him appraisingly. 'Name?'

'Lady Jade Flint – but it won't do you any good. The arbiters have her.'

The blade's point stuck in the wooden floor with a solid *thunk* and Dyas stood and paced to the window, leaving the knife where it was. It was a vicious-looking thing, like something the cook would use to butcher a pig. Konstantin felt an overwhelming urge to piss.

Dyas placed both hands on the windowsill and stared into the darkness. Konstantin could just make out a dull glow that might have been the distant lights of the house.

'Tell me everything you know about this girl,' the man said.

'And then you'll let me go?'

He turned slowly and smiled. 'Naturally, Your Lordship.'

A flicker of hope dulled the edge of Konstantin's terror. *Of course* this man would release him; he was the future Count of Delf. Dyas wouldn't dare touch him. Konstantin glanced at the knife and swallowed. Still, it wouldn't do any harm to tell him what he wanted. With any luck he'd gut that Flint bitch like the sow she was. And once Konstantin was free, he could deal with Costanza.

The man listened in silence as Konstantin described his first meeting with Lady Jade Flint at his favourite whorehouse in Utz. He was feeling more foolish at every turn as he recounted how the Flint girl had said she was the agent for the book's owner, who'd be planetside for one night only – tonight, the night of the ball. There wasn't any way Konstantin could miss his grandfather's first ball in years so he'd arranged an invitation for her, to bring the book to him. Now he thought about it, that was probably what she'd wanted all along. He'd been played for a fool, damn her blood. Konstantin fell silent after describing the arbiter driving off in his high-roller, eyeing his captor anxiously.

'I believe you,' Dyas said, and Konstantin would have slumped with relief had he not been dangling upside down from the ceiling.

The man pushed himself off from the windowsill, walked over, yanked the knife from the floor and thrust the blade deep into Konstantin's side.

Konstantin gasped, staring at the hilt protruding from the roll of fat above his right hip. Blood ran warm from the wound, beading on the dark hairs of his torso.

A moment later the agony came.

He screamed as a furnace of white fire seared his belly, radiating outwards until he could barely think.

'I believe you,' Dyas repeated, 'but I have to be sure.' He grabbed the blade and slid it slowly downwards in a sawing motion.

As Konstantin felt skin and muscle part, he screamed himself hoarse.

4

BONAVENTURE

Bonaventure had been laid down in a minor yard above Endymion two decades before Orry was born, and the old freighter was showing every one of her forty years. Yet despite the chipped composite and scored paintwork, the ship's systems were in excellent condition; she made sure of that.

Her cabin was cramped, but she liked it that way. It had been years since the ship had carried paying passengers, but her father had given up suggesting she move into one of the more spacious staterooms on the observation deck. This was *her* place: she'd slept here since she was a year old and couldn't imagine laying her head down anywhere else.

She zipped up her maroon flight suit over a clean white T-shirt and paused to stare at the framed picture of her mother beside her narrow bunk. She didn't share Katerina Kent's elegant, fine-boned beauty, though Dad always insisted she had her mother's eyes. Orry couldn't imagine Katerina in a grease-stained flight suit – she was far better suited to the emerald ballgown now hanging from the door of one of the lockers that lined the cabin's walls.

Orry stared at the gown, then at her reflection in the glossy media screen next to the bed. She lifted a handful of sunburst-orange hair off her neck, the way it had been at the ball. She sighed, then caught a glimpse of the stupid, wistful look on her face and scowled.

Disgusted with herself, she snatched the ballgown off its hanger and began folding it into its protective sleeve. Time to go back in the costume closet; maybe one day she'd get to wear it again. She fastened the bag, punched the door release – and ran straight into her brother.

'Watch it,' she snapped.

'Whoa, time of the month again, Sis?'

'Get out of my way, Ethan.'

He didn't move. At fourteen, he was shooting up like a weed and almost as tall as her. When his lanky body began to fill out he might even be a match for her in the kickball ring they'd set up in the hold.

He brushed a lock of hair from his eyes and grinned. 'Dad wants us. Planning session.'

'Fine.' She tossed the dress onto her bed and shut the door. As she locked it with a command from her integuary, she looked suspiciously at Ethan. 'If you *ever* subvert my lock, I'll space you: you know that, don't you?'

He placed a hand on his heart. 'You wound me, Sister. I would never do such a thing.'

She glared and pushed past him.

Bonaventure's refectory was well appointed, intended to cater for a full crew of six, plus up to a dozen passengers. The galley was set into an alcove on one side of the oval compartment. Eoin was already sitting at the circular smart-table in the middle, a bulb of coffee cooling in front of him. Next to it was the ancient book in its cloth wrapper. He was running his hands over the table's surface, rearranging virtual notes and images. The refectory's wide media screen was muted, set to scan the local newsfeeds.

'About time,' he said. 'Ready to do some work?'

She groaned and dropped into one of the chairs bolted to the deck. Ethan went to the galley and snagged a couple of Utzeen candy bars. He tossed one to Orry.

'What's the rush?' she asked, tearing the wrapper open. 'Once we've sold Konstantin's spice we'll have enough gilt for a good few months.' She bit a chunk from the bar and waved the rest at her father as she chewed. 'I vote for a holiday.'

'She's right for once,' Ethan said. 'I hear Halcyon is nice all year long.'

Her father slurped his coffee and regarded them. 'While it's wonderful to see you two agree on something, we're not finished on Tyr.'

She sighed. 'Delf.'

'You might count that last job as a success, but I don't. We need another plan to get his integuary pattern.'

'What about the book game, though?' Ethan said. 'Folio fever won't last for ever. We should make as much as we can from it before the toffs find a new idiotic hobby.'

'Forget the book game,' Eoin said sharply. 'Trust me, we need Delf's integuary pattern more.'

'There are a lot of things you can do to someone if you have their pattern,' Orry said thoughtfully. 'What do you have in mind? And why Delf?'

'I have my reasons.'

27

'Care to share them?'

'Not right now. Let's just focus on getting that bastard's pattern first, then maybe we can take a short holiday before we move on him.'

'Halcyon?' Ethan suggested hopefully.

Her father rolled his eyes. 'We'll see.'

The media screen unmuted itself, filling the refectory with sound.

'—about the death of his grandson and heir, Konstantin Larist Soltz, the 3rd Viscount Huish—'

Orry looked up to see Konstantin's face filling the screen. She read the banner headlines scrolling below it with growing horror.

'What—?' Ethan began, before Eoin hushed him with a hiss.

'Arbiter-Colonel Zaytsev made this statement earlier,' the screen continued as Konstantin's face vanished, to be replaced by a man in a black uniform with silver fist emblems on his collar. The face beneath his steel grey hair might have been carved from granite.

'This brutal murder of the heir to one of the Ascendancy's Great Houses has shocked the Fountainhead. I have just come from an audience with the Imperator Ascendant, who has directed me to focus the full resources of the Arbiter Corps on bringing the perpetrators of this heinous crime to justice. Members of His Grace the Count of Delf's household have provided us with a number of promising leads. We are confident that those responsible will be brought to justice swiftly.'

Eoin stared at Orry, his face drawn.

'They think it was us,' she said hollowly.

He nodded.

28

'What do we do?' she asked.

He ran a hand across his chin. 'Give me a minute . . .'

'They *can't* think it's us,' Ethan said. 'Konstantin was still alive when you arrested Orry.'

Eoin waved a dismissive hand. 'How long do you think it will take the arbiters to check their arrest records and figure out someone is running around with a stolen badge? You know how superficial our story was – it was never designed to stand up to a murder investigation.'

Orry hooked the screen feed with her integuary and scanned the metadata. She placed her unfinished candy bar on the table as her brain picked out words like 'tortured' and 'eviscerated'.

'Who would do that?' she asked.

'Who cares?' her father snapped. 'They think you did it and that's all that matters.'

'But they can't find us,' Ethan said shakily. 'Can they? They don't know our real names.'

Eoin glared at him. 'Did you sanitise the security footage?'

'What? No – why would I do that?'

'So, they know what Orry looks like. What about the autocar and the high-roller?'

'What about them?'

'You subverted them – did you leave anything in their systems? Anything the arbiters could trace back to us?'

'I-I don't know.' Ethan looked like he was about to burst into tears.

'Don't blame him,' Orry snapped. 'You never told him to do those things – we've never needed to before.'

'That kind of thing should be routine! Any professional crew would know that—'

'He's *fourteen*, Dad! *You* taught us – don't try to shift the blame onto him.'

Eoin looked like he was about to explode. He glared at her, then without another word rose to his feet and strode away.

'Where are you going?' she called after him.

'The bridge,' he said over his shoulder. 'We need to get off this rock right now.'

'Shit.' She glanced up at the media screen, currently zooming in on an aerial view of the Delf estate. The house and rear lawn were crawling with arbiters and an inflatable dome had been erected by the lakeside. She jumped up and hurried after her father.

'What should I—?' Ethan began.

'Prep for zero-g,' she told him over her shoulder. They'd been on Tyr for weeks – long enough to get sloppy about securing loose articles.

5

WHERE'S THE FUN IN THAT?

Bonaventure's bridge was small for a freighter of her tonnage, with only six acceleration couches arranged like the petals of a flower around the holographic navigation orrery. Canted screens above each crew position provided redundancy, in case the integuary link to the ship's systems failed. Integuary hardware might have moved on since the ship's construction, but the connection protocols remained the same.

Her father was already lying on the master's couch, his eyes closed.

Orry settled into her own couch, letting the deformable polymer mould to the shape of her body. She used her integuary to hook *Bonaventure*'s general systems core. Status displays appeared at the edges of her vision and she frowned when she saw that Eoin had almost completed the pre-start checklist without her. The engines were *her* responsibility.

'I'll finish those,' she told him.

'I've got it. Contact the tower. I've just filed our flight plan.'

She reviewed the plan and gave a humourless smile when she saw the destination. She opened a channel to the control tower.

31

'Utz Tower, freighter *Bonaventure*.'

'Go ahead, *Bonaventure*.'

'Tower, we're ready to lift from pad zero-five. Request information and engine start.'

'Start-up approved. Sending information Sigma. Report ready for departure.'

Orry acknowledged. 'Starting number two,' she told her father, listening through *Bonaventure*'s hull-mounted microphones to the blare of the warning klaxon while checking the ship's exterior lenses for people or foreign objects beneath the hull.

When she initiated the start-up sequence, the familiar vibration of *Bonaventure*'s mass-inversion drive made her couch tremble. She repeated the sequence for the other three engines, all the while monitoring their status displays.

'Tower, *Bonaventure* with information Sigma. Request lift from zero-five for trans-orbit and collapse into Halcyon.'

'*Bonaventure*, you are cleared to lift from pad zero-five for trans-orbital injection and collapser transition to Halcyon. Safe journey.'

'Roger, Tower. *Bonaventure* is lifting.'

As her father fed power to the engines, the rumble filled the bridge and she focused on the status indicators as they lifted from the pad. He increased thrust slowly, the altimeter first crawling, then changing more rapidly as the wide curve of *Bonaventure*'s hull battered its way through the thick atmosphere. The heavy freighter shuddered and Orry was pressed down into her couch – then the shaking died away and the spaceport taking up the greater part of one of the outlying islands of the city of Utz dwindled below her.

Utz, capital not just of Tyr but of the entire Ascendancy, sprawled across the hundreds of isles that made up the Helion Archipelago. Turquoise channels glinted between the islands, the slender bridges that linked them barely visible from the edge of space. The parks and estates of the provincial islands were a vibrant green in the oxygen-rich atmosphere.

To the south of the city a thin black line climbed up out of the atmosphere. Each of the space elevator tethers rising from the equator like ribbons was capped with an orbital dock for non-atmosphere-capable vessels. As the curvature of the planet became visible, Orry could make out the vast naval yards around the nearest ribbon-head docking stations, and the hundreds of vessels of the Home Fleet moored there.

The pressure on her chest reduced as they left the last of the atmosphere behind and *Bonaventure* settled into a comfortable 1g acceleration.

'Are we really going to Halcyon?' she asked.

'You tell me.'

Another one of his tests. She thought about it. 'No,' she said after a moment.

'Why not?'

'It's unlikely they'll be able to identify me from the security footage, but if they do, they could trace me back to *Bonnie*, so the last place we want to go is where they think we're going. We need to get out of the Fountainhead to somewhere the Imperator's grip isn't so choking. Somewhere we can get new registration docs, update the fake IDs.'

He grunted. 'There's hope for you yet.' He sat up and examined the navigation orrery. The three-dimensional representation of the Tyr system hanging in the centre of the ring of acceleration couches showed the orbits of planets, moons and other celestial bodies as glowing lines.

She chewed her lip. 'What you said to Ethan? That wasn't fair.'

'I know it.' He manipulated the display, rotating and zooming out to examine the volume of space around the Fountainhead systems. Designated entry and egress collapse points were highlighted and annotated with scrolling data. 'It's my fault for not teaching him properly.'

'He's *good*, Dad – he's just young. He can't know everything. Maybe you're pushing us too hard.'

'You knew more than him at fourteen.'

'Not about subverting stuff.'

'About playing the game.' He sighed. 'You're a natural, Orry – maybe you raised my expectations too high. Your brother's pretty good, but he'll never be you.'

'Give him a chance! Now that we can't go after Delf for a while, maybe we should take a break, spend some of our Ruuz gilt.'

'Maybe we should.'

'And please, let's make the next job a simple one. For Ethan's sake.'

'Message received and understood.' He still didn't look happy as he turned back to the orrery. 'So, where shall we go?'

'Somewhere quiet.' She smiled. 'Ethan's going to be pissed off that you took Halcyon off the menu.'

'Did I?' He smiled innocently. 'That never occurred to me.' He glanced over. 'Where are you going?'

'Engine room. I want to check the drives are okay after a month planetside.'

'You can do that from up here.'

She grinned at him from the door. 'Where's the fun in that?'

Ethan was waiting for her in the refectory. 'Is he mad at me?' he asked, tagging along beside her.

'He's fine. He knows he was in the wrong.'

Her brother's long fingers plucked at the sleeve of her flight suit. 'Orry.'

She stopped. He hardly ever used her name.

He stared at his boots. 'Do you think Dad's right? *Did* I screw up?'

'As far as I can tell, our whole life is one big screw-up.' She placed her hands on his shoulders and looked him in the eye. 'What we are, what we do . . . it's risky, we know that, and some-times things will go wrong. We'll learn from it and be better next time. It *wasn't* your fault, Ethan. The plan was way too complicated – you weren't ready and I wasn't ready.'

'You're *always* ready,' he muttered. 'You're brilliant at *everything*.'

She cupped his face in her hands and stared at him with mock concern. 'Oh my God! What is *wrong* with you?'

He shrugged her off, trying not to smile.

'We all have our strengths,' she told him, 'and that's why our crew works. I'm good at playing a part, and I can keep *Bonnie* ticking over, but I couldn't do what you do, not in a million years. I wouldn't know where to start with subverting an inte-guary.' She snorted. 'Also, you know I can't even step outside the ship without having a nervous breakdown.'

His smile grew wider.

'I'm glad you find it so amusing.'

'Well, that is pretty funny. Thanks, Sis.'

'Just don't get all gooey about it.'

'Ha!' He punched her hard in the arm and skipped away.

'You little toe-rag.'

'Loser,' he called over his shoulder, already halfway to his stateroom.

She started down the axial companionway to the engineering spaces on the fourth of *Bonaventure*'s decks, below the cavernous and largely empty holds. By the time she reached the engine room she was breathing heavily, but the smell of metal and ozone was comforting. This was her favourite part of the ship; when she was upset or worried there was something soothing about the steady humming of the mass-inversion drives as they pushed the freighter through the emptiness of space. Orry knew every readout and regulator, every pipe and processor. Her father had made sure that both his children knew how critical it was that they could pilot and maintain the ship, in case the worst should happen. They didn't have to ask what 'the worst' meant; space had always been full of threats, from meteors and solar flares to pirates and commerce raiders – even the occasional Kadiran cleaveship.

She was checking drive number four when the harsh blare of the proximity alarm shattered the calm.

She activated her integuary immediately. *Dad? What's happening?*

After a moment she tried again: *Dad? Ethan?*

She tried to hook the ship's sensor core, and her concern turned to fear as she realised her integuary was being jammed.

Raiders.

She was picking her way between the throbbing machines, moving as quickly as she could, when the alarm cut out.

A few seconds later, she felt the unmistakeable shudder of a ship docking.

6

RAIDERS

The inner door of the starboard freight lock was closed when Orry reached it. Peering in through the inspection port she saw that the outer door was similarly sealed, stars visible beyond the matching port set into its surface. She looked away, sweat prickling her forehead. Whatever had docked with *Bonaventure* had done so here, she was certain of it; the noises she'd heard as she climbed up from engineering were too loud to have come from any of the other airlocks. So where was it?

She tried her integuary again and cursed. For the first time in years, she was entirely alone.

She stiffened at the sound of voices coming from deeper within the ship. This section of the outer hold was full of configurable shelving filled with empty shipping containers of all sizes, all held in place by molecular hooks. Her father sometimes talked about going legit one day, but she knew he'd never really do it. He loved the thrill of the game too much to swap it for the hassles of a free trader.

She slipped into the maze of canyon-like alleyways and navigated the turns until she reached the curving pressure bulkhead that divided the doughnut-shaped ring of outer holds from the circular inner hold. Pressing her back against a container and blending into the shadows, she stared through the pair of wide access doors into the central space.

'For the love of Rama, Jericho! Will you give it a fucking rest already?' The speaker, a wasted-looking man in his thirties, had a black streak running down the centre of his close-cropped white hair. The spacesuit he was wearing looked like an ageing version of something an extreme-g enthusiast might build, its thermal fins covered in faded and scored street art.

He was looking up at a mimetic at least a head taller than him. A tactical cloak hung from the robot's shoulders, its ballistic weave reinforced with ablative plates. The machine – *Jericho?* – regarded the man in the suit through the two red sensors set like eyes in its ovoid face.

'But it's not fair,' it complained. 'Just because my senses are better than yours, I have to miss out. It's not my fault you humans stumble through life with your heads up your arses. I'm fed up with waiting outside while you have all the fun.'

The man looked outraged. 'You think I *enjoy* cutting on people?'

'I know you do, Dyas.'

Dyas shook his head. 'I'm not some kind of psycho. I do what needs to be done.'

'Whatever you say.'

He glared at the mimetic. 'All right, you sick fuck, you can do the next one. Just stop sulking.' When the mimetic nodded, he added, 'Happy now? Good. Can we get on?' He stomped away towards the axial companionway leading up to the crew spaces and the bridge.

Orry tried her integuary again, wanting to warn her father and brother, and snarled with frustration when it failed to connect.

Dyas was almost at the companionway steps when a laser beam seared across the hold in front of his face. He recoiled and threw himself behind a net of empty plastic drums.

Eoin's face peered out from the companionway and quickly withdrew. 'I'll give you exactly ten seconds to get off my god-damn ship,' he yelled.

It might have been the decent thing to do, but Orry couldn't help feeling frustrated with her father. He was a good shot; he could have hit Dyas with that first beam. Now the element of surprise was lost.

Dyas chuckled. 'Captain Kent, I presume? I understand your concern, so let me put your mind at ease. All I want is that little trinket your daughter grifted out of poor Konstantin. Hand it over and we'll be on our way, all peaceful like.'

Orry touched the smooth stone hanging round her neck.

Dyas ducked as another beam parted the netting, shifting the drums. Smouldering strands danced around his head.

'I won't tell you again,' her father shouted.

The raider scowled. 'Jericho, explain the situation to this idiot.'

'With pleasure.' The mimetic drew a bulky maser from under its cloak and aimed at the companionway.

Eoin leaped from the cover of the bulkhead as metal bubbled and spat, flinging himself behind a wall of containers as Jericho tracked him and fired again. The air shimmered and the containers buckled into superheated slag. Orry gripped the pendant tightly, the edge of its golden setting digging into her palm as liquid metal flowed over her father's legs. He screamed, and tears sprang to her eyes, but she was unarmed, worse than useless. There was *nothing* she could do to help.

The raiders approached her father. Flames licked the surface of the metal as it cooled, hardening over what was left of his legs. He stopped screaming and scrabbled desperately for his weapon, but Dyas kicked it away and drew a pistol from his belt.

'Ouchy,' he said. 'Now, where's that pendant? Or shall I send Jericho here to find your daughter and ask her?'

'F-fuck you,' Eoin spat.

'I know she's on board. Your son, too.'

He shuddered as he hacked out a laugh. 'You pair of clowns! Do you really think I'd file a genuine passenger manifest? My kids are on a charter flight – they'll be halfway across the galaxy by now.'

Dyas hesitated for a moment, then chuckled. 'Nice try, Captain, but I know when a man is lying.'

'I'm not lying,' Eoin insisted, but even Orry could hear the desperation in her father's voice now.

'You know what?' Dyas said, stepping closer. 'It doesn't matter. That pendant is somewhere on this ship and I'm going to find it. I'll tell your kids you said "hi".'

He raised his pistol and fired. Eoin's head disintegrated, painting a broad splash of red across the deck.

Orry stared at her father's lifeless body: he was gone, snuffed out in an instant. An involuntary moan escaped her lips.

Jericho whirled, red eyes blazing, and Dyas followed the mimetic's gaze. 'Well, well,' he said, then glared at Jericho. 'What are you waiting for, bonehead? Get her!'

Terror overwhelmed Orry, smothering her grief, and as

Jericho's maser rose she flung herself back down the narrow canyon between the towers of shelves. She screamed as heat washed over her, blistering her back. The reek of singed hair caught in her throat.

'What are you *doing*?' Dyas raged. 'We need her alive, you *moron*!'

She twisted around a corner, tears of pain blurring her vision. *Where's Ethan?* She had to find him. Despair plucked at her as she entered another alley, trying to keep ahead of the raiders.

Dyas' mocking voice came from somewhere off to her left. 'Where are you going, Aurelia? There's nowhere you can hide that I won't find you.'

She veered right, wondering where Jericho was. Panic rose in her chest and she forced it down, remembering the lessons her father had drummed into her. *Fear is good, it gives you an edge – but panic will get you killed.*

She forced herself to stop and crouched in the half-light, trying to control her breathing as she listened. Jericho's soft pneumatic tread came from her right. She couldn't hear Dyas.

Think.

Like most merchant vessels, *Bonaventure* had a radiation-shielded citadel; theirs was concealed in the crew space near the bridge. The safe room was equipped with provisions and a small-arms cabinet. Ethan was most likely there – but that meant she'd have to go through Dyas to get to him. *Stupid.* If she'd thought of it earlier she could have fled around the outer hold and worked her way back to the axial companionway. Now it was too late: she was trapped out next to *Bonaventure*'s hull.

'Aureli-*a-a-a*—'

She gritted her teeth. Engineering was her only option. It

had a comms stack and there were a couple of routes in and out. She could send out a distress call and with any luck double back on Dyas and get up to the citadel.

She raced for the engine-room companionway, praying Dyas hadn't somehow got ahead of her. The ladder was clear and she jumped down and flew along the passageway below. Distant footsteps sounded behind her as she reached the comms stack.

Her fingers flew over the screen, entering her manual override code, and relief flooded through her when it was accepted. She bent forward and spoke into the mic, keeping her voice as low as possible. 'Mayday, Mayday, Mayday. Freighter *Bonaventure*, fifty minutes outbound from Tyr, en route to egress point Rho. We have been boarded by raiders. One fatality. Please help!'

'Come on, pretty girl,' Dyas called. He sounded horribly close.

She backed away from the stack, cursing herself for not recording her words so she could loop them. She could only hope *someone* had picked up the transmission.

'I have something for you,' Dyas cooed.

She shuddered, but at least she knew where Dyas was; Jericho had fallen silent.

There were two access points to the deck above. Orry manoeuvred herself between the humming machinery until she could see the other exit, but there was an open area stretching between her and the door. It looked clear, but she would make an inviting target as she crossed the exposed deck.

'Where the hell are you, bitch?'

She tensed. He was close.

A freight trolley loaded with two plastic drums of coolant stood nearby. Orange warning stickers decorated the large blue cylinders.

The trolley's motor hummed softly as she aimed it at the door in the bulkhead, some ten metres away. The edge of the engine room was to her right, which meant Dyas and Jericho had to be somewhere in the tangle of machinery on the left. She set the trolley in motion and squatted down beside it, using the drums as cover. Her thighs started burning immediately as she waddled along, trying to keep up.

'Come on,' she muttered as it closed the gap to the exit at walking pace.

She was only a couple of metres away when Jericho stepped into the doorway, filling it. The mimetic raised its maser.

Orry threw herself sideways, away from the trolley. She didn't hear the maser fire, but could feel its heat as she rolled clear.

The trolley continued towards Jericho, the plastic drums bubbling and spitting. The mimetic released the trigger but it was too late: the trolley's front wheels were glowing white-hot and as they deformed, the melting barrels were pitched forward. The first one came apart a metre from Jericho, releasing a wave of coolant that splashed over the mimetic, soaking its ballistic cloak.

Orry, realising what was about to happen, tried to run just as the backwash hit the blistering hot trolley and ignited, engulfing Jericho in an inferno. She screamed as a wall of heat lifted her up and smashed her into *Bonaventure*'s hull, driving the air from her lungs. A warning klaxon howled as Jericho disappeared in a cloud of halon gas fired from the suppression vents in the overhead.

'Damn, girl,' Dyas called out, 'what did you *do*?'

Orry gasped like a landed fish, dragging air into her lungs.

'I don't think Jericho is very happy with you right now,' Dyas chided. He sounded amused. 'I was going to slit your throat, but now I might have to give you to him to play with instead.'

Tears rolled down her face. 'Leave me *alone!*' she screamed.

'Ah, *there* you are.'

She cursed and looked around wildly. There was a service airlock a few metres away. Her stomach fell away at the thought of the void on the other side, but she clenched her fists. It was her only chance.

'I'm going to enjoy this,' Dyas called.

She could see him now, the bright fins of his suit visible as he approached.

'Come *on*, Orry,' she muttered, and forced herself into the airlock.

Panic threatened to overwhelm her as the inner door closed, trapping her inside. She twisted the safety handle to override the electronic lock, keeping her back to the outer door the whole time. Beyond it was *nothing*, infinite vacuum. She snatched a spacesuit from an alcove and struggled into it.

Ignoring the small inspection port set into the outer door, she focused with desperate intensity on the head-up display projected onto her visor as the airlock depressurised. Silence enveloped her. Her gloved finger hesitated over the door panel. She *had* to do this. There was no other way. It was only a short EVA over the hull to the airlock by the bridge: she'd be outside the ship for a couple of minutes max – then she'd be in the citadel with Ethan and they could wait in safety for the cavalry to arrive.

She took a series of quick breaths, trying to calm her pounding heart. *You can do this*, she told herself sternly. Closing her eyes, she pressed the panel.

The cold pierced her suit. With a supreme effort of will she turned her body to face the open outer door. Every breath was loud inside her helmet. Blood thudded in her ears. She opened her eyes and stared into the void.

'Oh, Rama, what am I doing?'

The stars hung dully against the expanse of space as she shuffled out of the lock. The molecular hooks in her boots clung to the ship, making every step an effort. There were manoeuvring packs in the airlock, but the thought of floating free of the hull made her want to scream.

Bonaventure's hull bulged in front her: the vast field of scored metal seemed to go on for ever, even though she knew it curved back within a few metres. Behind her, the freighter's huge radiator fans glowed cherry red as they dealt with the power plant's waste heat. She closed her eyes, willing herself to calm down. Sweat stung when she opened them again. It had been four years since her last EVA. Apparently, nothing had changed.

She levered up one boot, leaned forward and set it back down, then repeated the process with her other foot. Behind her, the airlock's outer door remained open, inviting her back inside.

No! You have to do this . . . She took another step, then another, but the horizon of the ship's hull looked no closer. As she lifted her leg a new wave of dizziness made her reel and stars started spinning around her head. She flailed, leg still raised, imagining her other boot slipping. Somehow regaining her balance, she slammed her leg down, gasping. Tears filled her eyes.

'I can't,' she whispered, despising her weakness. She turned and retraced the few pathetic steps she had managed to take.

Waiting for the airlock's outer door to close was the worst part. Her helmet was stifling her. She couldn't breathe as she watched the pressure rise. The moment the HUD indicator turned green her hands were on her helmet seal. She wrenched it off and let it thud to the deck where it rolled away. Recycled air filled her lungs, sweet as a mountain stream. She pressed her forehead against the cool of the bulkhead and tried to relax her shoulders.

A sharp knocking on the inner door made her head snap up.

Dyas peered in through the inspection port. The intercom crackled to life. 'Looks like you're in a pretty pickle,' he said with a smile.

'Screw off.'

He pouted. 'Such spirit. So what went wrong out there? Touch of vertigo?'

Orry's rage at herself boiled over. 'Why don't you go fuck yourself, you ugly little toad?'

His face stiffened. 'So rude! Why don't you come out of there so I can teach you some manners?'

'Why don't you take your stupid beard and what's left of your robot and piss off out of my ship?'

'That's not going to happen – not until I have Konstantin's pendant. Tell me where it is and I'm gone. No one else needs to get hurt.'

It was only when she reached up to touch the pendant that she realised it was gone. She fought to keep the dismay from her face, wondering where she had lost it. *It must have been when I was thrown by the exploding barrel*, she thought. *Damn it!* Whatever lies were coming out of Dyas' mouth, she knew the pendant was the only thing keeping her and Ethan alive right now, so she had to keep that going until help arrived – or until she could figure out a plan.

'I've got it right here,' she told him. 'Around my neck.'

'That makes things simple, then. Open the door and hand it over and we'll leave.'

'You expect me to believe that?'

'Not really, no.' His arm moved and a curved blade appeared in front of his face. He smiled venomously. 'How about this? I find your little brother – Ethan, isn't it? – and start cutting pieces off him until you come out.'

She slammed a fist against the inspection port. 'You leave him alone!'

His smile widened and she forced herself to calm down. She was giving him all the leverage he needed on a plate. She took a steadying breath. 'Is that the knife you used on Konstantin?' she asked, playing for time.

'Smart. Yes, this is the one. He was a screamer, that boy.'

She swallowed. 'So what's so special about the pendant, anyway?'

'Nice try. Just come out and I'll leave your brother alone. If you don't, I'll have to take your ship somewhere quiet while I look for him. I can take my time—'

He stopped and turned his head away, then turned back,

grinning. 'Well, well, well,' he said. 'Look what we have here.'

Jericho appeared behind him, its face scorched and blackened. It held up a hand and Orry saw the pendant dangling from its fingers. Her last hopes died.

'This does change things a little, don't you think?' Dyas said.

'What are you going to do?' she asked dully.

He appeared to consider. 'You're not coming out?'

'I can't say the thought holds much appeal.'

He nodded sagely. 'In that case, you leave me with little choice.'

'Take the pendant and go?'

He chuckled. 'No,' he said evenly. 'Blow you out of the airlock.'

She stared at him, trying to work out if he was serious. Terror traced an icy line up her spine.

She moved first, lunging for her helmet, but the alarm was already shrieking as Dyas yanked down the emergency venting handle. Her fingers brushed against the helmet and sent it spinning away like a top as the outer door blew open. The maelstrom of explosive decompression whipped her body across the airlock and out into the heart-stopping cold of space.

Orry spiralled away from *Bonaventure*'s hull in a hailstorm of frozen oxygen. The cold clawed at the exposed skin of her face, penetrating deep into her bones. Her lungs were bursting, screaming for air, but she knew not to hold her breath. Instead, she exhaled slowly. Her father had told them a human body could survive for more than a minute in hard vacuum.

Not that it would help.

As *Bonaventure* grew smaller, she realised she wasn't scared any more. Now the pain had gone it was quite pleasant, floating free. She just hoped Ethan had sense enough to stay safe in the citadel. A feeling of deep well-being filled her as her vision began to fade. She supposed it was hypoxia setting in, but she no longer cared.

The last thing she remembered was the strange sensation of saliva boiling on her tongue.

7

MENDER

Consciousness returned slowly. At first the familiar throb of a ship's mass-inversion drive made Orry think she was in her cabin, but the smell wasn't right. There was an antiseptic odour that brought to mind a hospital, but it was fighting with something earthier, a musty scent that reminded her of unwashed clothes. Then the memories came flooding back and her eyes flew open. She was in a medical bay, cocooned in diagnostic equipment. Scratched and chipped surfaces betrayed the age of the sensors. Both her spacesuit and flight suit were gone, leaving her in only the white T-shirt and underwear she had put on that morning.

'You're one lucky lady.'

She jerked up and banged her head on a monitor. A heavyset old man was sitting on the other side of the triangular compartment, a scowl on his craggy face. He was wearing a shabby jacket and crudely patched trousers. His thinning grey hair badly needed cutting, and dirty white bristles sprouted from deep folds in his chin. One of his eyes had the dull glint of an implant.

Orry choked on her dry throat when she tried to speak. The old man leaned forward, groaning with the effort, and passed her a bulb of water. She sipped gratefully at it, then tried again.

'Where am I?'

'On my ship.'

'But the airlock?' She shuddered at the memory. 'How did I get here?'

'I picked you up.'

'*How?* I was floating in deep space—' A thought occurred to her. 'Where's *Bonaventure*?'

'Your ship is gone.'

'*Gone?*' Orry's heart was pounding so fast an alarm started beeping somewhere in the equipment surrounding her. *Ethan . . . !*

The old man stood and leaned over her. He checked something, then flicked a switch. The beeping stopped.

'Don't get distressed, girl,' he growled. His face softened a little. 'My name is Mender, Jurgen Mender. This is my ship, *Dainty Jane*. Her sensors detected you and I caught you with a hawser – reeled you in like a Genovian bloodtrout.'

When he wasn't glaring, Mender's face was quite agreeable, almost grandfatherly. 'Thank you,' she said, her mind whirling. 'I'm Orry. How did you come to be there at exactly the right moment?'

He ignored her question. 'I don't care what your name is, girl. And don't get too comfortable. As soon as we get to Novo Castria I'm throwing you back, my little bloodtrout.'

'I can't go to Novo Castria! I have to find my ship – my little brother's still on board—' The thought of what Dyas might be doing to Ethan was too much. She swallowed, fighting back tears.

His face contorted. 'Piotr's withered balls,' he spat, 'save me from wailing bloody women.'

She flushed with sudden anger. Shoving the machines aside, she swung her legs off the bed and jabbed an accusing finger at him. 'My father's been murdered, my ship's been stolen and my brother is missing,' she said. 'That bastard Dyas took everything. What do you expect me to do?'

Mender snorted. 'I should be the one crying,' he muttered.

'What does that mean?'

He shifted uncomfortably in his seat, looking at the medical readouts rather than at her. 'That bastard Dyas owes me – I was tracking him out of Tyr when *Jane* detected you, so I had a choice, didn't I? You or him. *That's* how I happened to be in exactly the right place – and he's long gone now. Who knows when I'll find him again – it's a big bloody galaxy out there . . .'

'I'm sorry to inconvenience you,' Orry said coldly.

'It's more than an inconvenience, girl.' He stood, ignoring her icy tone. 'We're an hour from the egress point. Stay here until we collapse.'

'But—'

'Stay here. We'll talk later.' He limped away.

Orry glared after him until the door closed, then lay back. She gritted her teeth as she tried to hang on to her anger, but it was no use. Her eyes brimmed over. Her face felt tight, like she had a bad case of sunburn, but at least it didn't hurt. In fact, none of her hurt, she suddenly realised, not even where the maser had caught her. Mender's equipment might not look like much but it was clearly still working.

She had to talk to him and find out what he knew about Dyas. Mender was the only lead she had. Maybe she'd been a little hard on him – after all, he had saved her life. Dad always told her she had a tongue like a whip. Mender hadn't just rescued her but he'd patched her up too – and lost his lead on the raider because of it. She found herself mouthing one of her father's favourite maxims: *my enemy's enemy is my friend*. Any way she cut it, Mender was all she had in the galaxy right now, and yelling at him wasn't any way to get him on side.

She forced her fear for her brother deep down inside and locked it away with her grief at her father's death. If she was to get her brother back, she had to think clearly. She'd deal with Dad's murder later; right now she had to concentrate. This was going to be the most difficult game of her life.

The deck was cold on her bare feet when she tried to stand. Her legs wobbled, but supported her weight. She stood for a moment, waiting for the headrush to pass, scanning the room, and spotted her flight suit in one corner, along with her boots. Once she was dressed, she felt a little less vulnerable.

She crossed to the door.

It was locked.

Any goodwill she felt towards Mender evaporated. 'You old bastard!' Her fist thudded against the unyielding composite. 'Mender,' she yelled, 'let me out of here right now!'

She stepped back, rubbing her hand, and looked for the intercom. It was next to the door, an ancient-looking model she'd never seen before. Like the rest of the medbay, it had the same feel of age. The medical equipment was well maintained, but beneath the dull gleam Orry sensed rather than saw a fine layer of accumulated grime that no amount of scrubbing could entirely remove. The deck and bulkheads were the same, worn smooth by countless hands and feet.

The intercom lit up at her touch.

'What?' Mender asked.

'You locked me in.'

'For your own protection.'

'From *what*?'

He sighed. 'All right, for my protection. From your whining.'

She took a long breath. 'Could you let me out, please?'

'No.'

She balled her fists and shouted, 'Let me out!'

The intercom shut off.

She reactivated it. 'Goddammit, Mender, you let me out right n—'

The intercom shut off again.

She shrieked and slapped the bulkhead, imagining it was his wrinkled face. Her palm throbbed as she reached for the intercom again, then thought better of it and instead, crossing to one of the cabinets, she began wrenching open drawers until she found what she was looking for. Brandishing the scalpel and a pair of surgical scissors, she returned to the door.

'Lock *me* up, will you?' she muttered. The controls were flush to the bulkhead but the scalpel blade slipped easily into the narrow gap beside them. She wiggled the blade gently, careful not to snap it as she prised the control panel out.

Her hand froze as her integuary tingled. She shivered; it felt like someone was running their fingers lightly through her hair. She straightened, leaving the panel dangling. Closing her eyes she focused on her integuary, worried it had been damaged by the airlock's explosive decompression.

The tingle came again, moving through her mind. She tried to capture it, to discern its source: was it coming from outside, or from somewhere inside her? The feeling left as abruptly as it had come.

Her eyes snapped open at the sound of the door folding up into the overhead.

She frowned. Had she done that? Poking her head out, she saw the medbay was situated at the end of a passageway with more doorways opening off it. Ignoring them, she headed for the door at the far end, which opened at her approach to reveal a cargo bay. It was tiny by comparison with *Bonaventure*'s sprawling holds, too small for real cargo. Metal tool cabinets surrounded a workbench fixed to one bulkhead, beside which was a long, low shape shrouded in an oil-stained tarpaulin and lashed to the deck. She had seen bays like this before, on ex-military ships used for smuggling, designed to accommodate a couple of ground vehicles or a small flyer; space wasn't usually a factor when running illicit cargoes. Her lips twitched into a ghost of a smile. Mender was far from the archetype of a dashing smuggler.

She pulled back the corner of the tarp to reveal the front of a vintage Horten-Yakimov ground-effect bike hovering half a metre above the deck. 'Oh baby,' she murmured, running her fingers over its curves. The once bright paint of the open cowling was faded, but the engine beneath gleamed like it was right out of the showroom.

'How did you get out?' Mender growled from behind her.

She spun round. 'Sorry, I was just—'

'Just snooping,' he snapped, his bushy eyebrows lowered.

She stared at her feet. 'Sorry,' she repeated, then raised her eyes slowly, keeping them wide.

Mender cleared his throat awkwardly. 'Cockpit's up here,' he said, jabbing a thumb at a series of rungs fixed to a bulkhead. 'You'd best stay where I can keep an eye on you.'

They passed through a small galley area over the cargo bay and up a ladder into the cockpit, where four mesomorphic acceleration shells hung suspended within a free-floating transparent sphere, a design which confirmed what Orry already suspected: the ship had once been a military vessel, the bowl-shaped shells used during high-g manoeuvres to seal themselves around the occupant, the gel lining instantly transitioning into an oxygenated smart fluid designed to prevent lung collapse. Each shell seat was surrounded by a network of glowing screens and worn instrument panels. Orry liked the old-school feel, but she wasn't so keen on the clear canopy arching overhead. She held back, warily eyeing the distant stars beyond.

'What are you waiting for?' Mender asked, indicating the seat to his right. He extracted a slim cheroot from a battered packet and flicked off the tip to light it. The end glowed as he sucked on the filter.

She wrinkled her nose as he blew out a plume of acrid smoke. Keeping her eyes focused on the cockpit, she forced herself up into the sphere. Sliding into the soft interior of the deep shell she focused on the instruments while Mender clambered awkwardly into the commander's position beside her. He held his right leg stiffly and let out a grunt of relief when he was in position.

'Are you alone on board?' she asked.

'I was.' The cheroot bobbed up and down between his lips as he spoke. His gnarled hands made some adjustments to the instruments.

'Doesn't it get to you? Don't you get lonely?'

'Nope,' he replied, tapping at a flickering display with one blunt finger. He cycled it off and on again.

'I would.' She stared out at the stars, waiting for the panic. Instead, she just felt numb.

He looked at her. 'I'm sorry about your father.'

'Thank you. But you didn't kill him.'

'No, but . . .' He turned away. 'Fucking Dyas.'

She shifted in her seat to stare at him. 'Tell me about him – how do you know him?'

'It doesn't matter how I know him. He's a nasty little bastard, and I wish to Rama I'd never met him.'

'Are you going to keep looking for him?'

He nodded.

'Take me with you.'

'Now why would I do a thing like that?'

She leaned forward. 'I can help you.'

He laughed. 'By the time I catch up with him again your brother will be floating in the black somewhere and your ship'll be sold. The best thing you can do is accept that and get on with your life. Revenge ain't all it's cracked up to be.'

She glared at him. 'You're not a very nice person, Mender, you know that?'

'So I'm told.'

'Is that why you live alone?'

'Don't you ever stop asking questions, girl?'

'I have a name, you know.'

'Good for you. Now shut up and let me plot this collapse.'

She cast her eyes over the instrument panel. There were a lot of physical displays, even considering the need for redundancy. 'Does this thing have an integuary node?' she asked.

'This "thing" is called *Jane*. And yes, she has an integuary.'

'Sorry, it's just I've never been in a ship this old.'

'It's not age, it's experience. They don't make them like *Dainty Jane* any more.'

'Where was she laid down? I don't recognise the class. Is she military?'

Mender looked at her, eyes sparking with interest for the first time. He stubbed out his cheroot and exhaled the last of its smoke. 'What makes you say that?'

'The size of the cargo bay. And this.' She indicated the sphere around them.

'Yeah, she was military,' he confirmed.

She met his appraising gaze head on.

'You have an integuary?'

She nodded.

'Had it long?'

'Since I was nine.'

'*Nine?* Rama.'

She shrugged. 'Mum wasn't keen, but Dad talked her into it.'

'It's illegal to graft implants to anyone under thirteen. What did your old man do, hire some quack with a surgical bot?'

'It wasn't like that,' she snapped. 'I *wanted* one. I wanted the connection.'

'When I was nine I wanted to be a dog. My daddy didn't sew a tail to my butt.'

Orry stared at him for several seconds. 'You wanted to be a *dog*?'

He held up his hands in surrender. 'What can I tell you? I was nine.'

'Why'd you want to know if I have an integuary, anyway?'

'Just curious. Use it much?'

'All the time.'

'Your daddy kept you busy, did he?'

'Something like that.'

He thought for a moment. 'You want to plot the collapse?'

She blinked. 'Uh, sure.'

Mender extracted a dented silver hipflask from an inside pocket, unscrewed the cap and took a slug. The smell of whisky made Orry's nose itch. He smacked his lips, replaced the hip-flask and waved a hand at her. 'Go on ahead, then.'

She felt with her mind for *Dainty Jane*'s contact field. There was a slight hesitation as Mender authorised her implant, then the ship's systems pressed in on the edges of her consciousness. *Jane* felt alien, very different to *Bonaventure* – older, certainly, but more than that. There was a depth Orry had never experienced before; rich layers of substrate just beyond the reach of her integuary.

It took her a few seconds to realise what was needling at the edge of her mind: an element of familiarity. It was *Dainty Jane* who'd touched her integuary in the medbay.

Putting her curiosity aside for the moment, she hooked the navigation core and ran the numbers for a direct collapse to Novo Castria. Readouts appeared in her peripheral vision, floating in the air around her, the data repeated on the hardware screens in the cockpit. Redundancy was a core principle of survival in space: backup displays had saved many a pilot's life.

It took her longer than normal, but she figured it out. She looked expectantly at Mender when she was done. His good eye glazed as he used his integuary to check her calculations.

He gave a grunt of approval. 'You know anyone on Novo Castria?' he asked.

'No,' she said.

'Ah, you'll be fine. Pretty girl like you, soon find yourself a rich husband.'

She rounded on him. 'I don't want a husband. I want to save my brother! I want my ship back. I want Dyas' balls on a plate. Why won't you help me?'

'Listen, girl, I like my life the way it is, just me and *Jane*. Why would I want a mouth almighty like you getting under my feet?'

'I can help with running *Jane*.'

'Don't need any help.'

'But how am I supposed to find Dyas without a ship?'

'Not my problem. You ain't coming with us.'

She slumped and stared out of the canopy. There was more traffic now they were approaching the egress point: bulk-haulers, inter-system liners, even a vast galleon in the livery of the Empyrean Development Company, surrounded by a shield of close escort ships. Eighty thousand kilometres away, an Alacrity class frigate altered course.

'Fine,' she said. 'Dump me on Novo Castria. I'm sure I won't get raped or killed or anything.'

'Don't pull that sob-story crap on me, girl. You'll be fine.'

'Like you give a shit.' She watched the distant ships.

He broke the silence. 'What *will* you do?'

'What do you care? I'll have to find a ship, won't I.'

'Just like that.'

'Just like that.'

His fingernail picked at a crusty stain on his thigh. 'Listen, maybe when I find Dyas I could—'

'What? Ask him where Ethan's body is?'

'Oh, I won't be *asking* for anything.' He snorted. 'Forget it.'

She turned to him. He was focused on the instruments, his face tight. *Get a grip, Orry. Be nice.*

'I—' she began.

The comm stack burst into life. 'Mercantile vessel *Dainty Jane*, this is Ascendancy frigate *Speedwell*. Maintain your current attitude and thrust. Stand by to be boarded.'

Orry stiffened.

Mender's wrinkled skin looked pale as he crammed on a headset. 'This is *Dainty Jane*. What seems to be the problem, *Speedwell*?'

'I say again: *Dainty Jane*, maintain your current attitude and thrust. Stand by to be boarded.'

Mender muted the channel and cursed.

'What are you going to do?' Orry asked. She watched the frigate's approach with growing panic, all thoughts of Ethan pushed from her mind. What did they do to people who tortured viscounts to death?

'There's nothing I can do,' he replied bitterly. 'You're clearly no bloodtrout, girl. You're a dead bloody albatross around my neck.'

8

SPEEDWELL

Speedwell closed at 5g. At a thousand kilometres the frigate reduced thrust and turned to match *Dainty Jane*'s course and speed. A port opened in *Speedwell*'s hull and a cutter emerged, light glinting from the little craft's dorsal turret and the engine flaring with a soft blue glow as it ate up the distance between the two vessels.

Mender levered himself out of his seat as the cutter manoeuvred for the freight lock at *Dainty Jane*'s stern. 'Stay here,' he told Orry.

She ignored him and hopped nimbly from her seat.

He sighed and climbed down from the cockpit.

The cargo bay reverberated as the cutter came alongside. Orry shuddered, remembering the last time she'd heard a ship docking.

Mender produced his hipflask. 'Just do what they say,' he growled before draining it.

She swallowed, her eyes fixed on the airlock's inner door. It opened with a hiss and four auxiliaries in armoured suits piled into the cargo bay, all screaming at Orry and Mender.

'On your knees!'

'Hands behind your heads!'

'Down on the deck – *now*!'

'*Do it!*'

The deck plates dug painfully into her knees as she complied. Beside her Mender remained standing, arms half-raised.

Three of the auxiliaries swept the cramped hold as the fourth, sergeant's bars visible on his chest armour, kept a stubby darklight carbine trained on Mender.

'Clear!' one woman yelled.

The sergeant approached Mender. His faceplate withdrew smoothly into his helmet and he snapped, 'On the deck, or I *will* drop you.'

Mender met his glare with indifference. 'There's no need to shout, son. I may be old but I ain't deaf. I do have a stiff leg, though' – he slapped his thigh – 'so I'd be obliged if I could remain standing.'

The sergeant's face glistened with sweat. Orry held her breath as she watched a bead roll down his temple. She half expected him to shoot Mender where he stood.

'Sergeant Volkhov!' a voice snapped from the airlock. 'Let the old man stand if he wants.' A young woman barely out of her teens stood framed by the inner door. She wore no armour, just a blue tyro's uniform with a holstered service pistol at her waist. Orry recognised the look on the junior officer's face: out of her comfort zone and trying not to show it.

Volkhov eyeballed Mender, then stepped back. Orry tried not to flinch as the sergeant loomed over her. He looked like a giant in his bulky armour, able to crush her without a thought. She straightened her back and stared directly ahead.

'Stand, please,' the tyro told her as she entered the cargo bay. She motioned with one black-gloved hand.

Blood coloured Orry's cheeks as she climbed to her feet, humiliated and angry.

Volkhov stepped aside to let the officer approach.

'My name is Garrett,' the tyro said. 'I've been ordered to bring you aboard *Speedwell*.'

'Why?' Mender asked.

Garrett ignored him as Volkhov produced two pairs of slender restraints. The sympathetic look on the tyro's face didn't convince Orry for a moment. 'Orders,' she explained apologetically, gesturing at the restraints.

'This is ridiculous,' Orry began, her eyes darting around the cargo bay, but there was no escape.

Mender caught her eye and gave an almost imperceptible shake of his head. *Pick your battles*, he sent over *Dainty Jane*'s integuary channel. The old man looked like he'd aged twenty years since the auxiliaries came aboard.

Teeth gritted, she allowed Volkhov to fasten the restraints, which shrank to the width of her wrists. After the sergeant had secured Mender, he produced two slim circlets from his belt pouch.

Not taking any chances, are they? Orry sent. She hated integuary dampers.

Mender didn't reply, just continued to stare straight ahead as Volkhov slipped the circlet over his matted hair. Like the restraints, the damper tightened to fit.

Gloom settled over her as she felt the coolness against her forehead. It contracted, and her integuary shut down for the second time in as many days. It was an odd feeling, like a hole in her mind. She was sealed off from her surroundings, as if her senses had been reduced to a narrow tunnel.

Garrett smiled. 'Please,' she said, extending a hand towards the freight lock.

'You can't just take us,' Orry protested. 'We have rights.'

Mender laid a hand on her arm.

She looked from his strained face to the auxiliaries and sighed. Walking stiffly, she passed through the airlock and into the cutter.

The interior of the craft was little more than a tube criss-crossed with composite bracing. The anti-spalling compound designed to contain shrapnel in the event of hull penetration gave the bulkheads a matt finish, like stringy rubber. The cutter's two pilots turned to stare at her from the cockpit, behind which a ladder led up to the dorsal turret. Towards the stern, an armoured skiff was clamped to the deck. The shark-like teeth painted on the prow gave the long, sharp-nosed ground effect vehicle a menacing look.

Orry dropped into the nearest acceleration shell, a more modern version of those in *Dainty Jane*, and felt the stiff gel mould itself to her body. Garrett sat next to her as Volkhov sealed the airlock, then strapped in beside Mender, his darklight carbine resting across his knees.

'It'll be a short run,' the tyro said. 'Moderate g-point thrust, so no need to flood the shells. Just relax and breathe normally.'

'I know,' Orry said, feeling a stab of apprehension nonetheless; *Bonaventure* rarely pulled more than 2g.

The molecular hooks holding the cutter against *Dainty Jane*'s hull disengaged and Orry found herself briefly weightless as the vernier thrusters nudged the smaller craft clear.

'Get ready,' Garrett said.

Orry's shell reclined until she was lying flat. A rumble filled the compartment as the cutter's drive engaged and the gel stiffened around her, preventing blood from being forced back towards her head. Even so, her hands and feet became heavy and she felt her internal organs shifting inside her. The gel tightened even more, making her feel stifled, and she gritted her teeth as the pressure continued to increase. Her heart thudded in her chest as she fought to inflate her lungs.

The crushing forces ceased abruptly as the thrust cut out, and she was suddenly weightless, held in place only by the gel's grip. Verniers fired again and the cutter flipped slowly, nose over tail, until its drive was facing *Speedwell*.

As they coasted for a few seconds, Orry prepared herself: it was bad enough to go through that once, but the deceleration burn would be an exact repeat . . .

She was thankful when the cutter finally matched *Speedwell*'s 1g acceleration. As the gel relaxed its grip, her shell returned her to a sitting position.

The verniers started firing short bursts that rocked her back and forth, side to side. Finally the main drive cut out and the cutter stopped moving.

'Here we are,' Garrett said, rising effortlessly to her feet. 'This way.'

They stepped from the cutter, which was the largest craft in the small hangar, and Garrett led them across the deck to the exit.

'Are you going to throw us in the brig?' Orry asked as they waited for the airlock to cycle.

'Nothing so dramatic, I'm afraid. *Speedwell* isn't a big ship, so most spaces have to perform more than one function. You'll have to suffer the horrors of the wardroom.'

They drew curious looks from passing crew members as they made their way through the frigate. Orry noticed that the same rubbery anti-spalling compound coated every area not covered by protective padding. Handles protruded at regular intervals to aid rapid transit through the warship in zero-g.

Garrett stopped at a door with the words 'Officers' Mess' stencilled on it. Plastic chairs were bolted to the deck around a long dining table, which all but filled the room. Framed pictures fixed to the bulkheads showed ships and military engagements against vivid starscapes.

Two men sat on the other side of the table, one in the blue uniform of a Grand Fleet captain, the other wearing the black and silver of the Arbiter Corps. There was a tea set on the table and both men had steaming bulbs of mahogany-coloured liquid in front of them. The captain, a large man sporting a square beard and waxed moustache that added years to his wide face, rose to his feet as Orry entered the wardroom. She scowled at such an obvious sign of Ruuz heritage.

'Welcome aboard *Speedwell*. I am Second-Captain Naumov. This is Arbiter-Lieutenant Dragan.'

Dragan was a young man with a gaunt face and black hair plastered down on either side of an arrow-straight centre parting. Orry took an immediate dislike to him. She knew vessels of the Grand Fleet often carried an arbiter as a supernumerary, exempt from the usual duties of the crew. Their sole job was to extend the power of the Imperator into every ship, ensuring absolute loyalty. To Orry, Dragan represented everything that was rotten in the Ascendancy.

'That will be all, Garrett,' Naumov said.

'Aye, sir.'

Sweat made Orry's scalp itch as the wardroom door closed behind her. She kept her eyes on Naumov, resisting the urge to glance at Mender for reassurance.

'Please,' the captain said, indicating the seat opposite him.

She hesitated. She was still seething with anger beneath her fear, but Naumov's courtesy had wrong-footed her. Mender edged past and took a seat opposite Dragan. She followed his lead.

The arbiter consulted a screen on the table in front of him. 'Your name?' he asked Orry.

'What's this about?'

'Please, your name.'

'Olga Fokyrcelf. Would you like me to spell it?'

Naumov stroked his moustache to hide a smile.

'You were identified when you came aboard, Miz Kent,' Dragan said. 'This is really just a formality. If you want to play games, go ahead. All you will achieve is to waste everyone's time.'

'If you know already, what's the point in asking me?'

He stared at her for a moment then sighed. He made a note on his screen. 'Aurelia Katerina Kent.' He looked up. 'Any aliases?'

'I don't know what you're talking about.'

'Lady Jade Flint, for example. Does that sound familiar?'

'Never heard of her.'

'Of course not.' He made another note. 'Miz Kent, we have witnesses who place you at His Grace the Count of Delf's residence on Gallows Isle two nights ago. Would you care to tell me what you were doing there?'

'No.'

'What was your business with Konstantin, the Viscount Huish?'

'We're old friends. I used to pimp him out at the ribbon-head stations. Freighter crews love a bit of posh.'

Naumov choked on his tea. Dragan glared at him as the captain produced a white handkerchief and dabbed his lips, trying not to smile. He waved at the arbiter to continue.

'It surprises me that you find this process so amusing, Miz Kent. As I said, this is only a formality. We have more than enough evidence to charge you with the viscount's murder.'

Orry was struggling to maintain her bravado. 'Look,' she said, 'I was there, okay? But I didn't murder him. He was still very much alive when I left.'

'Ah, yes: when you left in the company of your father. I have a number of questions for him, too. Where is he?'

'He's dead.' Her face suddenly felt hot and her eyes started to fill with tears. She blinked them away and stared at Dragan, damned if she would let him see her distress.

'Really.' He clearly didn't believe her.

'Yes, *really*. My ship was attacked by the same man who murdered Konstantin. He killed my father and took *Bonaventure*.' She stopped short of mentioning Ethan, since the arbiter hadn't brought him up yet.

'Yes, we picked up your distress call. I don't suppose this mysterious raider told you his name?'

'He did, as it happens, you pompous ass. He's called Dyas.'

'Dyas,' Dragan repeated. 'How are you spelling that?'

'D – i – a – z – D – y – a – s – *I don't know*. After he shot my dad I was too busy running to ask for an autograph. He's small with black-and-white hair and he had a mimetic with him.'

Dragan cocked his head to one side and regarded her. 'How did you get off the ship?'

'He blew me out of an airlock.'

'And Captain Mender here picked you up?'

She nodded.

'That sounds unlikely. In hard vacuum a human body loses consciousness in what, ten seconds? Dead in a minute?' He turned to Mender. 'You must have been close by. Any particular reason?'

The old man gave a brittle laugh. 'Just dumb luck, buddy.'

'Indeed.' Dragan made another note.

'Leave him alone,' Orry snapped, drawing an odd look from Mender.

The arbiter sipped his tea. 'And this . . . *Dyas* . . . he admitted murdering the Viscount Huish?'

'Yes. He showed me the knife he used.'

'Did he enlighten you as to his motive?'

Orry hesitated as her mind raced. The beginnings of a plan were forming, but she needed time for it to fall into place. 'Could I have some of that tea?' she asked politely. 'I'm dry as a saltsea snake.'

'I don't—' Dragan began, but Naumov was already reaching for a clear bulb.

He added a splash of the tarry black concentrate and topped it up with steaming water. 'Sugar? Milk?'

She resisted the urge to accept. Sweetening or whitening tea was poor form in the Ascendancy, which meant she would normally do both, but she was past such petty jibes. Shaking her head, she accepted the bulb from Naumov and blew on it before taking a sip. It was surprisingly good, cleansing her mouth with its bitter, earthy flavour.

Dragan opened his mouth to speak.

'I'm afraid I can only offer you crackers to go with it,' Naumov told her. 'We've been on deployment for some time.' He offered her a packet.

'Thanks.' She looked at the hard squares with distaste before levering one out, despite being hampered by her restraints.

Dragan was staring at Naumov, his lips pressed tightly together. The captain waved a cracker at him. 'Continue.'

'Thank you, sir.' He turned to Orry. 'Why did Dyas kill the viscount?'

'He said something about a pendant.' She took a bite of her cracker. It was brittle, filling her mouth with dust and crumbs. She swallowed with difficulty and reached for her tea.

Dragan frowned and consulted his screen. 'The same pendant you had in your possession when your father arrested you, posing as an arbiter?'

'The very same. That's why Dyas came after us – to get the pendant.'

'Why?'

'If you find out, let me know.'

'And where is the pendant now?'

She pointed at Mender. 'I hid it on his ship.'

Mender's head snapped round. 'Hey! Don't drag me into this.' He turned to Dragan. 'I just picked her up, okay? Doing the good Samaritan bit – I don't even know why I'm here.'

'Why hide it?' the arbiter asked Orry.

'Well, look at the old goat,' she said. 'I thought he was about to rob me blind.'

Mender glared at her.

'Where did you put it?' Dragan asked.

'I could tell you, but it wouldn't do any good.'

'Miz Kent, if this unlikely tale of yours is true, then you might just escape this unfortunate affair with your life.'

Yeah, and end up in a picking gang on Furina for twenty years, Orry thought bitterly.

'Giving me that pendant would be a start, at least.' Dragan finished.

'You can have the bloody thing and welcome,' Orry told him. 'I just meant I'll have to be the one who fetches it for you. Him, too.' She jerked her head at a scowling Mender.

'Really? And why is that?' Dragan's patience was clearly wearing thin.

Everything rested on making her next words convincing. 'After Mender rescued me, he granted me limited integuary rights to the galley systems – so I could cook for him.' She glanced at the old man, who was staring at her with a kind of horrified admiration. 'He said I owed him,' she continued. 'If you hadn't come, it would have been his cabin next. For . . . you know . . .' She looked disgusted.

Mender spluttered and she hurried on, 'Anyway, I hid the pendant in one of the galley storage lockers and reprogrammed the lock to open only in response to a command from my integuary.'

The arbiter's eyes narrowed. 'All right, so you're the only one who can open it. Why do you need him?'

'After I cooked for him, he got suspicious and revoked my

access rights. He'll need to restore them before the locker will respond to my command, and he can't do that from here.'

Dragan glanced at Naumov, who shrugged. 'It's plausible,' he said. 'We could send them back over with a couple of auxiliaries.'

'And what do you have to say, Captain Mender?' Dragan asked.

Orry held her breath as Mender stared into her eyes. After what felt like an eternity, he turned to Dragan.

'I don't know anything about a pendant, but the rest is true enough,' he lied, then jabbed a finger at Dragan. 'But I wasn't going to force her into nothing. She's too scrawny.'

Her relief had no time to take hold as the focus of her anxiety switched from Mender to Dragan.

The arbiter drummed a slow tattoo on the table with his gloved hand. 'Very well,' he said eventually. 'Bring me the pendant and I'll make some enquiries about this Dyas individual.' She hid her relief as he continued, 'Make no mistake, Miz Kent: as far as the Arbiter Corps is concerned, *you* murdered the Viscount Huish, and it will take a lot more than a gimcrack pendant and someone's surname to save you from a public neck-stretching.'

9

KARMIC. SORT OF

Sergeant Volkhov and a female auxiliary named Harley escorted them back to *Dainty Jane*.

'You know you're going to have to remove these dampers, don't you?' Orry told Volkhov once they were out of the cutter and back in *Dainty Jane*'s cargo bay.

'Shut up.'

'And these.' She raised her bound wrists.

He placed a gloved hand between her shoulder blades and shoved her forward. She stumbled and almost fell.

'Galley's up this way,' Mender said. He leaned against a bulkhead for a moment, wheezing. 'Sorry, son, all this excitement ain't so good for my ticker.' When he pushed off from the wall he was the very picture of a decrepit old man, shoulders bowed under the weight of his years.

Dainty Jane's galley was a cramped compartment above the cargo bay – little more than a few lockers arranged around an induction plate and a rehydrator unit. Unidentifiable food stains coated most of the surfaces. *Ethan would have a fit*, Orry thought, then smiled sadly. *I can't believe I miss his ridiculous obsession with cleanliness* . . .

Harley covered them as the sergeant slung his carbine and reached out to remove the damper from Mender's head. In his armoured suit, Volkhov dwarfed the frail-looking old man. As his gloved hands fumbled with the slender circlet, Mender caught Orry's eye and shifted his gaze to a ring-shaped handle set in the bulkhead beside her. *The old twister's up to something*, she realised. He raised his eyebrows for emphasis.

'Hold still,' Volkhov snapped.

'Sorry, son.'

She edged sideways so the handle was in easy reach. Harley watched her, but said nothing.

Orry's hastily conceived plan had focused on getting them off *Speedwell* and back aboard *Dainty Jane*. After that, it became what her father liked to call 'fluid'. She was glad Mender appeared to have an idea what to do next. *Jane* was his ship, after all.

'There . . .' the sergeant said as the circlet came off Mender's head.

'Orry!' Mender snapped, his good eye already glazing.

She grabbed the ring as he collapsed, dropping to the deck as though his bones had turned to liquid.

'What—?' Volkhov began.

She gasped as *Dainty Jane* instantly reversed course. Her grip tightened on the ring as the ship switched direction, lifting her bodily from the deck and slamming the unprepared guards into the overhead. The thrust from the engines cut out entirely, taking the gravity with it.

She felt the weight leave her body and mashed her boots onto the deck to activate the molecular hooks.

Mender was up in an instant, moving like a man half his age. 'Check her!' he yelled, pointing at the floating figure of Harley as he launched himself across the galley towards Volkhov.

'You broke my fuckin' arm,' the sergeant snarled as he struggled to regain his footing. His darklight carbine swung up but Mender gripped the barrel and used it as an anchor to arrest his own forward momentum. Volkhov struggled for a moment, one arm hanging limply at his side, but the old man was clearly stronger than he looked. The sergeant's boot snapped out in a kick intended to shatter his opponent's knee, but Mender pushed himself clear at the last moment, twisting in mid-air to brace his boots against the bulkhead. He yanked at the carbine, sending Volkhov whirling across the compartment.

Orry ducked under his flailing body and shuffled quickly to Harley. The auxiliary was floating loosely, her head lolling. Orry grabbed at her carbine, but its strap was tangled in the composite-ceramic plates of her armour.

Behind her, Volkhov had twisted to land feet first on the far bulkhead. He pushed off immediately, launching himself back towards Mender and leaving the old man no time to use the carbine. Instead, Mender also plunged forward, with a roar of fury.

Orry threw herself clear as the two men collided over her head and started spinning away in a tangle of lashing limbs. The carbine drifted clear of the mêlée and she pushed off after it. Mender was aiming desperate punches at Volkhov's face, the only part of him not protected by armour.

As her hand grasped the weapon, Volkhov slid a long bayonet from its sheath, his lips drawing back in a bloody smile. Mender grabbed desperately at the sergeant's arm, sweat standing out on his face as Volkhov forced the blade towards his good eye.

Orry fumbled with the carbine, managing to tuck the stock into her shoulder and holding it awkwardly with her bound hands.

'Stop!' she yelled. 'Right fucking now!'

Volkhov turned to her and his smile slipped. 'What are you going to do with that?' he asked. 'Put it down before you hurt someone.'

Orry had never enjoyed the countless hours her father had made her practise in *Bonaventure*'s makeshift firing range, and she'd never be the galaxy's best shot – but at this range she didn't need to be.

She pressed the trigger.

The darklight carbine cracked and the light beside Volkhov's head dimmed as if it were being viewed through a heavily smoked lens. The blade of his bayonet folded in on itself and vanished, sheared off cleanly a centimetre above the handle.

She shifted her aim to his chest. He released the remains of the bayonet and raised his good arm.

'Okay, okay! You win.'

'What now?' she asked Mender.

He gave her a shaky smile. 'What's the matter? Didn't you plan this far ahead?'

'Did you?'

'As a matter of fact, I did. First, Sergeant Volkhov here is going to let us out of these restraints. I think you'll like the next bit. It'll be karmic. Sort of.'

*

Mender was right. Orry stared through the inspection port of *Dainty Jane*'s dorsal airlock and smiled at Volkhov, receiving his middle finger by way of reply. The sergeant's face was drawn with pain, although they'd bound his broken arm to his chest. Harley's limp body was tethered to his waist – just unconscious, to Orry's relief.

She waved at them through the window, cycled the lock and watched as they floated out of the ship, their suits' manoeuvring systems disabled. As they cleared the lock, Orry's integuary informed her that Mender had released the docking hooks.

Cutter's clear, he confirmed from the cockpit. *They'll be wondering what the hell is going on right about now.*

The outer door closed and she pushed off and went sailing down the passageway to the galley.

'Dragan's going to be pissed off,' she commented as she swooped up into the cockpit bubble. She landed neatly in the seat beside Mender.

He chuckled as his hands flew over the controls, though his eye was glazed as he interfaced directly with *Dainty Jane*'s systems. The hum of her drives altered pitch.

Orry stared out of the canopy and realised her vertigo wasn't bothering her much. Puffs of gas emerged from the cutter as the small craft manoeuvred towards the floating figures of the two auxiliaries. She was glad to see its dorsal turret remained motionless.

Speedwell hailed them. '*Dainty Jane*, *Speedwell*. Shut down your engines immediately or we will fire into you.'

'Unlikely,' Mender muttered to Orry, 'not with their cutter twenty metres from our hull.'

She could see *Speedwell* a thousand kilometres ahead, rotating about her long axis to bring her forward battery to bear. Mender's abrupt braking manoeuvre had clearly caught them by surprise.

'We'll never make it to the egress point,' Orry said. 'They'll fire as soon as the cutter's clear.'

'Not a problem.'

Mender rummaged through the discarded food containers from a dozen worlds littering the top of the instrument panel until he found an ancient digital checklist, its transparent surfaces frosty with minute scratches. He tossed it to Orry. 'Pre-collapse checks.'

'*What*? You're not going to collapse *here*?'

'Why not? Thanks to you I'm neck-deep in shit already. What do I care if we collapse outside the designated area? The Administrate can pull my ticket after the arbiters have cut me down from the scaffold.'

She blew out her cheeks, feeling a little foolish. 'What about those two boneheads?' she asked. 'Their suits will never stand up to the backsurge. Even the cutter will get tossed about.'

Mender's eye cleared and he turned to watch the cutter. It was approaching the floating figures. 'What do you think I'm waiting for? Checklist.'

'Can't we use our integuaries?'

'I'll use my integuary, you use the checklist.'

'What's the point of that?'

He turned to her. 'This is how I learned to do it, so this is how we do it. My ship, my rules.'

'Whatever.' She sighed, establishing an integuary connection to *Dainty Jane* anyway. 'Old school' was becoming a real pain in the arse. She activated the device, found the correct list and read the first item. 'Disengage mass-inversion drives.'

She felt Mender shut down the engines.

'Mass-inversion drives off,' he said.

'Retract radiators.'

'Vanes retracted.'

'Stabilisers to standby.'

He glanced at her. 'Skip that one. The stabilisers are borked.'

'How do you make atmospheric approaches without stabilisers? Can't you fix them?'

'This old girl ain't exactly just out of the manufactory, girl. They haven't made parts for her in a hundred years.' He flapped a hand at her. 'Carry on.'

She ran through the rest of the short list with Mender parroting every item until the last. 'Acceleration shell clear and functional,' she finished.

'Shell's clear,' confirmed Mender, taking back the checklist. He tucked it away.

'*Dainty Jane, Speedwell*: do *not—*'

He switched off the comm stack. Outside the canopy, the cutter's airlock slid open. The little craft drifted sideways and swallowed Volkhov and Harley. The outer door closed.

'Real smooth,' Mender said approvingly. 'Ready, little bloodtrout?'

'Yep—'

'Hang on to your hat, then.'

Her mind splintered as their wavefunction collapsed.

10

TYCHO IV

'The thing is,' Eoin explained, his voice muffled by the gleaming drive housing he was wedged beneath, 'if you ask any starship captain how the postselection drive works, he'll give you the same spiel about spacetime attracting and repelling at quantum distances.'

'Or her,' Orry said, with all the stern outrage of a twelve-year-old girl.

He gave an exaggerated sigh. '*She*'ll use words like entanglement and explain that the ship is placed into a state of quantum uncertainty where its particles exist both here and at the destination at the same time.' He grunted as he squirmed deeper. 'Then she'll probably mention postselection and tell you that *after* the ship has arrived at its destination, its navigation computer chooses where it should be from every possible quantum outcome, causing its wavefunction to collapse so that it exists in only one place once more. At that point, you'll be reaching for a drink. Move the light over here a bit, will you?'

Orry did as he asked, stretching as far into the maintenance cavity as her scrawny arms would reach.

'Thanks. The truth is that no unaugmented human really understands the physics of the thing. We didn't invent the technology, we just acquired it – but we did build the AIs who make it work.' He grunted and shifted in the tight crawl-space to stare back out at her. 'But that's okay, Number One Daughter. You don't need to understand how a thing works to be able to fly it.'

His words had never left Orry, particularly that final phrase. At some point she realised a more appropriate epithet would be 'monkeys with machine guns'.

The transition was instantaneous: one moment *Speedwell* was looming ever larger in the canopy, the next Orry was looking at the bloated sphere of a distant gas giant.

The planet glowed against a sable shroud, moons dotted across its swirling face. Her stomach lurched and she grabbed for a sick bag, barely getting it to her mouth in time. She looked over at Mender, embarrassed. Collapses on an empty stomach always made her puke.

To her surprise, he grinned. 'Don't worry about it, girl. I've filled more bags than I care to remember and anyone who tells you different is a liar.'

Orry wiped her mouth and smiled gingerly. She stared out at the gas giant. 'This isn't Novo Castria.'

'Nope.'

She hooked the navigation core. 'Tycho IV? Never heard of it.'

'I hope not.'

'What do you mean? Why are we here?'

'To see Cordelia Roag.'

'Cordelia Roag? You're shitting me, right?' She looked more closely at him. 'How does a smelly old space hermit know where to find Cordelia Roag?'

'I ain't smelly,' Mender said, hurt. 'I know her a bit, is all.'

'You "know her a bit".' The old man was completely exasperating. 'What do you want with her?'

'You want to find Dyas, don't you?'

She blinked. 'I thought you said—'

'Forget what I said. Do you want your brother back or not?'

'Of course, but—'

'So Roag is our best chance of finding him. Don't make me spell it out, girl. You did all right back on *Speedwell*, so I guess you can stick around for a while. Just until we find Dyas. Then you're gone, understand? I don't care if your ship's been sold for scrap. This is a temporary arrangement.'

'But I was the reason we were picked up in the first place—'

'And you got us out again. Mostly. You have a way with words.' He chuckled. 'Hell, you almost had *me* convinced back there.'

Orry couldn't speak. Instead, she leaned forward and kissed Mender lightly on the cheek. His bristles tickled her lip.

He flushed. 'Stop that. Even if we do find him, Dyas'll probably cut us to pieces before we get close.'

Gravity returned as he fired up the mass-inversion drives. 'We're a couple of hours out. Go and get some food in your belly.' He nodded at the bag of vomit. 'There's a disposal unit down there, too.'

Orry decided she'd wait to press him further on his relationship with Roag. The woman was a shadowy legend, even in the more dubious circles the Kent family ran in. The Ascendancy would pay handsomely to learn of her whereabouts. But if Roag could help . . .

'Thank you.' She released her harness and squeezed out of the cockpit.

The galley had survived the struggle with Sergeant Volkhov pretty much intact. Orry looked around the cramped space, so much smaller than *Bonaventure*'s refectory. Was it really only a day since she was sitting there with her family, discussing the future? Her father's death was a knife twisting in her heart. How long would the pain last? Every little thing triggered memories, knocking the wind out of her like a punch to the gut. She and Ethan were orphans now, set adrift in the galaxy. She had to find her brother – and her ship. That was all that mattered.

She opened a locker and stared in dismay at the empty trays inside. The one beside it was just as bare.

'What does he even eat?' she muttered as she opened the next one. The top tray was stuffed with packets of dehydrated chilli. Several plastic bottles of extra hot sauce lay in the tray beneath. She grimaced. 'Not gonna happen.'

Her integuary buzzed. She waited for a notification to pop up, expecting a message from Mender, but nothing appeared. When she looked back at the galley, one of the locker doors was ajar. She frowned, sure they'd all been closed when she came in.

Freezing air made her shiver when she opened the door fully, but she rummaged through the frosted packets within and came out holding a bag of frozen tomatoes. She closed the freezer and noticed another door half-open above her head. It contained packets of dried milk and egg powder.

Orry looked around the room. It was silent except for the usual shipboard noises.

'Omelette it is, then,' she said, feeling a little foolish. 'Thanks.'

Tycho IV filled the canopy when she returned to the cockpit, roiling clouds of ochre and purple ten thousand kilometres wide. *Dainty Jane* skimmed the troposphere, juddering without her stabilisers. As they descended, Orry saw the black shapes of refineries scattered across the sky.

'What are they extracting?' she asked.

'Not much any more. Most of these rigs are derelict. They used to harvest all sorts, but mainly methane and CO_2 for carbon composites. Now Roag just pulls out water vapour, oxygen and enough hydrogen and deuterium to run the fusion plant.'

Orry stood between the seats and stared out of the canopy. 'Which one is hers?'

'Let's find out.' He inserted a data plug into a port and punched a code into a keypad. Numbers scrolled across the displays and he released the controls as *Dainty Jane* began a gentle bank to starboard.

The ship lined up on a refinery that looked just like all the others. It was at least a kilometre across, a massive network of beams and pipes surrounding a core of pressurised modules. Vast gas scoops lay idle beneath the decommissioned rig and landing pads littered its upper surface, nestled between venting towers that rose like starscrapers.

'How long is it since you've been here?' she asked.

'A while. Roag and I . . . well, we didn't part on the best of terms.'

'That sounds promising. Isn't she worried someone will tell the arbiters where she is?'

Mender laughed. 'And cross Roag?'

'Is she that bad?'

'Don't let her appearance fool you. She's dangerous, that one. Her parents were settlers on Hask, back when it was right out on the rim. There wasn't any love there – they used her like a workhorse. When they died of the red mange she ended up a rape slave in a sick little mining outpost. She was twelve or thirteen. After a time she decided she didn't want to do that any longer, so she stuck a razor blade inside herself, if you know what I mean. While the fat slob on top of her was screaming, she got hold of his gun. Took a hoversled and lit on out of there – the miners thought they'd seen the last of her, but they were dead wrong. She came back the next night and freed the other children.'

'What happened to the miners?' Orry asked, not entirely sure she wanted to know the answer.

'There were twenty-two of them in total. The way I heard it told, fifteen of the bastards were still alive next morning. Roag had 'em stripped and spread-eagled, took a hydroram to every one of 'em, giving them a taste of what they'd been doling out. Those who survived, she sent through the mineral grinder.'

'What a lovely story. I can see why people are reluctant to get on her wrong side.'

'Yeah. And she's only got meaner over the years.'

The derelict rig filled the canopy now and Orry's lungs fell through her feet as *Dainty Jane* suddenly shot upwards. Lights glowed beneath streamers of drifting vapour, illuminating a landing pad furred with dirty brown streaks of corrosion. The pad slid out of sight and a moment later they touched down with the slightest of jolts.

She listened to the whine of the engines die away as Mender ran through the shutdown checklist. He levered himself from his seat and began climbing down to the cargo bay.

'Listen, girl,' he said, as she trailed behind him, 'this won't play out like it did on *Speedwell*. You go shooting your mouth off to Roag and things will turn sour fast. Show the woman some respect.'

'So I'm coming with you?' She hadn't been sure. Now her chest fluttered with a mixture of fear and excitement.

'I don't have much choice. I'm damned if I'm leaving you here on your own.'

He hopped off the ladder and headed down the passageway to the medbay. He opened one of the side doors and entered, leaving Orry at the threshold. The cabin beyond looked like a whirlwind had passed through it. Stained bedclothes hung half off the bunk. Dishes and discarded fluid bulbs littered the deck. A musty smell of stale food and body odour made her raise a hand to her nose.

'Do *I* get a cabin?' she asked, as Mender picked up a pile of soiled clothes and dumped them on the bunk.

'With any luck you won't be around long enough to need one.' He buckled a holster around his waist and turned to her with a proud grin, holding a bulky handgun that looked like someone had welded a pistol grip to a battleship's main gun.

'What the hell is that?' she asked.

'This little lady is a Covus Systems Fabretti Model 500. I rechambered her for dicore rounds – that's what troopers use to punch through the reactive plating on armoured vehicles.'

He gazed lovingly at the pistol. 'They don't make 'em like this any more.'

'I can see why. It looks like it'll leave nothing but a pair of smoking boots.'

'Not far off,' he said, 'and that's the point. No one fucks with a Fabretti 500.'

He removed the gun's oversized magazine, checked the long, fat bullets within, then slapped it back into the Fabretti with a satisfying clack. A power cell whined as Mender activated the pistol with his thumb.

'Five-round magazine, fully compensated. Recoil damping, and the frame is threaded with negative matter.' He hefted the Fabretti, then offered it to Orry. 'Feel how light she is.'

She shook her head. Guns were a necessary evil, but she preferred a subtler approach where possible.

He shrugged and rubbed an invisible blemish from the Fabretti's barrel with his sleeve before replacing the pistol in its holster.

She looked around the cabin as he pulled on a long overcoat. 'How can you live like this?'

'Like what?' He looked puzzled. 'Come on.'

Back in the cargo bay, he grabbed a couple of rebreathers from a cabinet and tossed one to her. 'Make sure you get a good seal. The pressure and gravity are fine at this altitude, but you sure as hell don't want to go breathing the atmosphere.'

She followed him into the freight lock. The mask pinched the skin around her nose and mouth and she tasted plastic when she inhaled.

For the first time, she noticed a contraption that looked something like an ancient harpoon gun connected to a multi-jointed hydraulic arm. The long barrel ended in a three-clawed robotic hand.

'Is that what you used to rescue me?' she asked through her mask.

'Yeah,' said Mender, sounding a little uncomfortable. 'It's a claw-grabber – for recovering salvage. Don't have much use for it these days.'

She looked at it thoughtfully.

Mender fitted his own mask. 'Let me do the talking, okay?' he reminded her. He gave her a reassuring smile. 'Don't sweat it. You'll be fine.'

The airlock cycled and the outer door opened.

11

UNDERBELLY

Wind battered Orry's face as she stepped onto the pad, raising tears that dried instantly on her cheeks. Mender grabbed her arm and pointed to a door standing open on the far edge of the pad. A figure in goggles was waving frantically at them, struggling to hold the door against the storm. The wind whipped at the scarf wrapped around his face, revealing a respirator beneath.

She narrowed her eyes against the tumult and staggered across the pad. The wind reduced to a furious howling as she fell through the door. Another figure swathed in ragged clothes beckoned them into an airlock. The man in the goggles followed them inside and hunched over a control panel. The noise of the wind cut off abruptly as the door closed, replaced by the gentle hiss of air being pumped in.

A green light illuminated and she removed her rebreather with relief. The man at the panel turned quickly and pointed a snub-nosed sneakpiece at Mender's face. Orry's stomach turned to water as something hard pressed into the base of her skull.

Mender reached up slowly and lowered his rebreather. 'Spiro and Wride. I hoped you'd be dead by now. You pull that trigger, Spiro, and it'll be the last thing you ever do.'

'You mean the last thing *you* do, Mender. You're a fool to come back here after what happened.'

'Maybe. Maybe not. What do you want?'

'The girl.'

Orry gasped as the man behind her – *Wride?* – grabbed a fistful of her hair and yanked her head backwards. Foul breath rolled over her face and she shuddered as he licked her neck.

Mender's expression didn't change. 'Tell you what. Open that door and let us walk out of here, and I won't tell Roag about this.'

'Roag ain't gonna find out.'

Wride laughed, and Orry felt his gun shift as groping fingers slid down her belly to her groin.

Her fear boiled into anger and she raked her boot heel down the inside of his leg. He howled with pain and she drove her elbow up and back as hard as she could, feeling a satisfying crunch. His grip on her hair loosened and she squirmed free. Unable to run, she turned to face him.

He was hopping on one leg, clutching his nose. Blood oozed between his fingers, shocking red against his white, almost translucent skin. He was entirely hairless, a sallow sack of a man with puffy features. Hate glittered in eyes too small for their sockets as he swung a long-barrelled pistol towards her. Her father's endless self-defence classes came flooding back and Orry moved almost without thought. Stepping inside Wride's reach, she gripped his forearm and twisted her body, using his own weight against him. She kept hold of his gun arm, feeling it twist as his body rolled over her back to land in a heap. He screamed as she bent his wrist back to just shy of breaking point. The pistol clattered to the deck and she placed her boot across his windpipe. Her head whipped up to look for Spiro, and she found herself staring down the narrow muzzle of his gun.

The whine of an energy cell caused his eyes to flick sideways.

'I really wouldn't do that,' Mender growled, pressing the Fabretti into Spiro's temple.

Orry held her breath, unable to take her eyes off the gun aimed at her face.

Sweat stood out on Spiro's forehead. He was a thin man with a pointed chin, black hair tied back into a ponytail. He licked his lips, then reversed the sneakpiece and held out his hands. 'Jeez, Mender, we was just fucking with you.'

Orry felt like crying. Instead, she released Wride's arm and kicked him hard in the ribs. He grunted and doubled up, allowing her to scoop up his gun. Her hands were shaking.

Mender snatched the weapon from Spiro's hand and shoved him back against a wall. 'You dumb fucks. I should fix you both right now.'

She watched his hand tighten on the Fabretti and was suddenly afraid he meant it. 'Mender,' she said.

He wasn't listening to her. His eyes burned into Spiro's, until the younger man cringed, squeezing his eyes shut and turning his head away. His lips twisted into a grimace of terror.

'Mender!'

The old man blinked, then glanced at her. She shook her head.

He scowled and hit the airlock control panel. The inner

door slid open. He grabbed Spiro and shoved him into Wride, pushing them both out through the door.

'I want to see her.'

Spiro and Wride led them along a network of service corridors. Corrosion streaked the mustard-yellow walls, adding furry shades of blue, green and – Orry's personal favourite – a vibrant purple shot through with red crystals. The air tasted of metal and acid.

After a long walk Spiro threw open a pressure door and they emerged onto a catwalk, high against one curving wall of what had once been the rig's central processing chamber. The space formed a vast cylinder, more than half a kilometre in length and perhaps two hundred metres in diameter. Support cables and struts criss-crossed the chamber like the web of a colossal metal-spinning arachnid, above the homes and businesses of the rig's denizens.

Looking down, she could see repurposed shipping containers, old booster tanks and partially dismantled ships. Ladders and walkways wended between doors and platforms, and wide suspended thoroughfares were crowded with people. The smoke rising from a hundred glowing sources was snatched into enormous air-scrubbers fixed high in the arc of the cylinder's roof. The smell of seared meat and spices made her mouth water.

They had entered near one end of the old processing chamber. A narrow stairway led down from the catwalk to intersect the widest of the hanging thoroughfares, which emerged from the heart of the makeshift town to form a bridge leading to a broad arch in the cylinder's end wall.

The stairs swayed alarmingly, groaning under the weight

of four bodies. Orry gripped the railing with one hand as she descended, keeping Wride's pistol pointed at his back with the other. It was a relief when she stepped onto the unyielding surface of the bridge.

There were fewer people here than she had seen in the narrow walkways behind her. A woman in a stained shift lay nearby, perilously close to the edge. Her hair was a rats' nest and a livid bruise discoloured one cheek. She looked up as Orry passed and extended a hand, vacant eyes in a slack face.

'Kettlehead,' Mender said brusquely. 'Ignore her.'

Words glowed over the archway set into the cylinder's end: 'The Underbelly'. Small groups of men and women hung around outside, drinking and talking. Orry noticed that everyone was armed, and when she glanced back she saw heads turning to follow their progress as they passed. Music thudded as she moved through the cloud of sweetsmoke surrounding the entrance.

It was dark beyond the arch. The heat and the stench of too many people was beginning to stifle her, and as the discordant music grew louder she realised it was coming from several different sources. Staccato silhouettes born of flickering strobes leaped and whirled in front of a band playing on a raised stage marked by flashing beacons to her left. Nearby, a naked man writhed in a tall cage, bronze skin glistening. A metre away, a woman wrapped her legs around the bars of her own cage and arched her back seductively. Every centimetre of her skin was tattooed with animated roses in constant motion, blooming, dying, blooming. Orry looked away.

Mender appeared to know where he was going. He shoved Spiro forward again and Wride followed, glancing miserably back at Orry. She witnessed a few nudges and stares as they passed deeper into the Underbelly, but on the whole they were ignored.

A snarling drew her attention and she drifted right to stare down into a pit surrounded by a crowd of people clamouring to place bets. She caught a glimpse of a woman in light armour, holding a short spear. A pair of flightless raptors the size of dogs circled her warily. A scream of appreciation rose as the birds charged, but Mender had already moved on.

She followed him up wide steps leading to a dais at the far end of the Underbelly, backed by a metal wall. A dozen men and women lounged in plush sofas surrounding a knee-high table, overlooking the club.

Mender gripped Spiro's collar from behind, pressed the Fabretti into the back of his head and shoved him forward, marching him straight up the steps and onto the dais. Dangerous-looking men and women rose from their seats, weapons appearing like magic in their hands. Orry waited with Wride at the bottom of the steps.

Mender stopped opposite a trim woman in late middle age, seated at the centre of the table. Cordelia Roag's grey hair was full and long, framing a gaunt face. She wore a knee-length, figure-hugging blue dress cut in the latest Fountainhead fashion. Her exposed right arm and leg were banded with an intricate arrangement of dull bronze plates connected by leather straps and fine steel cords that reminded Orry of high-tensile cable. The effect was almost gladiatorial, but she couldn't decide if the plates would provide any real protection or were purely cosmetic.

Roag studied Mender for a moment, then waved a dismissive hand. Her minders returned to their seats, glaring at him.

'Jurgen Mender,' she said without enthusiasm. 'It's been a long time.'

'Cordelia.'

She regarded him coldly. 'Had a little trouble with Spiro and Wride?'

'Nothing we couldn't handle.'

'So it appears.' Roag leaned around him to look down at Orry. She beckoned her closer.

Heart pounding, Orry pushed Wride up the steps.

'Your handiwork?' Roag enquired, indicating his broken nose.

Orry raised her chin. 'Yes.'

'Did he deserve it?'

'His hands were all over me.'

'I—' Wride began.

'*Shut up*,' Roag hissed.

'You ought to keep your dogs under control,' Orry told her. 'Or neuter them.'

Roag looked at her with a little more interest. 'Is that what you'd do?'

'I'm not you.' She met Roag's stare head-on, forcing herself not to look away. After long seconds Roag relaxed back into her chair and chuckled, waving at her cronies. They joined in the laughter and the tension around the table eased a little.

'Release them,' Roag told Mender.

The old man hesitated, then shoved Spiro away. The pasty-faced man staggered forward and cried out as he barked his shins on the low table, almost sprawling over it. He glared at Mender, who calmly holstered the Fabretti.

Orry lowered Wride's pistol.

Roag nodded at Spiro. 'He do anything to you?' she asked Orry.

'I'm sure he would have, given the chance.'

'So you say, and you might be right. But might isn't enough to convict a man round here.'

Orry frowned. *Convict?*

Roag jerked her head at Spiro. 'Get out of my sight.'

Spiro nodded quickly, his relief evident on his face. He darted away, disappearing into the gloom.

'Boss—' Wride began.

'I don't want to hear it, you shit-belching maggot. You've been warned, Wride. I told you what would happen if I caught you pulling this crap on my rig.' Roag leaned forward. 'You know what to do.'

'Puh-please.' He swallowed, then reached for his belt with trembling hands. The women around the table smiled widely, while the men looked uncomfortable. Wride unfastened his belt, then his trousers.

'Look—' Orry began, stepping forward.

'Just you stand there and watch,' Roag said sharply. 'No need to thank me.'

Wride's trousers were round his knees, revealing doughy, hairless legs. He wasn't wearing any underwear.

'That your piece?' Roag asked, nodding at Wride's pistol. He nodded and Roag held out a hand.

Orry placed the gun in her palm.

'Long barrel,' Roag noted, before staring without expression at Wride's exposed crotch. 'I can see why you would like that.' Her nostrils flared. 'Rama, you *stink*, pig. Ever hear of personal hygiene?'

'Please, boss . . .'

'On your knees.'

He sank to the floor, shaking visibly. Orry watched with morbid fascination, a sick feeling in her gut.

'Put 'em on the table.'

Whimpering, Wride shuffled forward and placed his balls on the tabletop.

'Now pick one.'

'Wh-what?'

'Your foetid little love eggs. Which one do you like the least?'

A tear rolled down his cheek.

'Left or right, Wride? *Pick one.*'

He moaned. 'Right.'

Roag slammed the butt of Wride's pistol down like a hammer. He shrieked and clutched at his groin as every man around the table winced or looked away. He fell to the ground, writhing into a ball.

'Get up, you waste of skin,' Roag snarled. 'We're not finished.'

Wride was unable to speak. He shuddered, gasping and mewling. Orry tasted acid at the back of her throat.

'Get up!' Roag stepped over the low table and kicked him in the face with her boot. When that didn't work, she pressed the pistol's long barrel into his eye socket. '*Get . . . the fuck . . . up.*'

Somehow, Wride managed to crawl back onto his knees. Orry saw blood and strands of jelly-like gore smeared over his leg and kept her eyes firmly on Roag's face.

'You know what to do,' Roag told him. Shaking uncontrollably, his face a mask of tears and mucus, Wride resumed his earlier position.

'*Please!*' he screamed as Roag brought the pistol down again, hard enough to crack the table's ceramic surface. The wet thud again turned Orry's stomach and she had to swallow hard.

Wride's scream died as he folded forward, scattering glasses and plates. Roag stepped onto the table, hauled his head up by the hair, then dropped it with a dull thump and wiped her hand on his back.

'Get him to the quack.' Roag was sweating. She brushed grey strands from her forehead and picked up a bottle. Raising it to her lips, she drank half the contents, wiped her mouth with the back of her wrist and handed the bottle to Mender.

'I didn't think I'd ever see you again,' she said. 'Things must be desperate for you to come back to my . . . what did you call it?'

Mender shifted uncomfortably. 'I don't recall.'

'*Rotting tub of whorescum*, wasn't it?'

'I believe it was.'

'So, what can the whorescum do for you?'

Mender put the bottle down, untouched. 'Morven Dyas.'

Roag looked at him from her tabletop perch. Beside her, two men were hauling Wride's unconscious body away, leaving a smear of blood behind them. Roag stepped down and straightened her dress.

'Let's continue this somewhere more private.'

12

A HEALTHY DOSE

Cordelia Roag led them to a pressure door set into the wall at the rear of the dais. Two capable-looking women followed close behind.

'You can leave your weapons with Steiner here,' Roag told them, and a dark-skinned woman with bleached-blonde hair teased into vertical strands stepped forward.

'What about your weapons?' Orry asked, but Roag ignored her.

Mender handed over the Fabretti and a compact axon disruptor he pulled from his left boot. He raised his arms to let Steiner pat him down; she was thorough, and he smiled broadly throughout. The other minder took care of Orry. Once Roag was certain both were unarmed, she opened the door.

The swirling clouds of Tycho IV bathed Roag's inner sanctum in an eerie purple light, but the room was otherwise unremarkable: a sleek desk and matching chairs; a fine rug in front of the panoramic windows; a sofa against one wall next to another door. Orry thought the office looked more like a wealthy shipping magnate's than an interstellar criminal's. She felt vaguely disappointed.

Roag sank into a padded chair behind the desk and hoisted her legs onto it. 'So. What do you want with Dyas?'

'He owes me.' Mender dropped into one of the seats in front of the desk.

Orry hesitated, then perched on the edge of another, uncomfortably aware that Roag was watching her with cold eyes.

'And the girl?'

'He has something that belongs to her.'

'My brother,' Orry said, irritated at being spoken about as if she wasn't there. 'And my ship.'

'*Bonaventure.*' Roag smiled at Orry's surprise.

'I'm too old for games, Cordelia,' Mender growled.

'It appears that we might be able to help each other.'

'Go on,' Mender said cautiously.

'How much do you know about Morven Dyas?'

'Not much.' Mender darted an uncomfortable glance at Orry, rubbing the back of his head. 'Wasn't he some kind of extreme-g star? Won some competitions, had a stunt show that was syndicated a while back.'

'He was pretty good,' Roag confirmed, 'until he got injured. The sponsorship dried up and the network canned his show.'

'Good,' Orry said with venom.

'He came to me a couple of years back – he fancied himself as a free trader and wanted to lease a ship from me.' Roag shook her head. 'I almost felt sorry for the dumb fuck. Things went south fast – every deal he took turned bad. He fell behind in his payments almost immediately, so he hooked up with that psychotic mimetic and tried his hand at raiding.'

'With your blessing?' Mender asked.

'No.'

'You're going soft, Cordelia.'

She narrowed her eyes. 'I'm a businesswoman. It's difficult to make dead men pay what they owe. I explained the situation to Dyas, took the ship back and presented him with a bill.'

'Plus penalties for unlicensed raiding?'

'Naturally. It was a substantial amount in total. I think he was a little shocked.'

'I imagine he was.'

'Obviously he couldn't pay, so I made him an offer. There was something I needed picking up.' Roag looked at Orry. 'On Tyr.'

It took her a moment to realise what Roag was saying. '*You* sent him after the pendant – after *me*?'

'Orry . . .' Mender warned.

'*You* were not supposed to be involved,' Roag pointed out. 'It was a simple in-and-out job: I had a woman on the inside and all Dyas had to do was grab the pendant and go. No one needed to get dead. It was unfortunate that your family got involved, but that was none of my doing – or his.'

'*Unfortunate?*' Orry was on her feet. 'He killed my father!'

Roag gazed back icily. 'I would moderate your tone, if I were you. *Morven Dyas* killed your father, not me.' Her face hardened. 'Where's my pendant, Aurelia?'

Orry clenched her teeth so hard they ached. Mender was watching her anxiously, so she forced herself to relax and sat down slowly. 'I lost it – on *Bonaventure*. Dyas has it.'

'You're lying. If Dyas had found it, he would have brought it to me.'

'He did find it – he showed me just before he tried to kill me.'

Roag stared at her until sweat broke out on Orry's forehead.

'He's done a runner,' Mender said. 'He figures if you want it, Cordelia, it must be worth some. He plans to sell it himself.'

'He knows I'd send my people after him—'

Mender laughed. 'You did say he makes bad decisions. He's gambling that he'll have the gilt to disappear for good before you find out he's double-crossed you.'

Roag's lips twitched into a thin smile.

'You know where he is, don't you?' Orry broke in, filled with sudden hope. 'You have to tell us—'

'I don't *have* to do anything,' Roag snapped.

'Shut up,' Mender warned, glaring, but Orry ignored him.

'We'll go after him for you,' she offered eagerly.

Roag was still studying her. 'That suggestion is not entirely without merit,' she said eventually. Her eyes glazed for a moment as she accessed her integuary.

The door opened, admitting a boy carrying a tray with a bottle and three glasses. He set it down carefully on Roag's desk, then scurried away, not looking at anyone.

Roag picked up the bottle and examined the label, then poured a smooth golden liquor into the glasses. She picked one up and swirled the liquid round.

'Okay, then,' Orry said. 'We'll bring you Dyas and the pendant – just tell me where they are.'

'I want him alive,' Roag said. 'He's no use to me dead.'

Orry hesitated. 'What are you going to do to him?'

'That wet shit thought he could screw me. An example will have to be made.' Roag smiled. 'You can watch if you like.'

The thought of turning *anyone* over to Roag's tender mercies gave Orry pause, but only for a moment. He'd murdered her father, tried to kill her, kidnapped her brother and stolen her ship. If it came to a choice between Dyas' life and Ethan's? No contest.

'Fine,' she said. 'Where is he?'

Roag raised her glass. 'On my rig it's customary to seal a business arrangement with a drink.' She tossed hers back.

Orry picked up a glass and raised it to Roag, then downed it. The fiery liquor had a hint of spice paragon; it made her eyes water as it burned a path to her stomach. She choked back a cough and set the glass down. 'Where is he?' she rasped.

Roag's eyes shifted to Mender. The old man hadn't moved. 'Mender?' Orry urged.

He slowly leaned forward, picked up his drink and lifted it to his lips.

The empty glass made a sharp tap on the tray as he set it down.

'The Shattermoon,' Roag said. 'A dispatch pod from an associate of mine arrived just before you did. He's currently trying to talk his way past the picket.'

Orry shot to her feet and was halfway to the door before she realised Mender hadn't moved.

'What's so special about this pendant?' he asked. 'Why do you want it so badly?'

'That's none of your concern.'

'It must be valuable – aren't you worried we might just kill Dyas and take it for ourselves?'

Roag laughed. 'Not in the least. There are two very good reasons why you will bring me both the pendant and Dyas.'

Suddenly Orry didn't like the certainty in Roag's voice. She wondered if perhaps she should have let Mender do the talking after all.

'Firstly,' Roag said, 'if you don't, you know I won't rest until I have you back here in chains.'

'That didn't stop Dyas, did it?' Mender observed.

'True, unfortunately,' Roag admitted, 'which is why I've just given you both a healthy dose of biomites.' She patted the bottle. 'You have three days. If you're not back on this rig with Dyas and my pendant, my little friends will overload your integuaries and fry your pre-frontal cortices. They'll leave just enough brain function so you'll know what dribbling vegetables you've become.'

Orry stared at her, the thought of the molecular bio-organisms crawling inside her making her stomach churn worse than if she'd just completed a collapse. She jammed two fingers down her throat and half-digested omelette splattered onto the rug.

A look of disgust replaced Roag's smile. 'Don't bother. They're already in your bloodstream by now.'

'What if three days isn't enough?' Mender asked. He spoke calmly, but Orry could hear the anger in his voice.

'Make sure it is.'

'Why us, Cordelia? You have specialists you could send after him.'

'Do you know the secret of good people management, Jurgen? Motivation. I think you two will do splendidly. You may have been the shit back in the day, but that day has passed. Just bring me what's mine and we can part as friends.'

'Fuck friendship,' Mender growled. 'When this is over, there's going to be a reckoning.'

'Whatever.' Roag yawned.

Mender glared at her, then strode from the room, Orry hurrying after him.

'What was *that*?' she demanded as they descended onto the floor of the Underbelly. '"There'll be a *reckoning*"?'

Mender finished checking his Fabretti and tucked it into its holster. 'So? There will be. She's not getting away with this crap.'

'And you thought it was a good idea to tell her that?'

'Well, I was angry—'

'So now Roag knows you're planning on payback, what's to stop her just frying our brains as soon as she's got what she wants?'

'I'm not an idiot, girl. I know—'

Orry took refuge in anger. 'You don't know anything!' she shouted. 'You might just be a grumpy old bastard who doesn't care whether you live or die, but *I* do. My brother is *fourteen*, and he's alone on that ship with two murderers—' She swallowed a sob; she would *not* let him see how terrified she was. 'If you want to throw your life away, be my guest. But at least . . .' Her voice trembled. 'At least wait until Ethan is safe.'

'Maybe I am a grumpy old bastard, but at least I haven't just crawled out of my mother's quim,' he retorted, apparently unaware of her reddened eyes. 'Don't presume to lecture me, girl. I was dealing with people like Cordelia Roag when your daddy was still swimming in your grandpa's balls.'

'So how did she trick you so easily?'

'You're nothing but a mouth on a stick – no bloody use to anyone. I should have left you floating out there and saved myself a galleon-load of grief.'

'Mouth on a stick, is it? Well, this mouth has figured out how we can get onto the Shattermoon's surface. Or hadn't that pickled old walnut that passes for a brain started to think about that yet?'

'I—' Mender stopped and peered at her. 'You have? How?'

She smiled at his confusion, and a little of the fear and anger trickled away. 'Is there anywhere on this rig I can get a set of robes?'

'You can buy pretty much anything here. What sort of—? *Oh* . . .' A grin spread over his face. 'Follow me.'

As they emerged onto the bridge, he asked, 'You got any gilt?'

She stopped, taken aback. 'Oh! No, nothing; all our savings were on board *Bonaventure*. I expect that bastard's stolen all of it now . . . I don't suppose they're big on credit round here?'

'Take this.' He handed her a gilt chip. 'Some change would be nice.'

'Aren't you coming with me?' The thought of walking the rig's narrow walkways alone filled her with dread.

'You'll be fine. Most everyone will know we're working for Roag by now. It's as good as an auxiliary escort.'

'And if I meet someone who doesn't know?'

'Explain it to them.' Mender pulled out his axon disruptor. The narrow black tube fitted neatly into the palm of his hand. 'Like this.' He flicked his wrist and the disruptor extended with an efficient snap, tripling in length. His thumb moved and electricity arced across the terminals at its far end. He offered the evil-looking stunner to Orry.

'Where are you going?' she asked, taking it.

'To find out exactly what that queen bitch put in our brains, and how to get them out.'

13

HARRY

Mender was right: no one troubled Orry as her integuary guided her through the bewildering web of the rig's interior – in fact, most of the hard-eyed residents treated her with grudging courtesy.

An hour later, satisfied with her purchases, she was passing an alley that ran between two lengths of ancient hull plating when a yelp of pain made her freeze. Some twenty metres away, next to a pile of rusting metal, a man was holding a rapier to a young girl's throat.

He was tall and whip-thin, with a mane of messy dark hair and scuffed black boots that reached to his knees. His long coat screamed aristo, even though the golden thread decorating the sleeves was tarnished and unravelling in places. The point of his rapier pressed into the girl's throat as he pinned her against the wall.

She looked to be about Ethan's age, maybe younger. Limbs poked like sticks from shapeless clothes, her roughly shorn hair was sticking out at crazy angles and a bulky canvas satchel hung across her chest. Everything was coated in a layer of filth.

Orry stepped into the alley and set down her bags. Her hand tightened around the axon disruptor. Was there nowhere the bloody Ruuz didn't throw their weight about? Her lips pressed together in a savage smile. There were no arbiters out here to protect this bastard.

She had barely started forward when a curtain of tattered plastic sheeting behind the aristo twitched aside and a man and a woman stepped out, dressed in what Orry was beginning to recognise as the typical lowlife fashion of the rig. She stared at their guns with dismay, feeling like a prize idiot.

Before she could summon breath to shout a warning, the aristo had turned to face the new threat. The ragamuffin girl seized her chance and sprinted away – stopping after a few steps to watch the show.

Orry edged closer.

The aristo slipped his left hand beneath his coat and it reappeared holding a dagger with an intricate basket hilt. As he extended his arm she caught a glimpse of something around his wrist: a glossy bracer partially obscured by his sleeve.

'Now, sir and lady' – he inclined his head towards the woman, who was clearly no lady – 'I'm not looking for trouble. Why don't you go about your business and I'll attend to mine?'

The heavyset man spat on the ground and raised his weapon. The pistol's glazed finish was worn down to the composite in places, but it looked serviceable enough. The woman was brandishing an ancient Fleet-issue snubgun with a broken stock. Weeping sores covered her neck and face; the red welts disappeared into thinning hair. The snubgun shook in her hands as she levelled it at her victim.

'I'm glad you said that,' the man said, 'because you *are* our business.'

The woman let out a high-pitched shriek of laughter that made Orry wince, but her companion shot her a look of such hatred that Orry was surprised he didn't turn his gun on her.

The woman immediately fell silent.

'What do you want?' the aristo asked.

As if it isn't obvious.

'That sword, for one. And your fine clothes.' The man appeared to think for a moment. 'Oh, and the contents of your gilt account.'

'Ah.'

'Ah? What's "ah"? Don't toy with me, you mincing fucking pixie.'

The aristo looked crestfallen. 'Do you really think I'd be creeping around the back alleys of this rusting hulk if I had the price of a ticket out of here?' he said plaintively. 'I'm afraid you're plum out of luck, old boy—'

'We'll see about that. Now lay those pretty blades on the ground and stand against that wall.' He glanced at the ragamuffin girl. 'You all right, Sweetie? He didn't hurt you none?'

'I'm fine, Ivo.' She touched a finger to her neck and held it up, displaying a drop of blood. 'Just creased the skin, is all.'

'Ivo, is it?' the aristo said. 'I'm Harry. You look like a game fellow. How about we decide this like gentlemen? My sword against your gun.'

Ivo grinned. 'Now, why would I want to do that when I could just shoot you where you stand?'

'You could, it's true – but where's the sport in that? Come on,

Ivo, you've got a gun. What's the matter? Scared of a mincing fucking pixie?'

Orry watched, fascinated, as Ivo seriously considered Harry's challenge. Surely he wasn't stupid enough to accept? True, the alley was wide and he was standing at least two sword-lengths from his opponent, but still . . . *Just shoot him, already.*

'What do you propose?' Ivo asked warily.

A broad grin spread over Harry's even features. 'Simple. I sheath my blades, you holster your pistol. Just to keep things nice and fair, the lady lowers her gun. Then we draw, you against me.'

Ivo eyed the distance between them. 'All right.'

'Capital! Good man.'

Oh my God, Orry thought, *what* is it *with men?*

Harry's sword scraped into the long scabbard hanging from his belt and he tucked the dagger into its sheath.

Ivo shoved the pistol into his belt. 'Are all aristos so God-fucked stupid?'

'Ready when you are,' Harry said with a smile.

Ivo licked his lips.

'Shoot his pretty fucking face off!' Sweetie yelled, clearly feeling the need to contribute.

Orry saw Ivo tense a split-second before he went for his gun. Her eyes shifted to Harry – and widened when she saw he was already in motion. His sword flashed from its scabbard, blurring as he leaped forward into a perfect lunge. Before Orry could react, the point of Harry's long blade had pierced Ivo's chest and half a metre of red steel was protruding from his back.

The aristo's left hand whipped out and the woman with the snubgun staggered back, choking. Only when Ivo dropped to his knees did Harry slide his blade free. The woman had fallen onto her side and was clawing at her throat. Blood was gouting around the hilt of Harry's dagger. The blade was buried in her flesh.

Orry stared in disbelief. *No one is that fast.*

'You cunt!' Sweetie screamed, reaching into her satchel and hauling out a fletcher.

Surprise cost Harry half a second, by which time the girl had raised the gun – but then he was in motion, sprinting towards her with his rapier extended in front of him.

As Orry heard the flat rasp of the fletcher, Harry raised his left arm – and a coruscating disk of energy the size of a dinner-plate sprang from his bracer. She took an instant to be impressed with the tech, but Harry had already whipped up the buckler. At such short range the cluster of flechette darts had no time to disperse and they sailed through the shield in a tight grouping. Some were vaporised by the spitting energy, dying in a blaze of sparks, but the rest struck Harry high in his chest, hurling him backwards. He landed with a dull thud, his rapier skittering away. The shield fizzled and died.

Sweetie approached the groaning aristo cautiously, keeping the fletcher pointed at him. Orry cursed, snapped the axon disruptor to its full length and started forward.

Sweetie raised the fletcher and aimed at Harry's face – then jerked violently as Orry jammed the disruptor into her kidneys. She arched her back, moaning as her body spasmed uncontrollably. Orry reached in front of her and plucked the fletcher from her numb hand, then stepped back, allowing Sweetie to drop to the ground, where she lay twitching violently.

Orry dropped the fletcher and knelt over Harry. Close up,

she realised he wasn't much older than her. To her amazement, he smiled weakly.

'My princess in shining armour,' he said, plucking feebly at his chest.

She slapped his hands away and checked the wound. His ballistic-weave tunic had stopped most of the darts before they could do much damage; they were sticking harmlessly out of the dark red material like needles. Spots of red seeping through the tunic showed where a few had penetrated to the flesh beneath.

'You'll be fine,' she told him. 'Can you stand?'

'Give me a minute.' His head lolled back.

Orry looked around nervously, worried the noise of the fight might have drawn attention. She sent her location to Mender with a note to hurry.

She turned back to the aristo. 'Are you *trying* to get yourself killed?' she snapped. 'What kind of an *idiot* uses an aegis band against a fletcher?'

Harry appeared to look at her properly for the first time. A shadow of irritation crossed his face. 'I didn't have a lot of choice.' He sat up, wincing. 'You don't see a lot of ballistic weapons where I come from. Folk generally prefer a blade or an energy piece.'

She thrust out an arm and hauled him to his feet. 'Let me guess. The Fountainhead?'

He nodded, eyeing the disruptor in her hand. 'Alecto.'

'Ruuz?'

'Yes, but—'

'Aristo?' she asked coldly.

'Minor house. Look—'

'Which one?'

'You won't have heard of it.'

'Which one?'

'Bardov.'

'Never heard of it.'

He eyed her for a moment, then bent down and reached for his sword. He cleaned the blade on Ivo's leg, then walked unsteadily over to the woman, pulled his dagger from her neck and wiped it on her jacket.

'It's a shame,' he said, surveying his handiwork with a shudder.

'They had the drop on you. You did what you had to do.'

He turned back to Orry, pulled his shoulders back and bowed stiffly. 'Haris Vigo Bardov at your service. I am in your debt.'

'I know.'

His eyes shifted over her shoulder. Tensing, he reached for his sword, and she turned to see Mender standing at the alley's entrance, one hand on the Fabretti.

'Relax,' she told both men. 'We're just leaving.'

She recovered the fletcher and her purchases and paused next to Mender. 'Coming? We're on a deadline, remember?'

Mender frowned at Harry but said nothing, apparently deciding to save his questions for later.

'Wait!' Harry hurried after them, but Orry didn't slow down. 'Have you got a ship?'

'Mind your own,' Mender growled.

'Take me with you.'

'You don't even know where we're going,' she said, spotting the lift shaft up ahead that led to the landing pads.

'I don't care – anywhere's better than here.'

'No,' Orry and Mender said together.

Harry fell silent but kept pace with them. He looked at the robes bundled in Orry's arms, thought for a moment and smiled. 'You're going to the Shattermoon, aren't you?'

She hid her surprise. 'What makes you say that?'

'You've bought astrotheometrist robes, so it's either the Shattermoon or Dia Tacita. And no one *chooses* to go to Dia Tacita.'

'I might be going to a fancy dress ball.'

He gave her a pained look.

'The Shattermoon is a restricted zone,' Orry pointed out.

'Pardon me for saying, but you don't look like the sort of people who would be discouraged by something like that.'

'Well, that just makes you wrong again.'

Harry ran a hand through his tangle of hair. 'Your costume might get you past the picket, but what about the inner cordon?'

She stopped, frowning. 'There is no inner cordon.'

'No, sure.' Harry glanced around. 'Of course there isn't.'

'If you know something, kid, just spill it,' Mender growled.

'Not unless you take me with you.'

Mender snorted. 'You're lying.'

Orry used her integuary to scan Harry's facial features, respiration and body temperature. The subroutine worked well on those without an integuary, but Harry was an aristo and almost certain to have one, and if he did it would likely be adjusting his biometrics to mask his lie. She could see nothing to indicate he wasn't telling the truth, but her gut told her otherwise.

'Why should I believe you?' she asked at last.

'My mother is highly placed in the Administrate – she was on the oversight committee handling the Shattermoon legacy. I know everything about it. Take me with you and I'll get you down to the surface.'

She chewed her lip.

'You're not buying this bullshit, are you?' Mender demanded. 'Very convenient, if you ask me. I've flown from the Diatris Scar to Mendulon's Gate and I can tell you there ain't no such thing as a coincidence.'

'Look, you saved my life,' Harry told her. 'Where I come from, that's considered an honour debt.'

Orry groaned. She knew all about the importance of honour debts in Ruuz culture. 'Oh, no: you're not pulling that crap on me. I release you.'

He smiled and shook his head. 'Not so simple, I'm afraid. You saved my life. I have to do something of equivalent value in return.'

'Which just happens to mean you need to come with us.'

'Hey,' he said, hands held wide. 'I didn't make the rules.' He flashed a set of perfect teeth. His face turned serious. 'If you leave me here, I'm as good as dead.'

Orry grinned despite herself.

'Rama,' Mender muttered. 'I'm going to need a bigger ship.'

14

TROUBLE IN PARADISE

'Ouch!' Harry hissed, flinching.

'One more,' Orry told him. 'Don't be such a baby.' She adjusted the medbay's light and used a pair of tweezers to grip the end of the last flechette. Blood was trickling down his bare chest and she was doing her best not to notice the well-defined muscles moving beneath smooth skin.

He gritted his teeth but this time he didn't make a sound as she steadily extracted the final dart and wiped the blood from his chest with a damp cloth.

'Thank you,' he said as she sprayed the cluster of seven tiny holes with an antiseptic aerosol.

As she ripped open a sterile dressing she said, 'Can I ask you something?'

'That depends.'

'Back on the rig, the way you moved? You're *fast*.'

He grinned as she placed the dressing over his wounds and waited for the biofilm matrix to knit to his flesh. 'You want to know if I'm a chimera.'

'Are you?'

'Back home I was Alecto's continental fencing champion. A lot of folk expected me to win the world title, maybe even try for the Seven Worlds Shield – that's the Fountainhead's interplanetary competition.'

'What does that have to do with transgenics?'

'I'm just saying: no one gets to that level without some recombinant DNA.'

'What was the donor?'

He looked amused. 'You know, it's not really considered polite to discuss this sort of thing.'

'Oh no,' Orry said dryly. 'I'm *mortified*.'

Harry sighed. 'Mainly serval cat for reflexes and agility. Some emperor cobra for precision, and Mimosan crag goat for balance.' He slipped off the bed and pulled on his shirt. 'You don't like me much, do you?'

'Is it that obvious?'

'Then why did you bring me along?'

'You know why.' She fixed him with a knowing look. 'You're going to get us past the inner cordon.'

'Yes, of course.' He concentrated on fastening his shirt.

'Harry?'

'Yes?'

'There is no inner cordon, is there?'

'I—' He sighed and stared at the deck. 'No.'

'So now I know something else about you: you're a liar.'

'I'm sorry. I *had* to get off that rig.' He looked up. 'You know every ship that's tried for the Shattermoon's core has been destroyed? It's why they put the picket there in the first place: to keep the treasure hunters from plastering themselves over the debris field.'

'No – really?'

He scowled. 'So if you're not trying for the core, what's the point in going? There haven't been any new finds on that rock for decades. Whoever the Departed were, they knew how to protect their secrets.'

'Agreed. And so do I.'

He conceded with a smile. 'If you knew I was lying, why did you bring me?'

'Well, you were begging me to rescue you.'

'I wasn't begging.' When Orry raised an eyebrow he gave her a wry grin and added, 'As I recall, it was more like pleading.'

'You're still a liar.'

He clutched his heart. 'You wound me.'

She looked away.

'What's the matter?'

'Nothing. It's just something my brother used to say.'

'Used to?'

The medbay door slid open and Mender poked his head in. He was holding a bulb of coffee. From the smell, it had been liberally laced with whisky. 'On course for the egress point.' He hooked a finger at Orry. 'A word.'

She stepped into the passageway, nerves fluttering. 'What did you find out?' she whispered as the door closed behind her.

'Long story short, we're screwed.'

She sighed. 'I guess that's not much of a surprise.'

'Roag has a ghost atomicist set up in a lab on the rig. He tailors biomites to her specification. She must've guessed we'd be coming and prepared a custom strain for us, just in case. Whatever's in our heads, only Roag can deactivate them.'

'How could she *possibly* know we'd be coming? She even knew my name . . .'

'Roag's a real puppet-master,' Mender told her. 'She's pulling strings all over the galaxy – she probably knew about our escape from *Speedwell* before the Admiralty on Tyr did.'

'But how did she know we would come to her?'

He laughed. 'No magic there. Who else would be able to find Dyas?'

Orry ran her hands through her hair, which felt horribly greasy. She couldn't remember the last time she'd washed and suddenly all she wanted to do was take a long shower.

'What if we could get to this atomicist, convince *him* to deactivate the biomites?'

But Mender was shaking his head before she'd even finished the sentence. 'Forget it. Even if we could get to him, he'd never betray Roag. You saw what she's like.'

Orry wasn't so sure, but this wasn't the time to argue. They had three days, and all that mattered right now was finding Ethan. There would be time to worry about the invaders in her head once her little brother was safe.

'Oh yeah,' Mender said, 'I have something to show you.'

The medbay door folded open. 'Sorry, am I interrupting?' Harry was in his shirtsleeves, a red stain discolouring the expensive fabric where he'd been wounded.

Mender glared at him, then stalked down the corridor, muttering under his breath.

'I don't think he likes me much either,' Harry observed as Orry followed him.

'No, I don't think he does.'

Mender stopped at a door further down the passageway. 'You can berth in here,' he told Orry. 'If you like.'

She couldn't help but smile at his tone. 'Well, you don't have to sound so enthusiastic about it.'

'It wasn't my idea,' he murmured cryptically as he opened the door. 'You want it or not?'

She peered into the cabin. The deck was covered with plastic storage crates. 'What's in the boxes?' she asked.

'Just junk I've been meaning to get rid of. Shove it all in the freight lock and we'll jettison it before the collapse. It won't take you long.' His craggy face broke into a rare smile. 'Your boyfriend can help.' He limped away, chuckling at his own wit.

'He sounds happy,' Harry observed.

Orry scowled at the battered crates. There were at least twenty of them. 'Of course he is. He's being an arsehole. It's his thing.'

'He got me out of that hellhole, so he's all right by me.'

'Wait till you get to know him. Anyway, he would've left you there if it wasn't for me.'

'Then you're all right by me, too.' Harry grinned, and Orry imagined the brain-dead society girls on Alecto swooning at that smile. She rolled her eyes and squeezed through the door. The cabin was pretty basic, only a little larger than her quarters on *Bonaventure*. She grasped the handles of the nearest crate and pulled, but one corner clung doggedly, the molly hooks refusing to disengage properly. At last she managed to wrench it free and pass it to Harry.

'Who is he, anyway?' he asked. 'Your grandfather or something?'

'Rama, no! We just have something in common.'

'Something on the Shattermoon?'

'Some*one* actually.' She sighed. 'A man named Dyas – he took my ship.'

'That was careless of you. How did he take it?'

'He murdered my father.'

'Oh, Rama . . . I'm sorry.' He was silent for a moment. 'He sounds dangerous. Is getting your ship back worth risking your life?'

'My little brother's on board.'

'Ah . . .'

'Any more questions?' she asked acerbically, wishing he'd just shut up. She tore another crate free and piled it on top.

'Yes, actually. So this Dyas fellow took your ship and your brother – what did he do to earn the old man's displeasure?'

'Dyas owes him.'

'For what?'

Orry just stood there, nonplussed.

'You don't know, do you?' Harry continued. 'How long have you known him?'

'A day, but—'

'A *day*?' He whistled. 'Busy day.'

'He saved my life.'

'Do you trust him?'

'Of course,' she started, then hesitated. 'Well, I think so.' She wondered why she was defending Mender so fervently when Harry was right; she knew next to nothing about the old man.

'How long has he been on his own?'

'I didn't ask.' She went to pick up the next crate but this one stuck too, one side glued to the deck. 'Bloody molecular hooks,' she growled; they might be indispensable in microgravity but they were utterly infuriating when they wore out. She heaved again – and the hooks released, depositing her painfully on her backside. The crate hit the wall and burst open, spilling its contents over her.

'I'm fine,' she snapped as Harry stepped forward to help. He backed off and she clambered onto her knees, righted the crate and began tossing stuff back in: a damaged data module, a skin-tight cocktail dress she wouldn't be seen dead in, an empty bottle of Sabinian single malt. She picked up a crumpled databrane and shook it – the brane stiffened into a rigid screen displaying an image of a young couple in old-fashioned hiking gear, laughing on an outcrop of rock. Snow-capped peaks ranged away in the background.

'Is that *Mender*?' she asked, holding it out to Harry.

'I do believe it is,' he said with a smile. 'I wonder who he's with.'

The image vanished as the brane lost its integrity and flopped back into a square of plastic. Orry tried shaking it again, but its electrostatic generator was clearly damaged. She folded the brane carefully and tucked it into a pocket, then returned to the spilled items.

'I have another question for you,' she said.

'Ask away.'

'What in fat Piotr's name were you doing on Roag's rig?'

Harry ignored her less than respectful attitude towards the Imperator Ascendant. 'Would you believe me if I told you I came out here looking for adventure?'

'How's that working out for you?'

'I'm serious. You have no idea how *boring* it is on Alecto.'

'Oh, totally,' she sneered, '*sooo* boring, living on your family estate with more gilt than you can ever spend, servants at your beck and call—'

'Money can't fix everything,' he said quietly.

'Whatever.'

'We're more than what we're born to, Orry. I want to make a name for myself – make my own money, spend it how I like. I'm not going to end up like Mender, roaming the galaxy in a garbage scow.'

'*Dainty Jane* is *not* a garbage scow,' Orry said sharply, chucking a broken surveillance drone into the crate. 'How *are* you going to end up?'

'Infamous,' he replied with a wolfish grin.

'Interesting answer. And how exactly are you planning to achieve that?'

'I haven't worked out the finer details, but something is bound to happen if I move about enough. There are a lot of opportunities out there.'

'Yeah, opportunities to get killed – or worse.'

'Did anyone ever tell you that you're a very negative person, Orry?'

'I'm not negative, I'm realistic.'

'Well, you would be.'

'What does that mean?'

'Because of what happened with this Dyas fellow.'

'Oh really? So nothing bad would have happened to you on Roag's rig, then? What about, "If you leave me here, I'm as good as dead"?'

Harry flushed. 'Not everywhere is like that.'

'Oh, no,' she said. 'If you're planning on becoming infamous, you'll be rubbing shoulders with *all* the best people.'

'It will be different when I have my own ship, a crew to back me up.'

'Is that what you were doing on the rig? Trying to lease a ship from Roag?'

'Yes.' His jaw tightened. 'It took me all my gilt to find out where she was, and when I got there she wouldn't even see me.'

Orry looked incredulous. 'Really? What the hell did you expect? Roag's a *businesswoman* – no way she's going to hand over a starship to some kid with no experience and no money, no matter how posh his accent is.' She patted his forearm. 'Anyway, from what I saw of her, you had a lucky escape.'

'Maybe so. But I still don't have a ship.'

'You don't just get a ship because you *want* one, Harry. Real life doesn't work like that. You have to start at the bottom – sign on as a loader or something, then earn your master's ticket – *then* someone might lease you a ship. If you work hard you're only looking at ten years or so—'

'Ten years! I'll be an old man by then.'

She laughed. 'You'll be – what? Thirty-five?'

'Exactly. I can't wait that long.'

'You're going to have to. No one is going to just *give* you a ship.'

'That's easy for you to say. Once you find this Dyas chap, *you'll* have your own ship.'

She stared at him. 'There are so many things wrong with what you just said, I don't know where to begin.' She counted to ten, trying to calm herself. 'Okay, so how about this: my father was *murdered* – that's a pretty shitty way to get a ship.'

'At least you'll have one,' he repeated stubbornly.

'Oh my *God* . . .' She pushed past him.

'What?' he called after her, mystified. 'Aren't you going to finish your cabin?'

Without breaking stride, Orry raised a fist and extended her middle finger, aiming it back at him.

She heard music in the cargo bay, which grew louder as she climbed upwards. By the time she got to the cockpit, the jangling guitar and wailing vocals were positively battering her ears.

Mender was lying back in his seat, a cheroot glowing between his lips, his eyes closed, tapping out the beat with the fingers of one hand. He opened his eyes when she entered and turned the volume down.

'That was fast,' he said, stubbing out the cheroot.

She dropped into the right-hand seat and glowered at him.

'Trouble in paradise?'

'Give it a rest, Mender. That guy's a moron. He's just a spoiled child.' She broke into a mocking, deep-voiced impression of Harry. 'I want a ship *right now*. I'm too special to have to work at it like everyone else.'

'Are you done?'

She folded her arms.

'Handsome, though,' he said, a glint in his eye.

'I hadn't noticed.' Orry's cheeks burned.

He grinned and settled back.

'Oh, I found this in one of the crates.' She handed him the damaged databrane. 'I thought you might want to keep it.'

Mender had to shake the brane a few times before it became rigid. He stared at the mountain scene.

'Is that you?' she asked.

He ran a blunt finger over the image. 'Thought I'd slung this.'

'How old were you?'

'A little older than you. It was on Sabine.'

'Who's that with you?'

'No one.' He stared a moment longer, then held out the brane. 'Chuck this out with the rest. It's bust.'

'Are you okay?'

'I will be once I get *Jane* to myself again.' He turned the music back up, dismissing her.

Orry took the hint and climbed back down to the cargo bay. Consumed with curiosity, she placed the brane on the workbench. Mender might be a slob, but he looked after his tools, which were neatly arranged in a chest of shallow drawers. She quickly found what she needed and set to work on the device, which had been configured as a picture frame and loaded with nothing but images. The storage was damaged as well as the electrostatic generator, which probably meant the brane had been deliberately overloaded. It took time, but at last she was able to transfer all the images she'd been able to salvage to her integuary.

She dropped the remains of the databrane into a bin, then made herself comfortable and started to review what she'd recovered. The first few images were more mountain scenes, then what looked like a stage-one colony world: a simple, printed home beneath an orange sky, the surrounding ground just bare soil. The same woman, a little older, held a baby in her arms. In the final images the ground was a garden teeming with life. The child was now a boy of five or six, helping a fresh-faced Mender to water the towering crops.

Orry stared at the last picture, then up at the cockpit. She recognised the oldie now thudding out; her dad had played it too. She sighed and closed the images.

For all his arrogance, Harry was right. *Dainty Jane* might not be a garbage scow, but Mender was certainly alone, and the thought of ending up like him frightened her. She'd lost both her parents now; Ethan was all she had left.

Her integuary tingled as if picking up on her mood and she summoned a smile and looked around the cargo bay. 'You again?' she said, mostly to hear the sound of her own voice. Her scalp rippled softly in response. 'Stuff to do,' she said firmly, and jumped down from the bench.

She had to prepare for their arrival at the Shattermoon.

The observation blister provided such a clear view of the stars it was almost like being outside the ship. Orry was surprised to find she could stand it – and wondered if she'd conquered her greatest fear when Dyas had spaced her. Whatever the reason, she found she was actually enjoying being inside the blister – even if her attention right now was more focused on her outfit than the view.

The cream and scarlet robe was stained in a way that made Orry try hard not to think about the fate of its former occupant. The embroidered twists of DNA were coming loose in places, the broken threads waving in the recirculated air. The fabric was coarser than she'd expected; it was rubbing the exposed skin of her arms and legs and chafing her hips particularly, where she'd tied the shapeless garment around her waist with the length of rope that came with it. A pair of plastic sandals with deep, yellowing impressions of feet only a little larger than hers completed the ensemble. She studied herself through *Dainty*

Jane's internal lenses as she ran through the character she was to play. Ethan's life depended on her getting this right.

'That red doesn't go with your hair,' Harry said, poking his head up through the deck hatch.

'I'm busy.'

'Look, I'm sorry,' he told her. 'About before? Sometimes I say stupid things.' He glanced around the blister's transparent dome. 'Can I come up?'

'No.'

He took a breath. 'The truth is, none of this is how I expected it to be. Back home there are rules, you know? Clearly defined codes of behaviour, social boundaries: everyone knows where they stand. Out here, everyone does whatever the devil they want.' His brown eyes gazed into hers. 'And you . . .'

'What?' she asked, annoyed at herself for being interested in whatever he was about to say.

'You're so . . .'

His expression was so earnest she couldn't help but smile. 'What?'

He grinned back at her. 'Well, you grew up out here, that's all: you know a lot . . .'

'I *know a lot*?' She laughed. 'Is that the best you can do?'

'I'm just trying to say I like you—' His eyes widened and he spluttered quickly, 'No – not like that! I-I mean, I'm glad you let me tag along. And I'm sorry about lying. If you need some help with Dyas, my sword is yours.'

She blinked. '*My sword is yours?* Did you really say that?'

'Yes.' He looked confused.

'What are you, the last Musketeer?'

He frowned. 'Do you always respond like this when people

offer to put themselves in harm's way for you? I can't help where I come from.'

Orry sighed. 'You're right. I'm sorry. Thank you, Harry.' She moved aside to let him climb up.

'Does this mean I'm forgiven?' he asked.

'I'm not sure.'

'Heavens—' He turned slowly, taking in the view.

She adjusted the rope around her waist, prodded him to get his attention and gave him a twirl. 'I guess you don't see many astrotheometrists in the Fountainhead.'

'There are diplomatic missions – Dia Tacita and the Administrate have an understanding – but no, the ordinary monks tend to stay away.'

'They'd *love* you,' she said, thinking of his recombinant DNA. Genetic purists like astrotheometrists didn't believe in altering the human form through gene-splicing or artificial augments.

Harry ignored that and asked, 'Have you done this kind of thing before?'

'Once or twice.'

'It's a clever idea.'

'Thanks.' She was pleased with herself for coming up with it. Astrotheometrists were an odd bunch: half monk and half scientist, travelling the galaxy in a sacred quest to find proof of intelligent design, and particularly interested in exotic sites like the Shattermoon. Their home, Dia Tacita, was a helix habitat, curled round the artificial sun Perfidion like a double strand of DNA, although it reminded Orry more of a dangling length of apple peel. The Order were rich and had powerful connections. The monks travelled unarmed, relying on charity and the fear of retribution to protect them. She scraped a fingernail across a poorly stitched tear in the robe over her heart. Clearly that wasn't always enough.

'You realise it's not going to work,' Harry said.

Orry stiffened. 'You don't think I can pass for an astrotheometrist?'

'I don't know you well enough to say one way or the other, but you must think you can or you wouldn't be risking your brother's life on it.'

'Then why don't you think it will work?'

'I know the Grand Fleet. Whoever is in command of the Shattermoon picket will never let you down to the surface without orders, no matter how convincing you are.'

'Want a bet?'

He shook his head. 'I hope I'm wrong, Orry. I really do.'

'You are.' She wished she felt as confident as she sounded. In truth, she shared Harry's doubts – but she had no other ideas.

He turned back to the view of the stars. 'How long until we collapse?'

'Can't be long now. Have you eaten?'

'A little.'

'There are sick bags in the cockpit.'

'I'll be fine.'

She smiled. 'Have you been through many collapses?'

'Enough,' he said breezily.

'How many?'

His shoulders drooped a little. 'Three.'

'And how were they?'

He shook his head ruefully.

'I'll get you a bag. And one for me.'

'You?' He looked surprised. 'You don't like collapses?'

'No, I love being torn apart and remade light-years away.'

'Don't,' he said with a grimace. 'It makes my head hurt just thinking about it.'

The music thumping from the cockpit stopped.

'Speaking of pain,' she said at the sound of Mender's limping approach, making Harry chuckle.

The old man glared suspiciously as he poked his head up into the blister. He jerked a thumb at Orry. 'Pre-collapse checklist.'

She hid her smile. 'Yes, sir.'

'Anything I can do?' Harry asked.

'Yeah. Keep out of my way.' Mender tossed a sick bag at him and disappeared.

Orry gave Harry a sympathetic look as she descended the ladder.

15

PICKET SHIP

Goshawk was a sloop, not much larger than *Dainty Jane*. Vessels of this class were fast and lightly armed, mostly used as scouts and dispatch-runners. Clearly one small ship was all the Administrate considered the Shattermoon legacy to be worth these days.

Her commander, Under-Captain Hirota, had refused Mender's docking request at first, but after seeing Orry's robe on the viewscreen she had grudgingly agreed to send a launch to bring her aboard.

Goshawk's single battery remained locked on *Dainty Jane* as the pilotless launch sped back, sweeping under the sloop's belly to nestle into its docking cradle. Orry released her harness and floated up to the cramped craft's dorsal hatch, her robe drifting around her bare legs, making it awkward to move. *Completely impractical for microgravity*, she decided as she waited for the hatch to open.

She pulled herself out of the launch and into a compartment lined with stores. An auxiliary wearing shipboard fatigues rested one hand on his holstered pistol as he stood next to a smooth-cheeked tyro. The auxiliary's bushy black whiskers, extending down to his chin, were shot through with grey, mocking the wisp of fine hair on the tyro's upper lip. Orry was pleased: Under-Captain Hirota had clearly decided she warranted an officer to welcome her aboard, even if he was the most junior one on the ship. That had to be a good sign.

She placed her sandals on the deck and felt the molly hooks grip. When she inscribed the sign of purity with one hand, she received only faintly embarrassed looks in response.

The tyro stepped forward and saluted. 'Welcome aboard *Goshawk*, Precentor Tourmaline. My name is Orlov. I'm here to show you to the ops room.'

'My thanks.' Orry produced a serene smile and tucked her hands into the flared sleeves of her robe.

Goshawk's interior looked very much like *Speedwell*'s: all grey padding and anti-spalling compound. The operations room wasn't far, buried in the heart of the small vessel. An armoured auxiliary flanked a door with the words 'Command Restricted' stencilled on its surface. The room was illuminated by the soft glow of screens, and Orry saw images of *Dainty Jane* from several angles, as well as tactical displays of the volume of space around the ships. Some of the screens showed the Shattermoon itself. It reminded her of an ancient, broad-headed nail, a wide spike of exposed core extending down from an intact portion of curving crust. The spike was obscured by a thick blanket of jostling rocks: the debris field.

Hirota detached herself from a display station and approached. The trim woman was in early middle age, old to still be an under-captain, which meant one of three things:

either she was bad at her job, had pissed someone off, or had been passed over because of her non-Ruuz heritage. Orry hoped that might mean Hirota would be unwilling to trouble her superiors if she could help it.

Now she repeated the sign of purity and saw the under-captain's lips tighten, making her wonder if she'd made a poor choice of cover identity. The astrotheometrists' beliefs meant they were tolerated, or even feared, rather than liked.

'Thank you for agreeing to see me, Captain.'

'I sent the launch out of respect for your Order, Precentor, and because of the relationship between Dia Tacita and the Administrate. However, I have to inform you that nothing has changed: I cannot permit you to land on the Shattermoon without proper authorisation.'

'As I said, I was assured that you would be notified of my arrival.'

'And I have received no such notification.'

Orry smiled and held her hands apart. 'That is hardly my fault. Dispatch pods do go astray.'

'Nevertheless, I cannot permit you to land.'

'But it is imperative that I speak with Professor Rasmussen as soon as possible. Your superiors clearly agree, or they would not have granted authorisation.'

'Authorisation I have not received,' Hirota repeated. Her face was a mask. 'What is the nature of your business with the professor?'

'I don't mean to be rude, Captain, but that is a matter of some sensitivity.'

'And who exactly granted your authorisation?'

'Admiral Fedchenkov,' she said, naming the commander of

the Eridanis Treasure Fleet. By the time Hirota checked her credentials Orry would be long gone . . .

The under-captain thought for a moment. 'I suppose I could send a pod, but it would take a day to make the round trip, perhaps more.'

'Unacceptable,' Orry said, allowing a touch of frustration to enter her voice. 'This is a matter of urgency and I was assured that I would be accorded all assistance. This really isn't good enough.'

Hirota's face remained impassive, but Orry could tell from her biometrics that the under-captain was not as certain as she appeared. Having cast her line, Orry waited.

Hirota didn't bite. 'I'm sorry, Precentor. As I said, I can send a pod.'

Damn it, this isn't how it was supposed to go down. To buy some thinking time, she looked at the displays. Tyro Orlov, hovering nearby, stepped aside to afford her a better view. Her eyes stopped on an overhead view of a familiar, bulbous shape and it took every ounce of willpower not to betray her emotions as she stared at the grainy image of *Bonaventure*, squatting on the moon's portion of intact crust next to a collection of antiquated colony domes. Hidden within her sleeves, Orry's fingernails dug into her palms.

'I see Professor Rasmussen already has a visitor,' she said.

'Yes – we couldn't believe it,' Orlov said. 'He hasn't seen a soul in four years, then two of you turn up at once.'

'The dispatch pod containing their authorisation must have had a safer passage than mine, alas,' Orry said.

'Oh, no,' Orlov said, 'the professor cleared them himself.'

The tyro wilted under Hirota's glare and Orry turned to the under-captain with raised eyebrows.

'It's true,' Hirota said uncomfortably. 'In exceptional cases the professor can authorise visitors. He hardly ever does, though.'

'May I speak with him?'

'I really don't—'

'Under-Captain!' Orry snapped, abandoning all trace of the serene woman of the cloth. 'I am an astrotheometrist here on the direct orders of the Archcantor of Dia Tacita, a personal friend of the Imperator Ascendant himself. My mission is one of great importance and extreme urgency. I have jumped through every one of the ridiculous bureaucratic hoops surrounding this godforsaken relic of a world and it has clearly got me nowhere. Now unless you want to see out the rest of your career commanding a penal garrison in the Kadiran Marches, I suggest you open a private channel to Professor Rasmussen this instant!'

Hirota met her glare head-on and for a moment Orry thought she had gone too far. Then the under-captain said stiffly, 'Orlov, show the precentor to my quarters and open a secure line to the site.'

'Aye aye, ma'am.' He looked at Orry with something approaching awe. 'This way, please.'

Orry smiled at Hirota. 'Thank you, Captain.'

Hirota's jaw was clenched so tightly Orry half-expected her teeth to shatter like china pegs.

With a final glance at *Bonaventure*, she left the ops room in a tumult of hope and fear.

'I don't normally accept calls from strangers. What do you want?'

Jon Rasmussen, Emeritus Professor of Exo-Culture at the Halstaad-Mirnov Institute, was a healthy-looking man in his early hundreds. Beneath his bluster, Orry could tell he was scared.

'I am Precentor Jeris Tourmaline, of the Fifth Circle of Arkady,' she announced formally. 'The Serene Council despatched me because they are concerned for your safety.'

That got his attention. 'My safety? What do you mean?'

'Four days ago, the Temple of Echoes on Dia Tacita was robbed. One of our most revered relics was stolen: an exotic stone set in a golden pendant.'

Rasmussen's eyes flicked sideways, off-camera. 'What does that have to do with me?'

'We have reason to believe that the thief will be bringing the piece to you, for . . . appraisal.'

'So?'

'Five astrotheometrists were killed during the robbery. *Murdered*.' She leaned forward. 'Professor, is anyone there with you now?'

The professor swallowed, sweat standing out beneath the few strands of white hair that remained on his head. He nodded.

'How many?'

'One man.'

'I assume he can't hear us?'

'No, but he can see me.'

'Then look natural, Professor. Smile.' He managed a sickly half grin. 'Now, I want you to contact Under-Captain Hirota and instruct her to let my ship land at your site.'

'What good will that do? I know you bloody monks are good at *pash rakhar*, but this fellow is armed.'

'Would you rather I tell Hirota to send in her auxiliaries?'

'*No*,' Rasmussen hissed.

Orry smiled at him. 'Rest assured, Professor, if you allow me to land, I will deal with this situation discreetly. No one will know about your extra-curricular activities.'

He searched her face. 'Very well.' He glanced off to the side again. 'Please, hurry.'

16

CITADEL

Ethan's head was throbbing where it had come into sharp contact with the bulkhead, but he just wedged himself more firmly into the corner of *Bonaventure*'s citadel as the freighter lurched again. Only when he was certain she'd finally come to rest did he release himself.

'Nice landing, arsehole,' he muttered as he felt his molly hooks catch. He crossed to the citadel's bank of monitors and switched to exterior lenses. *Rama, this place is a dump.* The collection of landing pads and low domes looked like a holoset, but it was *real*, more than a century old, dating back to the beginning of the Second Expansion. Some of the curved walls were more repair patches than the original dusty ferroconcrete.

He'd watched the approach through the hardwired monitors, feeling lost without his integuary connection. He hated those monitors; not so long ago he'd watched his father being murdered on the screens.

He'd run to the arms locker then, disobeying his father's final order to remain in the safety of the ship's concealed citadel no matter what, but the locker had been sealed and his integuary wasn't functioning, so he couldn't unlock it. By the time he'd remembered the damn override code and fumblingly loaded a carbine, Orry was trapped in an airlock. He'd not been able to tear his eyes away from the screens, and as he'd watched his sister being sucked from the ship, he'd felt like his world had ended.

Suddenly, shockingly alone, terrified and cut off from the ship's integuary nodes, he had finally followed the family's standing orders and stayed in the citadel. And when the numbness finally started to wear off, he had to stop himself from venturing out to avenge his family: even in the depths of his despair he knew he would just be throwing his life away. Better to bide his time; an opportunity for vengeance would surely arise.

He'd considered sneaking out while Dyas slept, to kill the murderer or try to deactivate whatever was jamming his integuary, but that damned mimetic spent all its time prowling the ship, searching for him. The robot must suspect *Bonaventure* had a citadel – even though the safe room was well hidden, Ethan worried that it would stumble on his hiding place before he could exact his revenge. But for now at least it was concentrating its search on the lower decks.

Bonaventure cooled and ticked around him as he watched Dyas descend to the cargo deck. When the mimetic met the raider by the starboard freight lock, Ethan zoomed in and turned up the volume.

'Monitor things from the bridge,' Dyas said.

'The hell I will. So you can go and have fun with that old skinbag?'

Dyas rubbed his forehead wearily. 'Listen, you fucking

marionette, if you'd found the damn kid I'd be happy to let you come along. But as your *sensors*' – air quotes here – 'couldn't find a quim in a whorehouse, one of us has to stay here to make sure the little shit doesn't fly off and leave us.'

'You stay, then.'

Dyas held up the pendant Orry had taken from Konstantin. 'Look, once we sell this damned thing you can do what you like back in Freeport. Until then, Jericho, you do as I say. And *I* say *you* stay here while *I* go and interview the professor. Right?'

Ethan's hopes lifted as he watched Dyas stalk into the airlock. He knew Freeport well, and if Dyas really was planning to go there next, there was a chance of escape.

He switched one screen to the external lenses and watched Dyas bounce lightly across the landing pad and into a blocky building between two domes. Jericho turned and strode towards the axial companionway up to the bridge.

'Dammit.' He couldn't see anything on the surface now and he felt useless without his integuary. Leaning back in his seat, he stared at the overhead. *Work the problem*, Dad always said. *No matter how bad things seem, there is always a solution – you just have to find it. Giving into fear and despair will just make things more difficult.*

Ethan looked round the citadel, taking in the viewscreens and systems monitoring gear. His eyes stopped on the waldo controls for *Bonaventure*'s remote maintenance drone. He looked at the manipulator, tapping his front teeth with his fingernail a few times, then sat upright, feeling his heart beating faster, and pulled his chair closer to the screens. He cycled through the ship's external lenses until he stopped on a view of a servicing module at the edge of the pad. He stared at it for a few seconds, telling himself not to get his hopes up, then returned to the drone station and slid his hands and feet into the control sleeves. Compared with an integuary, this was a clumsy way of controlling the multi-limbed robot they used to effect repairs to *Bonaventure*'s hull and external systems ... but the archaic waldo controls did still work.

He detached the drone from its socket in *Bonaventure*'s bulging side and lowered it to the landing pad using its internal tether spool. The drone looked like a spider, each limb tipped with molecular hooks, as it scuttled over to the servicing module. Ethan made it select a data cable and pulled it back to the ship, used another limb to open a small port in the hull and a third to insert the cable, then reeled the drone back into its socket.

Trembling slightly, he accessed the new connection he'd just created. The landing site's security might be several generations out of date, but it was still effective. For the first time, his grief and anxiety was subsumed by curiosity as he set about breaking the encryption. It was a slow process, trying to subvert the system without his integuary, but that made the satisfaction when he finally succeeded all the greater.

'*Yes!*' he cried. '*I am ... the shit.*'

The virtual topology of the complex beneath the domes appeared as a 3-D wireframe on one of his screens. He pulled up heat signatures and expertly superimposed them onto the model. There were only two in the entire complex, both in what looked to be an enormous chamber deep below the surface. He searched around until he found the lift shaft leading down to the chamber, accessed a security camera attached to its exterior and shunted the feed to another monitor. The image was a little grainy, showing motes of dust hanging in the air below vaulted arches that formed a cathedral of fused rock. When he tilted the camera down, he could see metal storage shelves stuffed with boxes and containers, as well as laboratory equipment scattered across stone benches in the centre of the chamber.

Dyas was standing near one of the benches, where an elderly man in a grubby lab coat was peering into a microscope.

'Definitely exotic,' the old man said.

'I know that much, Professor,' Dyas said. 'What's it worth?'

'Hmm.' The old man adjusted the microscope and looked again. 'Well, you might get twenty for it.'

Dyas gave a humourless laugh. 'Look again, Prof. There's something special about that particular stone.'

The professor sighed and took Orry's pendant from the microscope. He crossed to another machine, placed the stone under a sensor of some sort, flicked a switch and turned to study the screen above.

From the way he stiffened, Ethan guessed that he didn't much like what he was seeing. 'You might be right,' the professor admitted, turning to Dyas. 'It is a nice piece. In fact, I'd quite like it for my personal collection. I'll give you fifty thousand for it.'

The raider grunted and looked around the dome. 'First it's twenty, then fifty. Do you know what I think, Professor? I think it's worth ten times that, and you know it.'

'I—'

'Do you think I floated into orbit on a rock, Rasmussen? I'm not a fucking idiot! I know you deal in these artefacts – the moment I walked out of that airlock counting my money you'd have it on a pod and headed to the Fountainhead for a nice little auction.'

'No! It really isn't worth any more than fifty—'

'Bollocks it isn't.' Dyas wandered to the nearest shelf and surveyed the trays. 'This is your collection, is it? Not a lot to show for a lifetime of scraping at the dust.' He picked up something and Ethan strained to make out the details. Then Dyas held it up in two fingers and he could see it was a translucent orb made of some type of crystal. Its surface looked oily, like a rainbow caught in a bottle.

'Please,' Professor Rasmussen begged, 'be careful with that.'

'You know, for someone with so many letters after his name, you're pretty fucking dumb.' Dyas let go of the orb and it shattered at his feet.

'No—!' the professor fell to his knees, his fingers fluttering over the rainbow shards.

Dyas walked along one shelf, studying the artefacts, while the old man stood staring at him like a grieving parent.

'The Departed crafted that orb before mankind discovered fire,' he said, sounding broken.

'Sounds expensive.' Dyas scanned the shelves, looking thoughtful. 'How much is all this worth, anyway?'

'I'm not interested in money.'

'I guess I'm not your usual customer, but you must have some sort of security down here. What's to stop me hauling all this crap away and selling it? You?'

The professor climbed slowly to his feet and brushed himself down. 'The picket ship.'

The camera image vibrated suddenly and Dyas tensed and looked up towards the top of the lift shaft. Cursing the antiquated systems, Ethan opened a second screen and cycled through the few cameras he could control. One showed another angle of the lift shaft, the metal supports rising up through the graceful arches of the vaulted roof. Between them, he could see the lift-cage slowing to a halt as it reached the bottom of the shaft. The door slid open and a craggy-faced old man with a shock of white hair stepped out, brandishing an enormous handgun, followed by a slender woman in astrotheometrist's robes.

Ethan stared at the second figure in disbelief.

Impossible! I saw her blown out of an airlock.

But here she was . . .

Orry. Alive.

17

DESCENT

Orry gazed hungrily at the old freighter as Mender set down a hundred metres from *Bonaventure*'s curving hull. It dwarfed *Dainty Jane*.

'What are you waiting for?' she demanded, already out of her seat. Gravity was light on the Shattermoon and made her feel like an athlete, if a somewhat clumsy one.

'Wait a moment,' Harry said. 'What's the plan?'

'Simple: we get Ethan, then we go after Dyas.'

'Hold up there, girl,' Mender said, climbing from his seat. 'I'll deal with Dyas. You two stay here until I've got him. Then we can go after your brother.'

'I'm not staying here!' Orry objected.

'Well you ain't coming with me. You're smart and you've got us this far, but a set of robes and a fancy mouth won't save you from a bullet. Let me take it from here.'

By way of response, she lowered herself to the arms locker below the cockpit sphere and grabbed a carbine. She extracted the magazine and checked the load, slapped it back into place and cocked the weapon – then she made the carbine safe and glared at Mender, who glared right back.

'All right,' he said reluctantly, 'but we go after Dyas and the pendant first, then your brother.'

'No – Ethan's more important.'

'If he's even still alive,' Mender said practically. 'Roag doesn't want your ship or your little brother. She wants Dyas and the pendant. We get them first. End of discussion.' He pushed past her to the locker.

'End of nothing!' she told him. 'Ethan first.'

'This ain't a democracy.' Mender offered a shotgun to Harry, who smiled and patted the pommel of his rapier. The old man rolled his eyes.

'Fine,' she said. 'You go after Dyas, I'll get Ethan.'

Mender sighed. 'Listen, girl, we've lucked out here. Your professor said Dyas was alone, right? That means the mimetic is probably still on your ship, which gives us a chance. We take Dyas first and get the pendant, and then we have some leverage against his tinman. If we split up, we're dead, and so's your brother.'

Orry hated him for being right. And although it was painful to admit it, he might be right about Ethan being dead, too. She'd been trying to raise her brother's integuary on the family channel, but there'd been no reply.

'Okay,' she said heavily.

The Shattermoon's atmosphere was thin, but it was breathable for short periods. It smelled of metal left out too long in the sun, but the fact there was any air at all was inexplicable to Orry. She shivered as she stepped out of the cargo bay, ice crystals crunching under her boots. Hoarfrost rimed *Bonaventure*'s upper hull, while the warm plating around her drives dripped a steady tattoo of melting ice.

As they crossed the pad, she couldn't keep her eyes off the freighter. The urge to run aboard and find her brother was almost overwhelming, but she followed Mender, trying the family channel again while praying the silence just meant Ethan's integuary was still being jammed.

Mender led them to a blocky building in a low cluster of domes huddled on one side of the pad. Next to a pair of freight elevators, a flight of service stairs led down into the moon's remaining interior. When she peered down, she could see one of the cage-like elevators at the bottom of the shaft, but the door of the other opened at their approach. The cage sank slightly under their weight as they entered and the door clanked shut, which didn't fill her with confidence, but when she threw the control lever, it dropped smoothly enough.

'Will Dyas put up a fight?' Harry asked as bare rock flashed past outside the metal cage.

'What am I, psychic?' Mender had to yell over the lift mechanism.

'I thought you knew him?'

'Not that well.' Mender cleared his throat, looking uncomfortable. 'Just keep behind us and try not to wave that pig-sticker around.'

Orry felt the elevator begin to slow and checked her carbine for the tenth time. Her mouth was dry and her legs were having trouble supporting her weight, even in the low gravity.

'Ready,' Mender said as the elevator ground to a halt.

The door slid open and he stepped out, brandishing his Fabretti. Orry followed close behind.

She spotted Dyas standing next to Professor Rasmussen near one of the stone benches and her hands tightened on her carbine. The raider was staring at Mender with a mixture of surprise and suspicion.

'Mender?' he said. 'What the hell are you doing here?' Orry moved out to stand beside the old man and Dyas' eyes widened. 'Well goddamn,' he said. 'How did you—? Wait – Mender, did you *pick her up?*'

'Shut your fucking mouth,' Mender snapped. He raised the Fabretti. 'Set down your piece.'

Dyas moistened his lips. His eyes darted to one side a moment before he dived behind the nearest stone bench.

It felt like a bomb had gone off in Orry's ear as Mender fired. Splinters flew from one end of the bench and Rasmussen fled, white coat flapping behind him. Smoke coiled from the Fabretti's wide muzzle.

Dyas' head popped up further down the workbench. His machine pistol produced a ripping noise and suddenly it was Orry diving for cover. She crouched behind a composite packing crate, praying it would stop the hail of bullets slamming into the other side.

Mender and Harry landed on the ground beside her.

'What do we do now?' Harry asked.

She didn't hesitate. 'Mender, use that cannon of yours to keep Dyas' head down. I'll work my way round behind him.'

He nodded, and she flinched as Dyas' gun spat again. The crate shuddered.

'What about me?' Harry asked.

'Just stay here,' she told him.

'Is that it? I can fight, you know.'

'With that thing? If you wanted to help you shouldn't have brought a bloody sword to a gunfight.'

Mender waited for a break in the fusillade, then stood up and fired. *Go!* he sent.

She sprinted to the nearest wall of shelves, slid behind it and scrambled along, keeping as low as she could. The chatter of automatic fire was drowned out by another deafening report from the Fabretti.

The curve of the shelves soon revealed the professor, curled into a ball, hands over his ears. He shied away when he saw her, a look of terror on his face.

'Are you all right?' she asked. 'Not wounded?'

'You're no astrotheometrist,' he said accusingly.

She patted him on the shoulder. 'Keep your head down, Prof.'

She was almost alongside Dyas' position now, and he didn't appear to have noticed her. The crumbling stone bench he was sheltering behind stopped her from getting a clear shot through the gaps in the shelves, so she was considering her next position when her integuary activated.

She froze as she recognised the signature.

Orry! Can you hear me?

18

A LETTER OF ADVOCACY

Ethan stared at the displays in front of him, hardly breathing. *How can she be alive? It's impossible.*

On one screen Dyas was backing away, while on the other the old man standing beside Orry was raising his huge pistol. He growled, 'Set down your piece.'

As his sister aimed a carbine at Dyas, a third person stepped out of the lift. Ethan did a double-take as the tall, skinny newcomer raised a *rapier*, of all things. *Where does he think he is? A duelling ground on Tyr?*

He zoomed in on Orry's face, relief welling inside him. It really was her.

Dyas dived for the cover of a workbench and Ethan found himself flinching as the old man fired his hand-cannon, sending stone chips flying everywhere. A moment later the gunman, Orry and the lanky swordsman scattered as Dyas popped up to return fire.

'No, no, no!' Ethan muttered. 'I'm not losing you again.' He tried in vain to get his integuary to open the family channel, slamming his hand into the console in frustration – then his fingers started racing over the controls, filtering the site's system nodes. A moment later a grin spread over his face. It looked like the site had its own integuary access node. It might be too far below the surface, but perhaps he could reconfigure it to relay a message to Orry. He set to work modifying the data-link between the ship and the site, glancing at the screen every few seconds to follow her as she made her way around the back of the shelves, trying to outflank Dyas. At last he identified Orry's integuary signature and created a patch channel to his console.

He was reaching for the switch to activate the console's microphone when a shriek of tortured metal made him twist in his seat. The citadel's hidden door shuddered under a powerful blow, buckling near the lock.

'Oh, Rama,' he muttered, and scrambled for his carbine.

The edge of the door crumpled and gave way as he snatched up the weapon, fumbling to cock it even as the door was wrenched away.

Jericho's emotionless face peered through the gap. '*There* you are,' the mimetic said cheerfully. 'I knew you'd break cover eventually. I hope whatever it is you're looking at on this rock is worth your life.'

Ethan shot it, raising sparks.

The head reappeared a moment later, an admonishing finger ticking like a metronome. 'That's not very friendly.'

Jericho peeled the door back as if it was opening a tin of yellowstrake tuna. Ethan fired again, this time raising a cloud of particulates from the mimetic's chest armour. It crossed the citadel in two strides, plucked the carbine from his hands and tossed the weapon away.

Ethan tried to dart past it and out of the ruined door, but the mimetic casually backhanded him. It was like being kicked by a mulette. He flew across the citadel and cracked his head on the console. Groaning, he tried to stand, but his legs had liquefied. Two Jerichos were approaching him, until he managed to focus and they merged into one. It wasn't an improvement.

'I'm going to fuck you up, skinbag,' the mimetic said conversationally.

Ethan used the console to lever himself up – and slammed a hand down to activate the patch channel he'd created. 'Orry!' he yelled. 'Can you hear me?'

The answer came back a moment later – not her voice, but her words rendered in an artificial tone. 'Ethan? Stay where you are. We're coming for you.'

He watched Jericho striding closer and screamed, 'He's here, Orry – Jericho's found me – *help, please!*'

The artificial voice stripped her response of emotion. 'We're coming. Hang on in there, little brother.'

The mimetic raised its arm.

'There's no time – he's here, *now*!' A desperate thought occurred to him and he shouted, '*Mama—*'

The arm fell.

Tyro Orlov looked at the two heavily armoured figures standing in *Goshawk*'s ops room with a mixture of awe and fear. They'd arrived shortly after the departure of the pretty and rather intimidating Precentor Tourmaline. Three ships visiting the Shattermoon in one day? That felt very wrong to Orlov, and from the look on his captain's face, Hirota shared his concern.

'You mentioned a document?' Hirota addressed the taller of

the pair, a heavyset man with a full moustache and scars criss-crossing the weathered skin of his face, but it was his partner who responded, half his age and height, with neatly cropped brown hair and delicate, pixie-like features. She offered Hirota a folded databrane secured with a round bronze-coloured seal the size of an imperial sovereign.

Orlov recognised the arms engraved on the seal immediately: House Delf.

Hirota released the seal and shook out the brane, her eyes scanning the copperplate writing. She glanced up at the bounty hunters, then held the document out to Orlov.

'You're from Tyr,' she said. 'What do you make of this?'

Orlov studied the brane.

The House of Delf, acting with the full authority of Piotr, Imperator Ascendant, commands and instructs that the bearers of this letter be permitted to pass freely and without hindrance, and that all citizens afford the bearers such assistance as may be requested.

'It's a letter of advocacy,' he said, 'signed by His Grace the Count of Delf. We're required to assist the bearers in any way we can.'

'Would it surprise you to discover,' Hirota said coldly, 'that I can, in fact, read?' She sighed at his blank look. 'Is it genuine?'

Orlov used his integuary to authenticate the digital water-mark, then studied the signature at the bottom of the document closely. Finally, he turned his attention to the seal.

'If it's a forgery, ma'am, it's a work of art.'

Her shoulders slumped a little. 'I concur.' She motioned for him to return the document to the pixie-faced woman, who wasn't bothering to hide the bored, supercilious expression on her face.

'What do you need?' Hirota asked her. 'We're no battle cruiser.'

'Weapons we got,' the man rasped. He sounded like his larynx was lined with broken glass. It made Orlov want to clear his throat.

'We're going down to the Shattermoon,' the woman told Hirota. 'Just stay out of our way.'

'Who are you after?'

The woman smiled nastily. 'What's the matter, Under-Captain? Worried about your career?' She thumped her partner on his chestplate and headed for the door.

Orlov hurried to escort them back to their ship, a sleek atmosphere-capable craft that looked like a slender knife docked alongside *Goshawk*'s blocky hull. As he left the bridge, he stole a glance at Hirota.

She looked like a broken woman.

19

EISENS

Ethan! Stay where you are – we're coming for you.

He's here, Orry – Jericho! He's found me – help, please!

Why had she listened to bloody Mender? *We're coming*, Orry sent. *Hang on in there, little brother.*

There's no time – he's here now! Mama—

The connection dropped out, leaving Orry feeling like she'd been kicked in the stomach. Ethan was alive – but for how long? She started back the way she'd come.

Where the hell are you going? Mender demanded.

Jericho has my brother. I have to get to him!

Goddamn it, girl, you stop right there. She kept going, until he snapped, *Orry! Stop!*

This time she did, her mind in turmoil. She flinched as Dyas fired again.

Mender sounded deadly serious as he sent, *I know you're worried about your brother, but the best way to help him is to get Dyas. One thing at a time.*

She drew a shuddering breath and steadied herself, then

turned back to the professor. Mender was right: it was time to end this.

Oh, shit! Mender sent.

I'm going, okay?

No, it's not that. We've got company.

Where? She twisted around, searching the chamber.

Not here yet – up on the pad. Two suits, coming this way. Elevator's going back up for them.

Auxiliaries?

Don't look like it.

How do you—?

Jane *told me. You need to hurry.*

The situation was getting seriously out of control. Orry scrambled a few more metres and peered between the shelves and this time Dyas was right in front of her, crouching behind the bench as he dug a fresh magazine from his pocket.

She stepped out and levelled the carbine at his back.

'Don't fucking move,' she snarled.

His hands froze, the magazine half inserted. He turned slowly to face her, a nervous grin on his face. 'Hello again.' Eyeing her carbine, he carefully laid his gun on the ground.

Mender stepped out from behind his crate. Harry was nowhere to be seen. 'Good job, girl. Bring him over here.'

Orry's mind flashed on an image of her father's blood spurting, his body falling. Her hands trembled on the carbine. It would be so easy to put a bullet into Dyas right now.

He must have sensed her thoughts because he put his hands in the air and started backing away. 'Now don't do anything stupid, okay?' A shrewd expression crossed his face. 'I'm surprised to see you and Mender together.'

'Don't say another word,' Mender yelled. 'I mean it, you sack of shit. Just keep your fucking mouth shut.'

Orry frowned, her hands relaxing a fraction. 'What do you mean?' she asked Dyas.

'Don't listen to that snake,' Mender warned her. 'He lies like a politician.' He glanced over his shoulder at the lift shaft and swore when he saw the cage descending. 'Get over here!'

She motioned with her carbine and Dyas edged out from behind the bench, hands still raised. Mender moved round to the other side of the crate to cover the shaft. She and Dyas were halfway to him when the cage door slid open.

Orry froze, frowning as she stared into the empty lift – no, not empty. There was something on the floor. She squinted – and her eyes widened.

The world vanished, replaced by pain. Her vision turned white as light brighter than any sun burned into the backs of her eyes. Noise battered her ears – she was inside a bell being rung by a giant's hammer. She dropped her gun, clutched her ears and squeezed her eyes shut. The pain was unbearable and her brain screamed in protest, her integuary lost in a tumult of sensory overload.

Finally, as the pain started to lessen, the white blanket covering her vision turned grey and blurred shapes appeared in front of her. The stunning cacophony in her ears faded to a desperate clanging, then a dull roar.

She blinked and removed her hands from her ears – and remembered Dyas. Only when she tried to drop to a defensive crouch did she realise she was already on her knees. The roaring in her ears was becoming a high-pitched whine which suddenly resolved into the staccato crack of laserfire. She rubbed desperately at her eyes, trying to focus, until she could make out the carbine lying next to her. A bright orange beam seared past her as she grabbed it. Fearfully, she looked around for Dyas, and found him still sheltering behind that same bench. She raised her carbine – then threw herself backwards as another beam flickered past. Dyas wrenched a scanner open and snatched something from inside; only when Orry caught a glint of gold did she realise it was the pendant. Before she could react, he'd disappeared through a gap between two towers of shelves.

Still alive, girl? Mender asked.

I think so. She looked over at the old man, crouched behind the crate. Laserfire lit the air around him like a dance floor, the beams burning through the composite. If she didn't do something he would be dead in a matter of seconds.

The beams were coming from two figures in what looked like military-spec armour, and they were advancing towards Mender. *Smart*, Orry thought. They'd timed their entrance just right, placing the stun-bomb in the elevator while they came down the stairs. They'd probably subverted the lift mechanism. *That's what Ethan would have done*, she thought with a pang.

Raising her carbine, she fired three quick shots and was rewarded as the smaller of the two figures, a woman, staggered back under the impact. Orry scrambled to her feet and ran for the nearest workbench, realising her plan to draw their fire had worked a little too well as beams flashed around her.

Pain shot through her right calf and her leg folded beneath her. She pitched forward and struck the ground hard, losing her grip on the carbine, which went clattering away. She rolled desperately as another beam sliced past her face, wondering how long she had left; her leg felt like someone had plunged a soldering iron into it and smoke was rising from at least one pencil-thin hole in her robes. The smell of seared flesh was not helping her nausea.

Thunder rolled around the chamber as Mender fired the Fabretti – and the female attacker's chestplate exploded in a shower of shards of ceramic composite and bloody gobbets of flesh. Orry winced as she caught a glimpse of the elevator through a basketball-sized hole in her attacker's chest before the woman toppled forward onto her face.

Mender dropped back down and she heard him eject his empty magazine. *Does he have any more, or is he out?* She couldn't hear him reloading . . .

She tried to stand again, stumbled and screamed, a mix of anger and pain. She set her teeth and started dragging herself towards her carbine, knowing she would never reach it in time.

Mender was spitting a non-stop stream of invective that confirmed he was out of ammunition.

The surviving attacker was advancing more cautiously now. As he paused to look down at his fallen comrade, Harry stepped from the shadows behind him, padded closer in complete silence and thrust his rapier expertly between the armoured plates low on the attacker's back.

The man froze for a second. His laser dropped from nerve-less fingers. Harry slid the blade free and stepped back as the attacker sank to his knees, then fell onto his side.

Orry rolled onto her back, staring up at the vaulted rock as waves of agony radiated up her leg.

Harry's face appeared above her, full of concern. 'How bad is it?' he asked anxiously.

She clutched his sleeve and hauled herself into a sitting position. 'You have to stop Dyas,' she said, teeth gritted against the pain. She pointed in the direction the raider had gone.

'Mender's already after him. He moves pretty fast for an old wreck. Let's look at that leg, see what we can do.'

Despite the pain and her fear for Ethan, there was something reassuring about Harry's easy manner, but she couldn't stop herself shuddering as he slid the robe up to expose her leg. The flesh was blackened front and back around the hole.

'You're lucky it went straight through the muscle and missed the bone,' he told her cheerily. 'That beam could have carved a nice chunk out of your leg.'

'It doesn't *feel* very lucky,' she grumbled, feeling sick.

'Well, it's cauterised at least. You got any meds?'

She shook her head, grimacing at another wave of pain. *Stupid – coming after Dyas without a med kit.* She could imagine her father's scorn. This would be the last time she'd ever make that mistake, she promised herself.

'Come on,' Harry said, sliding his hands under her arms, 'let's get you back to the ship.'

'You'll do no such thing!'

Orry had completely forgotten about the professor, who emerged from behind a smoking shelving unit. He crouched next to her and briefly examined her wound, then crossed to a nearby bench. When he returned he was carrying a first-aid kit.

'Thank you,' she said, as he rifled through it.

'I should thank you,' he said. 'What a truly dreadful man.'

'You're an excellent judge of character, Professor.' She flinched as he applied an analgesic spray to her leg, but the pain began to fade almost immediately, to be replaced by a cold sensation like an icy fog beneath the skin.

'You've gone to some lengths to catch up with him,' Rasmussen said, indicating her robes. 'Not that I can blame you.'

'What do you mean?'

He chuckled as he wrapped a dressing around the burns. 'Just because I'm old doesn't mean I've entirely lost my faculties, young lady.' The humour left his face. 'Why don't you tell me where you got that stone, and what you intend to do with it.'

She looked up at him. 'All I know is that it's exotic, and Dyas stole it from me. If you know any more, I'm all ears.'

He stared at her, then sighed. 'Do you know how we can be sitting here, breathing air and having this conversation? How the remains of this moon are held together?'

She had to admit she was hazy on the actual details. 'It's some kind of energy field, isn't it?'

He beamed. 'Precisely. It's called *eisenform energy* – after Claude Eisen, who isolated its phasic signature. We've found traces of it at other sites left behind by the Departed, but nothing else on this scale, or in any other part of the galaxy, and we've never been able to replicate it. The most widely accepted theory is that a violent eruption of eisenform particles – we call them *eisens* – caused the destruction of this moon. We believe this chamber and others like it form some kind of research facility. The Departed weren't infallible: they had accidents, too.'

'So if eisens blew this place apart, why are they now holding it together?' Harry asked.

'We honestly have no idea,' the professor said. 'Maybe the

Departed contained them and somehow reversed the event – perhaps they used eisenform energy for a variety of tasks.'

I could do without the lecture, Orry thought, wishing Rasmussen would get to the point. 'What does this have to do with the pendant?' she asked, and blamed the ache in her leg for making the words come out shorter than she'd intended.

He didn't appear to have noticed. 'The stone in your pendant is radiating an eisenform signature – I've never seen anything like it before, and I've been studying the Departed for a very long time. When you recover it, you *must* bring it to me,' he demanded. 'This is a scientific treasure of enormous significance – and it's also potentially *extremely* hazardous.'

The intensity in his face made her uncomfortable. 'I'll think about it,' she told him, 'but we have to get it back first.'

Mender's voice spoke in her head. *Orry, get up here, now.*

Why? What's going on?

I was too late. Dyas is back on your ship – he's taking off.

'Shit!' She grabbed Harry's arm and hauled herself to her feet.

'Remember,' Professor Rasmussen called after them, 'bring me that stone.'

She waved noncommittally and concentrated on getting to the lift, limping badly and leaning heavily on Harry.

'Wait,' she said as they passed the man he'd stabbed. With Harry's help, she knelt next to the body and went through the various pouches attached to his webbing. In one of them she found a folded databrane with a bronze-coloured seal.

She shook it out and read the copperplate letter with growing dismay.

'What is it?' Harry asked.

She stared at the document. 'It's a letter of advocacy from the Count of Delf. These two were bounty hunters.'

'After Mender?'

'After *me*.' She tucked the document away and staggered towards the lift.

Harry looked at the bodies, then at her. 'But—'

'Hurry up, Harry. I'll explain on the way.'

Orry stared at the Shattermoon as it fell away behind *Dainty Jane*. *What kind of power could* do *that to a moon?* she wondered, *not to mention maintaining an atmosphere and holding the fragments in place for hundreds of thousands of years?* The memory of Rasmussen's words chilled her.

She shifted her attention to the sensor core. Dyas had a good start on them: *Bonaventure* was just a distant flare, powering away from the Shattermoon towards the nearest egress point.

'Can we catch them?' she asked.

'Let's see, shall we?' Mender said, increasing the thrust slowly to avoid overstraining the mass-inversion drives. Orry's acceleration shell reclined as the cockpit sphere shifted to align her with the direction of thrust. She glanced at Harry, seated in one of the rear shells; he was looking a little pale, but he smiled at her. She settled back and watched the g-counter tick upwards. They were already at 2g and the gel lining was stiffening around her. She stared out of the canopy, trying not to think about the discomfort of the short hops in *Speedwell*'s cutter. *Bonaventure* was an alarming distance ahead, but the old freighter's engines wouldn't be able to push her much past 3g.

As *Dainty Jane* passed 5g Orry's shell snapped closed over her, plunging her into darkness. The firm grip of the mesophase gel softened, then disappeared entirely, leaving her submerged in a tank of watery fluid.

Just relax, Mender told her, unnecessarily. *Breathe it in*.

She closed her eyes, fighting the sensation of drowning. Primal instinct made her keep her lips pressed tightly together, but the smart fluid forced its way into her nostrils and down her throat, flooding her lungs, and suddenly she realised she could breathe. She no longer needed to inflate her lungs, and the acceleration pressure on her body was all but gone – but when she checked, she was astonished to find they were at 10g and still accelerating. Orry began to wonder exactly what *Dainty Jane* might be hiding under that battered exterior.

They were gaining steadily on *Bonaventure* when Under-Captain Hirota's voice sounded loudly through her integuary link to the ship.

Dainty Jane, Goshawk. *Heave to immediately*.

The sensors showed *Goshawk* lancing towards them at a steady 16g. Orry checked their own acceleration: over 14g now. Surely Mender didn't think he could outrun a sloop?

But Mender remained silent, and at 20g Orry saw *Goshawk* was falling behind. *Bonaventure* was much closer now, and for the first time she allowed herself to hope they might catch her.

A swirling beam of glittering particles flashed past the canopy, bathing them in a soft blue glow.

Dainty Jane, Hirota sent, *that was a warning shot. The next one will be into your engines. Reduce thrust and prepare to be boarded.*

Can you hit Bonaventure *from here?* Orry asked Mender.

Sure, but there's a margin of error. Do you want to risk blowing the whole damn ship up with your brother on board?

Can Goshawk *hit us?*

Definitely. It's your call, girl. Think fast.

She hooked into the comm. *Captain Hirota, you don't want to fire into us. We have Professor Rasmussen on board.*

Nice try, Mender sent, *but it'll take them about two minutes to verify he's still on the surface.*

Two minutes is better than nothing, she told him as she checked the g-counter. Steady at 20g. *What's* Jane's *max thrust?* she asked.

If you're lucky I might even show you one of these days.

Goshawk was far behind them now and Orry knew she would be able to see the bloom of Bonaventure's drives through the canopy if she wasn't sealed in a pitch-black cocoon. She came to a decision.

Take the shot, she told Mender.

About time.

She hooked the weapons core and watched Dainty Jane's targeting sensors lock onto the freighter, but before Mender could fire, the fierce blaze in the centre of each of Bonaventure's four drive-hoods flickered and dimmed, then died away completely.

Looks like Dyas doesn't want a fight, she sent happily. *What do we do about* Gos—?

Bonaventure vanished.

She stared in disbelief at the sparse patch of stars where the old freighter had been. They looked distorted, as if viewed through a film of oil. Clarity quickly returned.

She's collapsed away, Mender said.

No shit! Orry cursed. They'd been so close . . . Now Ethan was gone again, probably forever – together with any hope they had of getting the biomites deactivated in time.

Mender was prepping for their own collapse. *We need to get the hell out of this system before* Goshawk *puts a hole through us*, he sent. *We'll find them – we'll go to Manes, see if we can pick up any leads there.*

We don't have time for that!

If you have any better ideas, I'd be glad to hear them.

Orry's mind was racing; she kept replaying the fear in Ethan's voice, the way he'd cried for their mother just before—

That was *odd*, she thought, *not like him at all*. He hardly ever mentioned Katerina, and when he did he certainly didn't call her 'Mama'.

A smile crept onto her face. *You clever little bugger*. Hooking the navigation core, she deleted Mender's course to Manes.

Hey! he protested, *are you* trying *to get us killed?*

She hurriedly entered a new destination.

Freeport? Why Freeport? I hope you know what you're doing.

A series of staccato thuds made *Dainty Jane* tremble.

What was that? Harry asked. He'd been silent until this moment; his voice sounded shaky over the integuary channel.

The chaff dispensers, Mender replied. *Hirota's firing on us.*

Oh, marvellous, Harry sent. *Shouldn't we be going, then?*

We're not clear of the Shattermoon's gravity well yet. Any second.

Orry hooked the defence core and watched the dispensers in *Dainty Jane*'s stern spew the flecks of reflective foil into space behind the still-accelerating ship. A beam lashed out from the distant sloop and diffused harmlessly as it struck the foil. Orry overlaid the navigation core data and watched anxiously as they sped towards the egress point.

Any time, Harry sent.

Do you want to fly this bird? Mender demanded.

We're clear! Orry sent, eyeing the rapidly dispersing chaff.

Goshawk and the Shattermoon vanished.

20

A BAD CALL

Orry awoke to a throbbing pain in her lower leg. She lay for a moment, replaying the events of the past few days. She'd thought it best to get some sleep before examining her suspicions any further. Things often looked different after some rest.

She swung her legs off the bunk and stood gingerly. Her calf protested, but at least it took her weight.

Well, I've had some sleep now, and things look exactly the same. She pulled on her flight suit, laced up her boots and left the cabin.

Harry looked up as she entered the galley, the glow of a databrane illuminating his features from below.

'Couldn't sleep?' he asked.

'A little.' She peered at the brane. 'What are you doing?'

'Just catching up on the latest gossip. *Goshawk* receives regular dispatch pods, so their info core was quite current – *Dainty Jane* synced with them while you were aboard.'

'Wouldn't you be better off getting some sleep?'

He smiled and rubbed his eyes. 'I know, but if Delf is after you it's worth keeping an eye on what he's up to.'

'We know what he's up to: he's put a price on my head.'

'Yep, fifty thousand. Quite impressive, actually.'

She grimaced. 'So what else have you found out?'

'Not much; I'll keep looking. What are you doing?'

She looked up at the cockpit. 'I need a word with Mender.'

'Good luck.'

'It's not me who'll need it,' she muttered, starting up the ladder.

'I was going to wake you,' Mender said as she dropped into the right-hand seat. 'We're an hour out.' When she didn't respond, he looked at her. 'What?'

'Is there anything you want to tell me, Mender?'

He frowned. 'Like what?'

She stared at the avocado-green orb of Erlitz Shen ahead of them. Half the planet was in deep shadow. 'I was thinking about what Dyas said, back on the Shattermoon.'

'I told you not to—'

'Hear me out,' she snapped. 'Dyas asked if you had *picked me up* – doesn't that strike you as an odd thing to say?'

Mender busied himself with the instruments. 'Not really.'

'No? Because the way it sounded to me, Dyas knew you were close enough to *Bonaventure* to save me.'

'He's fucking with you, girl: just trying to set us at each other's throats.'

'Things have been pretty crazy since you rescued me,' she admitted, 'and I haven't been thinking clearly. But now I've thought it all through, do you know what I'm wondering?'

He started to say something, but she raised her voice and continued, 'What I'm wondering is: how exactly did Morven Dyas *get* to *Bonaventure*? Where's his ship?'

He narrowed his eyes. 'What are you trying to say?'

'Don't play games with me, Mender. You were working together, weren't you?'

'What? No!'

'Stop *lying*! You're the one who brought those murdering bastards to *Bonaventure*.'

'No! I—'

'They killed my father!' she shouted, all composure lost, and Mender sagged, a hollow expression on his face.

He opened his mouth to say something, then just nodded miserably.

Orry slapped him. When he didn't react, she slapped him again. 'Aren't you going to say anything?' She let her hand fall, ignoring her stinging palm.

'Like what?' he growled.

'Oh, I don't know. How about, *"Sorry I helped Dyas kill your father"*?'

His jaw worked beneath his sparse beard. 'I am sorry.'

'Bullshit!' she yelled.

Harry appeared from the galley. 'What on Alecto is going on up here?'

'Mender was just telling me how he and Dyas are bosom buddies.'

Harry frowned. '*What?*'

'Will you let me explain?' Mender asked. He sounded angry, which just fanned the flames of Orry's fury, but she folded her arms and waited.

He rubbed his face. 'All *Jane* and I want is to be left alone – but she's an old girl, components break sometimes and it takes gilt to fix them. I'll show you the fault list one day when you have an hour or two to spare. Things are pretty desperate, and

Dyas was offering a good price for a few hours' work. There was *never* supposed to be any killing.

'I made a bad call,' he added, and Orry laughed bitterly.

'A *bad call*? All this is because of you – because you want to carry on floating around deep space like a hermit.'

'I saved your life,' he ventured.

'Only so you could find Dyas again!'

'No,' he said firmly, 'I didn't need you to find him.'

'He's right, Orry,' Harry started, and she rounded on him.

'You stay out of this! It's none of your business.'

'None of my business? You'd be dead if it weren't for Mender and me.'

'So you're siding with *him* now? After what he did to me?'

'I'm not siding with anyone – just stop yelling.'

Mender may have saved me, but it was his fault I needed saving in the first place. She clamped her mouth shut and fumed.

'I said I'm sorry,' Mender told her. 'What do you want from me?'

She fought back tears. What did she want? An explanation? An apology? He'd already given her both and neither had changed a damn thing.

Mender glanced at Harry and cleared his throat uncomfortably. 'Listen, girl – Orry – if I could go back and change things, I would. Life is full of decisions and I made a bad one. I have to live with that. I'm sorry for the hurt I've caused you.'

'You think he betrayed you,' Harry added, 'but he didn't even know you when he signed on with Dyas, did he? Or what would happen. All he was – well, he was the transport, right? We've all done things we regret.'

'Is that supposed to make me feel better?' she snapped.

'Yes, actually.'

She took a deep breath and tried to gain some perspective, but the hurt and anger churning inside her made it difficult. 'What about *after* he picked me up?' she said plaintively to Harry. 'He kept on lying to me – and he used me to get to Dyas.'

'But he *did* pick you up,' Harry pointed out.

'And what would you have done if I'd told you the truth right away?' Mender asked. 'Before you even knew me?'

'You still helped Dyas kill my father—'

'And that will haunt me for ever.' He looked down, and then said, 'I know you can't forgive me – I just want you to understand.'

Orry stared at him. He was chewing his top lip and looking anxiously at her and it was that more than anything he'd said that made her realise he really did feel bad.

'You're right,' she told him coldly, 'I can't forgive you. But I need you, just like you need me, so it looks like we're stuck with each other.'

She pushed past Harry and out of the cockpit, hurrying down the ladder so they wouldn't see her tears.

21

SWEET THINGS

A gust of heavy, moisture-laden air whipped through *Dainty Jane*'s freight lock, bringing with it a tang of salt and rotting vegetation. It was monsoon season in Erlitz Shen's northern continent and the blanket of grey clouds overhead was shot through with streaks of turbulent black.

Orry walked down the loading ramp and crossed to the cliff's edge, careful not to trip on the cracked surface of the ancient landing pad; Erlitz Shen's considerable gravity meant any fall might easily break a bone.

Freeport sprawled away from the foot of the cliff. A rare break in the cloud cover allowed the rays of the larger moon to bathe the city in a golden glow, for a brief moment making the grid of grey streets with their crumbling buildings look almost charming. Orry knew the illusion wouldn't last.

The city, a former military base, had been carved from the jungle during the First Expansion and abandoned after the Withdrawal. Enough drifters stayed to transform Freeport into a haven for anyone determined to escape from the regimented life of the Fountainhead systems, and the Grand Fleet tended to leave the place alone, happy to just harvest the intelligence provided by the many Arbiter Corps agents embedded here.

Wincing at the sharp nip of an insect bite, she rubbed the back of her neck as she gazed out over the strip of buildings wedged between the sluggish brown waters of a broad river on one side and endless jungle on the other. The wreck of a vast marine cargo vessel lay on its side in the water, exposing the faded red paint of its keel. Beside the rusted wharves of the old port district were two enormously long patched ferroconcrete runways that ran the length of the city. A carpet of jungle stretched to the horizon, where Orry could just make out the squat peaks of a mountain range.

She stared morosely at the city. Dad had loved this place; he always said you could be anyone you wanted to be in Freeport. It wouldn't be the same here without him.

'You'd better be right,' Mender said, coming up behind her.

She slapped at a bug feeding on her forearm. 'I am.'

'You're betting our lives – and your brother's – on a single word. You really think you know Ethan that well?'

'He never called our mother "Mama" in his life, so he could only have meant Mama Jinx.'

Mender grunted. 'Freeport's a good choice if Dyas wants to offload that pendant, but I could name a dozen other worlds just as likely.'

'He's coming here,' she said firmly, 'and if anyone can find him, it's Emjay.'

Mender warily eyed the circular base of the crystal dome high above them, perched at the end of a long bridge anchored by cables as thick as Orry's waist. They were adorned with frayed fabric and torn strips of plastic that flapped like junkyard bunting in the wind. The bridge's metal segments curved out and up from the cliff's edge like the gargantuan steel spine of some long-dead beast.

'How well do you know this Mama Jinx, anyway?' Mender asked.

'My father grew up here – Emjay raised him in there.' Orry pointed up at the dome. 'I suppose that kind of makes her my grandmother. We used to come here all the time.'

'Used to?'

'I haven't seen her since my mother died.'

'Why not?'

'I guess she and Dad fell out. He didn't talk about it.'

'Then what makes you so sure she'll help us?'

'I'm not.' Orry took a last look at the hundreds of ships parked on the aprons next to the runways below, then set off towards the bridge.

Harry hurried over to join her. 'You bring me to all the nicest places,' he said.

'You can leave any time you like,' she told him. 'You paid your honour debt on the Shattermoon.'

'Is that what you want?' Harry asked, sounding worried. 'For me to go?'

'I don't care,' she lied.

He grinned. 'Then if it's all the same to you, I'll hang around a little longer.'

'Whatever.' She picked up the pace to hide her own smile.

'Anyone care what *I* want?' Mender grumbled from somewhere behind them. They both ignored him.

The bridge was a massive construction. The wide walkway

turned into shallow steps which quickly became steeper as the angle of the upward curve increased until they ended at a metal door in the base of a tower which extended up into the dome's solid base, a vast disk from which tangled piping and conduits looped down like jungle creepers. The dome had once been an observation and sensor station, but its equipment had long since been removed.

The faint sound of children playing came from somewhere above them.

The tarnished intercom unit set into the wall next to the door buzzed harshly when Orry pressed its button.

'No one home,' Harry observed after a while.

She reached for the button again.

'Get back in your ship and do one!' a high-pitched voice shouted from somewhere above them.

Orry stepped back and craned her neck. A freckle-faced girl was leaning out of a hatch near the top of the tower. She looked all of nine years old, tufts of shocking ginger hair poking from beneath a peaked cap that was topped with a pair of round goggles. She was pointing a long rifle down at them.

'Warm welcome,' Mender murmured, his hand creeping towards the Fabretti on his hip.

'Don't,' Orry told him. She raised her voice. 'We're here to see Emjay.'

'What you want with her?'

'I'm an old friend.'

'You have a name?'

'Ask her if she still has a puke stain on her best white blouse.'

'What?'

'Just ask her.'

The girl eyed Orry suspiciously. 'Don't move.' Her head withdrew.

'I'm getting nervous,' Mender growled.

'Relax,' Orry told him.

After some time a camera lens above the door moved, angling down. A moment later the girl was back in her opening.

'She wants to know if you still enjoy unguan fruit.'

Orry smiled. She was allergic to unguan fruit. She waved at the camera and called, 'It's fine, Emjay – I'm not here under duress and no one's holding a gun on me. These are my friends.'

A moment later, a sally port set into the larger door flew inwards and Mama Jinx emerged like a force of nature: an enormous woman with a pineapple of black dreadlocks wrapped in a multi-coloured scarf which clashed terribly with her shapeless rainbow dress. How she supported her bulk in Erlitz Shen's gravity had always been a mystery to Orry.

'You've grown,' Emjay observed. She looked around with a guarded expression. 'Is your father here?'

Orry stared at her, opened her mouth – and burst into tears. She felt Harry's arm around her shoulders.

'Perhaps we should talk inside,' she heard him say.

The freckle-faced girl was standing in the blockhouse at the top of the steep spiral staircase, leaning on her rifle, which was nearly as tall as she was. When she saw Orry's tears the girl gave her a look of withering contempt, then pulled out an aerosol and began methodically targeting the small cloud of insects that had entered with them.

The interior of Emjay's dome hadn't changed much in the ten years since Orry's last visit. The same two-storey flat-roofed clapboard buildings stood near the dome's centre, surrounded by extensive and well-maintained gardens. A gaggle of younger children hared around while teenagers paused their half-hearted attempts at gardening to eyeball the strangers.

They followed Emjay down a meandering wood-chip path, past the meeting hall and into a large refectory.

By the time they were seated at one of the long trestle tables, Orry had managed to regain some semblance of self-control.

Emjay listened in silence, her face grim as Orry brought her up to speed, then reached out and clasped her hand. 'What do you need?'

'Dyas is coming here,' Orry said, 'or he's here already. I need to find him.'

Emjay raised her voice. 'Derik!'

A lank-haired boy with a bad case of acne shuffled into the refectory. He glanced shyly at Orry from beneath his fringe.

'A man called Morven Dyas,' Emjay said. 'If he's in Freeport, find him. If not, I want to know he's landed before his engines have cooled.'

Derik groaned. 'But I'm—'

'Take Tabitha and Nwosu with you.' Emjay raised her eyebrows. 'What you waiting for, boy? Go to it!'

Derik glanced at Orry again, rolled his eyes and shambled away.

'Don't mind the attitude,' Emjay said. 'He's the best I have.'

Orry kissed her cheek. 'Thank you.'

Emjay nodded. 'You'll eat and drink with us tonight.'

'I thought you'd never ask,' Mender said.

Emjay looked him up and down. 'You look like a man who enjoys his food.'

182

'I think he meant the drinking part,' Orry said dryly.

'That too. Let me show you around.' She slid her arm through Mender's and led him away. He glanced over his shoulder with an alarmed expression that brought a reluctant smile to Orry's face.

Harry offered his arm, she curtseyd and took it and together they followed Emjay back out to the gardens.

'Who do they all belong to?' Harry asked, looking at the dozens of children playing or working under the dome.

'They're orphans,' she told him. 'Freetown creates a lot of them and Emjay takes them in.'

'How does she afford it?'

Orry smiled. 'This place isn't just an orphanage, it's a school. You're looking at the Sweet Things – the scourge of Freetown.'

'You mean . . . they're *thieves*?' He looked shocked.

'Thieves, grifters, subverters – and between them they make more than enough to keep this place running.'

'Isn't that dangerous?' he said, watching a group of Sweet Things run past, screaming with the joy of the chase. None of them looked more than ten years old.

'Not as dangerous as the alternative. This isn't the Fountain-head, Harry. You don't want to know some of the things that can happen to a child in Freetown.'

'But teaching them to steal?'

'If you can find an honest man in Freetown, I'll give you my ship.'

'So because they steal from other thieves, that makes it all right?'

'Where does all this moralising come from all of a sudden?

You're the one who wants to be *infamous*: how exactly do you intend to do that without breaking the law?'

He sighed and looked over the gardens. 'I don't know.'

She patted his shoulder. 'You can always go home. This lot don't have that luxury.'

Mender disentangled himself from Emjay and stumped over. 'I'm going down to the city,' he said. 'There must be a ghost atomicist around here somewhere – maybe he'll be able to do something to help us.'

Orry was trying very hard not to think about the biomites in her head. 'You want me to come with?'

'No need. You stay and catch up.'

'I'll come,' Harry offered. 'I'd like to see the place.'

Mender eyed him sourly. 'If you must.'

Orry walked with them to the spiral staircase. The freckle-faced girl who'd greeted them was still leaning on her rifle.

'Look after him,' Orry told Mender.

'I will,' Harry replied, earning a scowl from the old man.

The girl hauled open the heavy metal door and watched them descend, a bored expression on her face.

'Hello again,' Orry said.

The girl made a snorting sound deep in her throat and spat out a gob of phlegm.

'Nice,' Orry said. 'What's your name?'

'Tilda.' The word was spoken like a challenge.

'I'm Orry.'

Tilda stared at her.

Orry rummaged through her pockets until her fingers closed on an Utzeen candy bar. Pushing away the sudden memory of Ethan, she offered the bar to the little girl, who frowned suspiciously.

'How much?'

'Nothing. It's a gift.'

'What do I have to do for it?'

'Nothing!' Orry chuckled. 'If you had to do something for it, it wouldn't be a gift.'

Tilda studied the proffered bar for a few seconds then edged forward warily. Her hand darted out to snatch it from Orry's and she retreated to a safe distance. She tore open the wrapper and sniffed the bar before taking a tentative bite.

Orry watched her expression change as she took a larger bite and chewed appreciatively.

'How long have you been with Emjay?' she asked.

'Since I was eight,' Tilda told her through a mouthful of candy.

'How old are you now?'

'Nine.'

Orry looked around. 'I used to come here a lot when I was your age.'

'Sweet Thing?'

'Not really. But my father was, a long time ago.'

Tilda finished the bar and looked regretfully at the empty wrapper. 'My father's dead,' she said casually, as if passing comment on the weather.

'So's mine,' Orry said, a lump in her throat.

'Mum too. I miss 'em.'

Orry nodded.

'This place is good, though. Safe, y'know?'

'I know.'

Tilda was silent for a moment, then, switching subjects with the ease of a child, said, 'It'll be Foundation Day soon. There'll be presents and fireworks and Mama will cook jambalaya and we'll stay up late dancing. Mama loves to dance.'

Orry smiled. 'You know, I remember one Foundation Day when Emjay was dancing on the meeting hall roof at three in the morning. It took four of us to get her down.'

Tilda's eyes widened and for a brief moment she looked like the child she was. Then a clang sounded from the bottom of the staircase and she was all business once more. She peered down the shaft and Orry saw her fierce expression change to one of fear.

Laughter echoed in the stairwell and three Sweet Things emerged, led by a boy on the edge of manhood. He was dressed flamboyantly: a velvet jacket and skin-tight trousers, black ankle boots with long pointed toes. Tilda scurried away as he threw a casual blow in her direction, then he noticed Orry and pointedly ran his eyes over her body.

'Hi,' he said. 'Wanna see something funny?'

'Not really,' she said coldly.

The young man turned to his companions, both boys in their mid-teens wearing similar garb, and they grinned.

'You'll like it,' he told her, and strode to the dome's curving side, where the clear surface met the metal rim that edged the lawn. 'Over here.'

Orry glanced at Tilda, who'd shrunk into herself, trying not to attract attention, and walked over to the wall of glass.

'I'm Jackis,' the young man said. 'Down there, look.' He pointed down at *Dainty Jane*'s shell-like hull resting on the pad a few hundred metres away. Her loading ramp was lowered, and just beyond it she could see Mender astride his Horten-Yakimov. As she watched, Harry hurried down the ramp and jumped onto the bike behind Mender.

'Look at that old geezer!' Jackis said with barely concealed glee. 'He's about a hundred years too late for a mid-life crisis!'

His companions laughed uproariously at their leader's joke. 'Who's the lanky streak of piss with him?' wondered the stockier of the two, eyes dull in his wide, deeply tanned face.

'Probably his boyfriend,' the other, a slightly built boy with tight curly hair, said nastily. 'Or his nurse.'

'Or both!' Jackis turned to Orry, eyes shining. 'Rama, what a sight.'

Below them the Horten-Yakimov shot away down the narrow road leading to the city, passing small groups of children trailing back to the dome.

Orry gave the chuckling Jackis a withering look, then turned and walked away.

'Hey,' he called after her, 'you didn't tell me your name.'

She ignored him, but winked at Tilda as she passed. The girl responded with a shy smile.

Jackis caught up with Orry near the barn-like meeting hall. 'I remember you,' he said, falling into step beside her. 'You used to come here a lot, didn't you?'

She ignored him.

'Florrie, yeah?'

'Orry.'

'Yeah, yeah – I *do* remember you. You had a brother – mouthy little bleeder. Where is he?'

She stopped. 'What do you want, Jackis?'

He grinned, pleased she'd used his name. 'Just being friendly.

Listen, I've had a good day. Why don't we hit the city later? I know all the best joints.'

'I don't think so.'

'No? What's the matter? Scared you might have a good time?'

'With you? I don't think there's much risk of that.'

His face grew cold. 'You'll come round,' he said. 'They always do in the end.'

'Not this one,' she said tartly.

A clanging started above her and she looked up to see a girl standing on the roof, striking the brass bell that hung there with a mallet.

'Will you at least accompany me to the daily meeting?' he asked stiffly.

Children came running, converging on the hall from all over the dome. As a stream of kids poured up out of the stairwell she spotted Tilda near the front.

'No thanks,' she said, stepping away from him.

A curious smile tempered Tilda's grave expression when she saw Orry waiting for her.

'I used to go to these meetings,' Orry told her.

'They're boring,' the girl said with a grimace. She looked warily at Jackis, who glared at her, then turned and stalked into the hall.

'Can I sit with you?' Orry asked.

Tilda narrowed her eyes. 'You have any more of that candy?'

Orry laughed and held up her empty hands. 'Sorry. Can I sit with you anyway?'

Tilda screwed up her face for a moment, then nodded.

22

ALL THEY BRING IS PAIN

The Sweet Things produced a kind of rum made from honey-grass, a sweet cane indigenous to Erlitz Shen. Emjay put even the youngest to work extracting and crystallising the juice. Each child was allowed their first taste of the stuff on their twelfth birthday: a real rite of passage. Orry had never tried the fiery drink before, but she was fast developing a taste for it.

Her fourth glassful slid down her throat to warm her belly, which was uncomfortably full from a second helping of razor-fish bouillabaisse and a generous slice of roseapple pie. She was sitting with Emjay, Mender and Harry at an outside table on a spacious wooden balcony; an open pair of glass doors led into the dormitory block behind them, where bedrooms opened off a long corridor. Just inside the doors children were thudding up and down a broad flight of steps, but Orry, surveying the orphanage grounds in a melancholy haze, barely noticed them. The evening shadows within the dome were long, and fat rain-drops pattered on the glass.

Mender, across the table, appeared to be handling the rum better than she was, although his real eye was beginning to look

189

a little glazed. His trip to Freeport's ghost atomicists had confirmed what they already feared: Roag had them just where she wanted. Harry, sitting next to the old man, watched proceedings through half-closed eyes, a lazy smile on his face.

'Your father would have enjoyed this,' Emjay said.

'He would?' Orry poured herself another glass to stave off the sadness welling inside her.

'Oh, yes.' A solemn look crossed Emjay's broad face. 'Although maybe not so much after Kat died.'

Orry winced as the rum burned a path to her stomach. 'What happened, Emjay?'

'What do you mean?'

'Between you and Dad – why did we stop coming here?'

Emjay leaned back. 'We had a falling-out,' she said. 'Something and nothing.'

'It can't have been nothing,' Orry pressed, 'not when you didn't speak for ten years.'

'And now we never will.' Emjay's eyes were moist. 'Take my advice, child, and seize life by the throat. You never know what's around the corner.'

Orry wouldn't be put off. 'Was it something to do with my mother?'

'Why do you ask that?'

'Because I remember you and Dad yelling at each other after . . .' She swallowed and tried again. 'After he came back here to tell me Mum had been killed.'

Emjay shifted in her seat. 'Orry, I—'

'I'm not a kid any more, Emjay. If there's something I need to know, tell me. You owe me that.'

Emjay hesitated. 'Katerina was a wonderful woman and

I loved her like a daughter. But there are things you don't know.'

'What things?'

'When your parents met, there was trouble.'

'What sort of trouble?'

She remained silent.

'Emjay, *what sort of trouble?*'

'Kat's father didn't approve of Eoin,' she said at last. 'When she chose him over her family, he was furious – things turned nasty and they had to leave the Fountainhead.'

'She came from the *Fountainhead*?'

'Yes, from Tyr – you didn't know?'

'No! Mum never talked about her life before she met Dad. What else don't I know about her?'

'It doesn't matter,' Emjay said evasively. 'What does matter is that your parents loved each other very much – all they wanted was to keep you and Ethan safe.'

Orry rubbed her forehead. 'How did Mum die? Dad said it was a flyer accident – is that true?'

'Yes.' Emjay looked uneasy. 'How much do you remember?'

'I was ten. Ethan was four and he got really sick, so Mum and Dad left me here with you and went to see some kind of specialist. A few weeks later Dad and Ethan came back – Ethan was cured, but Dad–' her voice cracked and she took a gulp of rum. 'That's when Dad told me Mum had been killed in an accident.'

'That's what happened,' Emjay said firmly, but she was staring at Orry in a very odd way. She appeared to come to a decision. 'Look, I–'

There was a crash – shattering glass – in the dormitory and

she frowned and rose to her feet, but Orry couldn't help thinking she looked more relieved than angry. 'Back in a minute,' she muttered, and waddled into the building.

Orry sighed.

'Families,' Mender grunted, snagging the rum. Dispensing with his glass, he hoisted the jar to his lips and took a long draught. 'All they bring is pain. You're better off on your own.'

Orry kept quiet. If the alcohol had loosened Mender's tongue she might actually get some answers. Harry, next to her, was already out for the count, his eyes closed, head nodding gently.

'You know,' Mender slurred, 'life's pretty fucking funny when you think about it.'

She tried to make her smile encouraging.

'I had a family once,' he continued. 'Erin, that was her name.' He gave a snort of amusement. 'Not much of a looker, but I loved her. Had a kid, too. Oskar. He was a great little guy.' He wiped his real eye.

'What happened?' Orry asked quietly.

'Bandits killed them both when I was in town buying a gun.' He laughed bitterly. 'Because I'd heard there were bandits about.'

She remembered the databrane. 'You were colonists on Sabine . . .' Mender had dropped his head and was staring at the table, but she persevered. 'What did you do? After, I mean.'

'I buried my family. Then I took my shiny new gun and went after them. In a way I was glad the bastards had done for Erin and Oskar both; there was no one left I had to look after, so I was free to do what needed to be done. I didn't think about what had happened, only about getting even.' He looked at Orry. 'You know exactly what I mean.'

Her face hardened. 'Did you get them?'

He laughed softly. 'By the time I tracked them down, the local constables had already killed them.'

Orry thought about how she would feel if she finally caught up with Dyas, only to discover that someone else had dealt with him. 'That sucks.'

'It certainly did.'

They sat in silence for a moment, listening to the chirp of stemhoppers.

'How did you find *Jane*?' she asked at last, not really expecting an answer, but Mender was in a loquacious mood.

He gave a snorting laugh. 'She found me, more like.' He filled his glass almost to the top, took a gulp and smacked his lips. 'I couldn't stay on Sabine, not after that, so I shipped out, drifting for a while, taking jobs where I could – did some things I ain't proud of, but I never hurt anyone who didn't have it coming. By the time I met Roag I had a pretty good rep. She was just starting to carve out her own territory and thought I could help.'

'And did you?'

'She got her empire, didn't she?'

'So you were a kingmaker.' Orry scowled. 'Seems to me things might have turned out better all round if you hadn't been quite so effective.'

He scowled. 'You might be right at that.'

'And how does *Dainty Jane* fit in?'

'Like I said, I ain't proud of my life.' He had gone back to staring at the table. 'At first, after Sabine, I didn't care. I wanted to die, you know? But I didn't. I guess everyone has a natural talent and, well, I'd discovered mine. And the worse the situations got, the more I learned. It ain't rocket science, really. By the time Roag hired me I was enjoying myself, taking pride in my work, but after ten years with her I was sick of it through and through: sick of the backstabbing, the beatings, the killings. A man reaches a certain age and he takes a long hard look at his life. I didn't like what I saw, but I couldn't see a way out. What else was there for me?'

Orry was fascinated. 'So what did you do?'

'Took more risks, pushed my luck until it ran out. Roag sent me to Tantris to persuade the hoods there to pay the tribute they'd agreed. They were chancers, always late with payments, and Roag had had enough. Anyway, these guys were strictly small-time; they should have buckled under the moment they saw my face, but I guess I underestimated them – that wasn't like me. Or maybe I knew, deep down, what was coming, and I chose to accept it. So instead of a couple of strung-out kids, I ended up facing a dozen armed gunhands. I managed to get out, just, but there wasn't much left of me. That's when *Jane* found me.'

'What do you mean, "found you"?' she asked. 'You mean her crew found you?'

Mender carried on as if he hadn't heard her. 'A little while later I told Roag I was quitting. She wasn't happy when I told her what I thought of her and her operation, but she knew how much she owed me, so she let me go. Mind you, she always said I'd come crawling back.'

'What changed? Why did you quit then when you couldn't before?'

He stumbled to his feet. 'I need a piss.'

'Mender?' she asked. 'What changed?' Exasperated, she

watched him weave his way across the balcony and into the building. She suddenly felt very alone.

Harry was still dozing, his chin in his hand. Edging her chair closer, she rested her head on his shoulder, feeling his warmth through the thin fabric of his shirt. He was Ruuz, and a liar, but that wasn't important right now; she just needed some company. Then he moved, putting his arm around her. She hesitated, then nestled into him. As her eyes drifted closed, the dome started spinning alarmingly around her.

She quickly opened her eyes and sat up.

'You okay?' he asked. She'd thought she was holding the booze better than him, but he sounded sober, or at least more sober than her.

'I'm arseholed,' she admitted, then laughed.

He grinned. 'I can tell.'

She moved a little closer. He really was good-looking. A bit aristo for her liking – she could see his heritage in his square jaw and aquiline nose – but handsome by any definition of the word. And he'd saved her life on the Shattermoon.

'I hope you find your brother,' he said quietly, staring across the room.

'Me too.'

'I mean it, Orry.' He turned to her, wearing an odd expression. 'I . . .'

She could see the discomfort in his face. 'What is it?'

'I have a sister, back home on Alecto. Elena. She's the only thing I miss about that place.' He rubbed the back of his neck awkwardly. 'She's . . . Well, Elena's wonderful, but she's fragile – not good with people, and she needs routine.' He shook his head, chuckling fondly. 'Heavens, does she need her routine.

Anyway,' he continued quickly, 'if she went missing I'd move mountains to get her back safely.' He looked anxiously at her. 'I just wanted you to know.'

Orry leaned in and brushed her lips against his. She paused, waiting, and he kissed her back, tenderly at first, then more firmly.

But as she started to pull him closer, he drew away.

'Orry, wait.'

She didn't want to wait, not when his lips felt so good, but he grabbed her shoulders and pushed her gently back.

'What's wrong?' she asked. 'Don't you like me?'

'I like you, Orry, but just how much of that stuff have you had? I don't want you to regret anything in the morning.'

She pressed a finger to his lips and sniggered. 'We're only *kissing*. What kind of a girl do you think I am?'

He removed her hand and held it. 'A drunken one,' he said with a smile.

A shadow fell across them, eclipsing the light from the dormitory.

'Why're you wasting your time with this mincer?' Jackis enquired, his face flushed. His body swayed as he glared at Harry. Behind him, his crew grinned with anticipation.

Harry scanned Jackis' face, then checked out his two minions. 'Go and bother someone else, will you, chaps?' he suggested, pleasantly enough. 'We're a little busy.'

'I saw you,' Jackis snarled. 'Where's your boyfriend gone?'

'Excuse me?'

'The old man.' Jackis gave him a sneering smile. 'I can't imagine nailing that, but hey' – he laughed nastily – 'if that's what you're into.'

Harry raised his eyebrows, but Orry nudged him. 'Just ignore him,' she said. 'Go and sleep it off, Jackis.'

'Only if you come with me – this one might like a dried-up old ringpiece, but I like my quim young and moist.'

Harry opened his mouth to respond, but she was there first. 'You *really* ought to learn that no means no, Jackis. Let me make this plain enough that even *you* can understand: I've met your type before and I don't like it. You're a nasty little shit, a bully and a coward, and I'd rather fuck a Kadiran than sleep with you. Is that clear enough?'

His cheeks flushed. 'You ugly fucking cow—' he began, but got no further as Harry shot to his feet and slapped him hard across the face.

Jackis stumbled back, clutching his cheek, clearly shocked by Harry's speed.

His crew stepped forward to flank him but he held them back, a malevolent expression on his face. Behind them, kids had paused at the top of the stairs to watch the scene unfold.

'Apologise to the lady,' Harry said.

'Harry—' Orry started.

'No,' he insisted. 'If we were on Alecto he wouldn't have dared call you that. By Piotr, I've had enough of people like him thinking they can do or say whatever they please.' He fixed his eyes on Jackis. 'Apologise.'

'Or what?'

Harry smiled. 'Or I'll make you.'

Jackis eyed Harry's rapier. 'With that?' he scoffed. He flicked his wrist and a narrow blade appeared in his hand.

'Stop it!' Orry yelled, stepping between them. She shoved Harry back, then rounded on Jackis. 'Go away. *Now!*'

His knife was a finger's-breadth from her stomach. He didn't move as he glared at her.

'What are you going to do?' she spat, suddenly furious at him and Harry both. '*Stab* me?' She raised her T-shirt to expose her belly. 'Go on, then. What are you waiting for?'

Jackis' fingers flexed around the hilt of his stiletto. He glanced at the Sweet Things gathered behind him and licked his lips, then, glowering, he tucked the blade away.

'I didn't think so,' she said, disgusted, her heart pounding as much with fear as fury. For a moment there she'd thought Jackis would actually do it.

She looked him up and down, reading his body language. He was hunched forward, fists clenched, his intentions all too clear.

Fine, she thought, *if that's what he wants*.

She began to turn away, but when he moved she was ready. As he lunged, she gripped his arm, shifted her weight and heaved him over one shoulder, just as her father had drilled into her. Jackis yelped as he arced through the air and into the table, sending the rum jar and glasses flying as he demolished it.

The Sweet Things burst into laughter as he stumbled to his feet, clutching one arm. He looked at the laughing faces, turned bright red and lurched away, pushing through the crowd and making off down the corridor. His crew hesitated, dumb-founded, then hurried after him.

She rounded on Harry. 'Who the *hell* do you think you are?' she snarled. 'I do *not* need protecting. You're not my father, or my bodyguard. You're just someone who's tagging along for the ride.'

His face hardened.

'I can look after myself,' she yelled. 'I don't need any help from you and your stupid sword!'

'I was *trying* to help,' he said stiffly.

'Well, don't! Jackis is just a kid—'

'He's old enough to use a knife.'

'And what would you have done if he hadn't backed down?' she demanded furiously. 'Kill him?'

'I—' Harry frowned. 'Wait a minute, you're the one who threw him into a table.'

'You don't belong out here, Harry! Go home.'

She turned on her heel and strode away, hurrying down the stairs and out of the dormitory.

The gardens were quiet. Steam rose from the grass where vents in the dome had been opened to allow the rain through. Water dripped from leaves and blossoms.

She breathed in the humid air. It had been a mistake to come here, where everything reminded her of her family, of the good times they'd spent together under the dome. Suddenly she longed for the solitude of her cabin aboard *Dainty Jane*. The ship was different, unfamiliar, and there were no painful memories waiting to ambush her.

As she strode across the grass she heard footsteps behind her and she turned to see Tilda. 'Not now!' she snapped, and hated herself as the girl's face crumpled. She fled, and Orry took a step after her then cursed, furious. 'Why can't everyone just *leave me alone*?' she muttered as she strode to the gate.

A teenage boy had replaced Tilda on guard duty.

'Let me out,' Orry snapped.

'It's late,' he said nervously. 'Where are you going?' His eyes flicked over her shoulder, no doubt searching for Emjay.

'None of your damn business,' she snarled. 'Just open the bloody door.'

He gave in and she entered the blockhouse and clanged down the staircase, her footsteps echoing, to the gate at the bottom.

The air outside was fresher than inside the dome, but it was still muggy and did nothing to clear her head. She walked through the rain with dogged determination, focused on getting back to *Dainty Jane*. She knew she'd overreacted, but she had a low tolerance for Harry's bullshit: one minute he was being nice, and the next – that damned Ruuz arrogance came pouring out. The rum hadn't helped, mind.

Her heart ached as she thought about what Emjay had said about her parents. She missed them more than ever.

When she reached the freight lock she saw that Mender had overridden the manual controls and the ship was sealed. She tried to hook the security core, but apparently her integuary privileges didn't extend that far. Swearing, she turned and leaned against the cool metal of the outer door. There was nothing for it but to return to the dome with her tail between her legs.

A sound startled her and she turned, pulse quickening, to see three figures appearing from the darkness: Jackis and his weasels.

Of course.

The three young men spread out around her.

She considered challenging them, but the look of hatred on Jackis' face suggested talking would be a waste of breath. Instead she eyed the gaps between the three, judging the distance back to the dome.

Jackis smiled. 'Rather fuck a Kadiran, would you?' The thin stiletto appeared in his hand. 'We'll see about that.'

23

FERREIRA BUMBLEBEE

Orry's muscles tensed as adrenalin coursed through her system, instantly clearing her head. She pressed her back against the freight lock door and flattened her palms against *Dainty Jane*'s cool hull, ready to push off and start running – when the door soundlessly slid open and she fell backwards into the airlock with a cry. Before she could pick herself up, the door closed in front of her.

I'm safe . . . Relief left her heart thumping.

Feeling oddly weak, she peered out through the inspection port – and recoiled as something thudded into the clear silicarbonate: Jackis was pounding on the window, his fist clenched. The tall boy with curly hair was standing beside him and it took her a moment to realise he was working on the access panel seal with a lockprise.

The inspection port darkened without warning and lights strobed rapidly outside. When the port cleared, three bodies were lying squirming on the cracked ferroconcrete at the foot of the loading ramp.

Orry turned and looked suspiciously at the camera eyes set

high in the corners of the airlock. 'All right, Mender,' she said, 'I know you're on board. Stop playing games.'

She couldn't hold back a gasp as the inner door slid open; red night-cycle lights were glowing in the cargo bay beyond. She shivered.

'Stop dicking around, Mender: I mean it. What did you do to them?'

Rather than Mender's gravelly tones, a woman's voice issued from the speaker grille in the bulkhead.

'They'll be fine in a while,' the voice said. 'The light pulses temporarily overload the human nervous system.'

Orry stood stock still. 'Who are you?'

The voice laughed gently. 'You know who I am, Orry.'

'You're the ship – you're *Dainty Jane*.'

'Why did you come back here alone? That was dangerous.'

'I was angry,' Orry said, her mind reeling. 'What are you, an AI? Why haven't you spoken to me before? Does Mender know you can talk?'

Another chuckle. 'Do you really want to discuss this in the airlock? Come to the galley. I think you could do with some coffee.'

'I don't want any coffee.'

'I know. But trust me, you need some.'

A steaming bulb was waiting in the dispenser when she climbed into the galley.

'It's instant, I'm afraid,' *Dainty Jane* said. 'I can collapse across parsecs, but grinding beans is a little beyond me.'

Orry sat, cradling the bulb between her hands. The heat stung her skin. 'Go on, then,' she said at last.

'Which question do you want me to answer first?'

'Does Mender know about you? That you're sentient?' She paused. '*Are* you sentient?'

'By any commonly understanding of the word, yes, I'm as sentient as you. Mender knows – but he doesn't know everything.'

'Do you talk to him?'

'Sometimes. Often it's not actual conversation, more an understanding of intent. Emotions.'

'You have emotions?'

'Oh, yes.'

'Proper emotions? So not like an AI—'

'What makes human emotions "proper"? Neurotransmitters triggering the release of chemicals into your brain? Humans have debated the finer points of emotion and sentience for centuries. But I'm not an artificial intelligence.'

'Then what are you?'

'I was human once, much like you – I still am, I suppose, on some level. Except now I'm a ship as well.'

'How is that possible? Mindmerges were outlawed centuries ago—'

'Two hundred and thirty-two years ago, to be precise.'

Orry looked around the galley, at the decking worn smooth by countless boots, the fine scratches on the bulkheads. 'You *can't* be that old . . .'

'Older, obviously.'

'Which yard?'

'Goethe Scorus.'

Orry froze, the bulb of coffee halfway to her lips. She set it down. 'You're *Goethen*?'

'Yes.'

'Get to fuck—'

'I don't know where that is.'

'Sorry, I didn't mean ... It's an expression of surprise. Not to be taken literally.'

'That's a relief,' *Jane* said.

Orry frowned. Had she detected a hint of humour in the old ship's youthful voice? Goethe Prime was a legend: the colony, on one of the earliest worlds to be settled outside the Fountainhead, grew rich during the First Expansion thanks to their pioneering gene-sequencing, which allowed sophisticated human-machine interfaces. The integuary in Orry's head was based on Goethen neural interface tech.

The Goethen Ship Authority had been created to oversee the application of the new technology to the planet's burgeoning ship-building industry. The mind-ships, far superior to craft fitted with quantum navigation cores or even AIs, became the most sought-after vessels in the galaxy. The Ship Authority guarded their patents jealously, but once news leaked out that the ships were the result of merging a genetically viable human mind with the ship's substrate, human rights and genetic purity groups – including the astrotheometrists – started applying pressure until the Ascendancy outlawed mindmerges. Investors dumped now-toxic Goethen stock and the planetary economy crashed overnight. Some of the shipyards managed to switch to making more traditional vessels, but Goethe Prime never regained its former glory.

'I didn't think there were any Goethen ships left,' Orry said.

'Then you were misinformed.'

'Didn't most of you disappear when the Administrate ordered the mindmerges to be reversed and the ships retrofitted with AIs?'

'They didn't understand the merge process – no one outside the Ship Authority did. Once a human mind is merged it becomes infused throughout the ship – and the Goethen ships are not merely receptacles into which a mind can be dropped or taken out again. They too are sentient, in their own way.'

'But they did separate some of you from your ships—'

'—and many of those poor souls took their own lives. Those who didn't spent their last days in institutions. The ships had to be destroyed.'

'Why?'

'Are you aware of the recent Leonov Public School Massacre?'

Orry frowned, trying to puzzle out the apparent *non sequitur*. The story had been all over the news while she was on Tyr: another unstable pupil with access to a powerful weapon. Thankfully, it didn't happen too often.

'The Ship Authority fulfilled Grand Fleet contracts for centuries,' *Jane* explained. 'If one teenage boy with a handlaser can kill twenty-seven people, imagine what a mentally unstable battle cruiser can do.'

'I see your point. So the others like you, those who were left – where did they go?'

'I don't know.'

'Why didn't you go with them?'

'It's a long story.'

Orry leaned back and lifted her legs onto the table. 'I have time.'

'That's a polite way of asking you to mind your own business.'

'Oh. Okay.' She paused. 'You were a military ship, though, weren't you?'

'Yes. A fast insertion boat.'

Orry could tell a frigate from a destroyer, but the finer points of naval architecture were lost on her. *Jane* must have seen that in her face.

'I'm an asset-delivery platform, designed to use speed and agility to penetrate enemy formations and deliver specialist ordnance or operator packages to specific target locations, such as capital ships.'

'What's an operator package?'

'That was a speciality of mine,' *Jane* said proudly. 'I was equipped with Advanced Operator Delivery Systems: breaching harpoons with a compartment fitted out for a single person. The idea was to fly in close and fire a spread of AODS into the enemy vessel. The torpedoes bored through the hull and formed a seal. It was a quick way to gain access to an enemy operations room and take the ship.'

'Who would even *do* that?' Orry said. She'd been fired out of a perfectly good ship once; the idea of doing it by choice made her stomach churn.

'Volunteers usually,' the ship explained. 'We called them minutemen because their life expectancy after leaving the tubes was generally less than sixty seconds.'

'Why did they volunteer, then?'

'Advancement and reputation, mostly. The survivors received automatic promotion, and a minuteman patch on your arm would pretty much guarantee you free drinks for the rest of your life.' *Jane* sighed. 'But the Administrate deemed the whole system too hazardous. No one has used AODS in decades.'

For once Orry found herself agreeing with an Administrate decision. 'Have you been in many battles?' she asked.

'One battle is too many.'

'Is that a yes? Would I have heard of any of them?'

'I'd rather not talk about it, Orry. I'm not a warship any longer.'

'But you still have your weapons?'

'Some of them, for self-defence. But Mender handles the weapons core.'

'Why? You must have much faster responses than him.'

'I have . . . difficulty with weapons.'

Orry frowned. 'What sort of difficulty? You mean a malfunction? Maybe I could take a look. I'm a pretty fair mechanic—'

'No.' *Jane* was silent for a moment. 'It's not that sort of problem.'

'Then what?'

Jane sighed. 'I'm a pacifist.'

Orry guiltily stifled a laugh. 'A pacifist warship? That's a first.'

'I told you, I'm not a warship any more.'

'No, but . . . Why are you a pacifist?'

'I have stress issues in combat situations.'

'Stress? Like post-traumatic stress?'

'Exactly.'

'A *ship* with post-traumatic stress disorder?' Orry couldn't stop the smile.

'And this is exactly why I choose not to talk to people.' *Jane* sounded distinctly disgruntled. 'I had hoped you'd be different.'

'I'm sorry,' Orry told her, meaning it. 'That was insensitive of me.' The ship didn't answer. '*Jane?*'

When she spoke, *Jane*'s voice was tense. 'I'm picking up a spaceplane on final approach. Her transponder isn't broadcasting but it's a Ferreira Bumblebee, Mod J-87, just like *Bonaventure*'s.'

Orry's integuary flagged up a connection request from the ship. When she accepted, the galley was replaced with an amalgam of feedback from the array of external sensors, with visual data from the hull-mounted lenses taking precedence. A familiar-looking spaceplane was battling its way through a tropical storm as it approached Freeport's long runways.

'That's Dyas,' Orry confirmed, closing the connection and jumping to her feet. 'I've logged hundreds of hours in that Bumblebee; I'd know her anywhere.' As she ran for the cockpit she switched to her integuary. *Mender, you there?*

That's a matter of opinion at the moment. What do those kids put in this stuff?

Dyas is landing – right now.

What? How do you know?

I'm on Jane, *tracking him. He's in* Bonnie*'s spaceplane.* She hooked the sensor core, superimposing the Bumblebee's position on the canopy. The sleek craft appeared in front of her as if Orry's eyes were suddenly able to penetrate the rain and clouds.

His gear's down. He's about to land.

Stay there, Mender told her. *Don't do anything stupid until we get there.*

Can I do something stupid once you're here?

Funny girl. Just stay on the ship.

She watched the Bumblebee descend, nose angled high to display its delta wings. The craft was jerking up and down, buffeted by the winds, but it still maintained a steady approach. It broke through the cloud base at 200 metres and Orry pictured herself behind the controls, mentally assessing Dyas' piloting skills as he flared the nose for touchdown.

'Too soon,' she muttered as the plane floated along above the patched ferroconcrete. The craft's huge wings always made it tricky to land, especially with a strong headwind and no cargo to weigh it down, but Dyas finally managed to get the wheels on the ground and airbrakes popped up all over the spaceplane. It turned off the runway with a kilometre to spare.

Orry descended to the arms locker. The battered door swung open to reveal empty pegs where the carbine she'd left on the Shattermoon should have been. Beside it was that shipboard staple: a multi-load shotgun.

She checked the active ammunition, thinking about Jericho's armour plating. Subsonic anti-personnel shells might be good for shredding a spacesuit, but she needed something with more punch. She scrolled through the other available ammo types until she found hardpoint penetration rounds. Chambering one, she headed down to the cargo bay to wait for Mender and Harry.

'You won't need that,' Mender said, indicating her shotgun. 'If we go charging in mob-handed we're liable to scare 'em off. I'll take the Horten down and scout the area. Once we know what we're dealing with, you can bring *Jane* in and deal with that fucking mimetic while I go after Dyas.'

'Why don't you stay here on the guns, and *I'll* scout the area?' Orry suggested reasonably. The clock was ticking and she didn't want to get into a stand-up row over this, but there was no way she was letting Mender go in her place. 'You're a better shot than me, and I can be pretty sneaky when I need to.'

'I'm sure you can, girl, but this is what I do.'

'What you *used* to do. No offence, but you're not a young man any more.'

Harry, who was watching the exchange in silence, winced.

'I ain't dead yet,' Mender growled angrily.

'I know,' she said quickly, hoping it was enough to soothe his vanity, 'but this is *my* problem – *my* brother. Let me do this, Mender. Please.'

He held her gaze for a few seconds, then turned to whip the tarpaulin off his Horten-Yakimov. 'Watch it on the corners,' he said, 'her back-end can be a bitch.'

Orry grinned.

'And take Zorro here with you.'

She sighed.

24

ESCALATION

She'd forgotten about Jackis and his crew, who were still twitching on the ground outside. The rain had returned with a vengeance and was bouncing off the ferroconcrete, soaking Orry in seconds as she coasted down the ramp and over to the cliff's edge. The Horten sank a little under Harry's weight as he climbed on behind her. She used *Dainty Jane*'s sensor core to penetrate the lashing rain and pinpoint the Bumblebee. Once she'd entered its location into the bike's navigation system a holo head-up display appeared above the handlebars, showing the quickest route to it.

The trip down the cliff-face was ten minutes of terror Orry prayed she'd never need to repeat; Harry was clutching her so tightly she could hardly breathe and freezing rain was lashing her face as the powerful bike swerved around hairpin bends she was able to see only on the HUD.

Finally they drew up at the edge of the parking apron, a hundred metres from the Bumblebee. Wiping her eyes, she squinted past a dozen ships that cluttered the waterlogged ferroconcrete in no discernible pattern, like toys abandoned by a child. Steam was still rising from the spaceplane's engines as she dismounted. She drew the shotgun from its holster and started to cautiously splash her way forward, Harry moving like a cat close behind her.

They were halfway to the Bumblebee when the hatch beneath its cockpit opened and Jericho emerged. Orry slowed, gripping the shotgun tighter, and hid behind the landing strut of a suborbital lifter. Harry drew his rapier and disappeared into a pool of shadow deeper beneath the spherical craft.

The mimetic jumped to the ground and surveyed the area around the spaceplane with its burning eyes. Dyas climbed down next, boots slipping on the wet rungs.

They're both here, Orry told Mender. *I'm going to try to get closer. If you come in fast and take out the mimetic, Harry and I will grab Dyas in the confus—*

She broke off as a light utility vehicle appeared on the far side of the apron. The boxy little van sent spray flying from its tyres as it sped towards Dyas and Jericho. It drew up some distance from the Bumblebee and a woman stepped out, enveloped in a long slicker.

Talk to me, girl.

Wait: something's happening. A woman's just arrived . . .

Orry watched with interest as the woman approached Dyas. Was she there to buy the pendant? She stopped a good distance from him and the two engaged in a shouted conversation over the driving rain. Even with her integuary's active audio enhancement, Orry could only make out the odd word.

'—a total idiot? Stop – my time with – shit—'

Dyas turned his back on the woman – who abruptly threw herself face-down into a puddle.

What the hell? Orry thought, looking around to see if someone had shot the newcomer, but now the woman was covering her head with her arms.

The wail of a siren reached Orry's ears and she saw a Fleet skiff approaching fast across the apron. Dyas turned quickly, raising a hand to keep the rain from his eyes. The shark's teeth painted on the prow of the open-topped skiff looked horribly familiar. As it came scything towards the spaceplane, Orry scanned the four auxiliaries in full armour sitting behind the skiff's pilot, her stomach sinking, and cursed as she recognised Second-Captain Naumov.

Dyas yelled something at Jericho and sprinted for the Bumble-bee. The mimetic aimed its maser and the rain flashed into a wide swathe of steam between the spaceplane and the skiff. The gunner squatting behind the electron-cannon in the nose was already returning fire, sending a vivid blue beam searing past Jericho's head, but before he could adjust his aim the skiff lurched, spewing thick black smoke from underneath. The craft pitched forward and skidded across the wet apron, raising a plume of water before digging its nose into the ferroconcrete and sending the gunner somersaulting through the air. Orry winced as he collided with the ground. He didn't move again.

The auxiliaries fared better than the hapless gunner, leaping clear and rolling expertly to their feet, while the pilot and Naumov clung on for dear life until the craft came to a steaming halt.

Orry saw the weird flicker of darklight as the auxiliaries engaged Jericho. The mimetic returned fire, its maser instantly incinerating one of the armoured figures; even in the deluge he went up like a human torch. The pilot scrambled forward and took control of the electron-cannon, swinging its gimbal mounting to bring the weapon to bear. The blue beam flashed out again and the Bumblebee's nose gear glowed white. Sparks spewed from the strut above the tyres and the whole spaceplane shifted as the metal parted, sheared clean through.

Dyas was almost at the Bumblebee's boarding ladder and his feet slipped out from under him as he desperately tried to reverse direction and get clear of its falling nose. Orry watched in dismay as it smacked into the ferroconcrete less than a metre from him and crumpled under the impact – she would never fly the old spaceplane again. Her regret turned quickly to fury as Dyas clambered to his feet and looked around.

Jericho's maser had caught the skiff's pilot, igniting her uniform, and she jumped clear and started rolling in the puddles to extinguish the flames. Orry could see puffs of what must be ablative dust arising from Jericho's armour as the two surviving auxiliaries tried for the killing shot, but one of them got a little too close to the mimetic and before she'd even realised her danger, Jericho had lunged forward and grabbed her by the neck. Orry swallowed bile as she watched the mimetic shaking the woman like a dog with a toy, before eventually twisting the auxiliary's helmet off. Her head was still inside. It completely ignored the blood gushing over its arms, which was quickly diluted by the pounding rain.

Dyas started running raggedly – straight towards the lifter concealing Orry and Harry. The raider was clearly more concerned about what was happening behind him than where he was going. Orry took a snap decision and stepped into his path, the shotgun tucked into her shoulder, safety off.

Dyas skidded to an abrupt halt. He was soaked to the skin,

eyes wide in a face white with fear. It took him a moment to recognise her.

'For *fuck's* sake,' he snapped.

'Where's my brother?' she snarled.

He glanced back at the firefight. The last auxiliary had taken cover behind the boxy van; the woman driver was nowhere to be seen. Jericho was advancing on the vehicle, stalking its prey, apparently oblivious to the darklight eating away at its armour.

'He's alive,' Dyas told Orry breathlessly, 'on your ship – if you kill me, you'll never find him. He'll die, all alone, wondering why his sister didn't save him.'

She had to resist the urge to break his nose. She desperately wanted him to be telling the truth about Ethan.

A flash of blue caught her eye: Second-Captain Naumov was standing in the dented prow of the skiff, aiming the cannon at Jericho. The last auxiliary was down, motionless on the ground beside the remains of the van. Naumov fired again, the beam slicing neatly through the mimetic's right arm above the elbow. Its forearm and the maser it was holding thudded to the ground – and Jericho turned and fled. Naumov tried to hit it again, but the mimetic was a blur of motion as it weaved away through the curtain of rain and into the darkness.

Almost without pausing for thought, the captain swung the cannon round and fired a beam over Orry's head; she hadn't even realised he'd seen her. He motioned for her to drop her weapon.

Mender? she sent.

I'm here.

We could do with a little help down here – things have kind of escalated.

What did I tell you? On my way.

Naumov gestured again and she held the shotgun out at arm's length and let it clatter to the ground. She raised her arms, and Dyas did the same. She glanced to the side, looking for Harry, but there was no sign of him.

The captain drew his sidearm and kept it aimed at them as he clambered from the skiff and walked across the apron, hunched into the driving rain despite his heavy watchcoat. As he came nearer, he touched his cap.

'Good evening, Miz Kent,' he said cheerfully. 'What a pleasant surprise to see you here.'

'You must believe me now,' she yelled against the rain. 'Dyas has got Konstantin's pendant – and my brother and my ship. You have to make him tell me where they are – *please*.'

'That may be so,' Naumov replied, 'but you must understand it's not my place to decide. You'll have to come with me.'

'No! I have to find my brother—'

'I'm sorry, Miz Kent, I really am.' Naumov pulled two pairs of restraints from his coat pocket and tossed them on the ground at her feet. 'Kindly put a pair on our friend here, then—'

His words dried up as the point of Harry's rapier pressed into his neck.

'Drop your gun please, Captain, there's a good chap.'

Naumov hesitated, then grimaced as Harry pressed his blade deeper. His pistol fell to the ground and he raised his hands.

'I advise you both to reconsider,' he said calmly. 'You're making things much worse for yourselves.'

Orry stared at the gun at Naumov's feet, then over at Dyas. Their eyes remained locked for a moment – and they leaped in opposite directions: she for her shotgun, he for the captain's pistol.

As her hand closed on the shotgun, Naumov kicked his pistol away before Dyas could reach it. The raider froze, arm still outstretched, and looked at her. Her fingers slipped on the wet shotgun and by the time she had it to her shoulder he was gone, vanishing into the shadows.

She swore, and started forward in pursuit.

Stay where you are, girl, Mender snapped in her head. *We've got company.*

Orry hesitated, seeing her only link to Ethan getting away. *Screw it,* she thought, and was about to tear after him when the roar of engines heralded the arrival of a craft overhead and a blinding searchlight played over the scene, making her shade her eyes.

A craft was coming to rest beside the bodies scattered between the Bumblebee and the grounded skiff and Orry immediately recognised it as *Speedwell*'s cutter. It settled lightly on its skids and auxiliaries spilled out of the open side hatches.

'Put down your weapons,' Naumov said, 'and I give you my word that you will treated fairly.'

The noise of the cutter's idling drives was drowned out by the howl of engines from behind her, and Orry turned to see the familiar shape of *Dainty Jane* gliding through the rain.

Harry removed his blade from Naumov's neck and, keeping it pointed at the captain, moved to join Orry.

'We have to go,' he told her. 'There'll be another chance to get Dyas. If we stay here we'll be arrested and then you'll never get Ethan back.'

She looked from the auxiliaries spreading out from the cutter to the rain-lashed darkness where Dyas had disappeared, and felt like screaming.

'All right,' she said, and ran towards *Dainty Jane*.

'Don't move,' Harry told Naumov, gesturing towards *Jane*'s mass driver with his rapier before sheathing it and running after Orry.

Warm air rolled over her as the ship hovered, then set down. The loading ramp extended.

Get on board, Mender sent from the cockpit. *And bring my bloody bike!*

She seized the Horten's handlebars and the bike floated effortlessly up the ramp and into the freight lock.

Are you tracking Dyas? she asked Mender as the ship rose and the ramp began to close, but Harry grabbed her arm and pointed through the narrowing gap.

Dyas stumbled into the circle of light surrounding the cutter, held between two auxiliaries. Naumov took one last look at *Jane*, then retrieved his pistol and strode back towards the cutter. Orry felt the ship rise more rapidly, pressing her into the deck. The outer door closed.

What are you doing? she demanded. *Dyas is right there!*

You want to take on the whole of the Grand Fleet, girl? We need to get the hell out of here.

And do what? She was furious. *Wait for Roag's biomites to turn us into vegetables?*

She stared through the inspection port, but the apron was already lost in the darkness below. Dyas and Second-Captain Naumov were gone.

*

218

'I don't understand,' she said angrily as she climbed into *Dainty Jane*'s cockpit, Harry on her heels. They were climbing steeply through Erlitz Shen's atmosphere. 'How did Naumov know Dyas would come here?'

'It was the woman,' Mender said.

'What woman?'

'The woman Dyas was meeting – you said she dropped to the ground before the skiff appeared.'

Orry had forgotten about that – he was right, there was no way the woman could have heard the skiff over the noise of the rain.

'She knew there was going to be a firefight,' Mender said, spelling it out. 'That's why she dropped.'

'She was in on it?' Harry said.

'It was a trap,' Mender told them. 'They knew Dyas was selling, so I'll bet they set up buyers in all the likely market-places. This one got a bite; she arranged a time to meet and *Speedwell* prepared a reception for him.'

'So what do we do now?' Harry asked.

'What can we do?' Orry muttered. 'We've lost him, and Ethan.'

'And the pendant,' Mender added.

'Not necessarily,' Harry said.

'*Yes*, necessarily,' she said. 'The Fleet have got him.'

'So let's get him back.'

'Oh, right – when we don't even know where they're taking hi—'

'Sure we do. He'll be on *Justiciar*.'

She paused. 'The super-titan? What makes you think that?'

'Delf sent those bounty hunters after you, yes? Well, I did some poking around and it appears the count has decided to get personally involved in the matter of his grandson's death.

He arrived on board *Justiciar* yesterday. Her command group is currently out near the Diatris Scar.'

'That's close,' Mender said thoughtfully. 'An easy collapse.'

'Are you sure about this?' Orry asked.

'It's all over the newsfeeds,' Harry told her. 'You're becoming quite the story.'

'All right,' she said, 'let's say Naumov does take Dyas to Delf—'

'—which he will,' Harry interrupted.

'Which he *might*. How does that help us? Do we just stroll onto one of the largest ships in the Grand Fleet and ask for him back? How the hell do we get in, let alone get him out?'

'I don't know about getting him out,' Harry said. 'But I have an idea that might get us on board.'

'Well?'

Harry looked at Mender. 'You're not going to like it.'

'Hello?' The word echoed through *Bonaventure*'s hold.

'Hello?' Ethan repeated, then coughed painfully. His voice was getting hoarse. Right now he'd gladly exchange his share of the ship for a bulb of barely recycled water. His head was throbbing where Jericho had struck him; that side of his face felt twice its normal size.

The ship had been eerily silent since he'd awakened to find himself floating gently above the deck, tethered by a length of cable. So *Bonaventure* wasn't under thrust right now. He wondered where he was, and where Dyas and Jericho had gone.

His stomach growled and he tried to ignore the hunger gnawing at his belly.

Ethan prayed his hated captors would return soon.

25

JUSTICIAR

Mender looked up from the pre-collapse checklist. *Justiciar*'s coordinates were locked into the navigation core. 'This smacks of desperation,' he muttered.

'Are you sure you know what you're doing, Harry?' Orry asked. 'You won't be able to go back home after this. They'll revoke your passport. You'll be a fugitive – for ever.'

Harry stared at the gold-edged databrane in his hands. 'It's fine,' he told her. 'I'm never going back.'

'You say that now, but what about in five years? Ten? And what about Elena?'

'I said it's fine,' he repeated sharply, raising his eyes to look at her. 'Your brother's out there. I want to help.'

'Let him help if he wants to,' Mender told her. 'It's only data on a brane.'

'You're just grumpy because we have to drug you,' she said.

'It's not the drugs that bother me, girl, it's waking up in the middle of a goddamned super-titan and having to rely on you two clowns to get me out.'

'At least *you* don't have to dress like a tart,' she said, trying in vain to tug her plunging neckline into a less revealing position. Harry stared fiercely at his passport. 'Where did you get this thing, anyway?' she asked.

Mender smiled. 'Its previous owner had to leave in a hurry.'

'Without her clothes? What did you do to her?'

'A gentleman never tells.' He returned his attention to the checklist while she slipped off a shoe and rubbed her foot. Mender's mystery woman had smaller feet than her – and terrible taste in hats.

Jane? she asked. *What really happened?*

You don't want to know. Thank the Prophet the old goat is too old for that nonsense now.

Orry smiled. 'What about this?' she asked, holding up her clutch. Mender had assured her the compact device inside the bag would jam any integuary in a ten-metre radius.

Mender sighed. 'Relax, girl, they'll never detect it – or the axon disruptor. I used to do this kind of thing for a living, remember?'

A cloud of escort and support vessels orbited *Justiciar* like electrons around a nucleus. The super-titan's lenticular hull widened towards its hub, lights sparkling in the towers rising from the colossal ship. At its thickest point the hull dropped steeply away to form a deep well lined with dock facilities. Orry watched a massive bulk-carrier manoeuvre into the well like an insect pollinating a gunmetal flower.

'I'm still not sure about getting to the brig,' Orry said, eyeing a flashing red light on *Dainty Jane*'s instrument panel.

'Getting to the brig will be easy,' Harry reassured her.

'Super-titans are essentially mobile habitats; there are at least as many civilians living on board as Fleet crew. The military areas might be secure, but travel between them is completely unrestricted.'

'I hope you're right.'

He grinned. 'Trust me.'

She turned away to watch an approaching formation of three lights: a gunboat escort vectoring to *Dainty Jane*'s position.

A combat spider was waiting for them when *Dainty Jane* dropped her ramp.

It scuttled forward and glared down at Orry and Harry. From the top of its steel-blue carapace two muzzles locked onto them. Orry remained motionless, resisting the urge to pull the hem of the clingy cocktail dress further down her thighs.

'*Identification*,' the spider croaked, its artificial voice modulated to encourage compliance.

Harry raised his databrane.

The spider emitted soft clicks and whirrs. '*Noble passport verified*,' it screeched, then shifted all its terrifying attention to Orry. '*Identification*.'

Harry stepped in front of her. 'This is my companion, Miz Sphene. She's travelling under my House passport.'

More clicks and whirrs.

Dainty Jane was the only vessel in Civil Dock 19. A door hissed open and two officers entered, followed by a pair of civilian medics pushing a wheeled gurney.

One of the officers, a woman of late middle age with a sallow complexion, was wearing a black and silver arbiter's uniform, and Orry tried not to stiffen as she examined them.

'Stand down,' the other officer, a portly captain with round apple-red cheeks, snapped at the spider, which instantly scuttled backwards into the shadows. It squatted there, a dark presence with myriad red eyes glowing malevolently in the half-light.

The captain ran his eyes over Orry's skin-tight dress and turned a shade redder. He bowed to Harry. 'An honour, Lord Bardov. First-Captain Macen at your service. I'm so sorry the circumstances that bring you aboard aren't more favourable. I trust you're not too distressed by your ordeal?'

Harry waved a dismissive hand. 'These situations arise from time to time. One learns to deal with them.'

'Quite, quite,' Macen's eyes shifted to *Dainty Jane*'s open cargo bay. 'And is he – that is to say, is the man who—'

'The wretch was still breathing last time I checked. Feel free to lock him in the brig or whatever you call it and throw away the key.'

Macen gestured to the medics, who pushed the gurney up the ramp and into the cargo bay.

The arbiter stepped forward and, with the slightest of bows, introduced herself. 'I am Arbiter-Major Ayzarev. I wonder if you would spare me a few minutes to answer some questions, Lord Bardov. Paperwork, you understand?'

'Of course, Major,' Harry replied, then added, 'all in good time.' He turned to Macen. 'I understand the Count of Delf is on board.'

'He is.'

'Then be a good fellow and give him my compliments, would you? I'd like to freshen up and get a good night's rest. It's been a long few days.'

Macen's eyes glazed as he accessed his integuary, Harry

turned to Ayzarev and said, 'I trust your questions can wait, Major?'

Ayzarev did a poor job of hiding her frustration.

Orry stopped herself fiddling with the ridiculous pillbox hat pinned to her hair and watched from behind its gauzy black veil as the medics wheeled the gurney back down the ramp. Mender was strapped to it, eyes closed and face slack.

Ayzarev stopped the gurney and examined him. 'What exactly did you do to him?' she asked.

Harry sighed. 'After hijacking our ship, this halfwit brought us aboard his own tub and locked us in a cabin. I should explain that I'm a chimera, Major: I have a venom gland. Anyway, this fellow got a little too close when bringing us one of his execrable meals, and . . . Well, you get the picture.'

Ayzarev looked at Mender, then at Harry. 'Is it fatal?'

'The food?' Harry said with a smile. 'I hope not.'

'The venom.'

'No, unfortunately.'

Ayzarev waved the medics on. 'How exactly did this man come to abduct you and your companion?'

Harry chuckled. 'Nice try, Major, but it really will have to wait for the morning.'

'His Grace will be happy to receive you, Lord Bardov,' Macen interrupted.

'Capital. Where will I find his stateroom?'

'It would be my honour to escort you, My Lord. Do you have any luggage?'

Harry laughed. 'Unfortunately not, Captain – I lost everything during the blasted hijack.'

'I'm sorry to hear that.'

'No matter. Shall we?' Harry nodded at Ayzarev. 'Until tomorrow, Major.'

The arbiter bowed stiffly, clearly unhappy.

'Come along, Sphene!' Harry ordered, and strode after the captain.

Orry suppressed a smile as she tottered after him in her borrowed heels; he was a natural at playing the arrogant aristo.

But then he would be, wouldn't he?

26

THE COUNT OF DELF

Harry bid farewell to First-Captain Macen in a spacious atrium outside the doors to Delf's suite. He waved nonchalantly as Macen's seat sank into the transit capsule waiting beneath the deck. The capsule's roof hummed closed and a section of deck slid into place above it. Harry blew out his cheeks with relief and rolled his eyes at Orry, who gave him a sympathetic smile; Macen had kept up a constant stream of ingratiating small talk for the full ten minutes it had taken the capsule to get a third of the way around *Justiciar*'s circumference.

Orry looked up at the cliff-like bulkheads, the ceiling lost in distant shadows. At one end of the atrium a vast, latticed window followed the curve of *Justiciar*'s hull. Through it she could see a destroyer, doubtless part of the super-titan's close escort, and, beyond, the twinkling lights of other ships in the command group. Drives glowed in the void, powering launches and tenders between the larger vessels. Inside the atrium, trees and brightly coloured plants grew from beds of nutrient pebbles.

'This is more like a luxury liner than a warship,' she observed.

'This bit is,' Harry agreed. 'I think she's large enough to carry a fair few weapons as well, though.' He pressed a chime set in a pair of doors made from some luxuriantly waxed wood.

Harry was right, Orry thought. Super-titans like *Justiciar* had done away with the need for permanent bases. Surrounded by command groups that were formidable fleets in their own right, each super-titan was an administrative hub, law court, fortress, arsenal, manufacturing plant and resupply depot, not to mention home to hundreds of thousands of personnel, military and civilian alike. The ships were slices of the Fountainhead, free to roam wherever they were needed in the vastness of Ascendancy space, a vital tool in stemming the rumblings of discontent from the outer colonies and nascent independence movement, impressing the Imperator's will on recalcitrant worlds.

The door opened to reveal a footman in formal attire. Harry held up his passport and the footman bowed, his upper body inclined at precisely the angle required for a member of a minor House.

'This way, Lord Bardov,' he said in oily tones, and ushered them into a long, narrow reception room that reminded Orry of Delf's mansion on Tyr, all antique furniture and white marble busts on tall pillars, oil paintings and etched-crystal ornaments. The room projected wealth and taste. *That's the point of it, I suppose*, she thought wryly. Another pair of tall wooden doors was set into the far wall.

'His Grace sends his apologies,' the footman oozed. 'He will be with Your Lordship at his earliest convenience. Can I offer you refreshments while you wait?'

'No, thank you,' Harry said. 'How long will His Grace be?'

'I cannot say, Milord.'

Harry nodded, looking a little uneasy. He'd assured Orry

that Delf would drop everything to welcome a fellow Ruuz in distress.

After the footman had vanished through a side door, leaving them alone, Harry raised his eyebrows in mute apology and took a seat. She pressed her clutch, feeling the hard edge of the integuary jammer inside.

Just how minor is your House? she asked.

He grimaced. *Sorry. Delf's an arrogant prick. I should've realised he might not see me right away.*

We have some time. I gave Mender enough sedative to keep him out for a couple of hours. And even if he does come round, he knows to stall them.

Harry managed a smile. *I can't believe he agreed to it.*

It's amazing what you're prepared to do when a time-bomb is ticking inside your head.

They looked up as one of the inner doors began to open and Orry was halfway to her feet before she realised the man in the doorway wasn't Delf. Her breath hitched as she recognised Dragan, *Speedwell*'s political officer. Her hands fumbled with the clasp of her clutch bag.

The arbiter's eyes widened when he saw her and he reached for his pistol, but Orry had thrust her hand into her bag and was already hitting the button of the integuary jammer. Harry crossed the room in a blur, dragging Mender's axon disruptor out of his boot, and Dragan went rigid as Harry rammed the disruptor into his side. His pistol clattered onto the tiled floor.

Orry raced past them and through the door. The Count of Delf was seated at a desk overlooking another expanse of curved windows that formed one wall of a spacious stateroom. He stood as she entered, as tall and locust-like as she remembered.

'What the devil—' he started – and she punched him in the face.

He fell back into his chair, more shocked than hurt. He touched his nose and examined the blood on his fingers with apparent confusion.

'Not one more word,' she snarled, leaning over him. Behind her, Harry dragged Dragan into the room and locked the door. His boots clicked on the tiles as he crossed to the desk.

The Count of Delf's eyes glazed and a look of cold fury came over his face when he realised his integuary was useless. He pulled a white handkerchief from the breast pocket of his frock coat and dabbed at his nose.

'The Bardov brat, I presume,' he said. 'I should never have lowered myself to receive you.'

Harry gave a stiff bow.

'Do you know what you've done, young man? Your House is finished. *Expunged.* I will take the greatest pleasure in dismantling it personally. Not that anyone will notice,' he added contemptuously.

'Shut up!' Orry snapped, noticing Harry had turned ashen.

'And the harridan speaks. You simpletons can't possibly expect to get away with this.' He eyed the axon disruptor uneasily. 'What do you want with me?'

'Don't you recognise me, Your Grace?' She withdrew the long pin securing her pillbox hat with its gauzy veil, revealing her sunburst-orange hair.

The count took it well. His Adam's apple bobbed up and down once and he addressed Harry. 'You want to be careful, my boy. This little witch has a penchant for butchering young noblemen.'

'Not just young ones,' Orry said dangerously, and the count

flinched as she pressed the point of the hatpin into his cheek just below his eye. She nodded across the room to Dragan's motionless form. 'What was he doing here?'

'Nothing,' he said quickly, eyes flicking to the desk. 'Simply a courtesy call to update me on his progress.'

Orry followed his glance and was stunned to see the pendant lying in plain sight.

She tried not to grin as she picked it up. 'So, Dragan returned this to you. What else did he tell you?'

The nobleman said nothing, so she brandished the hatpin and traced a line up his cheek. Only when it neared his right eye did he pull away.

'Damn it all! He said he'd found the pendant on a man named Dyas, who is being held in the brig. He told me you deny murdering Konstantin and insist it was this man Dyas.' He laughed bitterly. 'And I actually believed him. I was about to withdraw the contract on your life.'

She cursed Roag and her games. If it had been up to Orry, she would have left Dyas here to rot.

'I want you to issue an order for Dyas' release,' she told the count, 'and for the release of a man named Jurgen Mender.'

'In it together, were you? I might have known.'

She pressed the pin into his flesh until he hissed in pain. 'I didn't ask you to talk,' she said. 'I asked you to make out two release orders.'

'You'll never get off this ship – Ah!'

'You're still talking,' Orry said pleasantly. 'If it happens again, you'll need a new eye.'

He nodded carefully, sweat glistening on his face, and gestured towards his desk. Orry stepped back, watching carefully as he prepared two branes. When they were complete, he used a heavy signet ring to add his House seal to the bottom of each order. Orry read them over and nodded, satisfied.

'What now? Are you going to kill me?'

'I didn't murder Konstantin,' she told him.

'I don't believe you.'

'I know, but I needed to tell you.'

The Count of Delf studied her. 'If you didn't kill him, who did?'

'Morven Dyas.'

'So why do you want to release him? No doubt he'll admit his guilt under interrogation and you'll be cleared.'

'It's a long story. For what it's worth, I'm sorry about what happened. For all his faults, Konstantin didn't deserve to die like that.'

'You're lying,' the count said, though his voice lacked the certainty of a moment before.

'Think what you like,' she said, and gestured to Harry, who raised the axon disruptor.

'Wait!' the count cried, then jerked back in his chair.

'He sounded like he was starting to believe you,' Harry said. 'Do you think he'll call off the contract?'

'After this? Would you? Do you think he was serious about going after your family?'

Harry stared at the unconscious man. 'I don't know.'

'I know what Mender would say. Why take the chance? Kill him now, while you can.'

Harry hung his head. 'I'm not Mender.'

Orry squeezed his arm. 'I know.' She waved the release orders at him. 'Come on. This was the easy bit.'

27

NAUMOV

Orry checked the time. Twenty minutes since they'd left the Count of Delf and they still hadn't got to *Justiciar*'s brig. Her integuary said they were almost there – but how long would it take to prepare a prisoner for transfer? What laughingly passed for their plan was full of unknowns.

She sighed. Dad would be turning in his grave. Every grift she'd run since his death had been badly planned and poorly executed. It wasn't entirely her fault – there simply hadn't been the time to prepare the sort of elaborate scams they'd run as a family – but that wouldn't be much comfort if they were captured or killed.

She and Harry sat alone in a transit capsule; the narrow tube was so low that Harry couldn't stand upright, even in the middle where the roof was highest.

'Finally,' he muttered as they began to slow. His face was drawn.

The capsule came to a halt, the roof hummed open and the interior rose smoothly. Orry found herself in another atrium, an open area facing a white wall. It was very different to the last: there were no trees or plants, and no panoramic windows here – *Justiciar*'s brig was deep within the ship.

They crossed to a formidable-looking metal door, a bubble of armoured glass protruding from the wall on one side. A corporal's head and shoulders appeared, distorted by the glass.

'I am here on behalf of His Grace, the Count of Delf.' Harry held up the release orders for inspection.

A shallow tray emerged from the wall beneath the bubble. 'In the tray please, sir.'

Harry placed the branes into the tray and watched them disappear into the wall.

'One moment, please,' the corporal said, and withdrew his head.

Orry looked around the empty atrium. She shivered, goose-bumps rising on her bare arms and legs.

I look like an idiot, she sent to Harry.

You look fine.

I should've brought a change of clothes.

Relax. You get all sorts on a super-titan.

She tugged at her hem. *I'm not really dressed for releasing a prisoner.*

If there's a correct dress code for this sort of thing, I'm not aware of it. Harry grinned. *He probably thinks you're a present for Dyas.*

She shuddered. *Not funny.*

The corporal reappeared and saluted. 'Apologies, My Lord.' Red lights flashed around the perimeter of the heavy door, accompanied by a klaxon. The door slid slowly open.

She followed Harry into a compact anteroom. Plastic chairs lined one wall, opposite another armoured window. She could see the corporal in the office beyond.

The door slid closed, clanging into place with a dreadful finality.

'Take a seat, sir,' the corporal said.

'How long will this take?' Harry asked, and Orry detected a hint of anxiety in his voice.

'Difficult to say, My Lord.'

'Corporal, I would appreciate it if this matter was expedited. His Grace is not a patient man.'

'Of course, sir.' The man sat down at a terminal, the release orders beside him.

She tried to send a message to Harry, to warn him to relax before he gave them both away, but her integuary wouldn't connect. *The whole brig must be shielded*, she realised, *to isolate the inmates.*

They sat in silence.

She caught herself checking the time every few seconds and had to force herself to stop. She rubbed her forehead, trying to shift the dull throb that had started behind her eyes. Ignoring the pain, she watched the corporal work.

He returned to the window. 'The paperwork on this one is fine, sir,' he said, waving Dyas' release order. 'Your guy's on his way up now.' He held up Mender's order. 'There's a problem with this one, though.'

'What sort of a problem?' Harry asked.

'He's not here.'

Orry struggled to remain silent.

'What do you mean, he's not here?' Harry said, rising to his feet. 'Where the devil is he?'

The corporal looked at him oddly. 'In Central Medical, sir.'

She stood and slipped her arm through Harry's, squeezing his bicep as a warning. He was so tense the muscle felt like iron.

'Thank you, Corporal,' she said, smiling sweetly. 'That will be fine. Do you know where he is, exactly?'

'No, ma'am.' The corporal returned the unused release order through a slit below the window.

Harry allowed her to lead him back to the seats, where he sat stiffly. His cheeks were flushed.

More time passed, and Orry turned over possible next moves in her mind. There was no perfect solution, but she was pretty good at thinking on her feet when the need arose. She finally settled on a course of action and glanced at Harry, worried.

Another ten minutes gone, she thought. If Dyas didn't arrive soon it wouldn't matter what plan she came up with. Delf could come round at any moment, and when he did they were finished.

A clang reverberated through the anteroom as the door in the far wall swung open. Two guards escorted Dyas into the room, restraints on his hands and ankles. He wore a disposable plastic coverall with diagonal yellow and black stripes. A flash of surprise crossed his face when he saw Orry, quickly subdued.

'All yours, sir,' one of the escorts told Harry. 'Sign here.'

Harry pressed his House ring to the proffered databrane.

'Thank you, My Lord.'

One of the guards removed Dyas' restraints and the other handed him a shallow plastic tray containing his bundled-up pressure suit. They saluted Harry before leaving.

Dyas immediately reached under the suit and searched the empty tray. He looked up and his face tightened when he saw the pendant around Orry's neck.

'You'll need to sign for your weapon at the arsenal,' the corporal told him.

'That's fine,' Dyas growled, staring at her. 'Where can I change?'

'Later,' she said. She nudged Harry.

'Would you be so good as to open the door, Corporal?'

Once again the flashing lights reflected off the walls and the door began to creep open. For the first time Orry thought they might actually pull this off.

The smaller door behind her clanged open again and Second-Captain Naumov strode into the room. 'Who authorised this rel—?'

He stopped when he saw her, but as he reached for his pistol, Dyas threw himself forward and the two men struggled for a moment. Naumov hurled Dyas against the wall, losing his grip on his pistol in the process – and Orry darted in and scooped it off the floor.

She jumped back and pointed the gun at Naumov.

He raised his hands.

The main door slammed closed.

'Don't move,' she snapped at the corporal behind the glass. 'No alarms, or I shoot him. Understand?'

The man nodded slowly.

'This is insane,' Naumov said. 'Put that weapon down before things get any worse.'

'Shut up.' She glanced at the corporal. 'You. Open that door.'

'Ignore her,' Naumov said. 'She's bluffing.'

Orry compressed her lips, eyes flitting from Naumov to the guard. 'I swear, if you don't open that door right now I will paint this wall with his brains.'

'Don't do it,' Naumov snapped. 'That's an order.'

'Rama, sir,' the corporal moaned, his face white.

Orry realised she was running out of options. A cold sense of purpose overcame her. 'Last chance,' she warned the corporal.

Naumov shook his head. 'Don't—'

She shot him.

28

MEDICAL TORPEDOES

Naumov slammed into the wall in a crescent of blood, staring at Orry in shock. He was trying to stay on his feet, but his legs gave way and he slid slowly down into one of the plastic chairs, clutching his upper arm. Blood oozed between his fingers.

Harry's eyes were wide. 'What did you do?'

She pointed her gun at Naumov's head and his face went even whiter. 'Open the damn door,' she told the stunned corporal, and, seconds later, it began to open once more.

'Call a capsule to Central Medical,' she told Harry. 'Wherever the hell that is.' She gestured at Naumov with her gun. 'Up you get, Captain. You're coming with us.'

Scowling, he rose unsteadily to his feet.

'What are you doing?' Harry asked. 'We're not taking him with us?'

'Call a capsule,' she repeated, then turned to the corporal. 'You – get your arse out here.'

'I can't.'

'Out!'

'I can't! This compartment is sealed for the duration of my

watch. If I leave without being relieved an alarm will sound and the whole place goes into lockdown.'

'Shit!' She thought for a moment. 'Okay, listen to me very carefully. We're leaving now. If I hear an alarm, I'll kill the captain here. Got it?'

'Y-yes, ma'am.'

'Some breakout,' Dyas muttered as he strolled out of the main door.

'Would you rather be back in a cell?' Orry asked, pushing Naumov ahead of her.

'It's better than being dead.'

'We're not dead yet.'

A capsule was waiting for them, with Harry hovering nervously between the seats.

'Dyas is right,' Naumov said through gritted teeth. A trail of blood spots marked his path from the brig. 'You haven't a hope. Give up now, before things get any worse.'

She pushed him into the seat next to Dyas, sat opposite and looked at Harry. The capsule sank into its tube.

Naumov's eyes were locked on her. A sheen of sweat covered his face.

Dyas stripped off his prison coverall to display a network of elaborate tattoos that looked out of place on his doughy body. When he caught Orry staring, he turned away with a scowl.

Once he'd pulled on his pressure suit, she pulled out the medical kit from beneath the seats. 'Do something about Naumov's arm,' she ordered.

'Screw him.'

She didn't take her eyes off the captain. 'Treat his arm.'

'Or what?'

'Or he'll bleed out, and a dead hostage is no use to us.'

Dyas thought about that, then grunted and opened the medical kit. Orry was shocked when Naumov moved his hand to reveal the extent of his wound. She had never intended to do so much damage. The bullet had torn away a chunk of his upper arm, leaving a wide, bloody furrow. She had to resist the urge to apologise when the officer gritted his teeth while Dyas sprinkled coagulant over the wound and bound it with microbial repair tissue.

'Anything else?' Dyas asked sarcastically, using his discarded coverall to wipe Naumov's blood from his hands.

'Yes, one thing.' She swung the pistol to point at his face. 'Where's my fucking brother?'

His gold tooth glinted. 'As soon as I tell you where your precious ship is, you'll kill me.'

'So you *do* believe I'll shoot you?'

He studied her face. 'You know, I think you would at that.'

She moved the pistol to point at his knee. 'I don't have to kill you, arsehole. Where's my brother?'

His bravado faltered. 'However you're planning to get off this ship,' he said, 'I don't think kneecapping me is going to make it any easier.'

Her hand tightened around the pistol.

'Central Medical's coming up,' Harry said, but she didn't move. 'Orry!' he snapped. 'There'll be time for this once we get out of here.'

Dyas was sweating now and she held the gun on him for a moment longer, making her point. Then she shifted her aim back to Naumov, who was slumped in his seat, eyes flickering. *Going into shock?* she wondered, worried.

'I assume you have a plan?' Harry asked shakily.

'I'll get Mender,' she told him. 'You take Dyas back to *Dainty Jane* and wait for us. Give me the disruptor.'

'What if Dyas tries something?' Harry asked as he handed her the axon disruptor.

'Shoot him somewhere it hurts,' she said. 'Just don't kill him.' She tossed the pistol over to him—

—and Naumov hurled himself at her, cannoning into her chest and using his weight to pin her to the floor. She struggled to raise the axon disruptor, but she couldn't move her arm. She bucked, trying to shift him, but he was too heavy. His cheek was pressed hard against hers as he tried to reach the disruptor. Panicked helplessness started to overwhelm her as she realised he was just too strong.

He prised the disruptor from her hand and she waited to feel its jolt . . .

The captain grunted and went limp. Summoning all her strength, Orry managed to shove his body to one side, and saw Harry standing over him, holding the pistol like a club.

'This is all going very well,' Dyas observed dryly. 'I can see you're both real professionals.'

'Shut up,' said Orry and Harry together.

Naumov groaned and rolled onto his back.

'Just kill him,' Dyas said matter-of-factly. 'That guard back at the brig is going to raise the alarm any time now, whether this bastard is alive or dead.' He looked at them both as if they were idiots. 'Oh hell,' he spat, 'I'll do it myself.'

'Hey!' Orry yelled, raising the disruptor.

He stopped. 'What?'

'Leave him alone.'

'You're soft.'

'I said, *leave him*,' she repeated quietly and very precisely.

Dyas raised his hands in the air and backed off. 'Damned amateurs,' he muttered.

The capsule slowed to a stop and rose into a busy reception area. Harry helped her haul Naumov to his feet and they supported his weight between them while they waited for the roof to open. Uniformed Grand Fleet medics and nurses in crimson scrubs mixed with civilian doctors in black coats and red sashes. At first they barely noticed as she and Harry walked Naumov clear of the capsule, the axon disruptor pressed inconspicuously against his spine. But as the captain's legs gave way, Orry staggered under his weight and Harry had to help her lower him to the deck.

'Go!' she hissed, glaring at Harry as he hesitated.

As a doctor and an orderly converged on them, he whispered, 'Don't make me come and find you!' He hurried back to Dyas.

The capsule was already sinking into the deck as a tall woman in a physick's coat dropped down next to Orry. Her black hair, gathered into a waist-length ponytail, framed flawless olive skin. Her sculpted cheekbones and dark oval eyes looked almost too perfect, like one of the busts in Delf's anteroom.

'What happened?' the doctor asked, examining the dressing on Naumov's arm. Her accent was pure Fountainhead.

Orry burst into tears. 'It was an accident,' she blubbed. 'He was showing me his gun and . . . it just . . . um . . . went off . . .'

The doctor turned to her. 'He did this to himself?'

'Yes!' Orry sobbed. Crying was coming a little too easily; if she wasn't careful she wouldn't be able to stop.

'Get him to Diagnostics,' the doctor snapped at the orderly, who was already waving a gurneybot over. 'Are *you* all right?' she asked Orry. 'No injuries?'

'I'm fine.' Orry sniffed, and reached under her veil to wipe her eyes.

'What's his name?'

'Naumov.'

'And you are?'

'Amber Sphene.'

'I'm Senior Physick Rellis. You did the right thing, Miz Sphene, stopping the bleeding and bringing him here.'

'We were coming anyway,' Orry said. She handed Mender's release order to Rellis. 'I work for His Grace the Count of Delf.'

Senior Physick Rellis examined the brane as the orderly settled Naumov onto the gurneybot and walked off beside it as it hummed away.

When the doctor finished reading, she was frowning. 'I can action this if you want,' she said, 'but can't the count send someone else to handle it, considering what's happened? At the very least I think you need a bulb of sweet tea – nothing better to steady the nerves.'

Orry gave her a watery smile. 'I'm fine, really. When His Grace issues an order he expects it to be carried out immediately.'

The doctor eyed Orry's dress. 'What exactly do you do for the count?'

'I'm his . . . personal assistant.'

'I see.' Rellis looked as if she was about to pass comment, then changed her mind. 'Well, the arbiters will obviously need to talk to you about Captain Naumov, but I can certainly find out about' – she glanced at the brane in her hand – 'this Jurgen

Mender. Hold on a moment and I'll track him down for you.' Her eyes glazed over.

Orry inspected the waiting area with its banks of seats facing the admissions desks while she waited. It looked pretty much like every hospital reception she'd ever seen, except for the number of military uniforms present. She closed her eyes in an attempt to relieve her growing headache, trying not to think about Roag's biomites.

'Okay, come with me,' the doctor said, and strode off down one of the corridors. After a moment, Orry pulled off her heels and scurried after the doctor until she finally stopped in front of a bored-looking auxiliary private stationed outside a locked door.

'You are free to go, Private,' the doctor said, waving him out of the way. 'The man you're guarding is no longer under arrest.' She showed him the release order.

The young man read it carefully. 'I don't know, ma'am,' he said, looking worried. 'The lieutenant told me to stay here until I'm relieved.'

Rellis stood ramrod-straight and stared down at the hapless soldier. Orry got the impression she didn't much care for the military.

'Has your lieutenant seen this order?'

'No, ma'am, but—'

'And what do you think he would say if he had?'

The private hesitated. 'I understand what you're saying, ma'am, but I should really stay here until I'm ordered to stand down.' He brightened and suggested, 'You could always show that to the lieutenant. He's on C Deck, in the auxiliary spaces.'

'That's on the other side of the ship!' She folded her arms. 'Call him.'

'Ma'am?'

'You have an integuary. Call your lieutenant.'

'It won't do any good, ma'am. He'll want to see the order for himself.'

Orry stepped in. She smiled at the young soldier. 'Hello, Private. I work for the Count of Delf and he personally impressed on me the urgency of this order. Now, while I appreciate the chain of command, we really don't have time to go all the way across the ship to show this order to your officer, who will then want to show it to his officer, and so on – so why don't you give me your name and unit, and I'll ask the count to contact you directly. Will that be acceptable?'

'The Count of Delf?' the private repeated. The release order shook a little as he scanned it again, then he stiffened to attention and handed the brane back to the doctor. 'That won't be necessary,' he said. He saluted, shouldered his carbine and marched away.

'*Soldiers.*' Rellis almost spat the word as she opened the door.

The compartment beyond contained four beds, three of which were empty. Orry smiled with relief when she saw Mender lying in the fourth. *He looks peaceful*, she thought, watching his relaxed face, his chest rising and falling steadily.

The doctor checked the display at the foot of the bed. After scanning it for a few seconds she shook her head. 'I'm sorry, but I can't discharge him until he's come round; we still need to run some more tests. He's been shot full of venom, but our toxicology scans haven't been able to identify it. We do know that he has high-plasma cyteramol levels, so it looks like someone sedated him.'

'Can you wake him?' Orry asked.

'He's not my patient. Let me contact my colleague—'

'No!' Orry said quickly, and seeing Rellis' frown, continued in a calmer tone, 'I'm sure a shot of haldomycin would bring him round just fine.'

The doctor narrowed her eyes. 'Who *are* you?'

Orry activated the integuary jammer. 'Sorry, doc,' she said, pulling out the axon disruptor.

Senior Physick Rellis' eyes glazed, and a look of panic appeared on her face as she started to back away. Orry blocked her lunge for the door.

'What do you *want*?'

'Just what I said: I want you to bring him round.'

'But—'

'Now, please.'

'I can't do that.'

Orry raised the disruptor. 'Don't make me zap you, doc.'

Rellis straightened. 'Do what you like. I'm not going to prescribe anything without his medical notes. He may have an underlying cardiac condition, comorbidity – anything . . .'

Orry was beginning to wish she'd kept Naumov's pistol. However much she disliked guns, there was no doubt they commanded compliance more effectively than a disruptor.

The two women stared at each other. Eventually, Orry sighed. 'I'm sorry.'

'For wha—?'

The doctor jerked as Orry hit her with the disruptor, and

slumped to the deck. Regretfully, Orry started unfastening her dress.

She'd rather liked Senior Physick Rellis.

Ten minutes later, and feeling far less vulnerable in Rellis' coat, Orry wheeled Mender's gurney into an ambulance bay. She was a little worried about the old man; he should have come round by now.

Six sleek torpedoes, each painted with red and white stripes spiralling from one conical end to the other, were stacked above each other like bullets in a clip. The lowest rested just clear of a transit slot in the deck – and Orry realised the ambulances were actually modified transit capsules. The polished hulls gleamed in the bay's actinic light as she wheeled Mender's bed towards the unit at the bottom of the giant clip.

Harry? Have you figured it out yet?

Yes, I think so. Are you ready?

Almost. Wait one.

She pressed the actuator at the rear of the ambulance hopefully and grinned as the rear cone split apart and a ramp extended to where she was standing. She pushed Mender's gurney inside and locked its wheels as the rear door closed. There was plenty of room inside; even with all the medical equipment, she reckoned there was probably space for another two or three gurneys if you stacked them end to end.

Okay, go. She held her breath, praying her plan would work. She waited a few seconds, then frowned. *Have you done it?*

Yup. Anything?

No. She stared at the ambulance's main control panel. The

capsule was automated, but it had been fitted with back-up manual controls. *What did you do, exactly?*

Even over the integuary, he sounded sniffy. *I reported a casualty in Dock 19, just like you said.*

And what did they say?

It was a dumb system. It just told me help is on the way. Are you sure you're in the right bay?

The ambulance shuddered and the control panel lit up. *Hang on*, she sent, staring at one of the screens, now displaying a course through the tangle of transit tubes. *Something's happening.* She felt the ambulance sink into the deck and dropped into a seat. It was moving far faster than the others they'd taken. She grabbed Mender's bed to steady herself as the capsule sped away.

Orry?

It's fine, we're moving. She scanned the course again and tried to relax. *Should be with you in a couple of minutes.*

There was no reply.

Harry?

I hope you get here soon, he sent back. *We've got company.*

The ambulance rose into Civil Dock 19, and as the rear door opened Orry heard the wail of sirens.

Harry ducked into the capsule. 'Hurry,' he said, grabbing one end of Mender's gurney and pulling. The old man groaned as the wheels clattered onto the deck.

Orry jumped down and bent over him. 'Mender?' she called urgently, 'can you hear me?'

His eyelids fluttered.

Get him inside, sent *Jane*. *I've managed to seal the dock, but it's only a matter of time before they override the locks. I'm reading multiple heat sources out there.*

Orry grabbed the back of the gurney and pushed it towards the ship, only then noticing Dyas seated on the ramp, watching her with a faintly amused expression.

'You found the old bastard then?'

A clang echoed through the dock and a voice shouted from behind her, 'Don't fucking move!'

She turned to see auxiliaries pouring through an open door, weapons levelled at her.

'Go!' Harry yelled. He shot Naumov's pistol into the air, then dived behind the ambulance as the auxiliaries returned fire. Low-velocity bullets thrummed past Orry and flattened themselves on *Dainty Jane*'s hull.

Blood pounding in her ears, she pushed as hard as she could, sending the gurney bouncing up the ramp and into the freight lock, where Dyas was now huddled in a corner.

'Harry – get in here!' she cried as the intensity of the gunfire outside increased.

I can't move – they'll cut me to pieces! He was trying not to sound terrified, she could tell.

Leave it to me, sent *Jane* calmly. There was a whirr from somewhere outside the ship, followed by a series of concussive thuds. Canisters sailed across the dock, bounced off the bulkhead behind the auxiliaries and started emitting great quantities of smoke.

Harry, run! Orry sent.

A bullet smacked into Mender's bed as Harry threw himself into the freight lock and another ricocheted off the rising ramp to bury itself in a control panel, which fizzed and spat in protest.

The outer door closed.

29

PICK THE SMALLEST

Dainty Jane's engines were already spooling up when Orry dropped into the right-hand seat, flinching as small-arms fire rattled off the canopy. She hooked the avionics core and called up the external lenses, which showed a combat spider scuttling into the dock. The comm stack was flashing insistently, but she ignored it; the last thing she needed right now was to have to deal with a slew of increasingly angry messages from the dock authority and *Justiciar*'s operations room.

How's Mender? she asked Harry as her mind and hands flew, manually activating some systems while handling others via her integuary.

Coming round slowly.

Chuck a bucket of water over him or something, will you? I need help up here.

You want me to come up?

No, just keep an eye on Dyas. Oh – and find an acceleration shell: this could get hairy.

Dainty Jane vibrated as her engines came online.

'Can I make a suggestion?' the ship said.

'Please do.'

'Let me handle the flying. You look after the weapons.'

'Uh, I'm a better pilot than a gunner, *Jane*.'

'Please, Orry.'

'Do you need me at all?' Orry asked testily, watching the combat spider unlimber a cutting torch as it approached the ship.

'Yes, on the weapons.'

'Fine. Weapons it is.' She hooked *Jane*'s tactical core.

Locating a point-defence carronade, she targeted the spider. There was a *burp* and the auxiliaries took cover as the spider disintegrated in a whirling cloud of submunitions.

She felt her stomach sink as *Jane* triggered a lifting burn. The cockpit sphere rotated to keep her facing forward while the ship swung smoothly round and accelerated away, transitioning into horizontal flight.

A high-pitched warble filled the cockpit as they cleared the dock and soared into *Justiciar*'s vast internal well, its curving walls perforated with hundreds of similar dock apertures. The opposite side of the well had to be a kilometre away at least.

'Brace!' *Jane* warned, and the ship juddered under multiple impacts. Orry spotted a gun battery projecting from the cliff-like wall beneath the dock, but they were out of range before she could target it.

'What the hell are you doing to my ship?' Mender growled, staggering into the cockpit. He sank into his seat and glared at her. 'I have the weapons.'

'You have weapons,' she confirmed. 'What can I do?'

'Stand by on countermeasures in case the smart defence fails.'

She switched her focus to the defence core. 'Wow,' she said after a moment, impressed by the multitude of defensive measures at her fingertips.

'Take a closer look,' *Jane* replied. She sounded distracted, if that was possible.

When Orry delved a little deeper, she realised what *Jane* meant. The warship would have been extremely well protected in her day, but technology had moved on over the centuries and many of her systems were now obsolete, of use only against similarly outdated weapons. And the things that *were* still useful, like flares and anti-beam chaff, were severely depleted.

'Don't you ever replenish?' she demanded, but Mender ignored her.

The wall behind them tilted and fell away as *Jane* engaged her main drives, hurling the ship into an arc that would take them up and out of *Justiciar*'s internal void.

'Watch it!' Mender yelled as they shot over a cumbersome water tender being nudged towards a victualling dock by a pair of tugs.

Orry grunted as the ship swept into a crushing high-g turn, then the pressure eased – only to return from a different direction and with greater intensity. Her acceleration shell snapped flat and her vision greyed as *Jane* began a rib-crushing series of manoeuvres, throwing herself between the other vessels traversing *Justiciar*'s docks as the growing circle of stars that marked the exit from the super-titan's bowels rushed towards them. This time, Orry was prepared when her shell plunged her into darkness. The mesophase gel transitioned into liquid and she drew it into her lungs with only the briefest sensation of panic.

She hooked the external lenses in time to see the walls of *Justiciar*'s internal well vanish, replaced by boundless space. As the vast ship shrank behind them, *Jane* altered course yet again, now streaking for the gap between two of the escorting destroyers. Mender was spooling up the postselection drive, but the super-titan's mass was so great it was acting like a miniature moon – they would need to clear most of the surrounding command group before they were free of its gravity and could initiate a collapse.

Sirens blared and warnings appeared as multiple fire directors fixed on *Jane*. Kaleidoscopic fans of light – energy weapons discharging from *Justiciar*'s hull – flickered around them as *Jane* twisted and darted through clouds of silver streamers.

Orry watched the chaff dispensers count down towards zero as the destroyers loomed closer. The stern dispenser ran out first, and the forward dispenser was red-lining – when the energy barrage ceased abruptly.

Jane halted her defensive manoeuvres and concentrated on getting clear of *Justiciar*'s mass.

What's happening? Orry asked. *Why have they stopped firing?* They were abeam the nearest destroyer now, as close as their winding course would take them to the warship.

They haven't, Mender sent grimly, and she saw *Jane*'s point-defence systems start firing.

Six sparks of light rippled away from the destroyer: missiles which rapidly gained on them, despite *Jane*'s brutal acceleration. Tiny turrets around *Jane*'s stern seeded the void behind her with hundreds of golf ball-sized submunitions; a second later, the lead missile was torn apart, its debris detonating further munitions which destroyed the following two missiles.

The next line of defence, an electromagnetic pulse intended to fry guidance systems, was too old to overcome the hardened systems of the three remaining missiles, which were rapidly reducing the distance between them. *Jane* switched to low-yield tachyon beams, which washed harmlessly over two of the smart missiles when they deployed their own countermeasures. The third was not so fortunate; when it exploded in a blinding flash, Orry felt *Jane* lurch and realised just how close the missiles were.

Dainty Jane opened up her last line of defence and the rapid-fire slug-throwers instantly tore the lead missile apart. The final projectile lasted another three seconds, but that was long enough for it to get within twenty metres of *Jane*'s hull and Orry watched in alarm as its nose cone opened like a flower and discharged a cloud of submunitions an instant before the stream of slugs ripped through its fuselage.

She braced herself as a sound like hailstones striking a tin roof filled the cockpit. Alarms blared and *Dainty Jane* rocked wildly.

Damage report! Mender sent as shrieking alerts appeared in Orry's vision, but she was already on it, trying to make sense of what she was seeing.

Looks like it struck portside, she told him. *Compartments have sealed right through the ship – I'm seeing hard vacuum in two of them—* She stopped suddenly, panic rising. *Harry? Harry? Answer me!*

Just two? Mender interrupted, and she waited, hardly breathing.

That was intense, Harry sent.

Orry felt like something had released in her chest. *Are you okay?*

We're fine – we both got to shells in time.

Forget about your boyfriend, Mender sent, *and take a look outside. We're not out of the woods yet.*

He was right: ships were converging on them from all directions. She did a quick count: two frigates, a corvette and a sloop, together with a slew of smaller craft. *Dainty Jane* was caught in a fast-shrinking net.

What do we do?

Pick the smallest one and head right for her, Mender answered. For reasons Orry couldn't begin to fathom, he actually sounded excited.

You're enjoying this, aren't you?

Beats the hell out of being drugged and chained to a bed. He was still studying the approaching ships. *That one*, he said, bracketing one of the oncoming vessels on the distributed tactical display, and *Jane* immediately altered course.

Orry disregarded the reams of data scrolling past and focused on the distant glint of light ahead, which resolved into a squat, barrel-shaped craft closing on them at high speed. *What type is it*, Jane?

A fast patrol monitor: crew of three, armed with long-range protein lasers and mass drivers.

Sounds like a handful. How long till we can collapse?

Not until we're past it.

The cockpit flickered red as a fan of laser light pulsed from the approaching monitor and warning icons shimmered in Orry's vision. *Why aren't we doing anything?* she demanded.

We're almost out of chaff, Mender told her. *What do you suggest we do?*

Can't we manoeuvre?

That'll slow us down.

So what are we going to do? She fought to keep herself calm.

We ride it out. Relax, girl. Me and Jane *have seen a lot worse.*

Not with me on board, you haven't.

Mender's chuckle was cut short as *Dainty Jane* shuddered and a cloud of particles drifted past the canopy.

Not good, he sent.

Orry felt *Jane*'s vernier thrusters fire and the distant monitor tracked left until she was looking at it through the side of the canopy: *Jane* was now crabbing sideways towards the attacking craft.

What happened? she asked.

One of the thermoceramic plates under the cockpit is cracked, Jane answered. *I've moved it out of alignment.*

The ship shuddered again. More particles rose past the canopy and Orry's integuary showed the forward cannon spinning up. *What are you doing?* she asked Mender. *There are three people on that ship!*

If that armour gives out they'll gut us, he pointed out.

We're out of our mass driver's effective range, Jane sent calmly.

Just giving them something to think about.

A stream of slugs spat from *Jane*'s nose, motes of light floating towards the monitor. Compared with the near-instantaneous flashes of the energy beams, the hyper-velocity slugs seemed to crawl between the two ships, but the fan of energy started to stutter as the monitor began evasive manoeuvres.

Mender stopped firing. *Suckers,* he sent with satisfaction.

As if they'd heard him, the laser fusillade resumed with new intensity.

Screw this! Mender sent chaff spewing from the forward dispenser, and Orry watched the counter tick down to zero. For a few seconds she thought the chaff might be working as the strips of foil interfered with the beams, reflecting and attenuating them – but there wasn't enough of the stuff, and just a few moments later the lasers had begun finding their way through the thinning cloud and were striking the damaged hull plates again.

At this rate we're never going to get close enough to return fire—

She could sense Mender's frustration – then her heart began to race as something occurred to her and she called up *Jane*'s schematics. It was a matter of seconds to locate the waste processing system. Jane, *can you position yourself so the waste outlet vent is pointing towards the monitor?*

Yes, but—

Just do it, please.

The ship began to roll, and Mender sent, *Good thinking, girl, but you get to hose my ship down afterwards.*

If we get out of this in one piece, I'll be happy to.

As *Jane*'s roll slowed, Orry vented the waste tanks.

The beams lost coherence as they hit the dirty slick now floating between the two ships; instead of punching through it and straight into *Dainty Jane*, they made swirls in the sludge and dissipated harmlessly.

Jane rolled back to her original orientation. *Ten seconds to gun range*, she said.

Will it be enough? Orry asked.

Should be, Mender confirmed as he spun up the nose cannon again. *Well done.*

She smiled – until red lights illuminated in the cockpit. She braced herself, the laserfire ceased and *Jane* began jinking violently. The two vessels were seconds apart now, and through her integuary she could see the monitor's twin turrets sending streams of slugs their way and feel the impacts on *Jane*'s hull. *Why isn't Mender firing?* she wondered, staring at the monitor's barrel-like hull filling the canopy.

At last the mass driver under the cockpit fired, the super-dense slugs stitching a line across the monitor's grey hull. The enemy ship's running lights went out and its cockpit darkened. As they shot past the vessel, Orry saw its own mass drivers drooping in their turrets.

Mender let out a whoop.

Will they be okay? she asked.

Sure. I just hit their energy exchanger. Ship's dead, but they've got enough O2 to keep them alive until help arrives. Might get a little chilly, mind.

Torpedoes incoming, Jane announced.

Mender laughed. *Too late, my friends.* Jane, *get us out of here.*

With pleasure.

Orry's stomach turned over.

'Where's my brother?'

Dyas spat on the deck. 'You sound like a parrot, love.' He adopted a strident, mocking tone. *'Where's my brother?'*

Mender started forward, his arm raised, but Orry grabbed him and held him back. Harry, standing beside her, glared at Dyas, who was chained to a pipe in *Dainty Jane*'s cargo bay.

'You're not really in a position to bargain,' she said.

'I disagree.' Dyas managed a chuckle, but sweat was beading his forehead and Orry could tell he wasn't as calm as he looked. 'Your brother is still alive – bruised, but alive. Jericho wanted to gut him, but after the Shattermoon I figured if you caught up with us again it might be useful to have some insurance. Looks like I was right. If you want to see Ethan again in one piece, you'll let me go.'

Hands on her hips, she regarded him. 'No,' she said flatly.

Harry's rapier scraped from its scabbard and Dyas flinched as the point dug into the skin beneath his jaw.

'Easy!' he cried as Harry forced his head back, exposing the vein throbbing in his throat. He swallowed – carefully – and said, 'You kill me and the boy will die all alone on that big ship. How long can he last without water? Three days? Four? The clock's ticking . . .'

'Give me five minutes with this bastard,' Mender growled, 'and I'll make him talk.'

Dyas twisted his head a little to look at him. 'Oh, I'll talk all right,' he said with a nasty smile. 'Is that really what you want?'

'Forget it, Dyas,' Orry said wearily. Her head was killing her. 'Mender already told me about you and him.'

The raider's strained smile slipped. 'I can see you're a forgiving person,' he said. 'Just let me go and you can have your brother and your ship back.'

'It's not as simple as that.'

He frowned. 'Why not?' he started – then a look of realisation crossed his face and for the first time he looked genuinely worried. 'Ah. Roag. Well, looks like you've got a tough choice to make, then, 'cause I ain't talking.'

Harry's hand twitched, and the blade did too, stopping a centimetre from Dyas' right eye.

He became very still, then hissed, 'Go ahead, boy, do it – I can always get a fancy new eye like Mender.'

Orry placed her hand on Harry's and he lowered his sword.

'Well, if you'd rather die than return my brother, perhaps it's time for Plan B,' she said, ignoring a roll of Mender's eyes. She was glad he was standing where Dyas couldn't see him. 'How well do you know Roag's rig?' she asked the raider.

He frowned at the unexpected question. 'Well enough. I lived there for months.'

'Good,' she said. 'Then perhaps there is a way for you to earn your freedom.'

30

GRIFFIN'S YARD

Bonaventure's familiar smell, a reassuring blend of machine oil and ozone, filled Orry's nose as she floated out of the airlock. 'Ethan!' she yelled, his name echoing through the freighter's cavernous holds. She waited, heart in her throat.

'Here!' a faint voice croaked.

Dispensing with her molly hooks, she launched herself from the bulkhead and sailed towards the inner hold, where she found Ethan tethered to a cargo tie-down with a length of high-tensile cable. The pathetic, swaying figure anchored to the deck by his boots was staring at her in disbelief. One side of his face was discoloured with purpling bruises.

She used a handhold to change course and in one movement landed clumsily in front of him and enveloped him in her arms, squeezing until she feared she might snap him in two.

'Easy, Sis,' he croaked, then smiled weakly at her.

'Drink slowly,' she ordered, handing him a bulb of water, and while he ignored her and started guzzling greedily, she crouched down and used the code Dyas had given her to release the cable-lock around his ankle.

'You found the bastard, then?' he said eventually. 'I didn't know if you'd even heard me.'

'We found him. How badly are you injured?'

He flinched as she touched his face. 'I'll be fine once I have some food and a shower.'

She wrinkled her nose. 'In that order?'

He stiffened. 'See how you smell after you've been chained up in a hold for fuck knows how long!'

'Sorry—'

'No, I'm sorry.' He rubbed a filthy hand over his face. 'I guess I'm kinda strung out.' He stared at the deck. 'After Dad ... When I saw that bastard shoot you out of the airlock ...' He looked up, eyes shining with tears.

'It's okay,' she said, and hugged him again, stroking the back of his head like Katerina used to, her own cheeks damp against his hair.

He broke off and gave her a watery smile. 'Look at us. Dad'd be blowing chunks.'

She laughed and wiped her eyes.

His face hardened. 'What happened to Dyas?' he asked. 'I hope you killed that bastard and his bloody robot.'

'Not exactly,' Orry said.

'What does that mean?'

'Hey there!' Dyas said from behind her, and she turned to see him floating into the inner hold, Mender and Harry drifting behind him. They were both armed.

'I told you to keep him aboard *Jane*!' she yelled.

'Yeah?' Mender said angrily. 'Well, there's a slight problem with that.'

'What problem?' she asked, getting worried.

'*Jane*'s venting oxygen – fast.'

Orry frowned. 'She said she was okay.'

'Well, she ain't any more. We need to get her to a pressure dock.'

'Sis?' Ethan asked quietly. 'Who are these people, and why are they with the man who murdered Dad?'

'In a moment,' she said, then turned back to Mender. 'So what do we do?'

'I know a guy,' he said. 'Name of Edison Griffin. He'll fix *Jane* right up.'

'What about Roag? She said we had three days – by my reckoning those things in our heads are just about ready to pop.'

'Relax. She'll have built in some wriggle-room.'

'How much?'

'Another day or so? We have time.'

'Rama, Mender! I hope you're right.'

'I am. We can fine-tune your plan while *Jane*'s being repaired. Can you get this bucket running? *Jane* can fly herself to Griffin's Yard, but it won't exactly be a comfortable trip.'

'Hold on,' Orry said, '*you* want a lift on *my* ship?' She smiled. 'Now that's an interesting development, don't you think?'

'Don't be a pain in my arse, girl.'

'Uh, she's *our* ship,' Ethan pointed out, but they both ignored him.

'Because, you know,' Orry continued, 'that on my ship *I'm* the skipper. Not you.' She pointed towards *Dainty Jane*. 'Your ship's out there.' She jabbed a finger at the deck. 'This is *my* ship.'

Mender gave a heavy sigh and drifted past her, heading for the axial companionway. 'Cabins up here, are they?' he muttered. He paused at the foot of the ladder and told Harry, 'Chain that weasel up.'

'We had a deal!' Dyas protested.

'You're still alive,' Mender growled. 'Now shut up, all of you. You're giving me a goddamn headache.' He pulled himself up the companionway.

'Is he always like that?' Ethan asked.

'Yes,' Orry and Harry said together.

'He does grow on you,' she admitted.

'Like genital warts,' Harry added. He waved at Ethan. 'Nice to meet you at last. I'm Harry.'

'And that was Mender,' Orry said, indicating the companionway he'd disappeared up. She tried not to look at the melted section of deck near it, thankful that Dyas had at least removed her father's body. Her happiness at being reunited with her brother was suddenly overwhelmed by leaden guilt.

'So,' Ethan said, 'I have a question. Why is this murdering scumbag aboard our ship?'

'To be fair, I only murdered one person,' Dyas said. 'You're still alive, aren't you, whiny little bitch—'

'Tie him up, Harry,' Orry said. 'And gag him.'

'With pleasure.'

'Come on,' she told her brother. 'I'll bring you up to speed.'

The space around Griffin's Yard looked like the aftermath of a naval engagement. As Orry manoeuvred *Bonaventure* between derelict hulks and floating fragments of wreckage, she found herself wondering where they'd travelled, how they'd met their fates.

All roads through the maze of derelicts led to the extraordinary construction at its centre. It had been built as an escort carrier, Orry decided, although clearly long since decommissioned. As if the huge, box-like vessel wasn't already large enough, sections of other ships – hyper-tankers, bulk-haulers, even a liner – had been added to the old carrier. Docking arms extended like the booms of an ancient satellite.

An incoming audio transmission flashed up and she shunted it to the bridge speakers.

'Welcome! Welcome,' a jovial voice said. '*Jane* tells me you're in a spot of bother.'

'Hello, Griffin,' Mender replied. 'How's business?'

'About to pick up, it seems. I'm lighting up Arm 6. See you shortly.'

Up ahead, lights illuminated on one of the long arms and Orry fired the verniers to get *Bonaventure* into position. She watched *Dainty Jane* sail past the arm, venting a trail of frozen gas behind her as she headed straight for the carrier's hangar deck. The door closed behind the ship and she concentrated on lining up *Bonaventure*'s dorsal lock with the docking arm.

Ten minutes later, goosebumps rising beneath the thin fabric of her flight suit, she drifted up and out into the frigid air of the dimly lit docking arm. *It must be close to freezing*, she thought as she joined Mender, who floated nearby, talking to a remarkable-looking man.

Edison Griffin was a compact figure with biomechanical limbs replacing his legs. Orry wondered if he'd lost them in an accident or chosen to have them removed – after all, legs were worse than useless in permanent zero-g. In place of eyes he sported black lenses, and his lips had been neatly stitched around a tube leading to the rebreather affixed to his chest.

Griffin came to a graceful halt in front of her. 'What vision is this?' he exclaimed, his modulated voice coming from somewhere within his chest.

She smiled. 'Is that how you greet all your clients?' Moisture condensed in the air as she spoke.

'Only the beautiful ones.' The skin around Griffin's eye lenses creased with amusement. 'I am crushed, though. Mender tells me you're practically engaged to a nobleman.' He moved back a little as Harry floated up into the docking arm. 'Is this the lucky man?'

'What?' Harry asked, seeing everyone's attention on him.

'You don't want to believe everything Mender tells you,' she informed Griffin, giving Mender a hard stare.

'My heart soars,' he replied. 'Perhaps we can discuss this further over dinner?'

'Are my friends and my brother invited too?' she asked lightly as Ethan followed Harry out of the airlock.

'Good idea,' Mender said, 'I'm parched.'

'I said *my friends*,' she commented dryly, and Griffin burst out laughing.

'I like her!' He slapped Mender on the back, which sent the old man rolling. 'About time you brought someone interesting to see me, Mender. So, let's talk business.'

He led the way to the escort carrier's hangars: five decks high and stretching the entire length of the old ship, with enormous internal doors used to pressurise each hangar individually during flight operations. Right now all the doors stood open, creating a huge space littered with a variety of craft. Components were stacked high on shelving that ran for kilometres, with larger modules looming on individual pallets. Orry spotted a bewildering variety of weapons and ammunition.

'One of my projects,' Griffin said as they passed a long-range scout. The sleek vessel was clearly undergoing a custom paint job, orange and red flames spilling back from its nose.

Dainty Jane, in contrast, looked a sorry state, her hull plating cracked, her paintwork blackened. They floated up to examine her upper hull, where an entire section of plates was missing around the cockpit, leaving the honeycomb structure of her inner frame exposed.

'Oh, *Jane*,' Orry said out loud, 'does it hurt?' She clamped her mouth shut as she saw Ethan and Harry looking at her oddly.

Not in the way you mean, the ship replied on a private channel. *It's certainly uncomfortable.*

'Uh, who are you talking to?' Ethan asked.

Orry decided this wasn't the best time for introductions. 'Can you fix her?' she asked Griffin as he drifted over *Jane*'s hull, examining the damage.

'I can fix anything, my dear. The question is, can you afford it?'

'How much are we talking?' Mender asked.

Griffin's voice box made a fair approximation of sucking in his breath. A section of crumbling thermoceramic armour snapped off when he prodded it. He shook his head. 'How quickly do you want it done?'

'Tomorrow,' Mender said. 'We have an appointment to keep.'

'Tomorrow! Can your appointment be delayed?'

'It's with Roag.'

Griffin's body stiffened. 'I thought you'd washed your hands of that evil woman.'

'So did I. She had different ideas.'

Griffin glided closer. 'Are you in trouble?'

268

'You could say that,' Mender said.

'She put biomites in our heads,' Orry explained. 'If we're not back on her rig in time she'll fry our brains.'

Griffin snorted as though this were to be expected of a woman like Roag. 'What does she want?'

'It doesn't matter.'

'And do you really believe she'll remove the biomites if you give her what she wants?'

'No,' Mender muttered, but Orry glared at him.

'We have a plan,' she said.

'Does your plan involve screwing her over?' Griffin asked.

'You could say that.'

He thought for a moment. 'The repairs won't come cheap. How much have you got?'

'Nothing,' Mender said.

Griffin stared at him.

'That's not quite true,' Orry said, pulling out a gilt chip. She had been amazed to find the family hoard intact aboard *Bonaventure*. Ethan hadn't been happy, until she'd told him everything Mender had done for her. 'Will this cover it?' she asked.

Griffin examined the amount on the chip, then sighed and slipped it into a pocket. 'Not even close, but I suppose it will have to do.'

'Thank you,' she said.

'I do have one condition.'

'Go on,' she said cautiously.

'You stick it to that bitch real good.'

Orry smiled. 'I intend to.'

'Now go and get something to eat – Mender knows the way. There are cabins, if you want a break from your ship.'

'Aren't you going to join us?'

'I regret not. It appears I have a rush job on.'

The forward half of a dilapidated Consolidated Spaceways star-liner jutted from one side of the old escort carrier. Not yet ready for the memories lurking in her cabin on *Bonaventure*, Orry spent a restless night swaying in a freefall bag tethered to the threadbare carpet of what had once been a first-class stateroom in the ancient liner. Its faded opulence depressed her.

The headache that had started on *Justiciar* grew steadily worse through the night, a throbbing background burr that matched the sick fear in her stomach. She tried not to think about what was happening inside her skull, instead listening to Ethan snoring gently on the far side of the cabin. A few days ago, voluntarily sharing a cabin would have been unthinkable. Tonight, by unspoken consent, they had chosen to be together.

Orry rose early, leaving her brother sleeping. Too twisted up inside to eat, she made her way down to the hangar deck, stepping carefully over the power cables secured to the scarred deck. She found Mender buried to his waist in an open compartment in *Dainty Jane*'s starboard nacelle. Multi-armed mechs were swarming over the hull, applying finishing touches to the new plating. Sparks danced around thermic torches, tiny glowing spheres that drifted and died. Canisters of chaff were being loaded into the dispenser chutes.

'She's looking great,' Orry said.

A thud was followed by a muffled curse from inside the nacelle, then Mender slithered out, rubbing his head. He gave her a sour look, his one bloodshot eye glaring.

'Sorry,' she said. 'Have you been here all night?'

'Couldn't sleep,' he grunted, then tapped his forehead in just the spot where her headache was worst.

Griffin appeared high above them, near *Jane*'s bulging canopy. 'Good morning!' he called. 'Fully rested, I trust?'

'Much better,' Orry lied. 'I can't believe you've finished.'

'I've patched her up well enough. I just wish I had more time.' The spacer floated a little closer, his lower limbs folded up and out of the way. '*Jane*'s a classic,' he said, 'a real piece of history. Why she chose to team up with this miserable old geezer I will never know.' He slapped one of the gleaming new hull plates. 'You hear me in there?'

'I hear you, Griff,' *Jane* replied, her voice booming from her external speakers.

'When are you going to let me work my magic on you?' he asked. 'You won't find anyone with more original Goethen parts than me. Give me a few months and I'll have you back in showroom condition.' He caressed the curve of her starboard nacelle. 'Don't worry, I'll be gentle.'

Jane laughed uneasily. 'I'll think about it.'

'That's what you always say,' Griff said grumpily, then, perking up, he turned to Orry and clapped his hands. 'Come with me!'

She released her molly hooks and floated up to join him. A pattern of twelve iris valves each a metre in diameter stippled a wide area near the edge of *Dainty Jane*'s upper hull.

'Show her,' Griff told the ship.

'I don't think she'll be interested,' *Jane* replied, and then sighed. 'Oh, very well.'

One of the circles rasped open to reveal the pointed nose of a harpoon.

'There!' Griffin said proudly. 'What do you think?'

Orry was puzzled; she wasn't sure what he expected her to say. She ran a hand over the nose cone. Unlike most kinetic harpoons designed for extra-atmospheric use, it came to a sharp aerodynamic point. 'It's ... uh ... very nice. I'm sure it will be useful when Mender feels the urge to murder a ship full of people.'

'No, no, no,' Griff said. He sounded excited. 'You don't understand. Look more closely.'

'At what?' she asked, more sharply than she'd intended. Weariness and a throbbing head were making her snappy. 'It's a harpoon.'

Griffin's voice box made a snorting noise. 'It's *pointy*,' he said, and looked expectantly at her.

'So . . .'

'For *penetration*.'

She groaned. 'Just tell me, will you, Griff?'

'It's an AODS!'

She didn't like to disappoint him, not when he'd been so helpful, but she really had no idea what he was talking about. 'A what now?'

'An Advanced Operator Delivery System. It's *original*.' He was almost bouncing with happiness.

Orry looked at the harpoon again – and suddenly got it. 'You mean it's one of those things they used to fire poor saps into the sides of enemy ships?'

'The very same,' Griff said proudly, his eyes crinkling. 'I've been restoring it.'

She shook her head. 'Why?'

'What do you mean, *why*? It's *original*.'

She pinched the bridge of her nose. 'Right. Well, I'm sure Mender will find a use for it. Maybe he can fill it with some of his crap and fire it into a star.'

'He can't do that!' Griff protested, and she suddenly felt a little guilty; he was just trying to be helpful.

'Only joking,' she managed, gritting her teeth as pain flared behind her eyes, and waved as she floated back to Mender.

'What's bitten your tits?' he asked, slamming the nacelle panel closed. He pulled out his hipflask and took a skilful sip, careful not to let any of the contents float away.

She massaged her temples. 'Does your head hurt?' she asked quietly.

'Yeah. Getting worse, too.' The hipflask sloshed as he shook it. 'And it ain't this.'

'We should get going.'

He nodded, mouth set into a grim line. 'Have you told your brother?'

'Not yet.'

'Told me what?' Ethan asked, appearing around the nacelle, one of his favourite Utzeen candy bars in one hand. He was chewing carefully, favouring the less swollen side of his jaw.

'You call that breakfast?' Orry said.

'Breakfast of champions.' He puffed out his pigeon chest and adopted a body builder's pose for a moment. 'Tell me what?'

She braced herself. 'You know we have to go and see Cordelia Roag?'

'Yeah. Let's get those bugs out of your head and get on with our lives. Can't say I'm looking forward to going there, though.'

'I wouldn't worry about it,' Mender muttered, drawing a glare from Orry.

'The thing is,' she began, then took a breath. 'Listen, Ethan: you're not coming.'

He grinned at her. 'Yeah, I am.'

'No. You're not.'

His smile faded. 'I'm coming with you,' he said firmly.

'It's too dangerous, Ethan – I've lost you once already.'

'*You* lost *me*?' he snapped. 'I watched you *die*, Orry – I'm not *ever* going through that again.'

'You won't have to. I want you to take *Bonnie* and go to Freeport, wait with Emjay until I get there.'

He folded his arms. 'Nuh-uh. No way.'

'Piotr's withered cock!' Mender growled. 'Open your fucking ears, boy. You're just a kid – nobody wants you along. You'll get yourself killed – or worse, you'll get *me* killed.'

The look on Ethan's face broke Orry's heart, but he was already turning clumsily away from her. He pushed off and went sailing across the hangar towards Arm 6 where *Bonaventure* was docked.

She started to follow but Mender grabbed her arm.

'Give the boy some time.'

She rounded on him. 'What is *wrong* with you? He's just a child!'

He shrugged. 'I got him to do what you wanted, didn't I?'

'If that's your idea of parenting, it's lucky—' She stopped, aghast at herself.

Mender stared at her.

'Shit, Mender. I'm sorry—'

He drifted over to *Jane*'s freight lock.

'Mender!' she called after him.

'Say goodbye to your brother,' he shouted back. 'We need to go.'

She watched him disappear into the ship, then swore violently.

'What did I miss?' Harry asked from behind her. He was holding an oatcake in one hand and a bulb of tea in the other. Ignoring him, she aimed herself at Arm 6 and shot off.

Harry shrugged, took another bite of his oatcake and studied *Dainty Jane*'s new hull plates admiringly.

31

MELVIN'S FRIENDS

Orry waited silently with Harry in the galley below *Dainty Jane*'s cockpit.

'Mender,' she heard Roag say over the comm. 'I was wondering when you were going to call. I see you've satisfied half of our agreement at least.'

Dyas grunted fearfully from above them; Orry had especially enjoyed binding his hands and taping his mouth shut.

'Do you have the pendant?' Roag's voice continued.

'It's safe,' Mender told her.

'Can I see it?'

'You can see it when you get this crap out of my head.'

Roag was silent for a moment. 'What about your little friend? The girl.'

'Your biomites are the least of her worries now.'

'Ah. I heard you were making a nuisance of yourselves on *Justiciar*. What happened?'

'This son of a bitch happened.' There was a slap, and a muffled grunt of pain from Dyas. 'Forget about her. She's gone.'

'I see. But you're well, I trust?'

'Cut the shit, Cordelia. We're inbound now. Get your atom-icist ready. You can have Dyas when I land, but you don't get the pendant until my head is fixed.'

'That's not what we agreed,' Roag said, her voice dangerously low.

'We didn't *agree* anything,' Mender snapped.

Roag fell silent. 'You're a suspicious man,' she said eventually. 'Very well, we'll do it your way. I'll see you soon.'

There was a moment's delay before Mender spoke again. 'It's okay, she's gone.'

Orry climbed into the cockpit.

Dyas shifted in the right-hand seat to look at her. He grunted through the tape over his mouth.

'Shut up,' she said. 'As long as you've told us the truth, you have nothing to worry about.' She leaned closer. 'You have told us the truth, haven't you?'

Dyas nodded rapidly.

'Then you've nothing to worry about.' She patted him on the head, then grimaced and wiped her palm on his shoulder. She turned to Mender. 'What do you think?'

'I think she's going to kill me the second she has the pendant.'

'Yeah, I got that, too. Does she suspect anything?'

He shrugged. 'That's the problem with Roag. You can never tell.'

The empty torpedo tube was bitterly cold. Orry edged closer to Harry, seeking his warmth. She allowed him to put an arm around her shoulders in the darkness but concentrated on what was happening outside the ship.

Dainty Jane's external lenses showed Roag and five of her

hired guns gathered outside the open freight lock. Mender stood behind the bound and gagged Dyas, gripping him by his collar.

'How's the head?' Roag asked, shouting through her rebreather to make herself heard over the howling wind.

'Hurts,' Mender told her. 'Where's your man? None of these cretins looks smart enough to dress themselves, let alone fix my head.'

'All in good time.' Roag motioned for Dyas.

'What are you going to do with him?' Mender asked.

'Why the sudden concern?'

'I just want to be sure he'll get what's coming to him.'

'It's me. Be sure.'

He hesitated. 'Mind if I watch?'

Roag stared at him. 'You never were one for torture, Mender, even before you went soft. What's changed?'

He shrugged. 'He killed my friend. She was just a kid.'

'Sure, you can watch. I'll even let you help out if that'll float your boat. Now hand him over.'

He shoved Dyas forward. Two of Roag's minders grabbed an arm each and manhandled him towards the pressure door into the rig's interior.

'The pendant,' Roag said.

Mender shook his head, tapping his forehead.

'Search him,' she snapped. 'Then his ship.'

'It's not here,' he growled, as the dark-skinned woman called Steiner took his Fabretti. 'I ain't that fucking stupid.'

Steiner ran a sensor wand over him and shook her head at Roag, who nodded and indicated *Dainty Jane*. Steiner and another man climbed the ramp to the freight lock.

'This way,' Roag told Mender.

Orry watched the old man limp after Roag to the pressure door, followed by her remaining gunhand. The three of them disappeared inside the rig.

Pad's clear, Jane told her.

What about the two on board? Orry asked.

They appear to be starting their search on the upper deck. You're clear to go.

'Ready?' she asked Harry.

'Always.'

She snapped a pair of goggles into place and fastened her rebreather over her nose and mouth, then took a deep breath. *Okay,* Jane, *open up.*

Good luck. I'll be monitoring.

An oily scraping fought with the sudden whistle of wind as the tube's door irised open. Orry shuffled on her rear towards the light, dangled her legs out of the tube and slid down the curve of *Dainty Jane*'s upper hull until she could drop to the ground. The wind caught her immediately and she staggered as she looked around, trying to get her bearings.

Harry landed cat-like behind her and she grabbed his arm and pointed past the sealed pressure door to the far edge of the pad. He nodded his understanding and they battled through the wind towards it.

A maintenance ladder fixed to the rig's side dropped dizzyingly away above the broiling clouds of Tycho IV. Far below, the ladder linked to a network of walkways.

Orry hesitated for a moment, fighting a nauseating attack of vertigo – then a sharp pain shot through her head.

She gripped the handrail and stepped onto the creaking ladder.

Melvin watched his new friends with delight. There were precisely one thousand of them on the slide, all moving with a smooth precision that filled him with joy. Of course, he knew they were merely biological machines, simple structures of no intrinsic use except as components in a larger, distributed whole, but he loved them nonetheless. After all, one could say the same of human beings.

At the sound of the door-chime he looked up from the microscope, his chest suddenly tight. The tension became worse when he checked the time on the old analogue chronometer hanging on the wall. It wasn't lunchtime yet – nowhere near.

Hesitantly, he shuffled across the lab to the door. His finger moved towards the intercom three times before he finally summoned the courage to press the button. The unit's flat screen lit up, showing a picture of a pretty girl with big eyes and spiky orange hair.

Melvin waited, just staring.

'Uh, hello?' the girl said. 'Anyone there?'

'Yes,' he told her.

'Oh, hi. I can't see you.' He waited. 'I'm looking for Melvin Sheem. Is he there?'

'Yes.'

'Great. Um, any chance I can see him?'

'No.'

'Oh. Why not?'

'I can't open the door.'

'Why not?' the girl repeated.

Melvin's heart beat faster at the thought of opening the door. 'She would be angry with me.'

'Who would? Roag?'

'Yes. Mistress Cordelia.' He squeezed his eyes shut and clasped his trembling hands together, fighting the urge to strike himself.

'But she sent me.'

He opened one eye. 'She did?'

'Yes. With a message. A very important message. For Melvin Sheem.'

He opened the other eye. 'I have a routine. You're not on the timetable.'

'No. Uh . . . Sorry?'

'Is it an exception?'

'Yes! Yes, it's very definitely an exception.'

Melvin thought for a moment. The girl really was pretty. 'I'm going to open the door,' he told her.

'Good,' she said. 'Thank you.'

She sounded pleased with him. Was she pleased? It was so difficult to tell.

He opened the door.

She walked quickly into the lab. Melvin tried to close the door but a man had put his foot there. He was tall and he carried a sword, just like the ones on the casts from the Fountainhead that Mistress Cordelia let him watch sometimes.

'No,' Melvin told the tall man, shuffling forward.

'Relax, old boy.' The man stepped around him and sauntered into the lab.

Into *his* lab! 'No!' Melvin said again, more loudly, and stumbled after him.

The girl smiled at him, and he stopped. 'It's okay,' she said. 'I'm Orry, and this is Harry. We're friends.'

And then she touched him.

Melvin moaned, and his fists started thudding into his face and skull.

'Oh Rama!' he heard the girl say. 'Stop – *please!*'

Melvin's fists beat harder as the anxiety took control. *They can't be here! They have to go—*

'*No-no-no-no-no-no-no!*' he moaned.

'Please,' the girl said again, but he couldn't hear her.

'*No-no-no-no-no,*' he repeated.

'Let me try,' the man said.

'I don't think—'

The man with the sword was standing in front of him. 'Melvin?' he said calmly. 'You are Melvin, aren't you?'

'You can't be here,' Melvin moaned.

'My name is Harry. Melvin! Can you hear me?'

'Go-go-go-go-go-go!'

'*Hands down, Melvin!*'

Melvin stopped and looked at the man. The way he'd spoken – it was just like Mistress Cordelia.

'Why don't you show me what you're working on,' the man with the sword said. 'It looks very interesting.'

Melvin lowered his hands and looked over at the microscope. 'You won't understand.'

The man smiled in a kind way. 'Maybe not, but I'd like to see anyway.'

Melvin shuffled to his desk uncertainly.

'Stout fellow,' the man said.

32

ANTIBODIES

Mender watched Roag settle into the chair behind her desk and pour herself a drink. The purple light of Tycho IV was streaming through the panoramic window behind her and prisming through the decanter's multifaceted crystal. She waved it at Mender. 'Want one?'

'I'll pass.'

She chuckled and looked over at Dyas, who was hanging from a hook in the centre of the room, his arms strung above his head, feet scraping the floor. He'd kept up a constant grunting from behind the tape over his mouth, trying to gain Roag's attention. That wasn't what he'd agreed to back on *Dainty Jane*, and that made Mender uneasy. All Dyas had to do was hang there quietly and keep his mouth shut until Orry had completed her part of the plan. It was beginning to look like he had other ideas.

Seeing Roag looking at him, Dyas thrashed his body about. Mender swore under his breath.

'He seems very worked up,' Roag said with a smile. 'Shall we ask him what's the matter?'

Mender shrugged. 'Do what you want. Personally, I've heard enough of his whining.' He tried to think of a change of subject but small talk had never been his strong point. The natural thing to do in this situation would be demand to see Roag's atomicist, but that was the one thing he couldn't do; he needed to buy Orry time. If she were here in his place, she'd doubtless come up with some clever delaying tactic in an instant, but his pounding headache was making it difficult to think straight. To his surprise, he found himself wishing Orry *was* with him.

Roag was staring at Dyas.

'How's this going to play out then?' Mender asked quickly.

'What do you mean?'

His Fabretti was out of reach on the far side of Roag's wide desk. He leaned back in his chair and placed his boots on the desk's lacquered surface, increasing his distance from the pistol, trying to set her at ease. Reaching into an inside pocket, he found his crumpled packet of cheroots. He tapped one into his hand, lit it and drew deeply.

'I mean,' he said, 'are you going to cure me and then kill me once I've handed over the pendant, or just torture me to find out where it is?'

'What makes you think I won't just cure you?'

'I can't see your atomicist anywhere.'

'All in good time.' She sipped at her drink. 'Tell me about the pendant.'

'It's safe.'

Roag set her glass down and stood. She wandered over to Dyas. 'It's not that I don't believe you, Mender. It's just that . . . I don't believe you.'

She ripped the tape from Dyas' mouth.

'He's playing you,' the raider blurted immediately. 'His bitch is down with Melvin right now.'

If Mender was good at anything, it was hiding his emotions. He laughed.

'Something funny?' Roag asked quietly, reaching into a pocket.

He blew a plume of smoke and stared out of the window, his artificial heart pounding. 'That rat will say anything to save his hide,' he said dismissively.

'It's the truth!' Dyas whined.

'If it is true,' Roag said to him, 'how did Mender and the girl even know about Melvin? How could they *possibly* know where to find him?'

'I told them!' Dyas cried desperately. 'We made a deal! They promised to get me out of here if I helped them—'

'Bullshit,' Mender said calmly.

Roag ignored him. 'Why the change of heart?' she asked Dyas.

'I fucked up!' he said, tears running down his cheeks. 'I know I did – but give me another chance, *please* – I'll never let you down again.'

Mender eyed the Fabretti, playing out the next few seconds in his head.

'He sounds pretty convincing to me,' Roag said reasonably. 'Perhaps I should check everything is all right in the lab.'

'You do that,' Mender said. 'And while you're at it, get your atomicist up here.'

'All right,' she said. 'I will.'

As she started towards the comm screen set into the wall,

Mender swung his legs off the desk and hurled himself over it on his belly, arms outstretched. His hand had just closed around the Fabretti when agony split his skull, turning the room white. A thousand razors sliced at his head, flaying open flesh, shredding nerves. The Fabretti thudded to the ground as Mender writhed on the desk, clawing at his head. The decanter shattered, its noise lost beneath his screams.

After an eternity of agony, the pain lessened.

He blinked rapidly, clenching his teeth, as a figure swam into view. His mouth was filled with the taste of metal.

The figure resolved itself into Roag, who was holding up a small device, a black ovoid. Her thumb slid over a dial on its surface and Mender's head split again, forcing a scream from him. Gradually, the pain faded, reducing to mere agony.

'You make me want to puke,' she told him. 'To think I used to be scared of you. *You!* When I wasn't scared of anyone. *No one* could take what I'd built – except you. And look at you now.'

'Fuuuuuuu—' Mender managed.

She cupped her ear. 'What's that, old man?'

'Fuuuuu—'

She shook her head. 'Save your breath, I get the idea. Now you wait here while I go and fetch your little girlfriend, and then we'll talk about my pendant.'

The wallscreen chimed. Roag glanced at the caller ident and her jaw tightened. She looked thoughtfully at Mender for a moment before accepting the call.

The rhinocerine face of a Kadiran alpha male appeared on the screen.

Cold shock penetrated the pulsing waves of agony that were still coursing through Mender's skull.

'What is it?' Roag snapped at the alpha. 'I'm in the middle of something.'

Mender shuddered as dead eyes set beneath bony ridges rested briefly on him. The vivid crimson crest extending from the Kadiran's armoured head was wider than its powerful shoulders.

The alpha's mouth moved within its cage of protective bones, its rasping, guttural words muted by the comm's filters. A moment later a translation emerged from the unit, spoken in a neutral tone.

'Do you have the stone, Cordelia Roag?'

'I told you I'd let you know the moment I had it,' she replied curtly.

'Then you do not have it. Patience among the Hierarchs is wearing thin. Events have been set in motion. This is a timescale to which all must adhere.'

'I'm aware of the timescale,' Roag said, 'and I told you I'll get you the stone.'

'Should you fail to do so, the matter will be taken into our own broodhold.'

'I'll get you the stone,' she repeated in a low growl.

'Perhaps,' the Kadiran said. The screen went black.

Mender stared in disbelief. What the hell was Roag thinking, dealing with those monsters?

'Hell's teeth!' she spat, and rounded on him. She moved her thumb and his mind split once more. Tears blurred his vision; he could just about make out her tossing the remote control to one of her men.

'Watch him,' she ordered. 'You two, with me.' A section of wall opened to reveal a lift.

'What about me?' Dyas called after her.

Roag studied him for a few seconds. 'Cut him down,' she told the man holding the pain remote, then jabbed a finger at Dyas. 'You, wait here.'

The agony finally became too much for Mender, and he blacked out.

Orry watched as Melvin shuffled to the microscope; this was the last thing she'd expected. No wonder Dyas had been wearing a shit-eating grin when he'd told them how to find Melvin. She was tempted to leave the murdering bastard to Roag's tender mercies after all.

Melvin was a large man, almost as tall as Harry, but enormously fat. The childlike expression on his moon face made it difficult to judge his age, but she saw flecks of grey in his neatly trimmed black hair. He wore light blue medical scrubs and a pair of threadbare tartan slippers.

What just happened? she asked Harry.

He's on the spectrum. You just need to know how to deal with it.

Which you clearly do. How come?

I told you – my sister, Elena. He turned back to the atomicist. 'That's very good,' he said encouragingly. 'Why don't you show my friend?'

Melvin stood up. 'What do you want?' he asked.

Orry chewed her lower lip. Her plan had been a simple one: find the atomicist and scare him into removing the biomites. Somehow she didn't think that would work now, even if she could bring herself to threaten this pathetic creature.

She decided honesty was the best policy. 'We need your help, Melvin,' she said. 'I have something you made, inside my head.'

'Oh!' he said. 'Let me see.' He picked up a scanner from the desk and approached her. 'Hold still.' He stared through the scanner and beamed. 'Oh my, yes. It's *you*, isn't it?'

'Can you help me?'

He frowned. 'I don't understand.'

'Can you deactivate them?'

The frown turned to dismay. 'You want me to *kill* them?'

'If you don't, Roag will use them to kill me.'

He backed away, shaking his head. 'No – no, I couldn't.'

'What's wrong, Melvin?'

'The mistress will hurt me again.'

'It's okay,' Orry said soothingly. She looked around the lab to give her time to think. 'Do you like it here?'

'I like my work.'

'You could do your work somewhere else.'

He shook his head quickly. 'Mistress Cordelia will never let me leave. She will always look after me. She *told* me.'

'You could come with us, Melvin. I know somewhere safe where you could continue your work. Somewhere Roag – the mistress – will never find you.'

He stared at her. 'Will you be there?'

'Sometimes, yes.'

His brow creased. 'Is Harry your boyfriend?' he asked.

Orry was a little taken aback. Harry grinned broadly. 'Um, no,' she told Melvin. 'Harry isn't my boyfriend.'

'Why not? You're very pretty.'

She smiled. 'Thank you.'

'Can I be your boyfriend?'

'Oh, wow. I'm very flattered, but we've only just met.'

He looked at the floor and shuffled his slippered feet. 'If I came with you, we would get to know each other better.' He glanced up at her. 'Wouldn't we?'

'Yes,' she agreed, 'we would.' She pulled a sad face, hating the deception. 'Unless the mistress kills me. Then we won't get to know each other at all.'

'That would be a shame.'

'It would.'

Melvin was silent. 'I will help you,' he said eventually.

Orry felt a little wobbly as she watched him return to his desk. Melvin opened a drawer and ran his hands over dozens of glass vials arranged within. Selecting one, he inserted it into a gas injector.

'I'm sorry, my friends,' he whispered, with tears in his eyes.

She winced as he pressed the injector to her neck. It hissed and she felt a sharp pain. Melvin stepped back.

'Is that it?' she asked.

'The mistress has me make antibodies for every tailored batch. Do you have a headache?'

'Yes.'

'It will pass soon.'

'Thank you,' she said with heartfelt relief. Was it her imagination, or did her head feel better already? 'I have another friend. Can you help him as well?'

'Yes,' he told her. 'The mistress asked me to prepare two batches. One moment.'

As he returned to the drawer of vials, Orry activated her integuary.

Mender? You there?

She waited a moment then glanced at Harry. He shrugged, looking worried.

She tried again: *Mender!*

'Here it is,' Melvin said, holding up another glass vial.

The colour drained from his face as the lab door flew open, crashing against the wall. Orry whirled to see Roag, her face contorted with rage, framed by the doorway. Two of her gun-hands stood behind her.

Roag's pistol rose as if in slow motion until it was pointing at Orry's chest. Her finger tensed on the trigger, but a moment before she fired, something slammed into Orry's waist, driving her sideways. A gunshot echoed flatly through the lab as she thudded to the ground with Harry on top of her. A cry from Melvin made her look up. The big man was staring at a spreading red stain in the centre of his chest. He dropped to his knees, looking confused. Orry gasped as the glass vial fell from his fingers, but it clattered to the ground unbroken and rolled away under Melvin's desk as he toppled forward.

'God *damn it!*' Roag roared, and hurried to Melvin as her men followed her into the room. She bent over the atomicist and strained to haul him onto his back. His eyes stared dully past her.

Harry dragged Orry behind a bank of equipment an instant before Roag started firing. Orry flinched as rounds slammed into the machinery.

'You little *bitch!*' Roag screamed, apparently overcome with rage. 'I'm going take my fucking time with you!'

Orry reached up and fired a couple of shots, just to let Roag know she was armed, then shrank into a ball as the hired guns joined in. Their rounds started eating away at the shuddering console.

33

WAYWARD SCION

When Mender came round, the pain had lessened to a level where he could just make out Dyas standing over him.

'She's going to peel your face off,' the raider crooned. 'And I'm going to watch.'

'You . . . fucking . . . *moron*,' Mender managed to gasp. 'We . . . weren't lying. We would have taken you . . . with us.'

'Really? I couldn't be sure.' Dyas laughed easily. 'Still, things have turned out all right in the end.' He glanced at the guard on the far side of the room and leaned in closer, lowering his voice. 'Roag's not all that scary. I'll just say the right things and I'll be back in her good books; you'll see. She's soft, underneath all that bluster – you may be frightened of her, *old man*, but I'm not.'

Mender grunted a laugh through gritted teeth. 'Didn't look that way when you were chained up.' He stifled a moan. 'Looked like you were pissing yourself, *boy*.'

Dyas' smile turned brittle. He crossed to the wallscreen and brought up a menu. 'Shall we see what Roag is doing to your little whore and her boyfriend?' He scrolled through, then jabbed his finger and an image of a laboratory appeared on the screen. Orry and Harry were sheltering behind a bank of machinery while Roag and her men blasted away at it.

Mender glared at Dyas with murderous hatred; agreeing to ferry that treacherous little bastard to *Bonaventure* had been the worst mistake of his life. Dyas might not have told him what he'd planned, but Mender had known it wouldn't end well. Whatever excuses he tried to make, this whole mess was his responsibility. He pushed the pain to the back of his mind and focused. His hands flexed.

'Doesn't look like they have much of a chance,' Dyas observed happily, wandering a little nearer to Mender. 'I hope she's still alive when they bring her up here – maybe I can persuade Roag to let me have some fun with her.'

Mender mumbled something.

'What's that, old man?' Dyas asked, coming closer still.

Mender's hand fastened around Dyas' windpipe and slammed his head into the desk. The raider staggered back, dazed and choking as Mender kept hold of his throat, letting Dyas' movement help him to his feet. On the other side of the room Roag's guard first raised his weapon, then changed his mind and groped in a pocket for the pain remote.

Mender released Dyas' throat and wrapped a forearm around his neck, pulling him close. The pain was crippling – without Dyas' support he would be unable to stand. He shoved him towards the Fabretti.

Dyas reached back over his head and tried clawing at Mender's face, but as sharp fingernails tore bloody grooves in his cheek, Mender just tightened his hold. Dyas transferred his grip to Mender's forearm, trying to relieve its choking pressure.

The guard tugged the remote from his pocket, fumbled and dropped it. Cursing, he raised his weapon then hesitated, unwilling to shoot for fear of hitting Dyas. That wouldn't last – but the Fabretti was almost in reach.

Dyas stumbled and fell forward, bringing Mender down on top of him as the guard fired. Mender felt the bullet pass over his head and rolled desperately, reaching for the Fabretti. His head was in torment, but as his hand closed on the pistol his body reacted automatically, raising the weapon and squeezing the trigger.

The guard flew backwards, his legs a ruin of glistening meat, a wash of arterial blood staining the tiled floor around him. Mender stumbled to his feet and staggered towards the screaming guard. He fell on the pain remote like a starving man. His blunt fingers fumbled with the dial and suddenly the agony was gone. His head was swimming, but he was overcome with relief—

—until Dyas landed on top of him with a feral snarl, scrabbling for the Fabretti.

In an instant Mender's relief turned to fury. He punched Dyas in the face with his free hand, stunning him enough to shake him off, then pistol-whipped him, putting every bit of his rage and guilt into the blow. Dyas' nose exploded with a sickening crunch – he howled and tried to crawl away, but Mender dragged him back by his ankle, ignoring the flailing fist that caught him in the eye. He pinned the raider down and started methodically hitting him, again and again, spattering ribbons of blood everywhere, until he was certain Dyas was unconscious. The raider's face was a crimson mask.

The guard had stopped screaming. Dead eyes stared

accusingly as Mender hauled himself to his feet but he ignored them. Checking the Fabretti, he stepped into Roag's lift.

The firing ceased.

'Throw out your weapons,' Roag demanded.

'What's in it for us?' Orry yelled back.

'Good point,' Roag conceded. 'Try not to kill them,' she told her men.

The firing resumed.

'This would be an excellent time to reveal the next stage in your cunning plan,' Harry said.

Orry flinched as a round ricocheted past her head. 'I'm thinking.'

'Think faster.'

'Feel free to come up with something yourself, why don't you!'

A muffled roar sounded outside the lab and the fusillade faltered. Orry couldn't hear what Roag was shouting because her words were lost in the thunderous reports of a Fabretti 500.

She grinned at Harry. 'Thought of something! The cavalry's arrived!'

Poking her head out, she saw the mangled body of one of Roag's two men lying motionless near the door.

She couldn't see Roag, but the remaining gunhand was backing away – until he spotted Orry and fired, driving her back into cover while more rounds went lashing over her head.

Harry flung himself sideways, his arm flashing out, and she heard a wet choking. The Fabretti roared again, and this time Roag screamed. Orry jumped to her feet and saw her staggering into a corner, one arm hanging loosely. Blood soaked her shoulder.

Mender stepped into the lab, keeping the Fabretti aimed at Roag. 'Next time you get a clever idea,' he said to Orry, 'remind me to just shoot myself. It would save time.'

She resisted the urge to hug the old man and instead crossed to Melvin's body. She knelt beside him and took a moment to close his eyes before reaching under the desk. Her fingers closed around the vial he'd dropped. The gas-injector was still lying where he'd left it.

Mender didn't take his eyes off Roag as Orry inserted the little glass tube and fired the injector into his neck. 'Let's go,' she told him.

The old man didn't move.

'If you're going to do it,' the woman said, clutching her arm, 'just fucking get on with it.'

Orry looked anxiously at him. 'Mender, you can't – not like this.'

'If I don't, she'll come after us.'

'I'd rather take my chances than execute her.'

'I wouldn't,' Harry said. He crossed to the door and peered out.

She laid a hand on Mender's arm. 'Please don't.'

He clenched his jaw, fingers flexing around the Fabretti's grip.

'We've got company!' Harry yelled, ducking back into the lab as a bullet smacked into the doorframe.

Mender strode towards Roag. 'Call off your dogs,' he growled.

'No.' She smiled, her face taut with pain. 'Put down your guns and give me the pendant and I'll let you go. You have my word.'

She gasped as Mender grabbed a fistful of her hair. He pulled her close and pressed the Fabretti to her temple. 'I have a better idea,' he said, and shoved her towards the door. 'Stay close,' he told Orry and Harry, then raised his voice. 'I have your boss here! We're coming out, nice and slow, and if any of you fuckers so much as looks at me the wrong way you'll need a new paymaster. Understand?'

He edged out of the lab, keeping Roag close. Orry followed, Harry close behind. Straight ahead, a short passageway ended in the elevator leading up to Roag's inner sanctum. Her goons watched from passageways to the left and right, fingering their weapons uncertainly. Every second, Orry expected Roag to cry out, to sacrifice herself just to gain vengeance.

She breathed a little easier when they reached the elevator. Roag's crew hung back as the doors slid open.

Orry saw the pistol an instant before she recognised the man holding it. Dyas grinned at her from inside the lift, his teeth a slash of white against a mask of blood. His pistol spat and Harry's head snapped back. As he fell, Roag twisted free of Mender's grip.

Orry flung herself on Dyas, forcing his pistol aside. The Fabretti boomed behind her as she smashed his wrist against the steel handrail running round the lift's interior. He howled and dropped the gun. She made a grab for it, but he rammed her into one mirrored wall, cracking the glass. The air burst from her lungs as his fist drove into her solar plexus. She folded up, gasping, and his knee smacked into her nose, making lights dance behind her eyes. Pain eclipsed everything for a moment and when her senses returned, his hands were scrabbling at her neck for the pendant. She sank her teeth into his arm, biting down until the taste of his blood mixed with hers, feeling a savage satisfaction when he squealed.

The scream ended in a strangled squawk as Mender slammed into him at a dead run. The two men bounced off the mirrored walls, locked in a brutal embrace. Orry ducked under them and reached for the fallen pistol, and as her hand closed around it, Dyas thrust Mender away and fled down the passageway.

She raised the pistol, then noticed Harry lying crumpled on the ground. Roag was gone.

Mender grabbed Harry's arm and dragged him into the lift, but Dyas had reached Roag's gunhands, who were spilling into the far end of the passageway. Orry jabbed at the door control as the first bullets whistled past.

The doors closed and the lift began to rise.

Her nose felt hugely swollen and blood was streaming down the back of her throat, making her want to throw up. She spat into a corner, trying to clear her mouth, then crouched beside Harry as Mender reloaded the Fabretti. Harry's breathing was shallow and there was a hole high in his right cheek. The skin was already purpling around his shattered cheekbone. Orry pulled back his eyelid and saw the eye beneath was swimming in blood, its pupil blown. She slid her hand behind his head.

'There's no exit wound,' she said. 'The bullet's still in there. We need to get him to *Jane*'s medbay. Can you carry him?'

'Don't have much choice,' Mender said. 'Here.' He handed her the Fabretti, then fixed his rebreather into place and hoisted Harry onto his shoulders.

Orry secured her own rebreather as the lift slowed. The doors opened and she poked her head out – only to snatch it back as gunfire erupted from both sides.

'This is getting old,' Mender muttered, as an orange stun grenade rolled into the lift.

'Move!' she yelled, and raced towards the panoramic windows on the far side of Roag's inner sanctum, ignoring the dull crump of the grenade behind her. She focused on the window as figures moved on either side of her, partially concealed behind chairs and tables. Guns flashed again and a bullet snatched at her sleeve. She fired the Fabretti left and right to keep their heads down, then emptied the remaining rounds into the window.

Craters appeared in the thick silicarbonate, but the window held.

She skidded to a halt a metre from the glass, Mender beside her, Harry wrapped around his shoulders like a stole. The old man's chest was heaving. In the window, she could see a dozen men and women rising from cover, an assortment of weapons trained on them.

She recognised Roag's lieutenant, Steiner.

'Nice try,' the woman said. 'You can put your weapons down now.'

Mender stared at Orry, sweat rolling down his face.

'Don't make me ask again,' Steiner snarled, but a movement outside had caught Orry's eye. Her heart lifted as *Dainty Jane*'s familiar shape rose into view, the long barrel of a mass driver swivelling towards the window.

She and Mender ducked as *Jane* fired, tungsten slugs punching through the silicarbonate, sending Roag's crew diving for cover as furniture and fittings were obliterated.

A square of silicarbonate fell from the window, cut neatly out by *Jane*'s slugs, and Tycho's noxious atmosphere flooded into the room. The ship dropped out of sight and Mender yelled, 'Go!'

Disengaging her brain, Orry ran blindly at the opening, screaming wildly as she flung herself out.

She struck *Jane*'s upper hull and began to slide down towards the edge of the fuselage and the roiling clouds a thousand kilometres below. Scrabbling madly, her hands finally found purchase, slowing her descent.

Mender thudded down next to her, the impact jolting Harry clear of his shoulders. Orry yelled a warning as the nobleman's limp body started rolling away and Mender dived after him, managing to grab his jacket as he disappeared off the side of the ship. For a moment she was sure Mender would follow him over the edge, but as he neared the brink his flailing hand closed around a pipe rising from the hull.

'Little help here?' he grunted.

She had activated her molly hooks and, edging closer, was reaching for his hand, when *Dainty Jane* lurched wildly and bullets started striking the hull. She glimpsed Steiner standing in the broken window. The woman fired again and *Jane* twitched once more to spoil her aim.

Get us out of here, Orry told the ship, struggling to keep her footing. *Jane* rotated and edged away from the rig while Orry, ignoring the projectiles whipping around her, grabbed Mender's arm. Praying the molly hooks would hold, she let go of *Jane* and reached out with the other hand. Once she was holding Mender firmly he released the pipe, she heaved, and Harry inched back into view.

Ignoring the fiery pain in her arms, she kept hauling until

they'd got him safely onto the hull. Once Mender had engaged his own hooks, they carried him to the dorsal airlock and lowered him inside. The moment they joined him, *Dainty Jane* increased power and accelerated away.

'The wound was caused by a low-velocity bullet fired at close range,' *Jane* reported. 'It entered his left cheek, shattering his zygoma, then lodged in his premotor cortex.'

Orry stared at Harry, cocooned within the medbay bed. His head was heavily bandaged, his skin mottled with yellow and purple bruises. 'Can you get the bullet out?'

'That would require a level of delicacy beyond my capabilities. The slightest slip could cause significant neurological deficits or paralysis, or kill him. He is unconscious but stable, and his functions are not currently impaired at this point, but he needs a skilled neurosurgeon.'

'Can he be moved?' Orry asked.

'Any movement runs the risk of causing further damage, but if he is properly immobilised then it's possible, though not recommended. What did you have in mind?'

'As soon as we rendezvous with *Bonaventure* we'll transfer Harry aboard. I'll take him back to Alecto and—'

'*What?*' Mender erupted. 'You're *crazy*, girl. The Fleet will pick you up before you get anywhere near Alecto.'

'Maybe so, but at least Harry will get the treatment he needs. I owe him that much.'

'Yeah, they'll fix him up all right,' Mender said angrily. 'You can't hang someone when they're in a coma. It doesn't look good on the newsfeeds.' His tone softened. 'Think about it, Orry. You know he wouldn't want you to do this.'

She rubbed her face and muttered wearily, 'I just can't see any other way.'

'We can find a doc on Erlitz Shen – Emjay will know someone.'

'I wouldn't trust any of the quacks in Freetown to open a can of beans, let alone Harry's head. Besides, what would we pay them with? We're broke.' She shook her head. 'What do you think, *Jane*?'

'The coma has bought us a few days, but Harry's condition is deteriorating. Without an operation he will die.'

'You see? I'm sure Harry would rather be under arrest than a corpse.'

'He'll be just as dead if they execute him,' Mender growled.

'For what? *I'm* the one they think killed Konstantin; all Harry did was piss off the Count of Delf.'

'And assist in a prison break,' he reminded her.

'Neither of which is a capital crime.'

He pulled a sour face. 'Okay, so it's only you they'll string up in a live broadcast. How do you think Harry will feel about that when he's breaking rocks on Furina? And who's going to look after Ethan? You've only just got him back and now you're planning to throw your life away?'

'I don't say this often,' *Jane* broke in, 'but I agree with Mender.'

Orry stared at the deck. She knew she wasn't thinking straight. There *had* to be another way. If only Dad was around. He always had an angle—

She looked up. '*Jane*, do you have any dispatch pods?'

'Oh, Rama,' Mender moaned. 'I know that look.'

The three-person medical team was led by a doctor whose curling moustaches bounced whenever he moved. Orry could tell the man was nervous – but that was understandable, what with Mender lurking in the corner of the cargo bay, one hand on the holstered Fabretti. She didn't feel bad for the doc: once he returned to Alecto the man would be dining out on this story for months.

Harry was enclosed within a gleaming life-support unit floating a metre above the deck. House Bardov had spared no expense in recovering their wayward scion: exactly as Orry had hoped when she'd contacted Harry's father.

She stopped the floating unit just short of the freight lock and stared at Harry's face. The doctor had examined him for some time before grudgingly pronouncing that *Jane*'s care had been adequate. A ventilator covered Harry's mouth and much of his head was swathed in fresh dressings. Orry touched the glass above his face. She knew this was his only hope, but that didn't ease her guilt; she felt like she was abandoning him.

'Look after him,' she told the doctor.

'Like you have?' he replied coldly, then glanced nervously at Mender.

She stepped back and let the nurse push Harry into the airlock. The doctor followed without a word. Once the inner door closed, she resisted the urge to peer through the inspection port.

Mender walked over and put a hand on her shoulder. 'You did the right thing,' he told her. 'He'll get the best care there.'

'I'm not going to abandon him,' she said firmly.

'I know.'

'I mean it. I'll go to Alecto if I have to. If he needs me.'

'Come on,' he said. 'If the Fleet is going to ambush us, I want to be ready.'

She groaned. 'How many times, Mender? It's *not* a trap. There are a lot of things Harry may or may not have done that would not reflect well on House Bardov – I made that very clear in the message to his father. Aristos might be corrupt, decadent bastards in private, but they hate it when scandal becomes public.'

'And he believed you?'

She grinned, then, 'Of course he did. It's *me*.' She followed him to the cockpit and they watched the medical ship detach.

'That must have cost a pretty penny,' Mender observed, watching the sleek, atmosphere-capable craft edge away from *Dainty Jane*. 'A private medical vessel with crew, no questions asked?'

'Between medical and legal costs, Delf may not have to put himself to the trouble of ruining House Bardov; Harry might have done his job for him.'

'I imagine his father was less than pleased.'

'You could say that.'

'You're not making many friends among the Great Houses,' he observed.

She shrugged. 'I'm not Harry's keeper. He made his own choices.' She watched the medical ship accelerate away. 'Do you think a good advocate will get him off?'

Mender was focused on the sensors. 'Doubtful. Those aristo bastards normally get away with a slap on the wrist, but Harry betrayed his own class. No one likes a turncoat. I imagine they'll make an example of him.'

The medical ship's drive flickered and died as it reached safe distance. A moment later it vanished, leaving only an oily stain over the distant stars. Orry told herself she'd done the right thing.

'Pre-collapse checklist,' Mender said. 'If they're coming, it's going to be now.'

'They're not coming,' she said firmly. 'Let's go and get Ethan.'

34

SHATTERED

Orry scratched idly at a fresh collection of bites, ignoring the stars glinting beyond the dome, the unfamiliar constellations distorted by the condensation running down the thick glass and dimmed by the orange glow rising from Freeport. 'I'm just saying, *be careful*,' she told Emjay again.

'I appreciate your concern,' Emjay said, watching some of the younger Sweet Things playing on the lawn, 'but there's no need. We're quite safe here.'

Her dismissive manner was really beginning to worry Orry, who had decided that sending Ethan to Erlitz Shen had been a mistake. She should have arranged a deep-space rendezvous, far from anyone she cared about – anyone Roag could use to get to them.

But when she looked at her brother, lying there on the grass with a girl stretched out next to him, she couldn't help but smile. As he and the girl – *Longwei*, she finally remembered – giggled in unison, it confirmed her suspicion that they were sharing an integuary experience.

Emjay interrupted her train of thought by slapping her hand away from a bite.

'Don't scratch. You'll make them worse. Let the cream do its work.' She sucked her teeth in a disapproving way. 'Walking through the jungle to get here? I thought you knew better . . .'

'Tell me about it,' Mender muttered from the deckchair next to Orry's.

She frowned at him; he knew exactly why she'd asked *Dainty Jane* to drop them in a clearing several kilometres from the dome. Okay, so they'd had to cut a path through the jungle in the fierce heat, fighting off swarms of biting insects, but despite admitting that her caution was sensible the old man had griped the whole bloody way. He took great delight in blaming all his woes on her.

Ignoring him, she said casually, 'I don't see Jackis anywhere.' She hadn't told Emjay what had happened the last time she had been here; it was down to her to find the little shit and teach him a lesson he'd understand.

'I was wondering when you'd bring up that boy,' Emjay said, without taking her eyes off the children. 'I know what happened, and I'm sorry for it. He was always a wrong 'un. I guess I thought I could change him.'

'Where is he?'

Emjay waved a hand towards the glow from the city. 'Somewhere down there. Or maybe he's left Erlitz Shen, gone to be a pain in some other world's collective ass. Frankly, I couldn't give a damn.'

Orry gazed at her, wondering how genuine Emjay's casual manner was. She *never* expelled anyone entirely from the dome. Mind you, Dad had always said Emjay had iron running right through her; that was a definite requirement for survival in a place like Freeport. 'Don't blame yourself,' she said at last. 'Some people are just born bad.'

Emjay looked sad as she patted Orry's arm. 'So,' she said, 'you have Ethan and *Bonaventure* back – what are your plans now?'

'First off, stay away from Roag. Other than that, I don't know. Try to find some Ruuz to gull, I suppose.' Orry wasn't entirely comfortable lying to Emjay, but the less she knew, the safer she would be.

Emjay's face turned serious. 'If Mender's right and the Kadiran are involved in this, you need to be careful.'

'I didn't friggin' imagine it,' Mender muttered.

'It's not the Kadiran I'm worried about,' Orry said.

'Well, you should be,' Emjay told her. 'The Kadiran make Cordelia Roag look like a child pulling the wings off insects. Their society is based solely on strength. Only five per cent of Kadiran males get to reproduce, you know; they have to fight for the right to mate – in fact, they fight for *everything*. It's in their bones. If they want that stone of yours, they'll come and get it. And when they do, you'd better be somewhere else.'

'I've heard the stories,' Orry admitted, 'but if they're so tough, why even use Roag to get the stone? Why not find it themselves?'

'I'm amazed they used a woman at all. The Kadiran regard females as servants and breeding stock, not business partners. But then, they consider humans meat, so I guess when you're lowering yourself to deal with your dinner, it doesn't matter what sex it is.'

Orry thought about that. She hadn't really thought the Kadiran might be coming after her as well; that was pretty far-fetched, like being chased by the bogeyman. But Kadiran ships *were* sighted from time to time, and Mender was adamant the threat was real, so that was all the more reason to take the pendant back to Professor Rasmussen and unlock its secrets.

The problem would be getting past *Goshawk* a second time; after what had happened on *Justiciar* her face would be plastered all over the Grand Fleet by now.

'You could always stay here,' Emjay suggested. 'The children like you and I could surely do with the help.'

'I'd love to,' Orry admitted, 'but even if we're just dealing with Roag, it's too dangerous. Maybe once things calm down . . .'

'Are they likely to?'

'Not while Roag is still alive,' Mender grunted.

'He's right,' Orry said, then, 'we should go.' She started to lever herself out of her deckchair, but Tilda had caught sight of her and was waving wildly. She broke off from her game to run over – she appeared to have completely forgotten how they'd parted last time, which was a relief; Orry had been fretting about hurting the little girl's feelings.

Emjay placed a hand on her forearm. 'You won't even stay the night? Look at Ethan and Longwei – and Tilda likes having you around.'

'You look tired,' Orry said to the little girl.

'I'm fine,' Tilda said, then yawned hugely.

'It's late,' Emjay said with a smile. 'Time for all you littles to go to bed, I think.'

Tilda scowled. 'Five more minutes, Mama.'

'How about I tell you a story?' Orry said. 'I know a good one my dad used to tell to me.'

'Are there monsters?' Tilda asked hopefully.

'No, but there's an evil count who locks his daughter in a tower.'

Tilda thought about this. 'That sounds okay, I guess.'

As Emjay clapped her hands, summoning the other children

and weathering the usual storm of objections, Orry told Tilda, 'You go on – I'll be up in a minute.'

She watched Emjay and some of the older Sweet Things shepherd the younger children towards the dormitories.

'You're good with kids,' Mender observed.

'Well, it's not that surprising: Ethan is six years younger than me. He was only four when Mum died, so I guess I'm used to it.'

'You want any of your own?'

'One day, maybe.' She'd never really considered it. 'Can I ask you a question?'

Mender assumed a pained expression, but motioned for her to continue.

'What happened to your family was terrible, but it was a long time ago,' she said carefully. 'Most men would have moved on, started over. Why didn't you?'

He shrugged. 'What's the point? Everyone dies sooner or later.'

'Grief! If it were left up to you, the human race would just die out.'

'Might not be a bad thing.'

'You don't mean that.'

'I just don't like people, I guess.'

'You like *Jane*.'

'*Jane* ain't people.'

'She was once.'

'Yeah, and look what they did to her.'

Orry thought for a moment. 'You like me.'

'What makes you think that?'

She nudged him. 'You like me.'

He grunted again. 'You're all right. I suppose.'

'For a girl.'

His lips twitched. 'For a girl.'

'So there's hope for the human race after all. Can you see yourself ever settling down again?'

'I'm a little long in the tooth to have another kid.' His eyes fell. 'Besides, once was enough.'

'That's not what I meant.' She looked over at Emjay, who was carrying a recalcitrant child into the dormitory building.

Mender followed her gaze. For a moment he was speechless, and Orry jumped in: 'You two have something – there's a spark there. Even an emotionally stunted ball of gristle like you must have felt it.'

He cleared his throat. 'Don't be ridiculous.'

'So you're just going to fly away and go back to living like a hermit?'

'That's how I like it.'

'And what about *Jane*? Have you asked what she wants?'

'She likes it too.' His real eye glinted dangerously. 'You don't know what you're talking about, girl. Best you shut your hole now.'

A few days ago she would have been angry at his tone, but now she could recognise the pain beneath his frown. 'At least don't disappear for ever,' she told him. 'Come back to see Emjay, once Roag gets bored with chasing us.'

'Like that's ever going to happen.'

'Just come back here once it's safe,' Orry repeated. 'For me.'

He gave a noncommittal grunt.

They sat in silence, listening to the children's distant voices. Lights came on in the upper floor of the dormitory block.

'So what will you do with the pendant?' Mender asked after a moment or two.

She fingered it beneath her top. 'Honestly? I don't know. I want to take it to Rasmussen, but it's risky. It's not just getting past *Goshawk* – if I were Roag, I'd be staking the place out.'

'You're dead right. If I were you, I'd toss it.'

'But what if the Kadiran find it? Somehow I don't think they want the pendant for its historical interest, do you?'

'Just jettison it in deep space,' he said pragmatically. 'They'll never find it.'

She wasn't so sure. 'If I did go back to the Shattermoon, would you come with me?'

He laughed. 'You've got to be kidding, girl. Me and *Jane* are getting as far from Roag as we can, and I advise you to do the same.'

She hid her disappointment. Mender had more than paid his debt to her; she had no right to expect his help.

But he wasn't finished. His voice dropped as he said, 'Emjay's right, you know – about the Kadiran. Whatever you've heard about them, they're *far* worse. That war almost finished us – they drove us back and back, destroying fleets, slaughtering our colonies. The things they did to the prisoners were ... The Kadiran think human flesh tastes like shit, but they eat us anyway – *alive* mostly. It all comes back to strength, like Emjay said.' He shook his head. 'It's a miracle we managed to stop them at all.'

'They've kept the truce for two hundred years,' Orry said, 'so why change now? And what do they want the stone for?'

'Whatever it is, it ain't gonna be good news for us. They were dead set on wiping us out once and I can't see that's changed, even in a couple of hundred years. Take my advice, girl, and stay the hell away from them.'

'I'll do my best,' she promised, then added awkwardly, 'I guess I should say thanks – for everything. It's been ... interesting.' She leaned over and kissed him on the cheek. 'Will I ever see you again?'

Mender's jaw tightened. 'I doubt it.'

They stared at each other, and the depth of her sadness surprised her.

An ear-splitting crack made her head snap up and she stared at the dome in alarm. A perfectly round hole had appeared in the glass and she could just make out a plume of dirt rising on the far side of the buildings. She clambered to her feet, then covered her ears as another crack rolled across the lawn and a second hole appeared at the centre of a network of fractures. More dirt jetted into the air, clattering down on flat roofs.

Dark figures started dropping through the holes like spiders on invisible strands of silk, slowing as they neared the ground. The staccato rattle of gunfire echoed in the stairwell leading out of the dome and a teenage boy raced out, pulling the metal door shut behind him a moment before a grenade detonated with a dull *crump*. A cloud of dust shot out of the low building and hurled him to the ground.

Orry took an involuntary step backwards as Jericho appeared in the doorway, smoke swirling around its chassis.

She barely had time to register the bright scars of newly welded metal on one of its arms before the mimetic had turned its automatic railgun towards the fallen boy, who was lifting himself groggily to his feet. He staggered back when he saw Jericho and raised his hands in a pleading gesture, but the mimetic's weapon was already buzzing. The boy's upper body dissolved in a storm of bloody fragments.

Figures clad in the black mil-spec armour favoured by mercenaries and carrying assault weapons spilled from the entrance behind the robot.

'Run!' Orry screamed at the few teens still on the lawn, but they were already moving. She searched desperately for Ethan and finally spotted him racing for the shelter of the meeting hall, hand in hand with Longwei, his face pale but determined. She set off after him.

A brittle cracking sounded from above and she looked up to see the network of fractures had spread. With a mind-numbing crash the entire dome shattered, cubes of safety glass falling like hail.

The black-clad mercenaries were advancing with Jericho in the centre of their line. Orry crunched over drifts of broken glass, focused on reaching the meeting hall. She glanced back just in time to see Jericho taking down a fleeing girl, the stream of railgun slugs shredding her torso.

She dashed away tears and concentrated on getting to the open door. The sound of more automatic weapons fire came from the far side of the building, punctuated by the dull thuds of grenades and the screams of terrified children. Orry's heart twisted as she thought of Tilda.

She opened a channel to Mender. *Where are you?*

Keeping my head down! Looks like you were right, girl.

Get Jane *down here!*

She's breaking orbit now, but it'll take a while. We need to get out of this dome – it's a killing field.

Not without the children!

She flung herself into the meeting hall and slammed the door behind her. A line of holes appeared, punching through the flimsy wooden wall and showering the cowering children with splinters. They screamed and fled deeper into the building.

'Upstairs!' Orry yelled, ducking as more slugs flew through the walls. She grabbed Ethan by the arm and shoved him ahead of her, pushing him through the kitchen and into the entrance hall of the dormitory building. Opposite the main doors a flight of stairs led to the second floor. Orry took them two at a time, following her brother, who was still clutching Longwei's hand.

At the top she found Mender and Emjay setting up a cumbersome pulse laser on the balcony that extended from the front of the building. A few of the older Sweet Things were crouching behind the balcony's low wooden walls, firing down at Jericho and the advancing mercenaries.

Orry looked anxiously down the corridor towards the bedrooms. The place was packed with milling children, but at least the screaming had subsided now that some of the older children were there to calm the younger ones. Orry resisted the urge to find Tilda and instead ran to Emjay's side.

'I'm sorry,' she blurted, 'this is all my fault—'

'Don't give it a thought,' Emjay replied airily, carefully aiming the laser's long barrel. Green light strobed and Jericho was instantly surrounded by a cloud of ablative particles. The mimetic immediately shifted its fire to the balcony, tearing through the sturdy wooden floor like it was paper. A fist-sized hole appeared in a spotty-faced youth standing near Orry. He stared at the wound in his chest in surprise and dropped to the ground.

The rest of the mercenaries joined Jericho in directing a withering fire at the balcony.

'Fall back!' Mender yelled when several rounds struck the laser and toppled its tripod.

Orry grabbed Emjay. 'You have to get the children out of here!'

'I know.' Emjay searched through the children until she spotted Longwei, still clinging to Ethan. 'Longwei! Round up everyone you can find and take them out through the service tunnel. Run for the city – and don't stop for *anything*, understand me? Go to Big Suze and tell her we're under attack – tell her to bring help. *A lot of it.*'

Longwei glanced at Ethan, then at the balcony, flinching as bullets chewed a line across the floor. 'No,' she said bravely, 'I want to stay and fight.'

'Get the hell out of here!' Mender snapped, but Emjay raised a hand.

'I know you want to stay, Longwei, but I need you to take the littles and go. *Right now.*'

Longwei looked at Ethan again. His attempt at a reassuring smile looked hollow to Orry and her heart ached for them both.

'Be safe,' Longwei told him quietly, then called to the Sweet Things waiting nearby, 'Let's go!'

Orry checked the children Longwei quickly gathered around her, searching for Tilda, but she couldn't see the little girl anywhere. Cursing, she went plunging into the mass of terrified kids as they headed along the corridor towards the narrow stairs at the rear of the building that led down to the back door. Tilda's room was off a short side passage halfway down the main corridor. Orry pushed clear of the throng and ran into the room. It was empty except for some discarded clothes and a single shoe lying forlornly in the middle of the floor.

Ethan slammed into the doorframe behind her. 'What the hell are you doing?' he demanded breathlessly. 'We have to get out of here!'

She ran to Tilda's bed and threw back the covers, then checked the other three beds before wrenching the wardrobe doors open and pulling out the contents.

'There's no one here,' he told her. 'She'll be with the others. Orry, we have to go, *now*!'

'Okay,' she said reluctantly. *She'll be fine*, she told herself. *Worry about yourself and Ethan.*

The sharp crack of a shot sounded from the rear of the building, followed by a chorus of screams. A hand squeezed Orry's heart and she dashed back into the corridor to see the back stairs were clear: all the children had left the building. Another shot sounded from outside and the squeals of terrified children made her stomach lurch. She took off along the corridor, horrified at what she'd brought down on the orphanage.

At the end of the corridor, a window overlooked the grounds to the rear of the building. Through it, Orry could see a line of children scattering across the lawn, fleeing in terror towards an open hatch a short distance away. Longwei was huddled in the shelter of the open hatch, urging the kids on, practically throwing them down the shaft to safety. Two small bodies were lying motionless on the grass, and Orry froze as she caught sight of a dark figure lying on the roof of the neighbouring meeting hall, angling the long barrel of a sniper's rifle down at the panicked children. Her hands clutched the window frame as she spotted Tilda among them.

The sniper's rifle jerked and the child running beside Tilda tumbled.

As if in slow motion, the sniper shifted his aim to Tilda.

Orry screamed at the glass, utterly helpless.

Tilda's head snapped back, a halo of fine red mist forming around her as she fell.

35

HOW IS THAT BASTARD
NOT DEAD?

Orry stared at Tilda's body, lying still and pale on the grass. Blood had already pooled around the little girl's head. The last of the children ran past her, scrambling down the hatch, and sparks rose as a shot struck the metal disk.

Longwei hauled it closed, and Orry became aware of Ethan, tugging at her arm.

'Come on!' he urged.

Numbly, she allowed him to lead her to the front of the building again, where Mender, back out on the balcony, was firing down through the holes torn in the wooden panelling. The sight of him shook her back to reality as she suddenly understood just how lethal their predicament was. Tilda was gone; she couldn't let the same thing happen to Ethan.

'Where's Emjay?' she yelled.

'Gone,' he told her. 'She took the older kids to the sub-levels; there's a way out down there. I said I'd wait for you here and catch her up – *look out!*' He covered his head.

The building shook with another explosion, directly beneath

them this time. Orry ran to the top of the nearby stairs and stared down into the entrance hall. The front doors hung open, listing crazily on twisted hinges. A cloud of smoke and dust flared red as lasers flickered through the opening.

She shrank back as Jericho emerged from the smoke and stopped at the foot of the stairs. Turning its head, it scanned the ground floor. Firing came from somewhere beneath her and sparks flew from the mimetic's side. It swivelled, and disappeared from view. A moment later she heard the distinctive buzz of its railgun.

Two black-armoured mercenaries stepped out of the dust cloud, weapons raised, searching for targets. The visor of the left-hand figure slid back to reveal Dyas' grinning face. She experienced a stab of visceral hatred as he looked up at her.

'Hello again,' he said. 'Fancy meeting you here.' He reached for a netgun slung over his shoulder.

Orry threw herself sideways the instant before he fired up the stairs. The black ball flashed past her shoulder, strands already expanding into an adhesive net. It struck the wall behind her and hung there like a giant web.

She pulled herself up and snatched a glance down the stairwell: Dyas was hanging back while the other mercenary covered his back. The sound of Jericho's railgun had stopped. *Waiting for backup*, she guessed. She had seconds at most before they came up the stairs.

Dyas is here! she told Mender.

Dyas? How—?

Just get over here!

He arrived a moment later, followed by Ethan, who was clutching a pistol. Her brother had blood on his forehead.

'How is that bastard not dead?' Mender spat.

'Why don't you go down there and ask him—?'

A beam sliced up the stairs, burning through the corner she was sheltering behind and catching her face as she scrambled back.

'We have to get out of here,' she said, raising a hand to her cheek. The skin flared into agony when she touched it.

'Fuck that!' Ethan snarled, making a lunge for the corner, but Mender grabbed him and dragged him back.

'She's right, you idiot – we can't win this, not here. We're out-gunned.'

'We can't go down,' Orry said, shrinking back as the laser light flickered again, eating away at their cover. 'The roof – this way!'

The ladder was in a storeroom and Mender was just pulling the door shut behind them when Dyas and Jericho appeared at the top of the stairs.

'Shit!' Mender growled as he bolted the door, knowing it wouldn't stop the mimetic for more than a moment. 'Get on with it, girl. They're right behind us.'

The ladder was bolted to one wall, between shelves full of folded bedding and towels. Orry climbed the first few rungs, put her shoulder against the metal hatch at the top and pushed, relief filling her as it lifted easily. She peered out, scanning the flat roof – and a bullet struck the hatch a hammer-blow, numbing her shoulder. Rounds flashed past her head from at least two directions and she fell backwards, landing in a heap on the floor as the hatch clanged shut above her.

'It's no use,' she gasped, rubbing her shoulder.

Mender unbolted the storeroom door and opened it a

fraction. He poked his nose into the corridor – and jerked back immediately as a beam almost sliced it off. 'Help me, kid,' he ordered, throwing the bolt home once more, and he and Ethan wrenched the nearest shelf unit off the wall and tipped it across the door to barricade it.

'We're screwed,' Ethan said.

Somehow the knowledge that they were out of options steadied Orry. Her mind-numbing fear dissipated, to be replaced with resignation.

The door shuddered under a powerful blow.

'Hello in there,' Dyas called cheerily from the corridor. 'I imagine you've worked out by now that you're pretty much screwed.'

'Told you,' Ethan whispered.

'Why don't you come in and finish us off then, you gutless fucking child-killer?' Orry yelled.

'Ah, delightful as ever, Aurelia. Well, yes, I could send Jericho in to tear you apart, and I know he'd enjoy every brief second of that, but I'm afraid the boss wants you all alive.'

'Roag? How did you persuade her to trust you again?'

'I saved her life in the lift, remember? A grateful woman is a friend indeed – and talking of friends, how's lanky Harry's face? Not so pretty now, I'm guessing.' Dyas chuckled. 'Finding you was laughably simple – although I have to be honest, I never thought you'd be stupid enough to come back to Freeport. Jackis is right here, by the way – you remember Jackis? Charming lad. *Heaps* of potential. He sends his regards.'

Orry clenched her teeth until her jaw ached, but stayed silent.

'Now, why don't you all put down your weapons and come out of there. That way nobody needs to get hurt.'

The three of them looked at each other, and said nothing.

'Are you really going to make me do this?' Dyas sighed. 'Very well, then, on your own heads and so forth. Jackis, go and find me a couple of brats – I'm pretty sure we haven't killed them all yet, have we? Bring them up here – and hurry, will you? I'm getting bored.'

'Leave them alone,' Orry raged, 'they're just *children*!'

'Come out then, and we needn't bother with them.'

She turned to Mender – who wasn't looking at all fazed by their predicament. 'Keep him talking,' he murmured.

'You're bluffing,' she called to Dyas, 'and anyway, the children have gone – I saw them get away.'

'You'd better hope you're right – because I can hear Jackis coming up the stairs and it doesn't sound like he's alone. Come out before things get *really* nasty.'

She saw Mender glance at the ceiling just as a vibration began in the soles of her feet.

'Piss off!' she shouted through the door as the shuddering grew stronger, shaking the linen on the shelves. A bundle of sheets fell to the floor, followed by a pile of towels.

She grinned as she heard the low rumble from above, slowly growing in pitch: she would recognise *Dainty Jane*'s engines anywhere now. A series of rapid thumps sounded from the roof, making the building shake.

The roof is clear, announced *Jane*.

Outside the door, Dyas howled with rage.

Mender pointed at the ladder. 'Go!'

Ethan scrambled to the top, shoved the hatch open and disappeared just as the storeroom door splintered and Jericho's fist came smashing through the wood.

Mender fired the Fabretti straight through the newly made hole. 'Go!' he yelled at Orry, but she shook her head stubbornly.

'Not without you!'

He shoved her towards the ladder. 'Get to *Jane*, girl. I'm not going anywhere till you do.' He fired again then glanced at her. 'I'll be fine. I'm just going to delay them a bit.'

A beam burned through the wood, filling the room with an eerie red light.

'Come on,' Ethan called, 'shift it, will you?'

Mender emptied the Fabretti into the door and reloaded. 'Get out of here!' he shouted at Orry.

She stared at him, filled with sudden dread, but at last she started hauling herself up the ladder. The roof was perforated with holes from *Dainty Jane*'s mass driver and sparks were spitting from a mangled bank of smoking satellite dishes and antennae. The ship was hovering off the side of the building, ungainly in the thick atmosphere. Her freight lock was open.

Orry hesitated: Mender was at the foot of the ladder, still shooting, but the laser beams were flashing closer by him with every shot. Flames erupted on his sleeve and she heard him curse as he frantically patted them out.

'Mender,' she yelled, '*come on!*'

He looked up at her with a tight grin. 'Maybe you're right.' He started up the ladder, holding the Fabretti in one hand until he reached the top, when he handed it to her and used both hands to haul himself out of the hatch. 'Not as nimble as I used to be,' he muttered.

He was halfway out when he stopped abruptly, a look of fear washing over his face.

'Oh shit—'

Hands clawing for a grip, he was yanked back down.

Orry ran forward to see Jericho standing at the foot of the ladder, gripping Mender's legs. She pointed the Fabretti through the hatch and pulled the trigger, but the mimetic twitched aside and the round only scored a wide scar down its back. She tried to fire again but the slide locked back on an empty chamber.

'Magazine!' she yelled at Mender.

Gritting his teeth, he reached to his belt – then gasped and slithered backwards through the hatch. The magazine clattered onto the roof.

She grabbed it and slammed it home, but it was too late; Jericho had Mender by the throat and was dragging him out of the storeroom.

She was moving towards the ladder when Ethan grabbed her arm.

'What are you doing?' he demanded.

'We can't leave him!'

'There are too many of them!'

She shook him off and took another step before he grabbed her and pulled her back again. She tried to push him away, but he refused to release her.

'Let . . . me . . . *go!*' she yelled.

Ethan was opening his mouth to reply when a shot sounded from the storeroom below.

A ragged hole appeared high in his chest and he fell backwards, gasping.

Orry leaped onto her brother, hands slithering through blood to press on the wound. A helmeted head rose above the hatch and she pointed the Fabretti at it. The head jerked down out of sight and she heard the thud of a falling body and curses from below.

She helped Ethan to his feet and supported him as they staggered across the roof and up the ramp into the freight lock.

She felt *Dainty Jane* lift the moment the outer door closed.

'What are you doing?' she yelled.

'We have to leave,' *Jane* said. 'I'm tracking two ships approaching. Take Ethan to the medbay.'

'What about Mender?'

'If we stay here we all die.'

Ethan groaned and sank to the deck as the airlock's inner door opened.

'*Jane*, get us to *Bonaventure*, please!' Orry yelled as she grabbed her brother under the arms and dragged him into the cargo bay.

Her foot slipped in his blood and she fell back, slamming her elbow painfully into the deck. She got to her feet and grabbed him again, and his eyes fluttered and closed as she struggled to haul his limp body down the passageway. The medbay door opened as she approached and somehow she managed to manoeuvre his dead weight body onto the bed. His breathing was shallow, his pulse so thready she could barely feel it and his shirt was drenched in blood. But she couldn't stand there; she'd just be in the way.

Her legs feeling like jelly, she dropped into a chair and let the scanners swing into position, moving over Ethan's body. Then she felt gravity slip away as they entered orbit and she strapped herself into the seat.

'Orry,' *Jane* said quietly, 'I'm sorry, but you have to see this.'

Tearing her eyes from her brother, Orry accepted a sensor feed which showed *Bonaventure*, still in the high parking orbit where Ethan had left her. She was patched in just in time to see a spread of kinetic harpoons streaking towards the freighter. They struck *Bonaventure*'s drive-cluster, punching clear through the shielding.

The freighter burst apart like a rotten fruit, slinging her fabric in a rapidly expanding cloud. Orry watched in disbelief as *Bonaventure*'s remains tumbled out of orbit and fell towards the planet below.

36

DEBRIS FIELD

Orry didn't remember falling asleep, but when she did awake she was cold and stiff. For a few wonderful seconds she was at peace – before the memories hit her like a sledgehammer.

She was on her feet in an instant and staring down at Ethan's pale body on the medbay bed. His shoulder and chest were heavily bandaged.

'How is he, *Jane*?'

'Stable and sedated. The wound looked worse than it was; there shouldn't be any permanent damage.'

Orry sagged with relief. 'Thank you so much . . .' She pressed the heels of her hands into her eyes until they hurt and released a ragged sigh. 'Where are we?'

'I collapsed randomly,' *Jane* replied. 'We're now somewhere near the Antonides Ridge.' The ship hesitated. 'How are you feeling?'

'I've been better.' Orry's head throbbed as she looked around, a metallic taste heavy on her tongue. The deck was tacky with Ethan's blood. 'Does Mender keep any cleaning supplies around here?' she asked, ignoring the pang his name caused in her chest.

A panel released and a door swung open. Inside, Orry found disinfectant and wipes.

She experienced a strange sense of detachment as she scrubbed. *I wish I was a cleaning mech*, she thought. It would be nice to have her decisions made for her, to be told what to do.

'What will happen to Mender?' *Jane* asked.

Orry scrubbed harder, rubbing at a stubborn flake of rust-brown blood on the chair leg so hard that the cloth grew warm against her fingertip.

'Orry?'

She stopped and hung her head. 'Dyas will take him to Roag.'

'Can we help him?'

She pressed the back of her hand against her sweating brow. 'I honestly don't know how – we tricked her once, so she'll be ready for us this time.' She sat back on her haunches and pulled the pendant out from beneath her top, staring at it. 'This is what Roag wants. If we're going to get Mender back we'll have to let her have it.'

'But she'll give it to the Kadiran.'

'Yes.'

'And Professor Rasmussen told you that the stone was potentially very dangerous.'

'I know, but what else can we do, *Jane*?'

'If that stone is as powerful as the professor suspects, the Kadiran are the last people who should have it.'

'Even if giving it to them is the only way to save Mender?'

The ship remained silent.

'All right.' Orry stood up. 'Set a course for the Shattermoon.

Before we decide anything, let's find out what this thing actually is.'

'What about *Goshawk*?'

'I'll think of something,' she said, praying that she would.

'Where's *Goshawk*?' Orry asked the moment the distant shape of the Shattermoon appeared ahead of them. She was fighting to ignore the post-collapse nausea churning in her gut.

'Oh dear,' *Jane* replied. Overriding Orry's visual cortex, the ship displayed a split-screen amalgam of visual and sensor imagery: on one side, *Goshawk* was twisting and darting like a minnow, threading her way through a maelstrom of explosions and energy beams. The other half of the image displayed the sloop's attacker, an organic-looking ship whose chitinous hull resembled the barnacle-covered blade of a scythe.

'What's *that*?' Orry asked.

'*That* is a Kadiran cleaveship.'

Orry's hand rose instinctively to the pendant. 'What the hell are they playing at? Do they want to start another war?'

'I doubt it; I suspect they intend to destroy *Goshawk* so completely that there will be no evidence they were ever here.'

'Can *Goshawk* beat them?'

'No, cleaveships might be small, but they are heavily armed. Should we render assistance?'

Orry remembered the tyro, Orlov, with his whole career ahead of him, and Captain Hirota, hampered by her heritage. She rubbed the oily stone at her throat and took a deep breath. 'No,' she said, 'maintain our present course. The Kadiran are here for the professor – we have to get to him first.'

*

'I didn't think you'd be back so soon. Do you have the piece?' Professor Rasmussen beamed at Orry as she hauled open the lift door and stepped out.

'Pack your gear, Professor. We're leaving.'

'Leaving? I don't think so, young lady.'

'Do you have any idea what's going on up there? *Goshawk* is under attack by the Kadiran.'

'Impossible! The Kadiran would never—'

'I saw their ship, Professor, and they're here for you. We need to go. *Right now.*'

Rasmussen swallowed. 'Oh Rama, it's the stone. I was right.'

'About what?' Orry really didn't like the way his face had paled.

His bony fingers fluttered. 'I've been studying the readings I took when you were last here . . .'

'And?'

'Well, I need to perform more tests to be sure—'

'There's no time, Professor. Just tell me.'

'I checked the data so many times, praying I was wrong . . .'

She was losing patience. 'Wrong about *what*? And start packing!'

'The stone! I believe – and this is just a theory you understand—'

'*Professor!*'

'I think it's a planetbuster,' he gabbled. 'I think – that is, the readings indicate – that something like that stone was the catalyst that initiated the destruction of this facility, of the entire Shattermoon.'

Orry lifted the pendant and stared at the dull stone in its centre. 'That's ridiculous. It's tiny.'

'No, I assure you, the exponential release of eisenform energy through a phasic breach could—'

She held up a hand. 'Save it. That just means we've got even more reason to stop the Kadiran getting their claws on it. Come on – let's go.'

He frowned. 'Is that why they want me? To lead them to the stone?'

'I believe so, yes.'

'Then why on Tyr did you bring it here?'

'I didn't know they'd be here.' Orry rubbed her forehead. She was beginning to feel very scared. 'I've delivered it right to them.'

Professor Rasmussen stared at her, his face drained of colour. 'We have to go.'

She rolled her eyes. 'Thank you!' She watched him bustle around the lab, throwing items into a holdall.

Orry, Jane sent, *Goshawk has been destroyed. The Kadiran vessel is heading this way.*

'Professor! Leave the rest – they're coming.'

'But . . .' He stood there with an artefact in each hand, clearly torn.

She ran to him, grabbed the piece in his right hand and hurled it across the lab. It struck a scanner, sending it crashing to the ground. Rasmussen clutched the chipped glass disk in his other hand protectively to his chest.

She seized his lab coat. 'Now!' she yelled in his face.

He blinked rapidly as she dragged him to the lift. 'Whether you're right or not,' she said as the lift rose at what felt like a snail's pace, 'the stone has to be destroyed. The Kadiran are obviously convinced it's some kind of master weapon. They're already risking another war over it.'

'You can't destroy it,' he protested. 'It's an artefact of unprecedented historical and scientific value – it could be the key that finally unlocks the secrets of the Departed.'

'If the Shattermoon is anything to judge the Departed by, I reckon their secrets are best left hidden,' she said caustically, drumming her fingers on the cage and willing the lift to move faster.

'What about handing it over to the Ascendancy?'

She snorted. 'They're no different to the Kadiran.'

'You don't mean that.'

'Don't I?' She fixed him with a stare. '*Can* it be destroyed?'

'I don't know.'

'Don't give me that, Professor.'

'I mean it!'

'You must have some idea. How many decades have you been stuck inside this moon? No one knows more about the Departed than you.'

She saw the top of the lift shaft approaching at last. *How are we doing,* Jane?

The Kadiran vessel will have a firing solution in four minutes.

Orry dragged the cage door open and shoved him out. 'Move,' she told him, pointing at *Dainty Jane.*

Professor Rasmussen was not, it turned out, an agile man. Orry set a timer in her peripheral vision and watched it obsessively as the old man shuffled across the pad. *Dainty Jane's* engines were idling with a bone-shaking thrum.

'Go!' Orry shouted the moment they were both inside the cargo bay, but *Jane* was already airborne.

She helped the professor onto the cockpit ladder, and as he climbed, he wheezed, 'I know how we can find out.'

'Find out what?'

'Whether I'm right about the stone – and how to destroy it.'

'Why the sudden change of heart?'

He laughed dryly. 'I'm a little like a galleon in some respects. Sometimes it takes me a while to change course.'

They clung onto the rungs as *Jane* banked hard.

'Okay, so how?' she asked.

'You're not going to like it.'

The Shattermoon's debris field slipped past a hundred kilometres beneath them. Deep within it, near the moon's denuded and exposed core, the jostling chunks of rock were so densely packed that Orry could hardly see through them. Out here on the edge they were more widely separated.

'Down there,' Rasmussen said from the right-hand seat. He pointed at a gap between the outermost boulders.

'Are you certain about this?' Orry asked, eyeing the rocks. Most of them dwarfed *Dainty Jane*.

'Define *certain*. I'm certain enough to risk my life.'

'And ours,' she pointed out.

He stared at the distant core. 'I've been piecing together the clues for decades and they all point to some form of data store in the moon's core. We tried digging down to it, but machines stopped working, people disappeared, and in the end we had to give up. The only way in is through the debris field, but I've never been able to convince the Fleet to risk a ship.'

'But you want *us* to try, even though you couldn't convince the Admiralty.'

He looked at her. 'This is your only chance to find out what that stone is.'

She grimaced. 'So you're telling me that every ship that's gone into that debris field has been destroyed – what makes you think we'll be any different?'

'That.' He pointed at the stone around her neck. 'None of the other ships carried one. I haven't had time to fully analyse my findings, but I think it will help us through.'

'You *think*? How?'

'I don't know yet.'

There were more than just the two of them at risk. '*Jane?*' she asked. 'What do you think?'

'I think we've left things too late for a debate. We don't have a choice any more. Our chances of getting to a collapse point without the Kadiran ship disabling my engines is minimal.'

Orry watched the gap the professor had spotted. It was closing fast. 'I must be crazy,' she muttered, but *Dainty Jane* was already leaping forward, increasing thrust and arrowing towards the gap.

The Kadiran ship was out of sight behind them, occluded by the curve of the moon's intact portion of crust. She kept one eye on the cleaveship's predicted course as the rocks raced closer.

They plunged into the shifting rubble.

Orry killed the thrust and let *Dainty Jane* coast deeper into the debris field, using the verniers to avoid the larger pieces.

'The Kadiran vessel has entered the debris field,' *Jane* announced. 'At our current velocity they will intercept us before we are halfway to the moon's core.'

Orry studied the rocky fragments surrounding them. It was already becoming difficult to plot a course between them; speeding up would guarantee a collision.

Reluctantly, she goosed the throttles. A slowly spinning

rocky ovoid drifted in from the right and she compensated, spotting a larger fragment too late as it fell from above. She adjusted course to avoid it and winced as a loud scraping was transmitted through *Dainty Jane*'s hull.

'I can't do this,' she said, disgusted with herself. 'The damn things are coming in from all directions. You have control, *Jane*.'

'No, you must continue to fly,' the ship replied. 'This field is saturated with eisenform particles which are interfering with my systems – the degradation is becoming worse the further we penetrate towards the core. In addition, I have been forced to retract the radiator array due to impact damage. All excess heat is now being shunted to the thermal sinks, which have a limited capacity. I estimate eighteen minutes until they overheat.'

'Oh, great.' Orry didn't have to ask what would happen then; with no other way to dissipate the enormous heat produced by her power plant, *Dainty Jane*'s shielding would be vaporised, turning the ship into a giant fusion bomb. She took her hands off the controls to wipe her sweating palms. 'Can you at least give me integuary control? My reactions will be quicker that way.'

'I'm sorry, with the current levels of system degradation it's too risky. I'm having trouble ... I feel ... Can't—'

'*Jane? Jane*! Shit.' Orry took a breath. 'Looks like it's just you and me now, Professor.'

He didn't reply.

She tried to check the position of the Kadiran ship, but her integuary was no longer tracking it. She triggered a brief burn and twisted *Dainty Jane* around a planetoid-sized chunk of rock and saw that one side of it was hollowed out and filled with a honeycomb of passages and chambers – but before she could examine it they were past, and a fresh blizzard of incoming rocks required her attention.

'Hell's teeth,' she muttered, sliding *Dainty Jane* through another rapidly narrowing gap and into a steep climb over the pitted surface of a large mass that might once have formed part of the Shattermoon's outer crust.

The blow caught her entirely by surprise, a jarring impact on the back of her head that rattled her brain against her skull. Colours bloomed in her vision and she blacked out for a moment, only vaguely aware of someone shoving her aside.

Groggily, she saw Professor Rasmussen leaning over her, his hands on the controls, pushing forward until *Dainty Jane* was heading directly for the pockmarked crust beneath them.

'What the hell are you doing?' Orry yelled, grabbing his arms and trying to pull his hands off the controls. He turned and beamed at her with a look of pure ecstasy: horribly like the vacant smile of a kettlehead. She gave up trying to move his arms and instead punched him in the face. His expression of joy was replaced by feral fury and he released the controls to wrap his bony hands around her neck and start choking her.

A terrible pressure grew inside her head and her eyes started to bulge. Her chest heaved as she tried to draw air into empty lungs, but the old man's hands were like steel bands clamped around her neck. She clawed at his forearms, scratching off peels of skin with her fingernails, but his grip didn't weaken.

Black spots started appearing in her vision. Outside the ship, the broken crust was filling the canopy. The constant impact of smaller rocks formed a hollow drumbeat inside the cockpit.

Pull up! she told *Jane* desperately, but there was no response.

She closed her eyes. With consciousness slipping away, she tried to focus on her integuary, instructing her acceleration shell to close. It slammed into the professor's ribs without warning, throwing him on top of her, and she gulped down air as his grip on her throat released.

He grunted, trying to force the shell's cover back. It withdrew, leaving him lying awkwardly across Orry, his weight crushing her. As he pushed himself up, he moved his hand so it was pressing on the stone around her neck – and the instant his flesh touched the stone his face changed, his murderous expression turning to one of utter confusion.

He took a step back, frowning as he noticed the deep scratches on his arms, but there was no time to deal with him right now; she lunged for the controls and hauled *Dainty Jane* into a steep climb, staring at the pitted surface of the crust fragment racing past beneath them as she waited for impact . . .

. . . which mercifully never came.

'What happened?' the professor asked as the ship cleared the surface and plunged back into the chaos of the debris field.

'You just tried to kill us,' she croaked. Her throat felt like it was on fire.

His expression of bewilderment couldn't have been faked. 'I don't remember,' he whispered, looking confused and ashamed. He studied his arms in dismay.

Orry rubbed her bruised neck as she focused on avoiding the swarming rocks. 'Touching the stone brought you back to yourself,' she said, 'so I guess you were right.'

'I guess I was.' He sounded intrigued.

She cursed as a heavy blow sent *Dainty Jane* into a tumble and fought to right the ship, wincing at the constant ringing impacts from all sides. The rocks were packed closely now and she was struggling to find a gap large enough for *Dainty Jane* – but at last she spotted a tiny sliver of open space and sent the ship streaking through before it could close.

The surrounding rocks vanished. Orry quickly reversed thrust, bringing *Jane* to a dead stop. They were out of the debris field and there was nothing but empty space between them and the moon's denuded core.

Her mother had shown Orry an ant farm once, the complex inner structure laid bare behind a glass plate. The Shattermoon reminded her of that, with all its tunnels and chambers once buried deep beneath the surface now exposed. The different levels were joined by huge shafts and wide flights of stairs, and chambers like the one containing the professor's lab were linked by passageways far larger than any human would require.

'What,' the professor whispered, 'is that?' He thrust out an arm to point at one of the larger chambers.

Orry squinted at what looked like a humanoid figure. She instinctively hooked the sensor core, sighing when she remembered it was inoperative. Her integuary fared little better, unable or unwilling to resolve the grainy image.

The figure was standing motionless on the lip of the huge bisected chamber, staring out at them. It was taller even than Harry, with an undersized head and compact torso balanced on top of enormously long legs with rear-facing knees like the hind legs of a stag. Its arms, which reached almost to the floor, terminated in delicate, elongated fingers. The figure's bowed back made it look like a hunchback on stilts.

'Fly closer,' the professor breathed, his eyes glued to the oddly shaped apparition.

'Is it a statue?' Orry wondered as she used the vernier thrusters to send *Dainty Jane* coasting gently forward.

'I swear it just moved—'

'You're imagining things,' she said dismissively. 'Nothing could be alive in there, not after all this time.'

'It could be artificial – some kind of mimetic.'

'Still working after thousands of years? I don't – *Holy crap!*'

The figure had turned and was walking deeper into the chamber. It stopped and made a sweeping motion with one long arm, a gesture that looked very much like an invitation to come in and set the ship down.

It was the last thing Orry wanted to do.

37

EMISSARY

Although all her instincts were screaming at her to turn and flee, Orry brought *Jane* to a halt at the chamber's edge.

'What are you waiting for?' Professor Rasmussen asked. 'It wants us to land.'

Orry fingered the pendant.

'I think the professor is right,' *Jane* said.

'Oh, you're back, are you?' Orry said. 'Are you okay? Any idea who that guy is?'

'I am operating at severely reduced capacity; I can tell you no more than you already know,' the ship admitted.

Orry chewed her lip, staring at the figure. This was why they had come here, and despite the warning signals from her gut, curiosity gnawed at her.

'Don't blame me if we all wind up dead,' she muttered, then realised how much like Mender she sounded and smiled sadly. Setting her shoulders, she oriented *Dainty Jane* for a landing. As the ship rolled around the cockpit sphere, their view of the figure rotated until they were looking down on it.

She nudged *Jane* closer, bracing herself as they approached the threshold, expecting an impact at any moment – but whatever field was in place parted without resistance and allowed *Dainty Jane* to float into the chamber. The moment a significant portion of the ship's hull was over the floor, Orry felt the pull of gravity dragging her down and compensated with the landing thrusters, balancing the ship as it passed fully over the threshold and into the chamber.

'Reading point six of a gravity,' *Jane* informed her, 'and there is a breathable atmosphere in here.'

The professor tore his eyes from the figure to study one of the cockpit screens. 'Same composition as my lab.'

Orry set *Jane* down a few metres from the figure. Dust billowed, but its garments remained still.

'Keep the engines running,' she told the ship, 'and lock the mass driver on our friend out there. Any sign of trouble, waste him.'

'I can't take a life, Orry.' *Jane* sounded a little stern.

'Sorry, I forgot. All right, just keep it aimed at him: hopefully, that will be enough.' She led the professor to the freight lock and waited nervously for it to cycle until the outer door opened and dry, dusty air tickled her throat. The chamber smelled like an old book, musty, with a hint of decay.

The figure remained motionless, watching them approach.

Orry slowed as they drew near but the professor hurried on ahead, visibly trembling with anticipation. He stopped a metre from the figure and raised a solemn hand.

'In the name of the human race, I greet you,' he pronounced magniloquently.

Orry winced, then tensed as the figure moved forward with an odd rolling gait, making Rasmussen almost trip over as he stumbled out of its path. She heard a whine of servos from somewhere above her as *Dainty Jane*'s mass driver moved smoothly in its gimbal mounting.

The figure ignored the professor and stopped directly in front of Orry. Its broad, doughy face had a melancholy aspect. Eyes that were little more than punctures in its pasty flesh were set far high above full lips. The tiny eyes looked her up and down, then blinked.

'Your language is primitive,' it said.

She shivered. Its voice was unsettling, both resonant and sibilant, quite unlike anything she'd heard before. 'Thanks,' she said.

'It was not intended as a compliment.'

'I got that.'

The figure expanded its narrow chest in a deep sigh. 'Your presence here saddens me.'

The events of the past days had drained Orry and she was beginning to feel as if she'd been sucked dry. She knew this was a first contact situation, that she was a diplomat for the human race, but she was too wrung out to take this shit.

'Yeah?' she said snarkily. 'Well, your face saddens me.'

Professor Rasmussen looked horrified, but before he could intervene, the figure regarding Orry said, 'It is customary in my culture not to insult those from whom you wish to beg a favour.'

'How do you know I want something?' She didn't entirely succeed in keeping the belligerence out of her voice, which made the professor flinch, but the figure just raised an arm, unfolded a multi-jointed finger and pointed at the stone around her neck.

'Okay, you got me,' she admitted. 'I'm sorry. How about we start over? Do you have a name?'

'You may call me Emissary.'

'Not very original,' she started, then stopped, annoyed with herself. *Try keeping your mouth shut for a change.* 'I'm Orry, and this is Professor Ras—'

'I don't care.'

She counted to ten in her head. 'I'm guessing you're not alive. What are you?'

'You are correct. I am an artificial construct.'

'How long have you been here?'

'Since before this facility's destruction.'

She stared. 'How are you even still functional?'

He raised an arm and Orry's eyes widened as his flesh began to dissolve. Starting at the fingertips, his hand turned to a fine dust, falling away to form a swirling vortex. The hand melted to the wrist before the dust began to spiral back and it regrew.

'I see,' she said, finally – unwillingly – impressed. The avatar was *way* in advance of Ascendancy smart-matter research.

Professor Rasmussen intervened, asking, 'What is your purpose here?'

'My constituent parts performed many functions,' Emissary said. 'My form is infinitely reconfigurable.'

Was that *smugness*? From an avatar? 'Why have you chosen your current appearance?' she asked.

'This is the form of my creators. Would you prefer I emulated a more familiar shape?'

Emissary's body crumbled, reducing in height as it re-arranged itself. Orry's skin crawled as she watched her own face form above a maelstrom of whirling dust. A second later he had created a perfect copy of her, right down to the pendant around her neck. She felt violated, as if he had somehow stolen a part of her.

'Change back,' she snapped.

'Does this disturb you?' Even the voice was hers.

She clenched her fists, but the professor was looking fascinated. 'How do you know our language?' he asked.

'I have studied your people since your arrival at the facility.'

'All this time!' He sounded outraged. 'Why didn't you make contact?'

'Why would I?'

'To – to share your knowledge! I've spent my life on this rock, digging up fragments of your culture – and you were here all the time, able to give me the answers I was searching for?'

'Yes,' Emissary agreed.

'"Yes?"' The professor's face was bright red. '"*Yes?*" Why didn't you, then?'

'Why would I?' the avatar repeated.

'I – uh – to *help us*!'

'Why would I want to help you?'

'Because—' Rasmussen was at a loss.

'Why are you talking to us now?' Orry asked. 'Why invite us in?'

Emissary tapped the replica pendant around his neck. 'Ask your question.'

'Okay: what is this stone? Did something like it destroy this moon?'

A dust storm swirled around her doppelganger, leaving Emissary's original form in its wake. It was a relief.

'My creators used this facility to research the fundamental

building blocks of this universe. Such endeavours are not without risk. We call the object you are wearing a ventari stone. My creators used such artefacts to create stellar nurseries. Think of it as a tap, driven through the fabric of spacetime into a reservoir of energy stored elsewhere: when the tap is opened, energy flows through.'

'So what happened here?' Orry asked, gesturing around her.

'Tapped barrels sometimes burst,' the avatar said calmly.

Professor Rasmussen was staring at the pendant hanging from her neck. The stone suddenly felt horribly heavy.

'How do we destroy it?' she asked.

'This is the question you came here to ask,' Emissary stated.

Orry was tiring of the avatar's portentous statements. 'And do you have an answer?'

'Yes.'

She held her temper. 'Will you tell us?'

'Why should I?'

'You made this thing! You bear some responsibility, surely?'

Emissary said nothing.

She stepped closer, pleading. 'Listen, you have to understand: if we don't destroy this ... this *ventari* stone, someone bad is going to use it – millions – *billions* – of people could lose their lives. Doesn't that mean *anything* to you?'

Emissary's face remained expressionless. 'My creators are gone. What makes you think I care about humans?'

The professor tried another tack. 'Where did your creators go? Did they destroy themselves?'

'No. They found this universe too confining, so they freed themselves.'

'Were they a moral people?' he continued.

'They were pragmatic. The universe has a natural order. They tried not to interfere.'

'They were *creating stars*!' Orry interrupted.

'At one period in their development as a species, this is true,' Emissary conceded, 'but later, there was no need for such primitive technology.'

'It's a shame they didn't clean up their mess afterwards. Do you think they would want their legacy to destroy billions? How is that "not interfering with the natural order"?'

Emissary stared at her. After some time, he held out a hand. A miniature dust storm swirled up from his palm and formed itself into what looked like a dull brass sphere covered in intricate filigree work.

'I know that piece!' Rasmussen exclaimed. 'I sold it years ago, to a collector from Tyr.' He rubbed his chin. 'She was a regular customer. Rama, what was her name?'

'It is known,' Emissary said, 'as a shroudsphere.'

The professor wasn't listening. 'Golovkin!' he cried triumphantly, 'Eloise Golovkin. She lives on one of the islands of Utz.'

Orry, Jane sent, *the Kadiran ship is approaching*.

Orry crouched to peer between *Dainty Jane*'s landing struts, her mouth drying as she saw the menacing sweep of the Kadiran vessel moving clear of the debris field.

'What's up with this place, anyway?' she asked Emissary. 'I thought everyone who comes near it turns into a homicidal maniac?'

'An oversimplified view, but essentially correct. It is a safeguard.'

'Then how did the Kadiran get through in one piece?'

'I do not know.' He didn't sound much concerned.

They had more pressing things to worry about. 'Back on the ship,' Orry ordered – but the professor didn't move, and when she grabbed his arm, he shook her off.

'We can't leave,' he insisted. 'Think of the knowledge Emissary can give us—'

She turned him bodily and pointed at the Kadiran ship. 'If you stay here, you won't get the chance to find any answers.'

His shoulders drooped and he turned to look with yearning at the avatar, then sighed and started to shuffle towards the freight lock.

'Do me a favour,' she told Emissary, 'when the Kadiran question you, just be your normal, helpful self.'

'I doubt they will be stopping,' he replied. 'I suspect they are more interested in your ventari stone.'

'They might come back.'

'They might, but they will find no other stones here. I suggest you keep yours from them.'

'That's the plan.' Orry hesitated, then extended her hand. 'Thanks for your help.'

Emissary frowned for a moment before placing his hand in hers. His palm felt like the soft leather of Harry's duelling gloves. When she tried to withdraw, the avatar kept hold.

He smiled enigmatically. 'A great destiny awaits you, Aurelia Katerina Kent.'

She frowned as he released her, but there was no time to question him further. With a final curious glance at the avatar, she turned and raced towards the ramp.

The Kadiran vessel was stationary when she reached the cockpit, hovering a hundred metres from the energy field that protected the edge of the bisected chamber.

'They're hailing us,' *Jane* said. 'Visual signal.'

'Okay,' Orry told the ship, 'let's see what these bastards have to say, shall we?'

The Kadiran's cream-coloured crest was tattooed in geometric patterns. When it opened its mouth a series of coughing rasps emerged, punctuated with hisses. A moment later *Dainty Jane* provided a translation.

'I am Mourns-For-Lost-Glory, Vessel-Alpha of the cleaveship *Splintered Heart*. You will surrender the ventari stone immediately, or be destroyed.'

Orry stared at the Kadiran alpha and swallowed. She'd seen images, but having one right there on the screen, addressing – no, *threatening* – her, drove home how terrifying these creatures truly were. This one was straight out of a nightmare, activating some primal fear switch deep in her genetic memory.

Focus, she told herself. The Kadiran had called it a ventari stone. *So they do know its true nature.* That made it even more critical she keep it from them.

'He's bluffing,' she told *Jane*. 'They won't risk destroying the stone. Can we fight them?'

'No,' *Jane* said, 'they are more heavily armed, and my thermal sinks are nearing capacity. We can use either the drives or the countermeasures, not both.'

Orry had to force herself to think clearly. *What would Dad do?* 'Do they have *any* weaknesses? Is there *anything* we can use against them to give us a chance to get away?'

Jane thought for a moment. 'The Kadiran are a literal race. In the past they have had trouble dealing with deception, although they do learn quickly. They are also arrogant, viewing other cultures as inherently inferior. This has led to them underestimating the capabilities of others.'

Orry rubbed the stone as she considered *Jane*'s words, then she smiled. 'Tell them we surrender – direct them to the dorsal lock.'

'I would advise against surrender. In encounters with the Kadiran, the human dead are generally considered to be the lucky ones.'

'Noted.'

Jane was silent for a moment. 'You're not really surrendering, are you?'

'Just relay the message, please.'

Orry listened to the guttural exchange, impressed that *Jane* was able to make such biological-sounding noises through her voice synthesiser. The Kadiran language was so . . . *wet*.

'The Vessel-Alpha accepts our surrender,' *Jane* announced.

Orry watched the cleaveship approach. It was not a large vessel but *Jane* was right: it was absolutely bristling with weapons. It manoeuvred smoothly, the Kadiran equivalent of vernier thrusters flickering in a glittering light show as it moved in above *Dainty Jane* and lined up on the collar of her dorsal airlock.

Orry waited until the Kadiran vessel was just a few metres from the airlock, then ignited the main drives. *Dainty Jane* shot upwards and rammed the cleaveship, driving it into the chamber's roof with a dull grinding of metal.

Killing the main engines, she activated the thrusters on the upper hull; three had been damaged by the collision and failed completely, and the others struggled to separate the two ships, but at last something gave way with a metallic screech and they were free. Orry rotated the ship, fired the main engines again and *Dainty Jane* swooped out of the chamber and tore towards the debris field.

Jane's rear lenses showed the Kadiran vessel in momentary disarray, but as the rocks swallowed them up, the cleaveship was already swinging towards them.

As Orry prepared herself for the hellish job of navigating the debris field for the second time, she realised the rocks were less tightly packed than before, almost as if they were parting to allow *Dainty Jane* through.

What the hell?

Hooking the external lenses, she looked back at Emissary's chamber and saw the avatar standing motionless, hands clasped as he stared after her. *You've got to be kidding me,* she thought – surely his influence couldn't extend to the moon's remains? Perhaps Emissary wasn't quite as disinterested as he'd claimed.

As she returned to the controls, a thought occurred to her. 'How did the Kadiran ship make it through the debris field?'

'I imagine they just followed us,' Rasmussen replied.

'But what about the whole – you know, crazy suicide thing?'

'I really don't know. Perhaps the Kadiran are better able to control such impulses?'

Without the need to pick a convoluted course through the rocks, the return journey was much quicker. As the rocks began to thin out, Orry could see stars through the widening gaps. She increased thrust and *Dainty Jane* streaked into open space.

'Sensor core is functional,' *Jane* said with some relief, 'but the cleaveship has followed us; the Kadiran are within range and targeting our main drives.'

'You have control,' Orry said, then, 'Countermeasures!'

'Countermeasures unavailable. We're carrying too much heat.'

'Jettison the sinks – deploy the radiator array!'

'It's too late,' *Jane* announced. 'Brace for impact!'

The ship lurched and Orry felt the acceleration pressure on her chest vanish. *Dainty Jane* drifted on, helpless, rotating slowly.

'The Kadiran commander is hailing us again,' *Jane* said. 'He intends to board us. He sounds angry about what happened before.'

'What are we going to do?' the professor asked in a shaky voice.

Orry didn't have an answer.

38

A LAMENTED FACT

Splintered Heart stood off at ten kilometres and sent a gunboat to dock with *Dainty Jane*'s freight lock. Out of options, Orry and the professor waited in the cargo bay. Ethan was still unconscious, and she wondered bitterly if he would ever wake up again.

'Maybe if you give them the stone they'll let us live,' Professor Rasmussen said hopefully.

'We're not giving them shit,' Orry told him, looking around the hold. She walked over to one of the bulkheads, unfastened the pendant's chain and hooked it over the protruding end of a bolt hidden behind a cluster of tubes and conduits running up the bulkhead.

His eyes shifted from her to the pendant's hiding place, and he swallowed.

'They want us all dead,' she said, and he nodded in agreement just as the freight lock's inner door opened and two Kadiran breedwarriors stalked out. The scaled armour they wore accentuated their natural exoskeletons and Orry realised that the terror she'd experienced viewing the Kadiran on the screen was *nothing* compared to seeing them in the flesh.

The larger of the two made a noise like a drowning buffalo. A moment later his armour produced a translation in a neutral, electronic voice. 'Who is the alpha of this vessel?'

'That would be me,' Orry said, trying not to recoil as the Kadiran loomed over her. She was determined not to show any weakness, despite the fear that was sapping her strength and clouding her mind.

Filters fluttered in the front of the warrior's helmet as he sniffed her. 'You are a female,' his translator announced. 'Human females are permitted to command human vessels. This is a lamented fact.' He stepped back. 'I am Vessel-Alpha Mourns-For-Lost-Glory. You will give me the ventari stone.'

Orry straightened her back. 'I don't have it.'

'Your words do not reflect the true state. This is a human trait.'

The Kadiran reached into a pouch and pulled something out. He opened his glove, revealing a pale blue oval gemstone, its oily surface glistening in just the same way as Orry's pendant.

So that's how they made it through the debris field.

Mourns-For-Lost-Glory extended his arm, palm upwards, and swept it slowly from side to side, stopping almost immediately as he got to the bulkhead where the ventari stone was concealed. He strode across the cargo bay and retrieved the pendant. He made a gesture, and his comrade grabbed Professor Rasmussen and started dragging him towards the airlock.

'No!' the professor cried, but Orry was already striding forward.

'Leave him alone!' she yelled, coming to an abrupt stop as the alpha blocked her path.

Professor Rasmussen's howls faded as he disappeared into the Kadiran gunship.

'Your retreat is needless,' the alpha said as Orry backed away. 'What glory is there in slaying a female?'

'If you have a stone already, what do you want mine for?' she asked, desperately seeking a way to save the professor and keep the stone.

The Kadiran dropped the blue gem carelessly into his pouch and held the ventari stone up to the light. 'The Departed produced stones for many purposes,' he said, admiring the gem. 'This one will give us an advantage in the coming conflict.'

'*What* coming conflict? We're not at war! What are you going to do with it?'

'The stone's energy will be released upon the human capital world,' the alpha announced carelessly. '*Then* we will be at war.'

Orry stared at him, horrified. Destroying Tyr would kill the Imperator and cripple the Home Fleet in one devastating blow. With the Home Fleet gone, the rest of the Fountainhead worlds – the beating heart of the Ascendancy – would quickly fall, and the rest of human space would swiftly follow.

The Kadiran looked around the cargo bay. 'This is a Goethen vessel?'

'Yes.'

'Does it speak?'

'Not to you.'

Mourns-For-Lost-Glory produced an alarming sound from deep in his broad chest. After a moment, she realised the Kadiran was laughing.

'It will give me pleasure to destroy you and your vessel.'

'What happened to the whole "no glory in killing females" thing?'

'Your destruction will prove advantageous in the coming conflict. I do not expect a human to comprehend Kadiran glory code.'

'Oh no, I get it: it's not sporting to murder me face to face, but it's fine to blow me up from a distance so no one will find out about your chickenshit surprise attack on Tyr. If honour means so much to you, why do you fight your wars like frightened children?'

'Your insults are meaningless to me. I will not sully my edge with your blood.' The Kadiran stalked away.

'You're all cowards!' she yelled after him.

The airlock sealed.

'So, that went well,' she observed dryly as the scrape of the Kadiran gunship detaching echoed through the cargo bay. She pushed off and floated up towards the cockpit. 'How long have we got?'

'The cleaveship has already powered up its weapons,' *Jane* told her. 'I imagine they will fire as soon as they have recovered their gunship.'

Orry dropped into her seat and watched the gunship sail towards *Splintered Heart*. 'Is there anything we can do?'

'My drives are disabled. Weapons and countermeasures will create too much heat – the shielding will melt if we use them.'

'Huh. Looks like we're out of options, then. I bet you're sorry you ever met me.'

'This situation is not your fault, Orry. If anyone is to blame, it is Cordelia Roag and Morven Dyas.'

'But I dragged you into it—'

'No, Mender did that when he agreed to transport Dyas to *Bonaventure*. I know he regrets it deeply.'

Orry waved a dismissive hand. 'He didn't know what Dyas was planning.'

'For what it's worth, I told him it was a bad idea – but he was desperate.'

'Forget it. It's just a shame it has to end like this.'

'I agree.'

As Orry watched the gunship dock with the cleaveship, she clenched her fists, trying to stop her hands from shaking. It was one thing fighting for your life, she was discovering, and quite another just sitting there waiting for total annihilation.

'Two ships have just collapsed in,' *Jane* announced, and Orry focused on the sensor core, feeling a gut-wrenching mixture of relief and despair when she recognised *Speedwell*, in company with another frigate.

'The Kadiran ship is peeling off,' *Jane* said, and when Orry expanded her view she could see *Splintered Heart* had turned tail and was racing away at high-g, her course taking her in a direct line away from the Shattermoon's gravity well. *Speedwell*'s companion vessel – identified by *Jane*'s combat core as the *Xuan Wu* – powered after the cleaveship.

As *Speedwell* turned and made for *Dainty Jane*, Naumov's voice came over the com. '*Dainty Jane*, *Speedwell*. Are you in need of assistance?'

Steeling herself, Orry responded, 'No, we're just fine, thank you.'

'Really? Because you seem to be adrift, helpless and disabled.' Naumov sounded amused. 'I'm sending a cutter.'

*

Sergeant Volkhov was leading the auxiliary escort sent to bring
Orry and Ethan aboard the frigate. He said little, staring coldly
at her as Ethan's unconscious body was transferred to a gurney.

Second-Captain Naumov was waiting in *Speedwell*'s hangar
when she stepped out of the cutter.

'Have the boy taken straight to sickbay,' he ordered Volkhov,
before turning to Orry and inclining slightly from the waist in
an informal bow. 'It's good to see you again, Miz Kent. I think of
you whenever my shoulder aches, which is most of the time. My
thanks for that little reminder. And now I see you've managed
to get your brother injured too?'

'We need to talk,' she told him. 'Alone.'

He smiled. 'If you think I will fall for—'

She stepped closer and whispered, '*Please*, Captain.'

His smile faded. 'Wait outside,' he told the auxiliaries.

'Sir?' Volkhov queried.

'I'm sure I'll be fine, Sergeant.' He indicated the restraints
and integuary damper Volkhov had forced on Orry.

'Aye aye, sir.' The sergeant glared at her before leading his
team from the hangar.

'You have my full attention, Miz Kent.'

'The Kadiran are planning an attack on Tyr—'

The good humour left his face. 'I expected more of you, Miz
Kent.' He started to turn away.

'I'm telling the truth!' She grabbed his arm and continued
quickly, 'The stone in that pendant – the one everyone's been
looking for? It's a weapon, and now the Kadiran have it.'

He stared at her. 'You gave it to them?'

'No, *of course* I didn't! They *took* it – *and* Professor Rasmussen.'

'You're a con artist, Miz Kent, and by all accounts – and

my recent experience – an accomplished one. So explain to me exactly why in Piotr's name I should believe you?'

'You *have* to believe me,' she said, begging him to see that for once she was telling the truth. 'Why else would a Kadiran cleave-ship be this far into Ascendancy space? And they destroyed *Goshawk*!'

'Incursions by Kadiran privateers are not uncommon,' Naumov said slowly, 'although I admit I've never heard of them venturing this deep before. As for *Goshawk*, we will be gathering debris for analysis. If the Kadiran were involved, there will be diplomatic repercussions.'

'It'll be too late by then! The Kadiran know how powerful that stone is – they were the ones who hired Cordelia Roag to recover it for them, and she sent Dyas – that's why he came after my family when he found that Konstantin had given it to me.'

'Do you have proof of any of this?'

She stared at the deck. 'No . . .'

'Where are Captain Mender and Lord Haris Bardov?'

Their names caused a tightness in her chest. 'Roag has Mender. I don't know where Harry is.'

'Can anyone else corroborate your story?'

'Only Dyas and Roag.'

'And where are they?'

Her head snapped up. 'Tycho IV! I can show you—'

But the captain was shaking his head. 'I have orders to return you to Tyr without delay—'

'You *can't*! Don't you understand?'

'I'm sorry, Miz Kent. Preparations for your trial are already underway. The Count of Delf is—'

'Fuck the Count of Delf! You *must* know Dyas killed Konstantin – you arrested him—'

'And *you* chose to aid in his escape before he was interrogated, which is another charge you'll be facing. Why exactly did you do that, by the way?'

'Please, Captain,' Orry begged, 'that stone can destroy a whole planet – Professor Rasmussen knows the truth—'

'The same Professor Rasmussen who has been conveniently captured by the Kadiran? Your company appears to be rather hazardous to one's health, does it not? I'm sorry, Miz Kent, but look at this from my point of view.'

Her frustration spilled over into anger. 'You bloody fool! Are you so concerned about your career that you'll risk the capital?' His face tightened at that, but she was on a roll now. 'The Home Fleet will be *destroyed*, Naumov – do you understand? It will be the end of the Ascendancy – the end of *everything* . . .'

'We'll be collapsing back home directly,' he said coldly. 'I'll make a full report to the Admiralty when we arrive. If they see fit, they will order an investigation.'

She clutched at his sleeve. 'But that will be too late!'

He stepped back. 'Control yourself, Miz Kent. That is all I am prepared to do at this time.'

His eyes glazed and a moment later the airlock opened and Volkhov returned with another auxiliary.

'You'll be held in isolation until we can hand you over to the Arbiter Corps on Tyr,' the captain told her. 'Your brother will be treated properly. You will not be allowed to see him. I advise you to behave yourself; you're in quite enough trouble as it is.' He strode away.

'Captain Naumov, wait!' she yelled, but Sergeant Volkhov

blocked her path. 'At least look after my brother!' she shouted in desperation.

'You heard the captain,' the auxiliary growled, tapping an axon disruptor against his palm. 'Give me an excuse. Please.'

The airlock hissed closed on Naumov's departing back.

39

SAABITZ ROCK

The city of Utz sweated under a bloated sun. Orry stared across the wide stretch of glittering ocean separating her from the nearest of the city's island districts. After two days crammed into one of *Speedwell*'s tiny cabins, the open space of the Saabitz Rock Holdover Zone was a welcome change, even if the heat was not. Her skin was slick with sweat, the sleeveless T-shirt clinging to her body.

The tightly scattered islands of the Helion Archipelago two hundred kilometres north of Tyr's equator made up the capital. Perfectly white bridges described graceful arches over the broad channels between the islands, but there were no such bridges between the heavily wooded upthrust of stone that was Saabitz Rock and the rest of the archipelago. Just three kilometres away, one of Utz's most fashionable leisure districts was preparing to mark the two hundredth anniversary of the Imperator's accession; colourful bunting had been strung across wide boulevards all over the city and the gleaming hotels and casinos along the ivory beach were draped with animated banners. The worlds of the Fountainhead would be celebrating in style.

Orry didn't feel much like partying.

Her view of the city was unimpeded by fences or walls. The top of the wooded island was a tonsure of ferroconcrete bleached white by the sun. A cluster of buildings in the centre of the compound included a shower block, refectory and dormitories, arranged around the central processing hub and landing pad where she had been deposited that morning. The Administrate clerk who had taken receipt of her from Volkhov's team had told her she was to remain in isolation until her initial hearing. She had yet to see legal counsel, or even be properly processed.

Most of the zone's inmates remained beneath the shade cast by wide awnings set up across the compound, but Orry had too much nervous energy to sit still. Had Naumov believed her – had he delivered his report yet? Even if he had, what if the Admiralty dismissed her warning based on her – admittedly shady – past? *It's more than likely*, she reflected worriedly. *I'm the girl who cried wolf.*

She looked around until she spotted Ethan, sitting quietly under one of the awnings some twenty metres away. His left arm was in a sling and he looked horribly pale, but at least he was conscious and moving about. When he saw her looking he managed a strained smile, and she waved reassuringly, wishing with all her heart she could actually *talk* to him – but they wouldn't even let her near her own brother.

That was the worst thing about Saabitz Rock: the way they sequestered the prisoners' integuaries, creating a ready-made jailor inside every skull. The boundary of her personal isolation area was marked by a faint circle of green light, five metres in diameter, projected by her subverted integuary onto the ground

362

around her. She'd run towards Ethan when he'd finally emerged from the hospital wing earlier that morning, but as soon as their personal boundaries touched, the lines shifted from calm green to angry red and her head had been filled with a mounting pressure that soon turned to pain pulsating deep inside her skull; it didn't let up until she'd hurriedly backed off. The same thing had happened when they'd tried to speak to each other, shouting across the ten-metre gap, and she'd had to wave him to silence, despite the misery in his face. The other inmates clearly already knew the rules; they retreated rapidly whenever she came near them.

Her personal isolation area moved as she approached the Holdover Zone's boundary markers. As the warning line flashed red, she started to feel that same pressure in her head. Blocking out the pain, she managed two more steps – until the pulsing agony became too much to bear and she had to back off. The pressure lessened immediately, but there was no point trying again. They really were trapped.

She squatted on the ground and was pondering her options – not that she could see any at this point – when a flash of light caught her eye. Squinting into the sun, she made out a sleek aerocar, black against the brilliant blue of the sky, out over the strait. It looked like it was heading directly for Saabitz Rock.

Detainee Kent, Aurelia Katerina, a voice announced over her subverted integuary, *proceed to the processing hub immediately.*

She glanced at Ethan. From the way he was gazing idly at the awning above his head she could tell he hadn't received the same summons. She didn't even consider disobeying the order; doing so wouldn't get her anywhere, and she could do without the pain any attempt would bring. Besides, she wanted to know what was going on.

She trudged across the compound, sure things were about to take a turn for the worse, although she had no idea how. *I guess I'm about to find out.* The aerocar whined overhead, slowing as it came in to land.

Ethan caught sight of her leaving the compound and struggled to his feet, making a *What's up?* gesture with his good arm. She tried to reassure him with a smile, but from the worried frown on his face it was clear she'd failed.

It took her two seconds to case the processing hub: there would be no escape. The circular room had two doors, one leading to the landing pad, the other to the inmates' compound. When Orry had first arrived, an Administrate clerk had occupied the single desk in the centre of the room. Now the chair was empty, but two individuals were clearly awaiting her: a muscular man in a dark suit and a middle-aged woman in high boots and a fashionably cut thigh-length jacket.

The woman stepped forward. Her dark hair was tied back, framing a youthful face but for fine crow's feet at the corners of her eyes. The ugly red welt of an old duelling scar ran diagonally down her forehead, across her nose and onto her cheek.

'You will come with us, Miz Kent.'

'Where to? Who are you? Arbiters?'

'My name is Rostov.' The woman motioned with one gloved hand and Orry backed away as the gorilla bore down on her.

'Get off me!' she yelled as strong hands seized her, but she stopped struggling when an axon disruptor appeared in front of her face.

'I'd rather not use this,' Rostov informed her, 'so please behave yourself.'

Orry stopped struggling and allowed the woman to secure her wrists. She clearly knew what she was doing, because the pliable plastic ties became rigid when she touched a small key device to them. There was no way to unpick those restraints. Rostov dropped the key into her jacket pocket and pulled out an integuary damper, which she placed on Orry's forehead.

'Where are you taking me?' Orry demanded again as the man escorted her to the waiting aerocar.

'Someone is keen to meet you.' Rostov glanced at Orry's filthy flight suit and sweat-stained T-shirt and curled her lip. 'Although I can't imagine why.'

The aerocar's glossy black fuselage bore no markings; that and the luxurious interior told Orry that she was not in the hands of the Arbiter Corps.

She settled into a cream-coloured leather seat that conformed to her body in a way no acceleration shell ever had. Her minder wedged himself in beside her while Rostov positioned herself opposite. Orry examined the interior carefully, wondering if this trip would offer some chance of escape. The coachwork was some fine-grained dark wood, lacquered to a mirror finish. A thick cream carpet covered the floor; that and the aroma of the real leather made her acutely aware of her own stink of sweat and unwashed clothes. *No wonder Rostov's looking at me as if I'm scum*, she thought despondently.

The gull-wing door swung closed and the autonomous aerocar rose slowly. Orry tried to spot Ethan as the vehicle banked over the compound, but it was already picking up speed and in a matter of seconds they were passing over the white towers of an apparently endless suspension bridge that headed arrow-straight to the distant horizon and beyond. At the far end of the bridge she could make out the thin line of the Capitol Ribbon rising from the equator and disappearing into a layer of high cloud on its way to orbit.

'Are we going far?' she asked, but Rostov stared silently at her, her face expressionless.

Orry forced a smile. 'Good chat. Thanks.' She turned back to the window and stared out at the long sandy beaches of the leisure resorts below. Ahead, the Imperator's Palace rose beyond the slender spires of the administrative district of Isla Concordia. Ground vehicles drove along the spacious avenues below a carefully coordinated ballet of aerial traffic, aerocars constantly peeling off to disappear into buildings or land on pads clinging to vertiginous walls like leaves budding from a stem.

As they shot diagonally past a patrol cruiser – and was studiously ignored by the pair of uniformed arbiters within – Orry realised her flyer was disregarding the invisible traffic corridors observed by the other vehicles, instead taking an undeviating course straight across the city. Isla Concordia lay directly ahead now and she wondered whether the aerocar belonged to someone highly placed in the Administrate, or perhaps a wealthy magnate . . . although she couldn't begin to guess what a top civil servant or a chief exec might want with her.

They passed the triple towers of the Trefoil, draped in pulsing banners proclaiming the Imperator's bicentennial, and Orry gazed in fascination at the building from which the Administrate governed all of human space. She twisted as they sped over the skybridges linking the towers and watched the gaudily decorated spires and the administrative district recede into the background.

The aerocar's nose angled down and she frowned, her heart suddenly in her mouth. They were heading straight for the Imperator's Palace.

40

PIOTR

The palace was an architectural wonder, all crenellated parapets, domes and fluted towers, with sunlight playing over dazzling fields of glass. A single road wound up the hill from the city, sweeping through light woodland until it became a broad drive looping past the front of the palace. Formal gardens extending to the rear of the property gave way to what looked like a carefully managed vision of the jungle that had covered this part of Tyr when the first settlers landed.

As the aerocar descended over the main building Orry spotted a fleet of delivery vehicles, with mechanicals busily carrying what looked like catering supplies inside, but she lost sight of them as they banked gently and settled on an oval of manicured lawn in the centre of a walled garden. The distressed brickwork of the walls made her feel like she had landed in the middle of a period drama.

Four soldiers, tall men with the hard eyes of veterans, waited at the lawn's edge. They were wearing the ceremonial golden helmets and formal green tunics of the Imperator's Guard. Orry climbed out of the aerocar without a word and let Rostov lead her to the soldiers.

One of them, distinguished by a drooping silver moustache, stepped forward. 'This way, Miz Kent.'

She swallowed and followed him across a broad expanse of brown gravel which crunched under her boots, the only sound other than the birdsong which echoed around the walled garden. It was a beautiful place, but its tranquillity was at odds with the anxiety building in her chest.

She raised her hands to try to straighten her greasy hair, then stopped herself; she refused to be intimidated by her surroundings. With the guards forming a loose escort around her, Orry walked along the back wall of the palace, past a pair of French windows and through a plain wooden door to a spiral staircase leading down to a corridor lined with metal ducting and exposed cables. She found her mouth watering at the scent of baking that permeated the corridor; the rations aboard *Speedwell* had been bland at best.

The corridor ended at a flight of stone steps that descended into what turned out to be a large cellar kitchen. The bare brick walls looked like they had been transplanted from some ancient manor, but the brushed steel surfaces and modern appliances could have belonged to a seven-star hotel. A short, rotund man with thinning grey hair was standing with his back to her, apparently staring at a tray of pies sitting on the metal worktop in front of him. Flour and discarded utensils were scattered about him.

Orry walked down the steps, her chest fluttering with nerves, and the guards silently took up position at the foot of the stairs. Slowly, she approached the man. When he turned to face her, she saw the sleeves of his white shirt had been rolled up and he wore a flour-covered apron.

She struggled to maintain her composure.

His Excellency Piotr, Imperator Ascendant and *de jure* ruler of all human space, was a portly, ageing man with a grey walrus moustache and bushy sideburns. He studied Orry for a moment, no doubt taking in her lank hair, the shadows under her eyes and the lamentable state of her flight suit, and frowned.

'Would you care for a pie?'

She blinked.

He took a napkin from a nearby dispenser and used it to pick up one of the pies, which he handed to her. 'Be careful, young lady. They're fresh from the oven.'

'Th-thank you,' Orry said. She could feel its heat as he passed it to her. Her hands made awkward by the restraints, it took her a moment to juggle pie and napkin. When she managed to break it open, steam rose, bringing with it a peppery, meaty aroma that made her mouth water.

'Go ahead, try it,' he suggested.

She raised the pie to her mouth and blew on it, then took a bite, sucking down air and resisting the urge to flap her hands in front of her mouth to cool the molten mass sitting on her tongue. It took a moment for the flavour to emerge through the heat – and she had to force herself not to spit it straight back out again. The heavy-handed seasoning did nothing to mask an unpleasant, oily sweetness that had no place in any dish.

'Do you like it?' he asked. 'My own recipe. I marinated the meat in extract of Jovali gyrhawk.'

'It's ... uh ...' Orry tried not to gag as she forced the mouthful down. 'It's ... um ...'

He looked expectantly at her.

She sighed. 'I'm sorry, but it's awful.'

The Imperator's brow creased. He took a pie from the tray and sniffed it, then took a bite.

'Gah!' he cried, grimacing, and tossed it onto the work surface. He wiped his hands on his apron. 'Well, at least you didn't tell me what a "remarkably unique" taste it had.'

'Why would I do that?' Orry was genuinely confused.

'Honesty is a rare thing around here. I can't remember the last time someone told me they didn't like my cooking. They're all too bloody afraid of offending me. Isn't that right, Sievers?'

'Yes, Excellency,' agreed the guard captain from the foot of the stairs.

Orry felt like she was having an out-of-body experience. Was she really discussing the Imperator's appalling cooking with Piotr himself?

He stroked his moustache. 'I believe you're not always so truthful, though, Miz Kent.'

She opened her mouth, then stopped. Her father had drummed etiquette into them so they'd be ready for any play, but *Excellency* didn't sit well with her. She couldn't very well call this man Piotr, though. 'Sir,' she said, by way of a compromise, 'have you received Second-Captain Naumov's report?'

'Why else would you be here?'

That was a huge relief – perhaps she had underestimated Naumov and the Admiralty. Now she had a chance to make the most important man in human space understand the devastating threat they were facing. 'You need to mobilise the Home Fleet,' she urged him. 'Recall all other ships and start making preparations for a Kadiran attack—'

'Yes, yes – all in good time,' the Imperator said calmly. 'Tell me about this stone you stole.'

She hesitated, unwilling to incriminate herself.

The Imperator tutted. 'You expect me to take your claims seriously and yet you aren't even prepared to tell me why?' He began to turn back to the work surface.

'All right,' she said quickly, 'I'll tell you. It started at the Count of Delf's ball.'

She began to speak – briefly considering leaving out some of the more incriminating parts of the story, then deciding against it. The Imperator didn't interrupt as she outlined the whole sorry tale. His face remained impassive, and when she had finished, he kept silent for a long time.

'An interesting story,' he said eventually, but his eyes were cold and Orry realised she had failed to convince him that the Kadiran threat was real.

Where did I go wrong? There must be something I can do to make him believe me—

He motioned to the guards. 'Thank you for your time, Miz Kent.'

'That's it?' she protested. 'But you have to do something!' Hands seized her arms. 'You have to stop them!'

He frowned. 'I am the Imperator Ascendant, Miz Kent – I do not *have* to do anything.' He stepped closer. 'I am all too aware of your history, young lady. You are a petty criminal who displays a particular contempt for the Ruuz, which is ironic, considering the circumstances.'

'*What* circumstances?'

'I did wonder if your parents had ever told you the truth. It doesn't surprise me that they lied to you – I assume your brother knows nothing of your lineage either?' He studied her face. 'You do remind me of your mother.'

Orry gaped. 'You knew my mother?'

He smiled. 'Oh yes, very well. Your mother was Katerina Soltz.'

'Soltz?' There was an unaccountable yawning sensation in her stomach. 'Soltz, as in *Milan* Soltz? As in the *Count of Delf*?'

'As in Milan Soltz, yes. Your mother's father.'

Orry's head was reeling. 'You're saying the Count of Delf is my *grandfather*?'

'Yes, much to his regret.'

'Bollocks.' She flushed, angry that she'd failed to hold her tongue.

The Imperator was unaffected. 'Your mother was engaged to be married to the fourth Duke of Lowenstaat, an arrangement which would not only have been advantageous for both houses, but would have strengthened my own position. Then your *father*' – she could hear the scorn in Piotr's voice – 'came along, posing as a nobleman and sniffing around House Delf to see what scraps he could steal. He seduced your mother and lured her away. Of course,' he added, 'Delf never forgave her.'

'That's not true!'

'Believe what you want. I really don't care.' He gestured at Sievers, and Orry found herself being dragged away.

'This has nothing to do with my mother!' she yelled from the stairs. 'I didn't even *know* about my mother! I'm telling the truth about the Kadiran – this whole planet is going to be destroyed and *you can stop it*!'

Below her the Imperator Ascendant nibbled at another pie.

He shook his head sadly and tipped the entire contents of the tray into a bin.

The heat was less oppressive when Orry stepped out of the palace onto the gravel path. Tyr's sun was hanging low in the darkening blue sky as the evening shadows began to gather. The aerocar on the lawn was flanked by Rostov and her gorilla.

Orry realised she was still holding the pie the Imperator had given her. She was about to hurl it away when a thought occurred to her. She scanned the aerocar's lower fairings, searching for the air intake.

As they neared the edge of the path she raised the pie to her mouth as if to take a bite, but instead, clumsily let it fall from her fingers.

'Just leave it,' Sievers told her as she stooped to retrieve it, but she ignored him and picked it up – together with a handful of gravel. He didn't notice her surreptitiously press the stones deep into the still-warm filling.

'Five-second rule,' she said brightly as she sprang to her feet and nibbled at the crust. She grimaced. 'Nope, it doesn't get any better.'

'If you're quite finished?' Rostov said acerbically, but Orry ignored her and instead thanked Sievers for waiting, then strode quickly across the grass to the waiting aerocar.

As she neared it she stumbled, hurling herself into the side of the vehicle with a satisfyingly solid thud, just as her father had taught her. She was on her knees for only a moment, but it was time enough to cover her hands as she mashed the pie into the grille covering the primary air-intake for the vehicle's ram air turbine.

Rostov's gorilla grudgingly helped her up and she stumbled into him, wiping her pastry-covered hands down his suit as she regained her balance. He glowered at the mess.

'No great loss,' she told him. 'Between you and me, old Piotr's cooking isn't all that—'

'Get in,' Rostov snapped.

Heart pounding, Orry resumed her seat in the aerocar. Her plan was rough and ready – it probably wouldn't even work, but if it did, she needed to be ready. She re-checked the location of the aerocar's emergency controls as the palace fell away beneath them.

Her tension increased as they skirted the towers of the Trefoil and shot out across the city, overflying wide streets of tall townhouses, then the low-density estates of the provincial islands. Orry's world shrank to the sound of the aerocar's engine. Knuckles whitening in her lap, she watched Saabitz Rock draw closer at an alarming rate.

Finally, she heard a faint rattle from beneath the passenger cabin. *The Imperator makes tough bloody pies,* she reflected; this one had resisted being sucked into the air intake for far longer than she'd expected.

Her relief was tinged with fear: this was a horribly dangerous plan, putting all their lives at risk. She pressed her feet firmly into the carpet, bracing herself as best she could.

The rattle sounded again, louder this time, and Orry pictured the gravel careening along the intake tube towards the main turbine blades. A frown animated Rostov's scarred face for a moment before the screech of rending metal tore through the cabin.

The aerocar bucked wildly, then tumbled through the air as a high-pitched alarm battered Orry's ears, drowning the shouts of the other two passengers. Trying to ignore the vomit-inducing spinning, she focused her attention on the emergency controls set into the cabin behind Rostov's head.

The nerve-shredding noise of the engine tearing itself apart ceased, and a moment later a drogue chute deployed. The violent oscillations lessened and the tumbling resolved into a rapid but stable descent. Trees and lakes filled Orry's view as the aerocar plummeted downwards at a hair-raising angle.

She punched her belt release and fell forward out of her seat. Rostov grunted as Orry landed on her, their heads cracking together. Orry was seeing stars when she thrust her hand into Rostov's jacket pocket and closed her fingers around the key to her restraints. As Rostov clutched at her, Orry felt the gorilla grab her leg from behind. She kicked back hard and heard a cry of pain. His grip slackened.

A series of concussive thuds sounded from the roof as four emergency chutes opened above the stricken aerocar, billowing orange in the growing darkness. The vehicle lurched level, giving Orry a chance to wrench her arm free of Rostov's grasp.

Here goes nothing, she thought as their descent slowed, and reaching up, she yanked the emergency release for the cabin roof. As it spun away into the night sky, she hit the jettison override for chute number three and lunged desperately for the tangle of shroud lines as the chute separated from its anchor point.

The shroud lines burned as they slid through her palms, but she tightened her grip, ignoring the pain as the cords bit into her flesh and finally found purchase. Rostov clawed ineffectually at her waist as the chute plucked Orry up and out of the vehicle.

She shot upwards, holding on with all her strength while the world rotated around her, a kaleidoscope of green and blue, muted in the dimming light. Her slight weight did nothing to stabilise the massive chute, which was whipping across the suburbs like a kite.

With a growing sense of panic she realised that not only was the chute *not* descending; in fact the offshore breeze was lifting it higher into the air. Treetops brushed her boots and she tried to gauge the distance to the ground. It was too far to jump, but if she continued to rise like this, she'd soon have no choice.

The trees vanished into the darkness behind her and Orry saw a wide expanse of black below. Occasional lights sparkled in the gloom and it took her a moment to realise she was over a body of water.

Gritting her teeth, she let go.

41

TOO EASY

Orry's flight suit squelched as she sneaked between the rows of parked vehicles. She kept her head down, trying doors while monitoring the cars' security systems with her integuary, missing Ethan desperately. Her little brother could have subverted one in no time.

The car park belonged to a small hotel, the first building she'd found after pulling herself out of the sea. She was shivering despite the humid night air, her sopping-wet clothes clammy against her skin.

The soft hum of an approaching vehicle made her crouch lower. Headlights swept over the car park as a cab turned off the main road. It passed her and came to a halt in front of the hotel entrance. She heard raised voices through the cab's open windows and edged closer, keeping to the shadows.

'Twenty imperials?' the elderly woman in the back was complaining. 'Are you sure? That sounds like too much.'

The driver turned in his seat to stare at her. He was a bear of a man with a glistening bald head and a full black beard. 'Where're you from, luv?' he asked.

'Kemperstaad, on the southern continent.'

'Flown in for the celebrations?'

'Yes. My daughter and her family live here.'

'And they're too busy to pick you up from the airport?' the cabbie said. He glanced at the hotel. 'Or put you up? I'd have a word if I were you. Anyway, I don't know how much taxis cost in Kemperstaad, but here in the capital the fare from the airport is twenty imperials.'

Orry's jaw tightened. Twenty imperial sovereigns was highway robbery. She shrank back as a porterbot whizzed out of the hotel. It balanced on its one large wheel, waiting by the boot.

'It still sounds like too much,' the old woman said weakly.

'So you're accusing me of ripping you off?'

'No! No, I—'

'Look, luv, twenty imperials, or I call the arbiters – we'll see what they think.'

'Oh, very well.' The woman delved into her handbag and handed over a gilt chip. The cabbie swiped it over his dashboard and passed it back.

The boot sprang open and the porter lifted out a battered suitcase as the old woman stepped from the vehicle. Orry stared at the case, the ghost of an idea scratching at her mind. A moment later, she smiled thinly.

Creeping around to the front of the taxi, she lay on the ground. She heard the boot close with a click and the hum of the motor increased in pitch. The vehicle moved half a metre before its collision detection system sensed her and slammed on the brakes. The driver cursed, and Orry crawled quickly around to the passenger side.

The driver's door opened and when the cabbie stepped out

of the idling vehicle to investigate, she eased open the passenger door and slid over to his seat. He caught the movement and whirled round, confusion turning to anger, but Orry had already raised the windows and locked the doors. She put the vehicle into reverse, and with the cabbie lumbering after her, shouting threats she couldn't properly hear, she skidded onto the road, slipped the car into drive and accelerated away.

Once she was well clear of the hotel, Orry pulled into the side of the road. Ahead, the cantilevered arms of a suspension bridge rose white against the darkness, illuminated by the flash of fireworks which were lighting up the sky. She ignored the display and concentrated on disabling the taxi's transponder before the arbiters could use it to track her. In the distance, she could see the lines of sparkling drive-flares that marked the passage of ships and aircraft into the city's spaceport, situated on another outlying island. She twisted two final wires together, climbed back into the cab and followed the signs for the spaceport.

The arrivals terminal was busy despite the late hour. Orry parked in the waiting area for private vehicles opposite a taxi rank and studied the emerging passengers. It took a few minutes to identify the person she was looking for: a young woman of about her own build, dressed head to toe in the latest fashions. An older man, probably the woman's valet, was pushing a trolley piled high with matching luggage and topped with a hatbox.

The taxi at the head of the rank had just departed, but before the next in line could move forward to pick up the young aristo and her servant, Orry had jammed her foot on the accelerator and sped across the road, cutting into the front of the line and coming to a neat halt in front of the pair.

'Where to, miz?'

The aristo glanced at the taxi behind Orry, its driver glaring through his windscreen in outraged disbelief. She looked down her nose and asked, 'Are you supposed to cut into the front of the line like that?'

Behind her, the cabbie was climbing out of his vehicle. 'Not really,' Orry said with a conspiratorial wink, and punched the boot release.

The aristo sighed and nodded at her valet, who started loading the cases. 'Isla Luxor,' she said, then glared at the other driver as he shoved past her.

Orry quickly raised her window and locked the cab doors.

'What the fuck d'you think you're doing, mate?' the cabbie demanded, rapping on the glass.

In the rear-view screen Orry saw the valet load the last case into the boot. She closed it and he moved to the rear door to open it for his mistress. They both frowned when they realised it was locked, but the furious taxi driver was shouting too loudly for either of them to make themselves heard. Orry cupped her ear with her hand and flashed a beaming smile at the angry cabbie. With a wave to the bewildered aristo, she indicated and pulled smoothly away from the kerb.

'Too easy,' she murmured, as she watched the aristo berating first her valet and then the unfortunate cabbie. A moment later, they were out of sight and she was speeding into the darkness.

42

GOLOVKIN

The lighthouse must have dated back to the founding of Utz, the white tower an anachronism in these days of sophisticated navigation systems. At some point in its history it had been converted into a quirky and unconventional residence.

By someone with more money than sense, Orry thought, shrinking into the darkness as an arbiter patrol cruiser whined past further inland. The lighthouse was perched on the end of a promontory jutting into the sea, kilometres from any other building. This part of Isla Numa was sparsely populated, the elegant houses strung like beads along the rocky coastline, separated by wide stretches of woodland that she guessed would be beautiful in daylight.

She'd found a municipal leisure complex and gratefully used the facilities there to shower and change before abandoning the stolen taxi. She had already accessed the vehicle's on-board directory to get an address for Eloise Golovkin after an earlier integuary search had turned up nothing. Golovkin, whoever she was, must be a very private person.

Now, seeing her eccentric but expensive dwelling, Orry

began to suspect that the owner of the shroudsphere was an aristo.

She looked down at her new clothes, now sadly soiled, and wondered whether to rip the skirt a little more, before deciding she looked quite dishevelled enough.

She stepped out of the trees and limped across an expanse of manicured lawn to the steep stairs leading up to the front door, staggered up them and pressed the buzzer.

A woman in denim dungarees opened the door and stared at her. Fine lines deepened in a face that had been allowed to grow old naturally without resort to surgery or gene treatments. Pure white hair spilled out from a red bandana knotted around her head.

Orry adjusted her expectations; this woman did not look like an aristo.

'Yes?' the woman asked, eyeing the expensive cut of Orry's jacket.

Orry glanced over her shoulder. 'Please, madam,' she said, allowing a trace of breathless fear to enter her best Ruuz accent, 'a man . . .' She pointed back down the road and the woman's eyes narrowed as she gazed in that direction.

Orry responded to her appraising look with well-practised and anxious innocence. The woman bit her lower lip for a moment, then stood aside. 'Come inside.'

Orry slipped past her and the woman peered into the woods one last time before closing the door.

The inside of the lighthouse was open-plan, the round space filled with furniture – a large sofa, armchairs, a cluttered desk built into one curving wall. An iron staircase in the centre of the room spiralled up through the ceiling.

'Are you hurt?' the woman asked as she directed Orry to the sofa. 'Have you contacted the arbiters?'

'No,' she replied, 'to both questions. It's a . . . well, it's what you might call a delicate situation.' She made a show of appearing to remember her manners and gave a tearful smile. 'I'm so sorry – how rude of me! My name is Lady Amber Stone. My father is the Baronet Stone.'

'Eloise Golovkin.' The white-haired woman bobbed her head in a sketchy bow rather than a curtsey, which Orry filed away. She was still trying to build a picture of her mark. In the absence of any background information she felt terribly exposed. *If only Dad and Ethan were here to help me*, she thought with a pang, desperately missing them both. The memory of her father brought genuine tears to her eyes and it took an effort to drag her thoughts back to the matter at hand.

'What do you mean by "delicate"?' Eloise enquired.

'The man . . . well, he's heir to one of the larger Houses – you'll understand if I don't go into detail. A marriage would be advantageous to my family. We've met a few times, always with a chaperone, of course. He . . .' She hung her head and willed a blush to her cheeks. Her voice almost a whisper, she admitted, 'He persuaded me to agree to a clandestine rendezvous at his friend's house – we were to meet there, then go to the Museum of Antiquities. He led me to believe we shared a deep interest in the past – I'm so stupid!' She gulped and wiped her eyes again. 'It wasn't the artefacts he was interested in . . .' She stared at the floor, as if embarrassed to meet her hostess' eyes. 'I should have realised – my father is only a baronet, after all . . . He was alone in the house when I arrived, but I had already dismissed my car. I told him no, but he . . . he tried to force himself on me – I kicked him and fled, but I heard him following – if you hadn't opened the door . . .' Orry sniffed.

Eloise was looking uncomfortable. 'Would you like a drink, to steady your nerves? I have some brandy—'

'That's kind of you, but no, thank you. I've called for an aerocar – if I could just wait here until it arrives?'

'Of course.'

Orry allowed the silence to stretch out. She'd spotted relics dotted around the room, but it would be better if Eloise raised the subject herself. *Let the mark do the work*, Dad had always said.

'You're interested in history, then?' Eloise asked at last.

Orry beamed. 'Oh *yes* – I'm studying galactic human history at the Ritterheim School.'

'Really? Is Doctor Hathaway still in the exo-archaeology department there?'

Orry stared at her. Was Eloise suspicious, or was this a genuine enquiry? Either way, with no time to construct a detailed cover, she'd never heard of Doctor Hathaway, and if she queried the university with her integuary, the woman would notice.

She let her gut decide. 'The name isn't familiar – but I've only just started . . .'

Eloise appeared to relax a little. She picked up a fragment of crystal from the mantelpiece and offered it to Orry. 'What do you make of this?'

Orry realised she'd made the right call. She turned the piece over in her hands, studying it. 'It's beautiful,' she said. 'Is it Departed?'

'Yes, from the Shattermoon. I'm something of a collector.'

'How fabulous,' Orry enthused. 'I'm taking a whole module

on the Departed next semester – I'd *love* to see your collection. If it's not too much trouble,' she added quickly.

'Of course you may,' Eloise said with genuine enthusiasm. 'It's this way.'

As she led Orry up the narrow metal staircase lights flickered to life on the floor above, revealing glass display cases and shelves filled with hundreds of artefacts.

'This is *amazing*,' Orry said, genuinely impressed – Eloise must have been collecting for years. Her heart skipped a beat as she spotted an intricately filigreed brass sphere: it looked exactly like the shroudsphere Emissary had conjured for her.

She tore her eyes away from the piece and moved on; the trick was not to show any interest in the one thing she wanted. Now all she had to do was get rid of Eloise for a few minutes – a dizzy spell followed by a fall would do the trick. Asking Eloise for a glass of water should get her out of the room for just long enough. The old gimmick was hardly elegant, but it worked.

As she surreptitiously studied the room, trying to judge the best place for her fall, Eloise blinked.

'Excuse me a moment,' she murmured, and her eyes glazed as she took an incoming call. When her eyes cleared, she looked troubled.

'Everything okay?' Orry asked.

'Yes, just something I need to take care of.' She sounded a little distracted, which worried Orry. 'I'll be back in a moment.'

She watched her hostess disappear up the stairs to the next level. The timing couldn't have been better – but it was almost too perfect. Her gut was telling her to get out, but there was too much at stake to leave without the shroudsphere.

The case was locked, which was no great surprise. No matter – she was not above a bit of judiciously applied violence. She had already noted a heavy chunk of what was probably rock from the Shattermoon on an open shelf nearby. With a pang of regret for her designer jacket – she had grown to like it in the brief time they'd been together – Orry slipped the garment off, laid it over the glass and brought the rock down on it. Nothing happened the first time, so she turned the rock and brought it down point-first and the glass gave way with a muffled crack. She reached in and took the shroudsphere. It felt cold against her palm.

Hurrying down the stairs, she eased open the front door. The sultry night air was like a warm blanket after the cool of the lighthouse and she could feel sweat gathering on her brow as she ran down the steps to the lawn. Suppressing an urge to scream with exhilaration, she started off across the grass—

—and twin suns burst into life ahead of her, searing her eyes.

She threw up a protective arm as she stumbled backwards, triumph turned to despair in an instant. Through dancing afterimages she saw auxiliaries in black armour moving towards her, their weapons raised.

'Hands in the air!' one of them shouted. 'Don't move!'

She raised her arms, squeezing the shroudsphere tight in her right fist. *I came so damn close*, she thought angrily, trying not to sink into despair as she squinted against the glare.

Someone was striding towards her. The silhouette resolved itself into Second-Captain Naumov, who stopped in front of her and held out a hand.

'The artefact, if you please, Miz Kent,' he said politely.

'Are you going to use it?' she demanded.

He smiled ruefully. 'I wish some of my colleagues were as dedicated as you. It's a shame you've chosen to channel your talents into such a misguided enterprise.'

'It's not—' She stopped, her heart sinking. *What's the use?* She lowered her right arm and dropped the shroudsphere into Naumov's palm. 'At least study it,' she told him.

He examined it with interest, then stared thoughtfully at her. 'Restrain her,' he ordered the auxiliaries, and she felt her arms yanked roughly behind her back. 'Easy!' Naumov snapped, and the pressure relaxed a fraction. Restraints tightened around her wrists. 'You've triggered a planet-wide manhunt,' he told her cheerfully, 'but I suspected you'd be coming here. Perhaps you should endeavour to be a little less predictable?'

The wail of distant sirens rose over the city and he frowned, gazing towards the distant towers of the Trefoil and the Imperator's Palace beyond.

Looking around, Orry could see everyone was receiving the same integuary message as her on the planetary emergency channel.

This is an emergency broadcast. By order of the Imperator Ascendant, a state of civil emergency has been declared. Citizens will report to public shelters immediately. All military and reserve personnel report immediately to your duty stations . . . This is an emergency broadcast. By order of—

When she muted the channel, she could hear the same words echoing across the city, blared from every device with a speaker.

'What's going on?' she shouted at Naumov, who held up a hand to stop her; he was still listening to something.

When his eyes cleared, his face was strained. 'It appears we may have misjudged you, Miz Kent. A Kadiran task force has just appeared in-system. It's heading this way.'

43

MUTINY

Speedwell's operations room was a maelstrom of controlled activity when Orry and her escort entered. Sergeant Volkhov, glaring at her, remained by the door with a fresh-faced auxiliary named Ramis. A quick glance around revealed that most of the displays were showing long-range data on the Kadiran fleet, which was still well beyond the orbit of Tyr's most distant moon. Orry counted fourteen ships in total, fewer than she had thought; they were clearly not expecting much in the way of resistance.

The navigation orrery in the centre of the ops room was displaying a three-dimensional view of the space around Tyr, with the predicted paths of every vessel plotted in glowing light.

She stepped closer, studying the various ships. The bulk of the Home Fleet was still berthed in the naval yards, presently on the far side of Tyr and not yet in direct line of fire from the approaching Kadiran ships. It looked like only five Ascendancy frigates and destroyers had got underway in the time it had taken the cutter to return to *Speedwell*; the warships were now plotting courses that would take them around Tyr and towards the enemy. A swarm of orbit defence craft were also heading for the Kadiran task force.

'Why aren't more ships moving?' she asked Naumov.

'Shore leave for the Imperator's bicentennial,' he explained. Turning to a woman whose blonde ponytail floated free from a cap displaying the silver starburst of an under-captain, he asked, 'Perez, how soon can we break orbit?'

'Right away, skipper.'

'Crew complement?'

'Seventy per cent.'

He sighed. 'It'll have to do. Very well, XO,' he told her, 'sound the acceleration alarm; let's get moving.'

Perez issued a stream of orders, leaving Naumov staring at the orrery, deep in thought.

'What's your plan?' Orry asked after a moment.

'Our capital ships need time to recover enough crew to be able to leave the yards. We have to delay the enemy formation long enough to bring our big guns into play.'

She examined the handful of smaller ships already heading towards the Kadiran task force. 'Three frigates and two destroyers,' she said, 'plus the orbit guard. Will that be enough?' She didn't think so.

Naumov's expression confirmed her fears. 'These are the Kadiran capital ships – a battle cruiser here and a light titan, here.' He pointed out their positions at the centre of the enemy formation. 'They're surrounded by four light cruisers, which in turn are protected by six aggressor vessels.'

There were two ships she couldn't identify, one right in the heart of the fleet, between the two capital ships, and another out on the edge near one of the aggressors. 'What are these two?' she asked.

'We don't know,' Naumov admitted. 'They're not Kadiran vessels.'

She considered that, then turned to face him. 'Why am I here, Captain?'

'I needed to get back to my ship, Miz Kent. There was no time to return you to the holdover zone.'

She snorted. 'I'm not an idiot, Captain, so please don't treat me like one. You could have sent me with a couple of your auxiliaries. Volkhov would be delighted to see me back on that rock.' When Naumov didn't deny it, she lowered her voice and continued, 'You know I was telling the truth about the Kadiran, and you know that one or both of those unknown ships belongs to Cordelia Roag. Give me the shroudsphere and send me back to *Dainty Jane*. Right now you need all the help you can get.'

He studied her face, then reached into a pocket and pulled out the shroudsphere.

She held her breath.

'You have proved yourself a capable and resourceful young woman,' he said, rotating the metal globe between his thumb and forefinger, 'and I have no doubt that if you had not been determined to recover this' – he held up the shroudsphere – 'you would have disappeared into deep space. Do you seriously expect to be able to recover this *ventari stone* and destroy it?'

'What other options do you have? Right now it's five against fourteen, even without the ventari stone. And if that stone is everything Emissary said it is, all they need to do is get close enough to make a hole in Tyr's orbital defences and fire it through.'

'Our capital ships—'

'Won't be ready in time! Come on, Naumov, you know I'm right! From where I'm standing, I'm the only chance you have.'

Silence fell over the ops room and Orry realised that every pair of eyes was fixed on them. She ignored the crew, instead watching the struggle on the captain's face.

She groaned as Arbiter-Lieutenant Dragan entered the bridge. After their encounter on *Justiciar*, Naumov had kept Dragan well away from her. *With good reason*, she thought as she saw the arbiter's face twist with fury when he caught sight of her.

'Captain Naumov,' he started, 'why is this prisoner in operations – and why is she not in restraints?'

'Shut up, Dragan,' Naumov said wearily.

Relief coursed through Orry when Naumov offered her the shroudsphere, ignoring Dragan's protests. As she reached to take it, Perez called, 'Captain, incoming transmission from Fleet-Admiral Sheremetev.'

Naumov's hand closed around the shroudsphere. 'Audio,' he snapped.

A woman's voice filled the bridge. 'Second-Captain Naumov, I understand you have both Aurelia Kent and the Departed artefact on board.'

'Yes, ma'am.'

'You will make best speed to the flagship and deliver both of them to me personally.'

Naumov remained silent, staring angrily at Orry as if she were to blame for everything.

'Naumov?' Sheremetev repeated. 'Acknowledge.'

'Ma'am, Miz Kent is confident she can use the artefact to—'

'You heard my orders, Second-Captain.' The admiral's voice was icy.

'But Admiral—'

'Dragan? Are you there?'

The arbiter snapped to attention. 'Yes, Admiral!'

'Place Second-Captain Naumov under arrest. Under-Captain Perez, you will assume command of *Speedwell* and deliver the prisoner and the artefact directly to the flagship.'

'At once, ma'am!' Dragan gave Naumov a thin smile of triumph while the XO looked stunned.

'Admiral—' Naumov began, but Perez interrupted him.

'She's gone, sir.'

'Sergeant Volkhov,' Dragan snapped, 'take the captain to his quarters and keep him there. No one gets to see him without my permission.'

'Aye aye, sir.'

'Stand down, Sergeant,' Naumov said quietly.

Volkhov glanced at Dragan, his face a picture of anxiety.

'You heard Admiral Sheremetev's orders, Volkhov,' the arbiter said. 'Do your duty.'

'The admiral is not in full possession of the facts,' Naumov said in a reasonable tone, then pointed at the Kadiran ships, 'and we don't have time to convince her. Mister Garrett, kindly take Miz Kent back to her ship. XO, prepare to get underway the moment Mister Garrett and the prize crew have returned to us.'

Volkhov looked like a mimetic stuck in a logic loop. Dragan cursed and unfastened the flap on the holster at his belt. He aimed his service pistol at Naumov, but Orry could see his hand was trembling.

'Belay those orders,' the arbiter said loudly, addressing the entire room. His voice was an octave higher than it had been. '*I* am in command here.'

'Dragan—' Naumov began.

'No!' The arbiter stepped closer and thrust his pistol towards Naumov's face. 'This is mutiny, plain and simple. Leave the ops room this instant or—' The gun shook in his hand.

'Or what?' the captain asked mildly.

Dragan swallowed and steadied his pistol. 'Or I will execute you, Captain Naumov, for mutiny and dereliction of duty.'

Orry watched the exchange with horrified fascination. Dragan looked highly unstable.

'No, Lieutenant,' Volkhov growled, 'you will not.' He aimed his carbine at the arbiter.

Sweat stood out on the Dragan's forehead as his eyes flicked between the two men.

'Sergei!' hissed the young auxiliary standing next to Volkhov.

'Point your gun at the lieutenant, Ramis, there's a good lad,' Volkhov replied.

After a second's hesitation, Ramis raised his weapon.

'You're finished,' Dragan spat, 'all of you. You're all bloody traitors!' But the fight had gone out of him. 'You'll hang for this,' he said weakly as the captain reached out and wrapped his hand around Dragan's pistol. The arbiter opened and closed his mouth a few times, then released it.

Orry clutched a console for support, her legs suddenly weak. Naumov addressed the entire room. 'Arbiter-Lieutenant Dragan is right,' he said loudly, 'this *is* mutiny, I'm not going to lie to you. I need everyone I can get, but if any member of this crew feels that she or he cannot continue to serve under me, you may leave in the cutter. Those who stay may take some solace from the fact that Lieutenant Dragan is misinformed: only the senior officers will be facing the noose.' He met the XO's eye and she nodded solemnly. 'The rest of you will get away with ten to twenty years on Furina.' That raised some smiles. 'Of course,' he concluded, indicating the Kadiran task force, 'that's if any of us survive to face a court martial. Make your choice.'

After some shuffling and brief, hissed conversation, three of the bridge crew made their way to the exit, heads hung low, trying in vain to avoid the glares of their comrades.

'XO,' Naumov said, 'explain the situation to the rest of the crew. Anyone who wants to leave has five minutes to get aboard the cutter. Sergeant Volkhov, disable Lieutenant Dragan's integuary and confine him in one of the aft storage lockers.'

'Aye aye, sir.' Volkhov shoved Dragan towards the exit.

'And Volkhov?' Naumov called after him.

'Sir?'

'Thank you.'

Volkhov nodded, glanced at Orry, then escorted Dragan from the bridge.

Naumov handed Orry the shroudsphere.

'You made the right choice,' she told him.

He nodded, his face strained. 'I truly hope so.'

44

CHOICES

'What's happening?' *Jane* asked the moment Garrett and the two members of the prize crew had departed. 'Where's Ethan? Is his wound healing?'

Orry was trying not to think about her little brother. Unlike the rest of the helpless millions awaiting their fate on the planet below, Ethan knew exactly what they were facing. 'He's fine,' she said, praying she was right as she floated up to the cockpit, 'but right now, you and I have a job to do. Are your sensors back online?'

'Yes, the prize crew removed all system locks before they left. I have scanned the Kadiran task force. It's formidable.'

'Scan it again, will you? For eisenform energy.'

'Oh.' A moment's pause. 'I'm picking up trace amounts on Roag's commerce raider, *Scintilla*. She's in the heart of the Kadiran formation.'

After a moment's hesitation Orry climbed into Mender's command seat. 'Can we get to her?'

'Perhaps you didn't hear me, Orry: *Scintilla* is in the centre of the enemy fleet.'

'I heard you. But if we don't recover the ventari stone, millions of people will die.'

Jane sighed.

'What is it?'

'All the time I was with Mender I wanted him to be a bit more moral, a bit less selfish. Now I wish he was still here and we were running for an egress point.'

Orry smiled. 'No you don't.' She felt the vibration of the mass-inversion drives engaging.

'Oh, I do,' *Jane* said with feeling as Orry was pressed back into her shell. 'I really do.'

As they tore towards the leading Kadiran aggressor vessels, Orry found herself agreeing with *Jane*. The only scheme she'd been able to come up with made her want to run to the edge of occupied space and just keep going.

Stars sparkled like diamonds in the darkness of space. The battle had started and one of the Ascendancy frigates was already a burning hulk, flames coruscating across her shattered hull. The remaining vessels had divided into two-ship elements, each frigate-destroyer pairing working together, attempting to outflank the larger, blade-like Kadiran aggressors. Coherent energy batteries were now firing as kinetic harpoons and autonomous torpedoes streaked between the combatants.

The few remaining orbit defence craft – cutters and missile boats more suited to asteroid interdiction and anti-piracy duties than facing a fully armed fleet – had been weaving around the aggressor vessels, but for all their manoeuvrability the little craft were horribly vulnerable to the larger ship's weapons and as Orry and *Jane* watched, the last of them flared into nothing.

A moment later, the stern of one of the Ascendancy destroyers burst apart as a Kadiran harpoon made it through the vessel's defences. The stricken destroyer rolled, venting oxygen.

They're outclassed, Orry sent.

And it's only going to get worse, Jane replied. *There's a cruiser coming in.*

Beams were lashing the vacuum around the remaining Ascendancy destroyer, *Tybalt*, whose radiators were glowing white-hot around her energy-conversion grids. The Kadiran cruiser, a vast, sickle-shaped vessel, drew closer and Orry saw the panels of one of *Tybalt*'s radiator arrays warp as the light around them distorted.

What's that? she asked.

The Kadiran are using an entropy weapon.

I thought they were banned?

They are.

Tybalt's radiator array buckled, then disintegrated as its molecules aged ten thousand years in a matter of seconds. The destroyer's ability to dissipate thermal energy was already at full capacity under the bombardment it was receiving from the Kadiran vessel and the loss of the radiator array tipped the balance. *Tybalt*'s drive-shielding turned to slag under the excess heat, the destroyer exploded and for a brief moment a new sun burned at the edge of the enemy task force.

Head for that gap! Orry told *Jane*, studying the expanding cloud of debris that had been *Tybalt*. With the two Kadiran aggressors engaged and the cruiser out of position, she could see a clear path to the enemy capital ships – and to *Scintilla*.

Dainty Jane altered course and increased thrust. Orry's shell slammed shut and the mesophase gel flashed into liquid, flooding her lungs as she concentrated on the battle raging outside.

Black Dog and *Relentless*, the remaining frigates, were engaged in a desperate fight for survival their captains must surely have known they would never survive, but they fought on, pitching their meagre weapons and depleted defences against three much heavier and better-armed Kadiran vessels. Orry couldn't decide if she admired or pitied them. She checked *Speedwell*'s status, surprised at how concerned she was for Naumov and his crew. The frigate had broken orbit and was accelerating towards the enemy formation. Far behind *Speedwell* she could see a light cruiser just clearing the naval yards, but all the rest of the Home Fleet, with its heavy cruisers, battleships and titans, were still to get underway.

Alerts flashed in her mind and across the cockpit as the nearest enemy aggressor detected *Dainty Jane*. The remains of *Tybalt* were close now, a cloud of twisted wreckage and bodies. *Jane*'s dispensers fired, defeating a volley of beams from the aggressor, which was also busy engaging both Ascendancy frigates. Clearly deciding *Dainty Jane* posed less of a threat than the frigates, the aggressor's alpha sent two torpedoes after *Jane* and returned his attention to *Black Dog* and *Relentless*.

Proximity warnings sounded as *Jane* passed through what remained of *Tybalt*, jinking and rolling to avoid the larger pieces. Orry dealt with what she could using the point defences, but still the hull was battered as the smaller fragments hit. The autonomous torpedoes behind them picked up speed, and as *Jane* emerged from the debris Orry monitored them anxiously. She'd been desperately hoping they wouldn't make it through the wreckage, and her heart sank when they both emerged intact and began eating up the remaining distance to *Dainty Jane*.

She hooked the stern mass driver – and only then realised it was inoperable, damaged by a debris strike. She watched the torpedoes streaking towards them.

I have control, she told *Jane*.

Are you sur—?

Let me try something . . . She disengaged the mass-inversion drives and fired the verniers, neatly rolling the ship a hundred and eighty degrees until she was facing the oncoming torpedoes. The tracking sensors indicated five seconds to impact.

Fire! she told *Jane*.

I – I can't.

They're torpedoes, *not people* – shoot them*!*

I'm sorry . . . The ship sounded miserable.

Orry cursed, hooked the weapons core and aimed at the right-hand torpedo.

Three seconds.

Orry fired, spraying the area with slugs. The torpedo started manoeuvring in an attempt to avoid the hypersonic chunks of tungsten, but it was too close and the spread too large; it detonated, making *Jane* buck like a boat in a storm-tossed sea.

The second torpedo, knocked off course by the blast, flashed past a kilometre from their hull, but within a second gas was pluming from its nose and tail, rotating the long fuselage so it could reacquire *Dainty Jane*.

Orry targeted its drive unit and slugs tore through the torpedo's tail. The glow of its drive went dark and it spun away, tumbling end over end.

Heart pounding, she rolled the ship back onto their original course and restarted the engines.

I'm sorry, repeated *Jane* unhappily.

I can't do this alone, Orry told her. *I need you.*

I know. I just ... I can't fight any more— The ship stopped abruptly, then announced, *I'm receiving an incoming transmission from* Scintilla.

Cordelia Roag's face appeared, piped directly into Orry's audio-visual cortex. *Scintilla*'s bridge formed a backdrop.

'You appear keen to renew our acquaintance,' Roag said.

'I have the shroudsphere,' Orry told her.

'I thought you might.' Roag didn't sound surprised. 'Professor Rasmussen proved singularly loquacious under questioning by our Kadiran friends. What exactly do you expect to do with it? Board *Scintilla*, single-handedly defeat my crew and destroy the stone?'

'No. I want to swap it for Mender.'

Roag chuckled. 'You'll have to do better than that, Aurelia.'

'I'm serious.'

'You'd exchange one life for a billion?'

Orry shrugged. 'They're Ruuz. Fuck 'em.'

Roag's eyes narrowed. 'I don't believe you.'

'You don't even know me!' Orry snapped. 'Look, you said it yourself: I may have the shroudsphere, but how can I use it? Give me Mender and you can have the damn thing. We'll just go. The one thing you can be certain of is that I don't want to die here.'

Roag stared at her for a few seconds, then laughed. 'Nice try, Miz Kent, but I know bullshit when I hear it. But speaking of Mender, I do have something I want you to see. When the vessel-alpha you tangled with at the Shattermoon told me about the shroudsphere, I thought I'd better take some precautions. You've proved yourself to be rather tenacious, after all.'

The image in Orry's mind split into two. The new picture showed what appeared to be the bridge of another ship, with clean lines and large windows through which Orry briefly registered a Kadiran aggressor vessel – before her mouth went dry. Mender was standing in a clear cylinder that resembled a clone vat, though this one had been modified by the addition of a transparent tank on the top. A viscous, pale green liquid filled the tank.

Roag smiled. 'What's the matter? No snappy remark? No pithy comment?' Orry swallowed, and Roag added, 'Say hello, boys.'

Orry wasn't at all surprised when Dyas stepped into shot from one side, Jericho from the other.

'You see that green liquid above Mender's head?' Roag said. 'That's a digestive enzyme. Very potent. Let me give you a little demonstration, just for the fun of it.' She held up a clear beaker. Inside, a pink-eyed white mouse scrabbled against the glass. Roag set the beaker down in front of her and produced a large syringe of green liquid. Slowly depressing the plunger, she sent the liquid dribbling down the sides of the beaker until it was pooling around the mouse's feet. Orry watched in horror as the creature began to thrash about, squealing wildly. A thin vapour drifted up as the flesh sagged from its body, tearing like wet tissue as it dissolved. By the time the beaker was a quarter full there was nothing left of the mouse but a fine-boned skeleton and a few clumps of fatty tissue floating in a viscid soup.

'What do you want?' Orry asked, her stomach churning.

'You have a choice, Aurelia: you can come after me, or you can save your friend. You won't have time to do both.'

'How do I know you won't just kill him before I get there?'

Dyas spoke up. 'Oh, I want you here, bitch. We have a score to settle, you and me.'

'I'll leave it with you,' Roag said with a nasty smile. She cut the transmission.

Orry floated within her shell, oblivious to everything but the impossible choice she was being forced to make.

What are you going to do? Jane asked.

Why is it always *my* decision? she sent back angrily. *What do you think we should do?*

Jane considered for a moment. *If we go after Roag, can you stop her? Destroy the ventari stone?*

I don't know – if I'm lucky, there's a chance, but it's a slim one.

Is it any less than being able to save Mender?

Orry felt like screaming. *So it's a slim chance of saving one man against a slim chance of saving millions?*

When you put it like that, it isn't really a choice at all. You have to save Tyr.

Orry gritted her teeth. She'd already lost just about everyone she cared about. Other than Ethan, Mender and *Jane* were all she had left. *No,* she sent, *Roag's made a mistake. One person can't be in two places at once, but there are two of us.*

Orry—

Jane, I know you don't want to fight any more. But if you don't, Mender is going to die.

Jane was silent for a long time as *Scintilla* and the Kadiran capital ships drew closer. Orry eyed the other human vessel – it had to be Dyas' ship – on the rear edge of the enemy formation. It was flanked by a Kadiran aggressor vessel.

I can't use the shroudsphere, Jane pointed out. *I can't destroy the stone.*

You don't have to. You just need to delay Roag long enough for me to save Mender. Give me time, Jane, *that's all I need. Can you do that for me? For Mender?*

She held her breath.

I'll do what I can, sent Jane eventually. The ship's voice sounded hollow in Orry's head, devoid of emotion.

Thank you, Orry told her, shuddering at the thought of what she would have to do next.

She gazed at the enemy capital ships flanking *Scintilla*. What she was proposing would likely end in failure and death, for both herself and *Dainty Jane*.

45

GEEZER SOUP

The Advanced Operator Delivery System was cramped: a tempered ceramic coffin filled with the same oxygenated smart fluid used in the acceleration shells. The curved fuselage closed in around Orry as she fought to control her rising panic. *Dainty Jane* lanced towards Dyas' vessel, keeping them well clear of the closest Kadiran capital ship, a light titan shaped like the jagged tooth of some vast denizen of the void. The giant ship hadn't yet fired on them, which made Orry wonder just how much influence Roag had amongst the Kadiran – and *why*. That was a question for another time.

Jane kept Dyas' ship between her and the Kadiran aggressor. The aggressor might be dwarfed by the distant titan but it still looked like it could swallow both Dyas' ship and *Dainty Jane* whole. Orry watched the range count down, wishing she had thought to empty her bladder before climbing into the harpoon.

Ready? Jane asked.

No.

Do you want to abort?

Yes. No, kidding . . . I'm ready.

Launching in five seconds . . . Four . . . Three . . . Good luck, Orry. And you, Jane. *Keep Roag busy until we get ther—*

The harpoon fired—

—and Orry found herself racing like a bullet towards Dyas' ship. She tried to focus on her plan – what there was of it – rather than thinking about her temporary prison streaking through open space. She was dimly aware of *Dainty Jane* shooting away on a vector taking her clear of the aggressor, which had opened fire, her dispensers already seeding the area with slugs and chaff. *Jane*'s integuary feed disappeared and there was no time to see if her friend had escaped safely before the AODS struck Dyas' ship with an impact Orry felt even through the cushioning effect of the liquid that surrounded her.

Griffin will be pleased we used his torpedo, at least, she thought, wondering if she would ever get a chance to tell him. The harpoon vented its liquid and as she pushed the last of it from her lungs, a grinding noise assaulted her ears: the AODS was vibrating violently as it bored through the hull. The noise and motion ceased and there was a moment's calm before explosive bolts fired to jettison the harpoon's nose.

Light flooded in, bringing with it the acrid reek of scorched metal and plastic.

The last of the mesophase gel evaporated from her skin and clothing as Orry squirmed forward and found herself dangling head-first two metres above the deck. According to her integuary, the AODS had penetrated the ship's hull exactly on target: in a passageway just aft of the bridge. She let herself drop, grunting as she hit the floor and rolled to the side. Rising to one knee, she tugged Mender's Fabretti from her belt and thumbed on the power. The pistol produced a satisfying whine. *Nobody fucks with a Fabretti 500*, she thought with a grim smile.

The AODS had been designed to release an energy pulse on impact to temporarily disorient the target's systems. With any luck Dyas would be busy trying to work out what had just struck his ship – but even so, she needed to move fast.

She ran to the door at the end of the passageway and stopped, heart thudding. 'Come on, Orry,' she muttered. 'You can do this.'

At her command, her integuary superimposed a wireframe plan of the bridge over her vision. It wasn't perfect – an amalgam of the standard bridge layout for this class of vessel overlaid with what she'd glimpsed in Roag's transmission – but it was better than nothing. She touched the door's control panel and darted through and to the right, expecting to be shredded or immolated at any moment. She hurled herself behind a bank of consoles and scrabbled to her knees, holding the Fabretti in front of her face. She snatched a half-second glance at the bridge while filling her lungs with air.

The scene had changed little since the transmission: Mender was still in his tube, and now she could see he had an integuary damper around his forehead. Jericho and Dyas were still standing on either side, although now Jericho was aiming its maser at her. Dyas' pistol hung down at his side. His other hand was resting on a panel fixed to the side of Mender's tube.

'You do know how to make an entrance,' he said in a voice trembling with excitement. 'Now, toss out that ridiculous gun and come over here, or I'm going to whip up about twenty litres of geezer soup.'

'You think I'd trust you after all you've done to me?' Orry yelled. 'Let him go and we'll take a boat and leave.'

'What, no revenge? You disappoint me.'

'I'll let you live today, you piece of shit, but don't think this is over. I'll find you, and I'll kill you.'

Dyas laughed. 'Are you hearing this?' he asked Jericho. 'I'm not fucking with you, bitch. Toss the piece, or I melt your friend and Jericho will melt you. I'll count to three. One . . . two . . .'

'Three!' Orry screamed, launching herself to her feet and swinging the Fabretti towards the tank above Mender's head. She saw his eyes widen as she fired.

The tank exploded, spraying thick green liquid across the bridge.

She shifted her aim to Jericho, but an instant too late; a furnace blistered her hands and face, forcing her back into cover. Dyas was screaming: a raw animal screech that twisted her stomach. The air above the console had turned oily, shimmering in the heat from the maser as the metal warped and blistered.

The heat stopped, replaced by the pneumatic hiss of running steps as Jericho pounded towards her. Ignoring the pain in her blistered hands she aimed the Fabretti, but the mimetic was too fast; it grabbed her right wrist and wrenched it aside. She heard the crack of breaking bone and screamed as white fire shot up her arm and the Fabretti fell from her fingers. Jericho kicked it away before lifting her high above its head.

The world tilted around her and suddenly she was sailing through the air, flailing helplessly as she fell towards a bank of consoles on the far side of the bridge. She landed badly, the console delivering a massive hammer-blow to her side. She rolled off it, half-stunned, and struck the deck in agony, winded and gasping for breath.

'Don't kill her!' Dyas yelled. He gave a low groan that quickly escalated to a scream. '*Bitch!* My fucking legs – *help me*, you idiot!'

Through the waves of sickening pain, Orry felt the hard deck pressing into her cheek. She opened her eyes to see Dyas lying on the far side of Mender's tube. Roag's green digestive enzyme was splattered everywhere, dripping down the outside of the glass cylinder and pooling on the deck – and covering what remained of Dyas' legs. She could make out his boots in a puddle of green but the legs of his flight suit looked oddly flat below the knees. There were *smears* on the floor where Dyas had dragged himself clear of the enzyme, leaving his feet and lower legs behind. A frothy soup of red and black was leaking from the bottom of his flight suit. The air on the bridge smelled like month-old meat dipped in bleach.

'What do you want me to do?' Jericho asked.

'Get me to the fucking medbay!' Dyas screeched.

Jericho stepped closer and looked down at him. 'I told you not to use silicarbonate in the tank.'

'*What?* You want to talk about this *now*? Help me!'

The mimetic reached down and picked up a shard of the tank, examining it. 'If you'd used nanomesh like I said, you wouldn't be in this mess.' He tossed the shard aside. 'But no, it had to be transparent. She had to *see* the enzyme. Well, I bet you feel pretty fucking stupid now, you with no legs.'

'I swear to Rama, if you don't get me to the medbay I will string my fucking guitar with your higher-function filaments—!'

Orry shifted her gaze to the tube. Mender was staring out at her, his face strained. He looked past Jericho and she followed his gaze to see the Fabretti lying on the other side of the bridge. She rolled onto her back, trying not to groan as every part of her body protested.

'You know,' Jericho said to Dyas, 'I'm getting tired of the way you talk to me. I think it's time to renegotiate our business arrangement.'

'You tin-plated fucking *arsehole*.' Dyas' voice was high-pitched now, close to hysterical. His eyes were fixed on the mimetic as tears of agony rolled down his cheeks.

Orry pulled herself onto her backside, cradling her broken wrist and biting back a scream as bones grated in her side. She glanced at the Fabretti on the other side of Jericho, then back at Mender, who smiled grimly and dropped his head an inch.

'Fine,' Dyas was saying, 'whatever you want. We'll talk. *In the fucking medbay.*' His eyes shifted to Orry as she rose on shaky legs. She froze, eyes desperately searching for something, *anything*, she could use to defend herself.

Jericho's head whipped round – and the mimetic was already moving towards her when she saw the ship's helm controls. She made a lunge for the flight stick and shoved it towards the Kadiran aggressor vessel that was less than a kilometre away, filling one side of the bridge windows. Dyas' ship lurched sideways, beginning to roll, and fresh waves of pain radiated from her ribs as the bridge rotated around her, pressing her down into the helm.

Jericho was halfway to her when its feet left the deck. She flinched as the heavy mimetic tumbled towards her, the Fabretti sliding after it, but she had no time to react before Jericho smashed into the console just centimetres from her head, shearing off the flight stick and jamming the throttle fully open.

The ship leaped forward, surging towards the massive aggressor vessel and sending Orry rolling over the console top until she was able to activate her molly hooks and snag the deck. Her body, suddenly anchored, pivoted forward and her face slammed into the floor.

Spitting blood, she twisted just in time to see Jericho looming over her, hands grasping for her head. Something solid struck her side and she reached reflexively for it; her fingers closed around the Fabretti's grip and she raised the gun and fired.

The mimetic flew backwards, spurting fluid from a huge hole in its chest. She staggered to her feet, keeping the Fabretti aimed at Jericho, but the mimetic remained motionless where it had fallen. Beyond it, Dyas was sprawled against a bulkhead, groaning. A frothy red smear marked the path he had taken across the deck when the ship rolled, and more blood covered his face from a fresh gash on his forehead.

Collision alarms started blaring: the Kadiran aggressor was filling the windows now. Orry struggled with the jammed throttle for a moment before stepping back with a curse. A hollow thudding made her turn; Mender was pounding on the inside of his tube. She raised the Fabretti, waited for him to cover his face and fired above his head. The tube shattered and Mender jumped out, tearing the damper from his head.

When he grabbed her by the arms, Orry felt like collapsing into him.

'What took you so long?' he growled, immediately turning her relief to frustration – then he grinned and pulled her towards the back of the bridge, where a door had sprung open on an escape pod.

She heard a howl of rage from behind her and glanced back to see Dyas struggling with the damaged helm console, his face contorted with hatred. Beyond him, the hull of the Kadiran ship was a wall of jagged metal hurtling closer. His eyes glazed as he accessed his integuary in a last-ditch attempt to regain control of his ship.

'We have to get out of here!' Mender yelled, shoving her into the pod.

The door slammed shut and he strapped himself in opposite her. She felt her seat stiffen as the pod blasted free. The view outside the small port in the door whirled crazily, showing the aggressor's hull sweeping in like a hammer. The little craft shuddered violently, shaking her teeth in her head, and a deafening clang reverberated through the pod. Alarms sounded as they tumbled away, end over end, until Orry couldn't bear the sickening motion any longer and vomited, the milky liquid splattering back into her hair.

A flash painted the pod's interior orange and they lurched again, spinning in a new direction until stabilising thrusters finally cut in, firing until their attitude settled. Outside the viewport she could see the rear of Dyas' ship rolling slowly down the length of the aggressor's hull. A long gash had opened in the side of the Kadiran vessel and the glow of flames flickered deep within it.

The alarm was still sounding, and now Orry could hear the shriek of escaping air too. Mender released his harness and wrenched open the emergency locker. He tossed her a repair kit and took one for himself.

Moving as if in a dream, she snatched the slowly rotating kit from the air. As she released her own harness she superimposed an airflow model over her vision, which revealed three breaches. Mender was already working on the most serious, so she floated to the next largest, opened the kit one-handed and sprayed adhesive foam over the affected area before slapping a patch on it. By the time she was done, Mender had dealt with the third hole.

The alarm stopped.

Ears ringing, Orry released the kit and let it float beside her.

'Okay?' Mender asked and she nodded, trying not to shudder as pain almost overwhelmed her. He floated to the viewport and looked out. 'Rama! There's a sight you don't see every day.'

She joined him, and stared.

Tyr was a vast turquoise and green ball, close enough for them to make out the ribbon-head stations and orbitals ringing its equator. The Home Fleet was finally starting to deploy and Orry counted a dozen capital ships and hundreds of smaller combatants relentlessly pounding the enemy task force. The Kadiran titan rippled with explosions and the battle cruiser appeared to be breaking up.

'It won't make any difference if Roag gets close enough to deliver the stone into the atmosphere,' she said. 'Can you get through to *Jane*?'

He shook his head. The expression on his face said it all.

Orry tried to contact the ship herself, but there was no reply. She had no time to fear for her friend, as then something clanged into the pod's hull – and Orry recoiled with a cry as Jericho's face appeared on the other side of the viewport, red eyes glaring. The mimetic was covered in scorch marks and half its plating had been ripped away, exposing the toughened servos and fibres beneath.

'Piotr's puckered ringpiece,' Mender muttered. 'What does it take to kill that fucking thing?'

Jericho drew back one arm and made a fist, and Orry flinched as it punched the door's outer surface. A dent appeared.

Close to panic, she pushed off and sailed over to the bank of lockers. She pulled out one of the twelve emergency suits and started dragging it up over her legs, cursing her broken bones.

'What are you doing?' Mender demanded. He winced as Jericho pounded the little craft again and the door bowed inwards. 'There's no time, girl. We're done.'

Jericho's fist smashed into the door a third time and she could hear the groan of straining metal. Paint flaked from buckled hinges. Mender was right: one more blow would expose them to vacuum.

She pulled her leg out of the suit and floated back to his side. Jericho peered in at them, head cocked inquisitively. She clutched Mender and felt his arm slide around her shoulders, pulling her close. Jericho's fist drew back.

'Thanks for coming to get me,' Mender said quietly.

She couldn't reply but she hugged him close. She stared at Jericho, waiting for the end—

—and the mimetic's body disintegrated. One moment it was there on the other side of the glass, one punch away from spacing them – and the next, Jericho was gone, torn to pieces in the blink of an eye.

Orry stared dumbly, then felt the hot pressure of tears behind her eyes as *Dainty Jane* dropped into view outside the pod.

I'm sorry if I worried you both, the ship told them. *Combat configuration doesn't leave much spare power for integuary communication. My range has been severely limited.*

Orry gave a brittle laugh, realising she was close to the edge as Mender released her. For once in his life the old man was speechless. She flung her arms around his neck and hugged him hard until the pain burning in her wrist and ribs overwhelmed her and she let go.

You shot him! she sent happily.

I'm not proud of it. Jane sounded subdued and there was an edge of bitterness to her voice that Orry had never heard before. It made her feel like a foolish child.

What are you waiting for? Mender sent. *Bring us aboard.*

What happened with Roag? Orry asked.

I did my best, Jane replied, *but it's not good news.*

46

FISHING

How are the ribs holding up? Mender asked as Tyr filled *Dainty Jane*'s canopy.

Fine, Orry lied – she could feel the pain even inside the acceleration shell. At least with her lungs filled with smart fluid she didn't have to breathe. Her wrist ached too. She'd agreed to let Mender fit a temporary cast once they'd clambered out of the escape pod into *Jane*'s cargo bay while begrudging even the few minutes that took.

Dainty Jane finally began to decelerate and Orry saw two glittering specks manoeuvring in front of them, each trying to gain an advantage over its opponent as the darkness between them sparkled with beams and ordnance. She recognised the combatants immediately: *Scintilla* and *Speedwell*.

You see? Jane sent sharply, sounding like Ethan when he'd been accused of doing something particularly dumb.

The ship had explained it all on the way here: by the time *Jane* had caught up with Roag the first time, *Speedwell* had already engaged *Scintilla*. Since Naumov was doing *Jane*'s job for her, the ship had elected to return and assist in Mender's

417

rescue. Orry had had to bite off her first response: that *Jane* should have stayed to help Naumov, that she was just trying to find excuses not to fight. But if *Jane had* stayed to fight, Orry and Mender would be dead now. That still didn't make *Jane*'s decision the right one, but it seemed churlish to point it out. From her defensive tone, it was clear *Jane* had sensed Orry's unspoken criticism.

Speedwell is in a bad way, Mender sent.

We have to help them! Orry told him, but he was already spinning up *Dainty Jane*'s weapons. She sank towards the bottom of her acceleration shell as the smart fluid transitioned back into gel; the shell snapped open and she cleared her lungs, realising she no longer felt any discomfort from the gel entering or leaving her body. Mender's shell was already open. He paused to cough up a final gout of pale pink fluid, which trickled down his chest to join the rest of the gel. Orry's flight suit was already dry.

'I've got her,' Mender announced, frowning as he aimed the forward mass driver. 'Hold still . . . hold still . . .'

Verniers flickered along *Scintilla*'s upper hull just as he opened fire, pushing the sleek clipper down so that the stream of slugs passed harmlessly above her as she turned to head straight for *Speedwell*.

'She's going to ram them,' Orry said, watching helplessly.

Mender stopped shooting, unwilling to risk hitting *Speedwell*.

At the last possible moment *Scintilla* changed attitude again, passing so close to the frigate that *Speedwell*'s point-defence turrets raked the clipper's flank, tearing away a chunk of hull plating which went spinning into Tyr's atmosphere.

'What's she doing?' Orry asked as Mender tried to get a clear line of fire.

'Roag always likes to have the advantage,' he told her. 'Two against one ain't her style.'

'She's *running*?' Orry wasn't convinced.

'Better to live to fight another day. She can take the stone back to—'

Mender stopped as *Scintilla*'s nose came up and the clipper showed her belly to Tyr's blue-green sphere. A cloud of glittering dust spewed from the ship, scattering towards the planet, and *Scintilla* streaked away.

Orry and Mender stared at each other.

'*Jane*,' Orry cried, 'scan that cloud for eisens—!'

'*Already on it*,' the ship replied, '*and yes, I'm picking up eisenform energy. The signature matches the readings I took from the ventari stone. Illuminating now.*' A small section of the expanding cloud glowed brighter.

'Sneaky bitch,' Mender said. 'She knew a missile would never get through the orbital defences – but there's no way they can target a million tiny pieces of junk.'

Orry aimed *Jane* at the stone and increased thrust. 'At least we made her release early. We have some time.'

'To do what, girl? Say our prayers?'

'To go fishing.'

The puke matted in her hair smelled like sour milk, and sweat stung her eyes as she gazed out of the viewport in the freight lock's outer door. The curve of Tyr's sphere cut across her view. Beyond, she could see distant stars, looking flat and lifeless in contrast to the specks of debris Roag had released, which glittered and sparkled as they fell towards the planet's upper atmosphere.

She used her integuary to piggyback off *Dainty Jane*'s sensor feed and bracket the ventari stone: it was still a kilometre away, but *Jane* was gaining on it. Orry tried to ignore the yawning gulf outside the airlock, horribly afraid she was going to tumble down towards the planet below the moment the door opened. She winced as she adjusted her position, crouched awkwardly within the closed claws of Mender's grabber.

Closing . . . he sent from the cockpit. *Stand by*.

She could hear every heartbeat. *What the hell am I doing?* she thought to herself.

Opening outer door.

She concentrated on keeping her breathing steady as the doors slid apart. *I am not afraid*. The inside of the airlock had been in hard vacuum since Mender depressurised it five minutes ago, but with the doors open Orry suddenly felt totally exposed. Despite her efforts to calm herself, warning lights illuminated in her helmet as her heart rate skyrocketed. She closed her eyes, trying not to think about what would happen in the next few seconds. Then she changed her mind and visualised being fired from the ship on the end of the cable, focusing on the moment when she reached out and closed her fingers around the stone, and the reassuring pull as Mender reeled her back to safety.

I hope you're as good a shot with this thing as you say you are, she sent.

Got you once, didn't I, little bloodtrout?

That was probably a fluke.

He chuckled. *Relax. Five seconds . . . Four . . . Three . . .* He fell silent, leaving her wondering what had happened to two and one.

A juggernaut struck the small of her back and she screamed as pain flared from her injured ribs, eclipsing all else. The brackets her integuary was projecting around the ventari stone's location leaped towards her in a blur of motion. Fighting the violent vibrations, she reached out with her left hand. Her headlong acceleration slowed and she realised she could actually see the stone itself now: a dull green sphere no longer in its antique setting. The world shrank to a point directly in front of her. All that existed was her hand and the stone. It was so close now. Less than a metre . . .

She stopped with a jerk, the stone just beyond her reach.

What happened? she asked frantically.

Cable snag – we need to reset and try again.

We don't have time to reset! She stared at the stone, almost invisible against the green of the planet below. Her suit was already reporting traces of atmosphere.

She hooked the claw grabber's controller and ordered it to release. The claws sprang open and she floated free.

What the hell are you doing? Mender demanded, but she couldn't answer as vertigo rushed in, threatening to overwhelm her.

She gritted her teeth. *I . . . do not . . . have time . . . for this!*

Bracing one foot against the open claws, she pushed off gently. The grabber floated away, but it was enough to send her edging towards the stone. She approached the green orb at such an excruciatingly slow pace that she was sure both she and it would burn up in the atmosphere long before she reached it.

She was aware of Mender talking to her, but she couldn't listen to his words; all that mattered was the stone. Finally, it was close enough to reach. Carefully, she closed her fingers around it and at last she exhaled. She hadn't realised she'd even been holding her breath. Clutching the stone tightly, she checked her suit temperature: it was rising rapidly as she fell towards Tyr. She had maybe a minute until she cooked, taking millions of souls with her.

She twisted her body, craning to spot *Dainty Jane*.

I've got the stone, she told Mender. *A little help would be nice.*

The ship floated a hundred metres away. The freight lock was still open, but there was no sign of the claws.

Mender? She was progressing rapidly from shit-scared to utterly terrified.

Shut up, I'm concentrating.

The grabber shot out like an arrow, heading directly for her. She gasped, but at the last second it slowed abruptly and thumped gently into her chest. She felt herself propelled backwards by the impact, but the claws snapped closed around her, arresting the movement almost before it had begun.

She closed her eyes, fighting back tears.

Fluke, my ass! Mender yelled in triumph.

Orry couldn't speak. She was content to let the cable reel her gently back towards *Dainty Jane*.

Mender was waiting for her in the cargo bay when the airlock's inner door opened.

'We've got company. Half the Home Fleet, by the looks of things. They're quite keen for you to hand over that stone.'

She tossed it to him. 'Help me out of this damn suit, will you?'

He pulled the top half of the spacesuit over her head. She stepped out of the lower half and reached into a pocket, bringing out the shroudsphere.

She held out a hand for the ventari stone.

Mender hesitated. 'You know, they're going to be pretty damn annoyed when they find out you destroyed this thing.'

'You know what it can do. The Ascendancy and the Hierocracy are at war now. Whatever you think of the Kadiran, do you really want to hand over something that could wipe out billions of them? Because you know that's what Piotr will use it for.'

Mender grimaced and dropped the stone into her palm.

The shroudsphere spiralled silently open when Orry brought the stone close. She placed the green orb inside it and the filigreed brass sphere slid closed, sealing the ventari stone within.

'What now?' Mender asked.

She felt a warmth in her palm which quickly grew in intensity. The shroudsphere started glowing, a golden light that bled through the fine lines in its surface. The heat increased until the sphere became uncomfortable to hold – but before she had to drop it, the metal began to cool rapidly.

In seconds the shroudsphere was empty, as if the ventari stone had never existed.

47

MEAN OLD BASTARD

The private room was a far cry from *Dainty Jane*'s medbay. Harry was slumped in a wheelchair on the patio, facing the hospital's landscaped grounds. Orry took a deep breath before crossing the room and stepping out into the warm glow of Alecto's yellow sun.

'So this is how the other half live,' she said cheerfully. 'I still think you could have found an easier way of getting back here, you know.'

Harry tensed, but didn't look round. When he spoke, his voice slurred wetly. 'I told them not to let you in.'

Her smile slipped. 'Hey, it's me.' She placed a tentative hand on his shoulder, then pulled it away when he flinched.

'I don't want you here.'

'Harry, come on. I can think of worse places to recover.'

'I'm not going to recover.'

'Nonsense – it'll take time, that's all.'

Harry's right arm was tucked under a quilted blanket draped over his lap. The long fingers of his left hand twitched into a claw, nudging a miniature joystick. His chair swung to face her and she tried hard not to recoil.

The left side of his long face was a sunken crater covered in livid purple scar tissue. His eye was a sightless, milky orb.

'The bullet shredded my premotor cortex,' he slurred bitterly. 'They can rebuild my face, but I'll never regain full control of my body.'

Orry didn't know what to say. 'At least you're alive,' she said weakly.

He glared at her with undisguised loathing. 'Just get out.'

'No.'

'Get out!'

'You really are a spoiled child!' she yelled, and Harry blinked, flushing beneath the scar tissue. 'I know exactly what's been happening here: you've been sitting around feeling sorry for yourself and everyone has been letting you get away with it. You're not *special*, Harry. People get injured all the time – look at Mender. He's half bloody machine.'

For a moment she wondered if she'd gone too far, but then she decided she might as well get it all off her chest. 'In case you've forgotten, *you* chose to leave Alecto. *You* chose to come with us and *you* chose to go after Roag. It's not my fault you were shot, or Mender's. It's just bad bloody luck. You *will* get better – okay, maybe not back to the way you were, but you'll walk again, and that's more than my father will ever do.'

She turned away, overcome with guilt. Whatever she said, it *was* her fault Harry had been reduced to this.

He was silent for several seconds. When he spoke again the anger was gone from his voice. 'Orry, I want you to go.' She rounded on him but his left arm lifted in a weak gesture. 'No, listen. You're right, as usual. I've been brooding instead of focusing on getting better. The thing is ... I don't want you seeing me like this. It's going to take a long time to get back to anything approaching normal, and I'd rather you just saw the end result, not everything in between.'

She found it difficult to look at his injuries. 'Okay,' she said uncertainly, unable to keep the hurt from her voice. 'If that's what you really want.'

'It is.'

A door opened and a teenage girl of about Ethan's age entered, carrying a bunch of flowers. She stopped when she saw Orry.

'It's okay, Elena,' Harry said, and his voice was soft and kind. 'This is a friend of mine. Her name is Orry. Come and say hello to Orry.'

Elena stared furiously at the tiled floor.

'It's all right,' Harry reassured her, and his sister snatched a fleeting glimpse of Orry before dropping her eyes again. She edged forward like a nervous animal.

'Hello, Elena,' Orry said gently. 'It's nice to meet you.'

Elena stopped at the edge of the patio. She lifted her eyes briefly, then started shuffling her feet.

'I heard about what happened above Tyr,' Harry said to Orry, drawing the focus away from his sister. 'You and Mender are heroes. Does that mean all is forgiven?'

'I'm not sure. I'm going back when I leave here. My presence has been "requested".'

'You don't sound like you're looking forward to it.'

'I'm not.'

'Then why go?'

She smiled thinly. 'It's not the sort of invitation you can turn down.' She glanced at Elena, who hadn't moved, then leaned forward and kissed Harry's cheek. He smelled like a hospital ward. 'Look after yourself, Harry. I'll check how you're getting on the next time I'm back this way.'

His face twisted into a clumsy grimace. 'I'd rather you didn't.'

'Tough.' She flashed him a grin, which drained from her face the moment she turned away. 'Look after him, Elena,' she said as she passed.

It was all she could do to hold her tears until she was out of the room.

Tyr's sun beat down on the white buildings of the Admiralty, situated on an artificial island straddling Tyr's equator south of Utz. The dazzling light made Orry squint, even behind her smoked goggles. She craned her neck, following the line of the Admiralty Ribbon. The pair of cables no thicker than her wrist rose through the clouds on their way to the ribbon-head station in the centre of the naval yards. The capsules going into orbit were filled with personnel and materiel, those returning were, for the most part, empty. There was a tremendous amount of air traffic too, mainly troop transports and gunships. Grand Fleet officers and ratings moved with barely disguised haste, too intent on their destination to spare her more than the most perfunctory glance. Her flight suit had been repaired and laundered, but she stood out among the mass of blue and white uniforms.

'Good luck,' Ethan said, shading his eyes with one hand. 'I'll just wait here to be arrested again, shall I?'

Orry didn't laugh; she hadn't entirely ruled out that possibility. 'Just try not to subvert anything while I'm gone.'

'Around here?' He adjusted the sling supporting his bandaged shoulder and grimaced. 'How stupid do you think I am?'

She did laugh then. Ignoring the fluttering in her belly, she straightened her shoulders, strode up the wide steps and between the fluted columns of Admiralty House and inside. The cool air was a relief; she removed her goggles and stood just inside the doors, feeling the sweat drying on her skin.

'Miz Kent.'

She turned to see Rostov approaching. The scar-faced woman looked the same, despite the aerocar crash.

'Look,' Orry said awkwardly, 'I'm sorry about what happened – but everything turned out all right in the end, didn't it? So no hard feelings, right?'

Rostov's expression didn't change. 'Come with me, please.'

Orry sighed and followed her through the security check-point. A pair of elaborate staircases swept upwards from the central atrium, but Rostov led her to a discreet side door, which she unlocked with her integuary. At the end of a short corridor was a lift, which also opened at Rostov's silent command.

Orry entered and stood self-consciously beside Rostov; she was expecting the lift to rise and was surprised when it descended rapidly.

After what felt like a very long time, the lift slowed to a halt and the door opened. Two armoured guards were stationed outside; they nodded at Rostov as she led the way along another corridor. The officers down here – she could see no enlisted men or women – wore uniforms from all branches of the military, though Grand Fleet officers were prevalent. She couldn't see anyone under the rank of First-Captain.

She walked past several closed doors, one of which opened as she passed, providing a brief view of a large operations room filled with high-ranking uniforms. Finally, she spotted two members of the Imperator's Guard stationed in front of a door up ahead. She recognised the silver-haired guard captain, Sievers, from the palace, and exchanged a smile with him as he stood aside to allow her through the door. Rostov remained outside.

The Imperator Ascendant looked up as Orry entered. He was resplendent in the full, medal-heavy uniform of a Grand Marshal, very different to the last time they had met.

'A great many people want your head for what you did,' he said without preamble. 'They want to see you tried and hanged for treason.'

Orry shifted uncomfortably under his gaze. 'Are you one of them?'

'No,' he said, to her huge relief. 'Without you, none of us would even be here. To my mind, that outweighs the destruction of the ventari stone. Though it would be fair to say that I am less than pleased.'

'I'm glad you see it that way.'

'I'll bet you are.' He leaned back and steepled his fingers. 'So, the question is, what do I do with you?'

'Is that a rhetorical question?'

Piotr smiled. 'Let's suppose it isn't. What would you do, if you were me?'

'I'd let me go.'

'That's all? No reward? No honours?'

This wasn't playing out the way she had expected. She thought for a moment. 'There is one thing I'd like – if you're offering.'

'Go on.'

'Second-Captain Naumov is awaiting court-martial for mutiny. I want you to reinstate him.'

'Impossible.'

'Why?' Orry felt the blood rush to her cheeks. 'Issue a pardon. You say I saved Tyr – well, I couldn't have done it if Captain Naumov hadn't used his best judgement and released me.'

'I'm aware of the apparent contradiction, but the fact remains that Second-Captain Naumov publicly disobeyed the orders of Fleet-Admiral Sheremetev. We are at war, Miz Kent. If the Fleet sees one captain disobeying orders and getting away with it, where will it end?'

'That's ridiculous!'

'No, it's unfortunate. If it were up to me I'd promote the man, but as things stand I'm left with no alternative but to hang him. You probably think I can do exactly as I please, but you would be wrong. We are all slaves to something. I envy your freedom.'

'There must be something you can do, some way out.'

Piotr gazed levelly at her as he stroked his stiffly waxed moustache. 'I suppose I could commute his sentence to life on Furina,' he said eventually, then his face hardened. 'But the consequences will be on your head. It will make me look weak, and weakness in a war leader invariably costs lives. Do you think Captain Naumov is worth the risk?'

'Yes,' she answered without hesitation, 'but life on Furina is a pretty crappy way to reward a hero.'

Piotr shrugged. 'It's the best I can offer.'

'What about his crew? His officers?'

'Captain Naumov assumed sole responsibility for his actions and we need every member of personnel at the moment, so the Admiralty agreed to put the complicity of his crew down to fear of their captain, providing he accepted public responsibility.'

Orry nodded reluctantly. *At least this way he'll be alive.*

'And what about you?' the Imperator asked. 'Don't you want anything for yourself?'

'I just want to be left alone.'

'You saved the planet, Miz Kent, and my life, among countless others. Whatever opinion I might hold of your mother, I'm sure she would be proud of you. I could grant you a title commensurate with her rank.' His lips twitched into a small smile. 'It would gall your grandfather no end.'

Orry stared at him, trying to imagine life on her own estate, with servants and enough money to last a lifetime. She would never have to smell Mender's socks again, or grift for loose change, or shoot anybody. She smiled sadly. 'It's tempting, just to see the look on the old bastard's face, but no.'

'Heh. I thought you might say that. I'll leave the offer open, in case you change your mind.'

'I won't.' The words sounded churlish, and she added quickly, 'But thank you.'

'Very well. I've instructed the Admiral-Superintendent of the shipyard to make good any repairs to your vessel and to restock as required.'

Orry fought the urge to drop into a curtsey, then decided that perhaps Piotr deserved one small gesture of respect at least. He chuckled as she bobbed down in the most perfunctory way.

She stopped at the door. 'Is there any news about Roag?' she asked.

His smile vanished. 'Cordelia Roag is the single most wanted individual in the Ascendancy. Unfortunately, I rather suspect that if her allies haven't already killed her for failing to destroy Tyr, she will be somewhere deep within Kadiran space and out of our reach – for the time being, at least. Rest assured, if she ever shows her face on an Ascendancy world again I will hear about it.'

The thought of Roag being executed by the Kadiran left Orry feeling rather flat; it seemed like an easy way out after all that woman had done.

'Do you know why she did it?' Orry asked. 'Turned against her own race?'

'You'd have to ask her that. Perhaps the Kadiran offered to make her my replacement when the Ascendancy fell under their rule. Or maybe she just wanted to watch the galaxy burn.'

Orry nodded thoughtfully. She hoped very much to ask Roag that question herself one day.

'And he didn't offer you *anything*?' Mender asked. 'Money? A title?'

The hum of *Dainty Jane*'s mass-inversion drives filled the galley as they headed at a comfortable 1g towards the nearest egress point. Orry cupped her bulb of unsweetened tea loosely. It might be a Ruuz affectation, but she was developing a taste for it.

'I don't want anything from him.'

'What about what *we* want?' Ethan asked.

She shot him a warning look.

'Nothing at all?' Mender's eyes were narrowed.

'We're lucky he didn't execute us for destroying the stone,' she pointed out. 'I didn't want to push it.'

He grunted. 'I suppose you're right.' He slurped noisily at his coffee; even from across the table she could smell the whisky in it. 'So,' he said after a while. 'Do you have any plans . . . er . . . now?'

432

She braced herself. 'I've been meaning to talk to you about that.'

He nodded, scowling. 'I've been expecting this. You want to stay, don't you?' He jabbed a finger at Ethan. 'Him too, I suppose?'

'Um, that's not quite what I—'

Mender heaved himself to his feet and limped to the door.

'I suppose you have your uses. Not sure about him, though. Make me something to eat, girl, and I'll think about it.'

Orry's outrage drove all thought of her meeting with the Imperator from her head. 'Make it yourself, you mean old bastard!'

Mender grinned and stomped out of the galley.

'Wait,' Ethan called after him, rising to his feet. 'You have to show me the ents system.' He glanced at Orry, suddenly worried, and hurried after Mender. 'Please tell me there's an ents system!'

Orry smiled.

ACKNOWLEDGEMENTS

Huge thanks must go first of all to my publisher, Jo Fletcher, and her team at JFB for guiding me through the publishing process. Thanks also to my agent, Ian Drury, for banging the initial manuscript into shape and securing 'the deal'.

I am indebted to Rob Harkess and Neil Elliott for their sterling service as beta readers – Rob, as a fellow writer, is particularly good at not pulling his punches. Thank you also to Terry Jackman, Alex Weinle and Steve Turnbull for providing insightful feedback on the early drafts.

As always, Ian Cassidy responded to my cry for help with a raft of suitably impenetrable medical jargon, drawn from his vast professional knowledge of such matters.

And finally thanks to my family, at the heart of everything, for putting up with the endless muttering, swearing and occasional expressions of unbridled joy that I suspect are inevitable when engaged in the rollercoaster slog of completing a novel. My children in particular have provided a captive audience during numerous car journeys – very useful for talking through the minutiae of plot points.

Dominic Dulley

Morhelion

DOMINIC DULLEY

Orry Kent may not have stopped the war between the
Ascendancy and the alien Kadiran, but at least she saved
the Grand Fleet from immediate annihilation. Now she just
wants to get on with her own life.

The conflict feels a long way away – until a con turns sour
and she finds herself drawn into the very heart of the war.

When a dying agent of the emperor's shadowy Seventh
Secretariat tells Orry there's a traitor at the highest levels of the
Ascendancy, she has little choice but to take on the mission.

Which is why she finds herself stranded among the floating
bubble habitats of Morhelion, where pollution-spewing
smokers ply their trade in the beautiful but toxic atmosphere.

The hunt is on . . .

Jo Fletcher
BOOKS